I0651805

GRAND OAK BOOKS

The Complete Short Stories of Émile Zola

Published by:
Grand Oak Books Publishing, Ltd

ISBN-10 0983473803
ISBN-13 9780983473800

Library of Congress Cataloging-in-Publication Data:

Zola, Émile (1840-1902)/The Complete Short Stories of Émile Zola, Volume. ii
p. cm.

First Edition

The Complete Short Stories of Émile Zola

VOLUME II

Edited by Stephen R. Pastore

Introduction by Emily Pardoe

Grand Oak Books
2011

The Complete Short Stories of Émile Zola
VOLUME II

INTRODUCTION to The Complete Short Stories of Émile Zola in Four Volumes

by Emily Pardoe

The relative or sometimes complete unavailability of texts has been the major factor in depriving non-French admirers of Zola's novels of the rewarding and exciting literary experience of reading his tales and short stories. The present volume is unique in providing a conspectus of these works, ranging from his first collection, Contes à Ninon, published in 1864, to his last story, 'The Haunted House' (Angeline), which appeared more than thirty years later. The stories provide many pleasures of recognition: readers will find a variety of theme, a dramatic power, a minute observation of physical detail, the narrative invention, the social scope, which bring a whole epoch of French life into vigorous relief, and with which his novels have made them familiar. There are also, however, stimulating differences: they will be spared the irritation they may have felt at the novelist's occasional jejune determinism and his tendency to over-play (though not, thank God, in his best novels) the importance of so-called laws of heredity and environment. They will meet in the short stories no attempt to apply his half-baked and totally misplaced theories as to the possibility of turning the novel into a sort of experimental research laboratory to observe and deduce the laws of human behavior. They will even find the novelist's dramatic sense enhanced by the enforced concision of the short story form. And they will discover an accuracy of details that owes more to experience and intuition than to documentation, as the more anecdotal nature of the stories gives them an added liveliness.

But above all, from the very first tale (which is, significantly, in the first-person narrative), readers will become aware of a new dimension, a noticeable difference in tone, which may best be described as a sort of wry playfulness, used variously to mitigate or heighten an underlying seriousness. This different tone covers a wide range. It takes the form, for instance, of broad, even farcical humor, in 'Coqueville on the Spree' (La Fête à Coqueville)—a particularly interesting example, since Coqueville, as the epitome of the closed society, isolated in space and time, could have lent itself excellently to a painstaking study of the influence of heredity and environment, whereas Zola chooses to treat the village and its inhabitants, largely as a huge joke. Mainly, however, this playfulness finds expression in a wide range of irony: the savage irony of 'The Attack on the Mill' (L'Attaque du moulin); the cruelest irony of all, with 'Captain Burle' (Le Capitaine Burle), perhaps the only story where the tone is almost unrelievedly tragic; and, more frequently, a gentler irony, as in the story of Monsieur Chabre (Les Coquillages de Monsieur Chabre), or in 'The Girl Who Loves Me' (Celle qui m'aime). The irony is sometimes blatant: sections of 'Priests and Sinners' offer good examples of this; at other times far subtler, as in 'Absence Makes the Heart Grow Fonder' (Jacques Damour), which ends on at least two different levels. Whatever form it takes, the irony is rarely unadulterated, and here again, I think, readers of Zola's short stories will have a further advantage over someone who knows only his novels, where irony is generally in rather short supply, and often obtrusive when it does appear. The

eponymous anti-hero Burle, for example, excites compassion at the same time as he evokes an ironical smile of contempt, and the same can be said of Jacques Damour. Indeed pity, aroused, be it noted, obliquely in accordance with Zola's tenet of realistic impartiality, by ostensibly objective depiction rather than direct appeal to the reader's emotions, is a predominant element in many of these stories, and this skilful blending of contrasting suggestions arouses a similarly ambiguous reaction in the reader, a reaction more complex than that provoked by most of his novels, and which for many readers will more than adequately compensate for the lack of the epic quality of the better novels, well-nigh impossible to produce in a short story-although the spree at Coqueville is a binge of epic proportions, albeit on a mock-heroic scale.

Quite apart from the differences inherent in the genres, there is a deeper underlying distinction to be drawn between the novels and the short stories. For Zola the novelist, ambition and fame are the spur and the epic tone clearly forms part of the grand manner which will enable him to challenge a giant such as Balzac; but the charm of the short stories springs from the more urgent spur of economic necessity, the need to survive. The majority of these stories, in fact, form an important part of Zola's considerable and sometimes feverish production as a journalist, most of which falls between 1864 and 1880.

In 1865 when he left his job as head of the publicity department of the newly formed publishing firm of Hachette which he had joined two years before, Zola had to support his mother as well as himself, for his father had died when Émile was only seven years old; and incidentally, it should be mentioned that being the only son of a widow proved to have compensations: he was exempted from military service and had the additional bonus—his war stories make it plain that he must have considered this a bonus—that he escaped the servitudes and hardships and dangers of soldiering during the Franco-Prussian war. It is interesting to reflect that his numerous writings on the subject of war were based on hearsay and imagination, not on experience, which may explain why he fails to realize, in 'The Attack on the Mill'', that in modern warfare, shells had replaced cannon-balls.

Zola's economic straits, already bad enough, were shortly to become even worse when, very soon, a further mouth was added to the two he had to feed: that of his mistress Gabrielle-Alexandrine Meley, whom he was to marry in 1870. Something had to be done; it had to be done quickly; but it takes a long time, weeks or months, even for someone of Zola's methodical and industrious routine, to write a novel. It can take even longer to reap any considerable benefit from royalties, even if, with luck, you have the good fortune to have your novel accepted for publication in serial form, a method which Zola was able to adopt in later life. But as an unknown writer, there was only one possibility: journalism. Articles and short stories can be dashed off in a few days or even hours and, with luck and a reliable editor, you can eat and drink.

Zola's journalistic output never consisted solely of short stories; throughout his career as a journalist, a large part of his time and energy was devoted to criticism and reviews, not only of literary and dramatic works but also of painting, as we are reminded when reading 'Fair Exchange' (Madame Sourdis); and Zola, like young Ferdinand Sourdis, was a modernist, not surprisingly since he was a schoolmate of Paul Cézanne whom he continued to frequent for many years. One of his earliest public controversies arose from his support of the unfashionable and 'iconoclastic' painter, Édouard Manet.

Zola in his day, however, was best known as a journalist for his short stories and tales, some barely a couple of pages long, others of thirty pages or more, of which he wrote more than eighty over a period of more than thirty years, although of this number only 'Angeline' was written after 1880. The reason for the cessation of his activity after this date was simple: the resounding success of his proletarian novel L'Assommoir in 1877 brought him fame overnight and proportionate wealth shortly afterwards. The spur of financial necessity had gone; the contract which he had secured in 1875 through the good offices of the friendly Turgenev to provide articles and stories to the Russian periodical Vestnik Evropy (European Messenger) was to expire in 1880. The years of grinding poverty which Zola had experienced in the mid-sixties were now but a memory; they had, however, been useful in providing personal knowledge of a way of life which appeared in both his novels and his short stories. Henceforth his novels were to bring him enduring fame of a magnitude that he could never have expected as a critic or a short story writer. All the same, as a journalist, Zola obviously learned many of his skills during this period and it could be argued that he might even have done well to carry some of them over more fully into his novels. If journalism has disadvantages, it can also bring benefits.

The potential disadvantages are obvious. Paid by the word or by the page, a journalist can easily sacrifice quality to quantity. A very stern critic might, I fancy, find some wordiness in parts of Zola's short stories; but we should not forget that a more leisurely age than ours would be happy to linger over charming descriptions of Guérande and Piriac (in 'Shellfish for Monsieur Chabre') or of L'Estaque, in 'A Flash in the Pan' (Naïs Micoulin), all the more willingly if such descriptions have the charm of exoticism as well, since many of these short stories were written for Russian readers. Furthermore, as a realist, Zola is concerned to create as complete an atmospheric background as possible. And the occasional lengthy description, far from being purely decorative, serves to prolong our suspense and even, as in a good detective story (I think again of 'A Flash in the Pan'), the trivial, apparently unnecessary detail can provide a clue to the dramatic dénouement.

Another danger facing the journalist is that topicality is often expected to be one of his ingredients; especially in his earlier works, Zola takes his starting point from a contemporary event or a matter of current interest. Here again, Zola manages to survive relatively unscathed, and in any case, his output was sufficiently considerable to enable a selection to be made which avoids minutiae unlikely to interest a modern reader. In much of his later work, Zola avoids any such danger by deliberately choosing a topic of general import (as in 'Priests and Sinners') and inventing a dramatic framework to illustrate his point.

But the benefits of journalism are so considerable, at least for someone of Zola's temperament, as to outweigh the disadvantages. Writing quickly, you will find yourself writing briskly and crisply; you will seek to be lively. Writing for different editors and different reading publics gives you practice in flexibility. Parisian readers have different attitudes from those of the provincials, while Russian readers—for most of the stories were written under contract to a Russian periodical—require a good deal of background information, a requirement which admirably suits Zola's technique; and they have their special expectations and preconceptions with regard to French society. Could this perhaps explain some of the flippancy—'French sauciness' is perhaps the better word—of 'The Party at Coqueville?' But, above all, people will not, I suggest, read short stories to be preached at or indoctrinated, even if they are not averse to having their prejudices flattered. So didacticism, that scourge of Zola's criticism and his later novels, has no place in his short stories, although he has his own methods of inferring a moral. In fact, the best way of entertaining males—and more females than they may perhaps care to admit—is by the slightly scabrous or the quasi-erotically suggestive. However, from what we know of Zola, such a tone was not one which represented his own inclinations and here again this sort of constraint can only have furthered his development as an artist: he has to be careful to avoid too forthright an expression of strongly held personal views; artistry is more important than outspoken sincerity. It is, of course, an attitude which squares very well with the realist's avowed aim of depicting people and society in their everyday life, however dull and even hateful, people as they are and not as we would have them be. Such suppression of personal feelings is bound to have its limits, of course: particularly as a young man, Zola was much given to sentimentality which can sometimes sink to mawkishness and he had a strong melodramatic tendency which he never threw off. The sentimentality diminished with age and self-discipline but he never seemed able to accept Hardy's dictum that while nothing is too strange to have happened, there is a good deal that is too strange to be believed. Once again, we have been saved by the quantity of Zola's output: with over eighty stories to choose from, it is easy to weed out the mawkish or over-melodramatic, which might, indeed, have appealed to a Victorian reader but would now be found unacceptable.

Zola's short story writing falls into two easily distinguishable periods, with 1875 as the dividing line, when he was, in fact, at thirty-five, in the middle of his career, though his life was to be forcibly abridged. The first period contains largely very short pieces, some little more than a couple of pages long; the majority are mere sketches illustrating Parisian life (one of the collections of this typically journalistic production, first published in 1866, was called Esquisses Parisiennes). These sketches were a very prevalent genre at the time, a chronicle, and its author, the chronicler, writes of his personal impressions, usually basing his story on an odd event, an anecdote, real or imagined, a genuine or fictitious personal memory; he strolls through Paris noting things that strike his fancy or people who seem perhaps odd or even 'typically Parisian'; topics on which he can talk out loud, personally, inviting the reader's complicity. Occasionally, the tale will invite the expression of a hope or a non-censorious moral, although we should beware of accepting any such expression of emotion or judgment at its face value. It is pleasant chat and much of it, where Zola's contribution to the genre is concerned, is now read only by critics in search of influences or anxious to find in it the seeds of his future novels. These chronicles were largely published in the many newspapers and magazines which proliferated in Paris in the declining years of the Second Empire; and they tend to have a sameness of tone, a sort of slickness which quickly palls. All the same, some have sufficiently strong ironic edge and an observation of permanent human foibles accurate enough to amuse a modern reader. Five have been included here, out of a total of over fifty.

The second period of Zola's activity as a short story writer is very different; no longer sketches, the stories all have a plot and characters. Although still writing for a periodical, he is relieved of the need to crave the suffrage of the French reading public and can avoid any direct editorial pressure; the obligation to provide slick entertainment and instant dramatization is lifted. On his much broader canvas of more than ten thousand words, he can exercise his realistic technique of detailed observation, he is free to develop situations in accordance with views that from other evidence we know to be closer to his heart but which he has learned to express with artistic discretion. All except one of the remaining translations of the stories are taken from this collaboration: ten stories in all, exactly half of Zola's total output of short stories for the Russian periodical (he also wrote more than forty other pieces, articles on literary and other topics). One or two of the stories have retained the impressionistic stamp of his earlier journalism, not surprisingly since he occasionally borrowed from earlier sketches to put his Russian pieces together; and one or two of them are too essentially topical for inclusion here, for instance, a series of short sketches recounting some of the electioneering and voting in the important French general election of 1878, which are of greater interest for the historian than for the general reader.

We have mentioned the importance of drama in the short story to offer the reader an unexpected twist, a surprising turn of events or a sudden striking revelation of character. Zola well understood the desirability of this technique and in many of these stories he keeps the reader on tenterhooks. What exactly is going to become of the sexually obsessed Captain Burle? Who is going to be shot—or is anyone going to be shot—in 'The Attack on the Mill'? In 'Absence Makes the Heart Grow Fonder', what possible solution can be found for Jacques Damour's agonizing problem? Is that rather unpleasant young Frédéric Morand, so perfectly adapted to his rich middle-class background, none the less riding for a serious, if not fatal, fall? These are a few of the major dramas which combine with interlocking minor dramas to provide complex suspense for the reader. But it would be underestimating Zola's inventive narrative talent to assume that he places exclusive reliance on what are, after all, fairly ordinary basic skills which, if indulged in to excess, can turn into mannered devices. Zola has other strings to his bow and in all his full-length stories the questions are more subtly posed: it is not so much what is going to happen, as when and how is what we can expect to happen actually going to happen. Far less common is the question why something happens. Zola rarely probes motives nor, indeed, does he generally need to do so for the mainsprings of most characters' behavior are plain, although not necessarily simple. All the same, in one or two of these stories, there is greater ambiguity: Jacques Damour's final resolution, in "Absence Makes the Heart Grow Fonder' is not explained. When Zola does choose thus to respect the uncertainty of human motive, his realistic technique stands him in good stead, relying as it does on the external recording of behavior rather than on omniscient authorial probing: here actions or even gestures speak louder than words and the reader can ponder the motives at leisure.

But there is no doubt that the question of how something happens is most important for Zola and is worth examining in some greater detail. 'Shellfish for Monsieur Chabre' is as good an example as any. Now, it is surely not necessary to be particularly sophisticated or cynical to realize very early in the story that Monsieur Chabre's balding head is going to be adorned with horns and we know quite well who is going to put them there. The main suspense thus centers on the question of how, and this is where Zola shows his artistry. We see in great detail the physical background and contributory events which foster the growth of a relationship between a shy young man, becoming progressively and charmingly less shy, and a respectable and spirited young wife, becoming progressively less respectable; a relationship which not only unites two bodies—both equally beautiful bodies—but reveals a marriage of minds which share the same feeling for nature and a similar sense of beauty as well as the same sense of fun, the same interest in life's oddities. All these aspects of the links between the two young people are observed with careful and selective realistic detail, never over-explicit: the reader is not taken into the exact workings of the protagonists' minds or the minute development of their feelings but is left to surmise and deduce—and to be amused. Woven into the tale are Zola's own holiday impressions of a specific district of France which is realistically portrayed in considerable detail for the foreign Russian reader, no doubt fascinated—as American readers may well also be—by a glimpse into an excitingly beautiful landscape or a charmingly picturesque old town. More importantly, the impact of such joint impressions on the young couple in creating a stimulating bond between them is central to the plot; it seems clear that here is no description for the sake of description and even the long drawn out account of the shrimping expedition has an important functional role; it increases our suspense as well as suddenly revealing a breakthrough in the couple's relationship. The net result is that what could have been a banal and sordid adultery, a quick seaside 'petticoats up and trousers down' on the beach, becomes a lyrical celebration of the beauty of natural forces set in a convincing and fascinating specific French background, in a specific French milieu. Even the chief victim is not entirely a caricature black-and-white character. Paunchy and absurd though he is, Monsieur Chabre is a living person and not really a bad sort of fellow—he's mannerly and considerate towards his wife; and, in the end, Zola lets him come to no harm. He's nobly eaten his loathsome shellfish and the reader is delighted when he gets his reward in the shape of a bouncing son and heir; it's a sort of nineteenth-century form of in vitro fertilization. And quite apart from the sexual problem, we may feel that, through his truth to life, Zola has, as it were incidentally, given us an intriguing and plausible glimpse into a perennial mystery: how can rich businessmen, so shrewd and expert in their particular sphere, prove so ineffectual and stupid outside these activities?

I have spent time on 'Shellfish for Monsieur Chabre' because it is an excellent example of Zola's narrative technique, albeit one of many, whereby he succeeds in turning a relatively predictable what into a far more uncertain how. Beyond simple comedy or drama, we are taken into more enriching regions of the mind while at the same time our attention is constantly held by the convincing and accurate depiction of many different milieus. By the manner of their telling, we are persuaded to overlook the familiarity or even banality of the events being told; the realist Zola has, strangely, achieved a sort of classicism, the classicism of 'what oft was said but ne'er so well expressed'.

Zola's stories extend through a very wide range of French society, almost as wide as his novels, though the typical nouveau riche character of the period is not well represented; Durandeau in 'Rentafoil' (Les Repoussoirs) is the nearest approach to the crafty Second Empire speculator lavishly depicted in the novels. Apart from this, we see specimens from the aristocracy down to the peasantry and proletariat: indeed, in two of the stories here reproduced, 'How People Die' (Comment on meurt) and 'Priests and Sinners', there is a deliberate juxtaposition of the attitudes of different classes, although in the second of these, the emphasis is placed more on a particular type of priest rather than on the class of society to which he was ministering. If realism is deemed to depend exclusively on observation, there must be some difficulty in considering such works as realistic: Zola had no direct or personal experience of most of the milieus he was depicting, the aristocracy, the upper-and lower-middle classes, the proletariat or the peasantry. His own frequentations were largely of journalists, of literary and artistic Parisian bohemians. However, in his years of poverty in the early and mid-sixties, he would certainly have rubbed shoulders with the working and poorer artisan classes and he would have seen something of provincial life and peasantry in his boyhood in Provence. The life of the aristocracy and the upper-middle classes must have remained a closed book to him, to be learnt about from other writers' works or from other people's conversation. Critics have taken Zola to task over this. However, Zola had very sensitive antennae and a lively imagination; he was to need less than a week 'in the field' in Beauce when gathering material for his superb peasant novel La Terre and since both Balzac and Proust, in their different ways, seem to have overcome similar shortcomings in their novels, it would be prudent to let readers judge for themselves as to the authenticity of Zola's portrayal of classes of which he had limited direct knowledge.

From our knowledge of Zola's strong feelings about social injustice, we might have expected the aristocracy to have suffered harshly at his hands; in fact, they do not come off too badly. True, they appear as heartless, hypocritical and sexually promiscuous but they are shown as possessing good manners, decorum and a certain panache, a conventional picture, of course, but Zola's invention of incident, the petit fait vrai of Stendhal, and the accurate background detail make perfectly plausible and interesting stories out of this unoriginal material. The middle classes at all levels had been the butt of most of the important poets and novelists of the nineteenth century in France and Zola similarly belabors them for their materialistic greed, their snobbery and, particularly the women, for their bigotry; again, it is the manner rather than the matter that is original. Predictably, the lower-middle classes, harder pressed by economic circumstances, are treated more sympathetically, although Monsieur Rousseau, the stationer in the third section of 'How People Die', however sincerely he may mourn his wife, still has a nagging grievance against her: what a pity she had to die on a day which forced him to close the shop! It is far easier to arouse compassion for the wretched working classes and Zola does so; nonetheless, his code of impartiality leads him to show a few warts: the working-class inhabitants of the tenement block in the fourth section of 'Priests and Sinners' are notably uncharitable in their judgments as well as drunk and disorderly in their communal lives. On the whole, the peasantry come out best; they have a simple fatalistic dignity springing from their close contact with natural forces; but this does not prevent Zola from drawing a devastating picture of their appalling superstitions in the first section of 'Priests and Sinners'.

In a word, Zola's view of mankind is unflattering but it must be said that if there are few wholly admirable characters, there are also not many really despicable ones. Indeed, it could be argued that his characterizations in his short stories, because of his frequent humorous or ironic touches, is more rounded than in his novels; and the narrower canvas still gives him room to etch in some convincing, often slyly funny vignettes of minor characters.

As we might expect, one of the major characters of his short stories is the carefully drawn environment. Zola invites the readers' close attention to the influence of social and other circumstantial conditioning on our behavior; and this conditioning not only helps to explain our complexities, it also serves as an extenuating circumstance. In 'A Flash in the Pan' (Naïs Micoulin), for instance, Naïs' father is a wife-beater, a harsh father who knocks his daughter about, and a would-be murderer; yet this sort of uncouth savagery is shown as rooted in the desperate struggle to survive in a pitiless drought-ridden region, as well as in the still living tradition of a French male-dominated society whose pride in family honor is the mainstay of his existence. Similarly, the stupid Father Pintoux in the first part of 'Priests and Sinners' is as much a victim of circumstance as his pathetically superstitious flock of Breton peasantry; his life is almost as hard as theirs and his belief in hell fire as strong; and if the Monsignor of the fifth section of the same group is ruthlessly ambitious, it is his early military training which is partly to blame for his insensitivity. Zola obviously considers professional military training as one of the most pernicious environments. It results in a besetting sin which incurs his ultimate condemnation of any human being: lack of imagination. No amount of courage or loyalty can make up for this failure: the jaunty, gallant French officer in 'The Attack on the Mill' as well as the dour, pathetic, doggedly courageous and strictly honorable Major Laguitte in 'Captain Burle' are both ultimately condemned, insofar as Zola allows anyone to be condemned, as blinkered automata.

A further reason for Zola's distaste for the military is that, through their association with war, which he vies as a deplorable but inevitable human infirmity, they are closely associated with death. Zola had a streak of morbidity which finds explicit expression in 'Dead Men Tell No Tales' (La Mort d'Olivier Bécaille), and which no doubt will find an echo with many a reader. We know from other sources not only of his fear, which proved to be prophetic, of meeting an untimely death but also of being buried alive, and the story plainly owes much of its initial impact to this autobiographical element. However, as always, Zola constructs a plot and a situation which go far beyond any personal feelings. Fear of death and of burial alive turn out to be the most superficial, if perhaps the most dramatic, of the levels at which the story works; the real subjects are the fragility of the marriage vows, the pressure of economic necessity, the portrayal of women as creatures possessing habits and customs rather than morals, and finally, a favorite theme in Zola's short stories, the justification of sexual desire, an interesting contrast to the depressing view of sexuality revealed in the novels of the Rougon Macquart cycle; it seems almost as if in this portrayal of the successful fulfillment of young love, a vein of sentimentality persists from the early Contes à Ninon which was ruthlessly excised from the later novels. Let it be noted, by the way, that if women are sternly treated at times, the men have nothing to crow about: the motives of men's actions are usually social advancement or material gain, with love as a secondary commodity.

In later life, Zola became a very active political figure in his support for Dreyfus; but politics and politicians are skeptically viewed in his stories. The political Monsignor of 'Priests and Sinners' is a rabidly reactionary self-seeker while, at the other end of the spectrum, the left-wing Berru of 'Absence Makes the Heart Grow Fonder' is a rascally rabble-rousing firebrand who takes good care of his own skin. Big Michu's father, in 'Big Michu' (Le grand Michu), is mentioned as a brave and honest 1848 Republican; but Jacques Damour, in 'Absence Makes the Heart Grow Fonder', also brave and honest, is shown as a credulous simpleton whose Communard activity is closely linked to the few francs a day which he receives as a National Guardsman. Politics are in fact largely the preserve of a corrupt aristocracy and a conservative and ambitious upper-middle class and Zola shows us no evidence to suggest that any of the lower-class aspirants to political power are likely to be very different. In a word, politicians are members of the human race, of which someone wrote:

> I wish I liked the human race,
> I wish I liked its silly face,
> And when I'm introduced to one
> I wish I thought: What jolly fun!

Such indeed, here expressed in humorous Anglo-Saxon terms, which need not exclude a hidden anguish, is a sentiment that can be seen to run through Zola's short stories. It is a cry from the heart of many French writers, from Molière and La Rochefoucauld, Chamfort and Voltaire, Flaubert and Céline. In Zola, it is no isolated disenchantment, for his picture is very complete. He takes us into aristocratic bedrooms and dining rooms, into drawing-rooms in Paris and in the provinces, into little shops and wretched garrets, into a garrison town, seaside resorts, the Faubourg Saint-Germain and Ménilmontant, a Lorraine village and an assortment of cemeteries. He peoples his accurate backgrounds with convincing characters: men-about-town, middle-class money-makers, pretty bourgeois, soldiers, fishermen, peasants, bricklayers, shopkeepers, artisans and other manual workers, not forgetting the odd kept woman; conservative reactionaries as well as uneasy liberals and opportunistic republicans; and they are all seen in action, often dramatically and frequently ironically. We see a well-composed and authoritative fresco, of a wide range in full color, of French society in the second half of the nineteenth century. But this is not just a period piece: Zola's themes—love, young and fierce or tired and disillusioned, maternal, paternal, filial, married or adulterous; death, natural or violent; money (or lack of it); religion (or lack of it); work (or lack of it)—are always with us and to many of them he gives a strikingly modern, even prophetic, slant. His general theme is, after all, various forms of recognizably modern conflict: the dilemma of the tormented Abbé de Villeneuve is similar to that of the worker-priest; fundamentalist religious fanatics, in the line of poor Father Pintoux, are today, in many parts of the world, a commonplace; we can all think of gifted men destroying themselves through drink and dissipation; the lures of high pressure are familiar bogies; and many people have an uneasy suspicion that there may still exist those who hope to be able to cry, like the French captain in 'The Attack on the Mill', 'We've won! We've won!' on piles of corpses and flattened buildings. It would seem very likely therefore that, having survived for a century, these brilliant stories, so varied in theme and tone, will continue to engross and entertain readers for a long time to come.

The Complete Short Stories of Émile Zola

Volume II

PRIESTS AND SINNERS

I

FATHER PINTOUX had been the parish priest of Saint-Marchal for the last forty years. He was now a little old man of seventy, dried up by his open-air life; with his brick-red, weather-beaten face and his shabby, threadbare old cassock he looked like a peasant in his smock.

The story of his life was a simple one. He was a woodcutter's son from the neighboring village of Mériadec. A puny boy, bullied by his brothers, he had had the good fortune to be taken up by a patroness who arranged for him to be admitted to the little seminary of Guérande. Physical labor had always been anathema to him and the thought of wielding an axe to cut down trees scared him so much that he would have preferred to become a tramp. He had moreover always possessed a childlike faith which persisted at the seminary, together with an equally blind submission to authority. He believed everything his teachers told him and, never having been very bright, he avoided the need for thought by telling himself that God would do his thinking for him. He had taken holy orders with the same unquestioning submissiveness and with one single idea in mind: to exercise his ministry undisturbed. At first, the bishop of Nantes sent him round to a couple of smaller parishes and, finally realizing his simple-mindedness, innocence and complete lack of initiative, he had packed him off to Saint-Marchal and thought no more about him.

Saint-Marchal is a tiny hamlet in the wilds of Lower Brittany. The Nantes to Brest railway did not pass within twenty-five miles of it; it was real wolf country, set on a high plateau battered by storms raging in from the Atlantic, which can be seen as a thin green line on the horizon. Saint-Marchal had almost four hundred inhabitants and poverty was widespread, for the soil is stony and there is a great shortage of water. The wretched villagers seemed to belong to quite a different world from that of the average Frenchman. And it was in this poor hamlet that Father Pintoux had grown old.

Little by little, the priest had settled into his narrow round of routine, like some old riding-school hack. Mass in the morning, catechism in the afternoon; and in the evening, a game of cards with a neighbor. Since it was quite impossible to live on the few hundred francs he received from the parish, he had been forced to overcome his distaste for hard work and take to wielding a mattock in the vegetable garden at the back of his presbytery, where he grew beans and cabbages. He could be seen in his shirtsleeves, bareheaded in the sun, grappling with a stony soil far too hard and heavy for his puny arms. Afterwards he would put on his cassock and go off to hear confession from the girls of the village, still out of breath from his exertions and searching his memory for the Latin formulas which he trotted out automatically.

Father Pintoux had a whole collection of ready-made phrases and gestures which he had been using for the last half-century and from which he never deviated. For him, religion had become purely a matter of outward observance. His services went like clockwork. His devotion of earlier days had turned into mere empiricism and found satisfaction in the repetition, at every opportunity, of the same details culled from his missal. Had he returned to earth in the shape of one of those peaceful oxen lumbering stolidly through their pastures, he would have bowed down to the sun with the same conviction that he showed in kneeling before the figure of Christ.

Meanwhile, over the last forty years, he had officiated at the weddings of most of the villagers and baptized a whole generation of children. He was the patriarch of Saint-Marchal. At church festivals, they would bring him gifts of eggs and butter. It was he whom they consulted on any matter of importance; he conducted lawsuits, reconciled families and shared out inheritances. There was, indeed, nothing more natural than this regal status of priest, for he alone was capable of reading the books, he alone was in communication with science and with God. He represented authority even more than the mayor, for he spoke in the name of the Lord whereas the mayor spoke only in the name of the government; and Heaven, which metes out hail and thunder, is the only power feared by peasants, the only one before which they would bend the knee.

In the whole village, there was not one single unbeliever. On Sundays, the church was packed, with the women on one side and the men on the other. When the priest came in carrying the chalice, he could see at a glance if everyone was present. As soon as one of his flock was an absentee, he would be required to offer an excuse, such as an illness preventing him from leaving the house; otherwise the priest would call down God's wrath upon the head of the lost sheep. From the pulpit; he would fulminate dire threats against the ungodly, conjuring up the horrors of hellfire, with cauldrons of boiling oil and souls in torment roasting on red-hot iron bars. Strong men and women would blench and after the service little children would be haunted by nightmares for the whole week. In fact, the priest would not have harmed a fly; but he was repeating sermons that he had heard from others and he himself lived in awe of the divine wrath of a jealous God; he really believed these cruel and miraculous tales and legends. So Saint-Marchal lived in a state of humility and terror, like a primitive tribe prostrating itself beneath a cloud streaked with lightning and always on the point of loosing its thunderbolts.

One Sunday, having noticed that Marianne Roussel was not in her usual place beside the font, Father Pintoux set off after lunch to find out if Marianne was ill. He had the stiff, halting gait of an old man; the only signs of life now left in his stolid, leathery old face were his tiny grey eyes, as sharp and innocent as a child's. On the way, a few peasants stopped him to ask him what the weather would be like tomorrow and he looked up at the sky, wagged his head and finally promised that it would be fine. A few steps further on a woman's washing caught his eye, then he went into a backyard to look at a brood of chicks. For everybody in the village he was one of the family. The only thing which differentiated him from the other villagers was his cassock; he shared their ideas and their speech and he, too, looked as if he was walking in his sleep.

Finally, he reached the Roussels' cottage. Marianne was outside, looking perfectly well and chatting to her tall neighbor Nanette.

"Well, Marianne, what's all this about? You missed Mass this morning!"

And without giving her a chance to explain, he launched into his attack: it was wrong, the Devil was always lying in wait and she would certainly end up in Hell if she didn't go to church. In the end, Marianne managed to explain:

"It's my little girl, Father . . . She's very poorly. This morning I thought we'd lost her . . . So I had to stay at home."

"Little Catherine isn't well?"

"Yes, Father, we've put her in our bed. Come and take a look."

In a large bed at the far end of the gloomy room, a little girl about ten years old was lying with flushed face and closed eyes shivering with fever. The whole of her poor little body was trembling under the sheet. The priest went over and looked at her silently for a moment. Then he said slowly, "It's the good Lord punishing you, Marianne. You've offended Him by your bad example and He has laid His hand upon you."

He jerked his chin to emphasize each word, as if to indicate his approval of such divine vengeance. And Catherine had not been a very good girl, either. The previous Thursday during catechism, he had been obliged to send her out of church because she had been laughing and disturbing the other children. It happened to have rained very heavily that afternoon and, not daring to go home for fear of being scolded, the little girl had been drenched to the skin in a shower.

"She must have caught it last Thursday," her mother murmured. "She came home in a dreadful state."

"God is punishing her as He is punishing you," the priest went on. "Do you think He is happy when He sees a naughty little girl making fun of Him in His own house? Everything must be paid for, you know."

Nanette crossed herself and old Roussel, who was eating a bowl of soup at a table, nodded his head in approval. Yes, everything had to be paid for. If there had been a hailstorm last April, it was because the people of Saint-Marchal had displeased the Virgin Mary by not offering such fine bunches of flowers as in previous years, on the feast of the Assumption. If old Lazare's mare had died, it was because the old man had forgotten to make the sign of the cross as he walked past the Calvary.

However, as the Roussels had no recollection of having given any cause for God's anger, they hoped that their young daughter would recover, with the help of the angels. And if things were no better after a couple of days, they could even send for the doctor who lived at Pontenac, some fifteen miles away. Nanette gave a shrug; as far as she was concerned, doctors were of no use at all. Once Heaven had passed judgment on someone, there was certainly no doctor who could save him. And besides, the doctor at Pontenac was a heathen; everybody knew that you could see the Devil standing at the foot of the bed of any dead man whom he'd been treating and who had his medicine inside him.

"Rub her temples every hour with holy water," said the priest, "and say three Paternosters and two Ave Marias."

Then he knelt down and mumbled a quick prayer. The Roussels and Nanette said "Amen" with him and crossed themselves vigorously.

"It's not going to be anything much," said the priest as he left. "The child's body must cast out all its wickedness . . . I'll be back tomorrow."

But when Father Pintoux came to see the Roussels next day, he was greatly agitated and in a voice trembling with emotion he recounted the appalling story that he had just been told by his bell-ringer: Catherine had committed an act of sacrilege. On Thursday, after being sent out of the catechism class, she had slipped off to play for a moment in the sacristy, where the bell-ringer had seen her take off the crown of the large plaster statue of the Virgin Mary and put it on her own head, making several curtsies all by herself as she did so, doubtless in order to make fun of the Mother of God. The priest could not understand why Heaven had not struck her down on the spot. But now she was surely doomed. Her illness had come from on high.

"But she did come home soaked to the skin on Thursday." Marianne said again." Perhaps, after all, if we were to get her into a good sweat . . . "

"Oh, she's ill, very ill," old Roussel said in a low voice, sitting in a corner with his hands on his knees.

And the poor little girl seemed indeed on the point of death as she lay in the large bed with her short blonde hair all disheveled, gasping feverishly for breath through her burning lips; behind her half-closed lids, her eyes were glazed and staring and in her fever she kept moaning: "Oh, it's hurting me, it's hurting dreadfully!" It was pitiful to see this tender young girl in such pain, clenching her tiny fists in her lonely struggle against death.

Meanwhile the story of the sacrilege had spread through the village and all the neighbors had come flocking to the house. It was rumored that Father Pintoux was going to attempt to chase out the Devil who had got into the body of the Roussel girl. Soon there were a dozen people gathered in the front room. They were all whispering together and recalling other well-known incidents of the same sort. Three years before, another little scamp had stolen a holy wafer and pinned it to a tree for fun; the tree had immediately started to groan and red liquid had begun to stream out of its trunk while large drops of blood had dripped from every branch. Nanette swore that she had seen it happening, adding that at any rate her sister had seen it. But the group of villagers were even more impressed by another story: on one Shrove Tuesday, some young lads from Saint-Nazaire were walking round with cardboard masks on their faces and when a priest had gone by carrying extreme unction, one of the young rascals had decided not to remove his mask which had then stuck so tightly to his face that he had started screaming with agony and they had been forced to tear the mask off piece by piece, pulling the skin away with the cardboard.

After listening to these examples, no one was surprised that Catherine had been struck down with a dreadful illness for having dared to put the Virgin Mary's crown on her own head. A feeling of anxiety mingled with awe filled the room. Although it was broad daylight, the men felt rather uneasy and the women kept glancing apprehensively over their shoulders, half expecting to see a cloven hoof and a pair of horns.

"She was such a quiet well-behaved little girl," said her father. "Something must have got into her, that's for sure."

The priest had started praying. He walked round the room, reciting his Latin Prayers and, dipping a box twig into a plateful of holy water, each time he reached the child he sprinkled some over her, making a sign of the cross in the air. Catherine was still moaning, writhing and arching her back while she babbled incoherently in her delirium, laughing and sobbing simultaneously. Suddenly she started up with staring eyes, calling out to the people she saw around her; then she fell back, singing a children's song until her voice died away into silence.

The men and women in the room shrank back trembling, afraid of seeing a monster spring out of the poor feverish girl's open mouth. She must certainly be possessed by the Devil if she jumped like that as soon as a drop of holy water touched her. Surely the Devil was going to throttle her and put an end to it all. He put a box twig into a plateful of holy water, each time he reached the child he sprinkled some over her, making a sign of the cross in the air. Catherine was still moaning, writhing and arching her back while she babbled incoherently in her delirium, laughing and sobbing simultaneously. Suddenly she started up with staring eyes, calling out to the people she saw around her; then she fell back, singing a children's song until her voice died away into silence.

The men and women in the room shrank back trembling, afraid of seeing a monster spring out of the poor feverish girl's open mouth. She must certainly be possessed by the Devil if she started like that as soon as a drop of holy water touched her. Surely the Devil was going to throttle her and put an end to it all.

At the foot of the bed, Marianne was in tears: Catherine was all she had and now she was going to lose her without even knowing what had caused her death. Once more, she mentioned a doctor and begged her husband to drive quickly over to Pontenac; but old Roussel was still slumped stupidly in his corner and merely shook his head apathetically in reply. He was resigned to the death of his daughter, like all old peasants who submit to higher powers which they cannot understand. Why bother to send for a doctor when Father Pintoux had announced that God wished to take away their child? Father Pintoux certainly knew better than anyone. All you can do is to submit; your turn will come, too, and the best thing was to be always on your best behavior.

When he saw that the holy water was making the little girl suffer and not bringing her any relief, Father Pintoux clapped his hands lightly, as he did in church when he wanted the congregation to kneel. They all fell on their knees. He remained standing for a moment, saying:

"Let us pray together and ask our Lord to perform a miracle."

His brown leathery face lit up with the radiance of his faith and, despite his stoop and his weather-beaten peasant-like appearance, he had a majestic look as he fell on his knees and, with all the fervor of his seminary days, prayed God to show mercy on the poor sinner. The murmur of prayer grew louder and the anxious atmosphere in the room was filled by the icy chill of superstition, the helpless ignorance of people crushed by life's adversity. The little girl gave one final convulsive shudder and then lay flat in the bed, gasping as if in relief. Then, all at once, she gave a deep sigh and lay still. She was dead.

"Requiescat in pace," said the priest, raising his voice.

"Amen!" came the response from the villagers.

And they all rose to their feet and left, greatly affected by the scene, while Marianne stifled her sobs in her apron and old Roussel, utterly bewildered and unable to realize what he was doing, opened his clasp-knife and cut himself a slice of bread.

When Father Pintoux left he was greeted by the whole village as the representative of the dread Master who can exercise his power of life and death at any time. It so happened that Municipal elections were being held on the following Sunday and the villagers clustered round him to ask him how they should vote. He repeated the instructions which he had received from the bishop's palace the previous day. Next Sunday, not one of the villagers failed to attend Mass and the bishop's candidate was elected without a single dissenting voice. Father Pintoux ruled in Saint-Marchal like God himself, like some old rough-hewn, wooden idol with power to dispense thunderbolts and horrible diseases.

II

Every Friday, Father Michelin would hear confession from his lady clientele in the Dominican chapel in a little street in the Faubourg St-Germain. It was a very cozy little chapel, more like a large drawing-room, scented and intimate in its dim light from the stained-glass windows. It was considered the acme of good taste for ladies not to go to confession in their own parish but to come here instead, far from the common crowd of penitents. It placed them on another plane; they could imagine that God was offering them a more elegant absolution of their sins.

Father Michelin was a tall, fine-looking man of thirty, brown-haired and white-skinned, who was at that time enjoying a considerable vogue in high society. The son of a glass and china dealer in the Rue du Bac and born in that aristocratic quarter, he was now confessing the daughters of the countesses and marchionesses who had been his father's customers. This fact had not, however, gone to his head; he had succeeded in striking the exact balance of manner between the deference of an inferior and the all-powerful authority of the priest; this had given a special piquancy to his exercise of his ministry.

His schooldays were obscure but he was said to have been a good student at his seminary. He was basically a pleasant young man, fully determined to enjoy life and to be adaptable. While still a youth he must have had dreams of forcing an entry, in a position of authority, into those aristocratic drawing-rooms which he had till then been able to glimpse only through half-closed doors. His ambition was to move in select circles where he could satisfy his taste for fine things, choice meals and elegant women, everything that smelt nice. As far as religion was concerned, he looked upon it as a decent veil to throw over human ugliness. Without religion, polite society was impossible.

On that Friday, Father Michelin was hearing confession from the young Countess de Marizy, an adorable blonde as yet barely twenty-two years old, whose beauty had become proverbial in the social columns of all the newspapers. It was she who set the tone and no party was complete without her. The priest had become a friend of the family after a stay in the count's country seat of Plessis-Rouge in Normandy.

The countess was kneeling as she waited her turn. Her dainty little chin was resting on her clasped hands and she was pondering while gazing vaguely in front of her at the pale pink light from the stained-glass window. It did not take her long to examine her conscience: she had only one major confession to make and she was merely deliberating with herself how best to make it. She briefly toyed with the idea of not revealing her lapse, because it was a very difficult matter to speak about; however, it was that very difficulty which attracted her; she felt a feminine urge to relate to this tall handsome young priest how, unfortunately, she had been so far forgetful of her wifely duty as to yield to the solicitations of the Marquis de Mauroy, a sort of cousin of hers whom she had been in love with before her marriage.

Meanwhile, her turn had come. She stood up and went over to the confessional with a slight involuntary curl on her lips which provided a charming foil to the contrite expression which she had felt it proper to assume. No doubt she had found the appropriate approach and turn of phrase needed to make her task easier. She knelt down slowly and stayed there for a good half hour. Nothing could be heard, no voices were raised, there was not even a creak from the woodwork. Then she came out of the confessional, her eyes demurely cast down, and it was impossible to read anything from the expression on her face; she still had the slight involuntary curl on her lips which brought dimples to her pink cheeks.

Father Michelin confessed his men in the Dominican chapel on Mondays. So, on the following Monday, the Marquis de Mauroy was kneeling in exactly the same place as the countess had knelt, similarly awaiting his turn. The marquis was slightly built and delicate-looking young man, with a rather pretty face. Despite his dissipated way of life, he had never stopped regularly practicing his religion, considering it as forming part of his duty to society.

While kneeling, he was, like the countess, pondering and at the same time watching the pale pink light from the stained-glass window. He was wondering whether it would be wise to reveal his relationship with Madame de Marizy to Father Michelin. No doubt the secrets of the confessional were sacrosanct; but the priest might unwittingly betray what he knew by certain pointed glances in the count's presence. The marquis decided on a middle course: he'd confess his lapse while keeping the lady's name secret. Having set his mind at rest by this decision, when he reached the confessional, he went briskly down on to his knees.

Monsieur de Mauroy took less than five minutes to put his conscience in order but he came out looking extremely cross. The priest had refused to let him finish his rigmarole and had informed him very sternly that it was extremely remiss of him to have taken advantage of a gentleman who had welcomed him to his home as an old friend of the family. He had mentioned the count by name and shown that he knew all about the whole affair. To hell with all women! They couldn't go to confession without blurting out their whole story and often even embroidering on it!

It was now seven o['clock but the count had still not come in; they waited for a good quarter of an hour longer. The countess apologized for her husband's late arrival: he had so many important commitments. Everyone nodded understandingly although they all knew that the count's only commitments were the self-imposed ones which he undertook with the better-known amongst the actresses playing in Paris's smaller theatres. Indeed, his friends considered him too incompetent to go into politics.

"Monsieur de Marizy must have been delayed by the ministerial crisis," said Father Michelin. "No doubt he's being consulted."

"Yes, that must be the reason," murmured the marquis, looking at the countess with a sly smile.

She was playing with a scent-bottle and seemed completely unmoved. Father Michelin's remark had been made purely out of politeness, for he too knew quite well where the count must have been delayed. He even knew the name of the little singer at the Italian opera whom Monsieur de Marizy had just presented with a house in town. This actress, who went by the name of Bianca, was a Bordeaux girl who would gobble up the count in three months if she didn't show him the door before. The priest had caught a glimpse of her once in the Bois de Boulogne. A really lovely little creature . . . And, still thinking of her to himself, the priest said out loud, "Yes, Monsieur de Marizy will certainly be at the Ministry."

Eventually the count appeared. Although barely fifty years old, he had a grey, careworn face, receding hair and a morose expression which made him look like a distinguished statesman, prematurely aged by the burden of public office. He made his excuses, complaining that he was snowed under with work. They moved into the dining-room.

The food was delicious. At table, the conversation continued in an undertone but, during the second course, one very old gentleman raised his voice to ask the count who was going to be the new minister. The count did not hear him; he was looking worried and anxious. The old gentleman had to repeat his question.

"Well, as a matter of fact they haven't yet come to any decision," stammered the count finally. "It's a serious situation, very serious indeed . . . . We've never been in such a serious situation."

Everyone had stopped talking to listen to him and he was obliged to go on talking, which he found great difficulty in doing.

"Yes, it's a very dangerous situation. There's been some very violent disagreement . . . I expect they'll be able to patch things up."

Looking at the count, Father Michelin thought to himself that little Bianca must have got hold of the fire-tongs and sent him packing. That would be the violent disagreement to which the count had referred. At this same moment, the priest overheard the countess and the marquis, sitting close to him, exchanging rapid whispers.

"Why didn't you come?"

"I waited for you all day. You don't love me any more. Laura!"

"Be quiet! I'll come and see you tomorrow at two o'clock."

The countess had notice that the priest was listening to their conversation. She turned towards him with an engaging smile: after all, he was in the secret too and wasn't it his duty to show sympathy towards human frailty?

"Father, I know you're fond of game . . . Jean, offer Father Michelin some more partridge."

The priest remained calm. He would certainly know how to deal with the countess as she deserved next time she came to confession; but here, in her own dining-room, he was merely a guest and he was too much a man of the world to show the slightest trace of sternness, which would have been a gross breach of manners. And so dinner continued with the priest still hearing whispers on his left while at the same time looking at two pink spots he had just noticed, two little scratch marks beside one of the count's eyes. Meanwhile the wines were perfect, the dining-room was filled with the fragrance of fresh fruit, the whole meal was being served with the utmost elegance and decorum.

"Are you not preaching at Ste-Clotilde* next Saturday?" an old lady enquired from the priest during dessert.

"Yes, Madame de Beauvoisin. I'm preaching in aid of the charitable institution of Our Lady."

The conversation turned to this organization whose aim was to save the souls of orphan girls who were in moral danger. The countess was one of the lady patronesses.

"We're doing all we can," she said. "There are so many poor girls who go wrong because of the lack of a sound religious upbringing. Once a woman has learnt to know God, she is safe from all danger."

The Marquis de Mauroy gave wholehearted approval to the countess's remarks. Without religion, morality was impossible. Even the count rose to the occasion with a splendid homily, "As I was saying to two senator friends of mine only the other day, if you want to raise the moral level of the masses, you must force them down on their knees in the churches. And they agreed with me. They're intending to introduce a bill making the observance of the Sabbath Day compulsory. We must set an example, gentlemen, we must set an example!"

Exhausted by the effort of making this speech, the count seized the opportunity, as they were leaving table, to take his hat and slip discreetly away. Work is such a hard taskmaster!

The party was drawing to its close. The tow old ladies were the first to leave, followed by the other guests. Finally, only Father Michelin and the marquis remained with the countess. The countess was sitting on the left of the fireplace, the marquis on the right, with the priest in the middle. Conversation became desultory and monosyllabic. Father Michelin realized that he was balking the two lovers but he was tactless enough to want to make his presence felt in order to discipline the young couple and recall them to their sense of duty. He made no reference to the matter but he had promised himself not to leave before the young man.

Half an hour dragged by. The priest's situation was becoming more and more embarrassing. In the end, the man of the world won the day over the priest. Father Michelin stood up to take his leave. At this the countess and the marquis became extremely affable and, as he was going through the door, they called out to him:

"Good night, Father! You know we'll be there to hear you on Saturday."

On the following Saturday, the church of Ste-Clotilde was full of flowers and draped overall in red velvet. In the pulpit, Father Michelin had taken as his text the supreme virtue of the holy state of virginity, a theme of considerable delicacy which he handled in the choicest and most subtle terms. Amongst the congregation, the Count and Countess de Marizy could be seen sitting in the front pews, together with the young Marquis de Mauroy. After the sermon, at the consecration of the host, all three went devoutly down on to their knees. And Father Michelin could congratulate himself on having risen from his father's china-shop to the choir-stall from which he was now able to look down on these reverently bowed aristocratic foreheads. But there was one thought which tempered his elation: he knew that in his church religion was above all a matter of pomp and ceremony and that although these pious attitudes were his to command, he had little power over the souls of his congregation.

III

There was a small private dinner party at the Robinots', a wealthy middle-class family. No more than four people were present: Monsieur and Madame Robinot, their daughter Clémentine, and the parish priest, Father Gérard.

"Do help yourself to a piece of sole, Father," urged Monsieur Robinot. "I know you're fond of fish, so you can't refuse."

"Now Father, you must have some mushrooms," said Madame Robinot in a confidential undertone. "Do me the pleasure of taking these two."

And even Francoise the maid, busily uncorking a bottle, whispered into the priest's ear, "Some Chambertin, Father?"

And Father Gérard beamed affably to his left and right at his host and hostess and made polite replies; he even gave a sly friendly wink to thank Francoise. He was being spoilt, really he was. But the sole was superb and he'd be very happy to have a few more mushrooms. Then he leant back in his chair and drained his glass of Chambertin with half-closed eyes.

Father Gérard was fifty years old. He was fat but he was so ready to poke fun at his paunch himself that nobody would think of blaming him. He boasted a large, found, pink face and a fresh complexion which bore witness to his level-headed, peaceful and happy existence. The son of well-to-do lower middle-class parents he had gone into the church with a gentle smile on his lips rather than with any passionate faith in his heart; he had shrewdly weighed up the pros and cons and come to the conclusion that the life would suit him. Some of the very best livings had fallen to his lot and his superiors had never failed to further his advancement, and were still furthering it, for they saw in him one of those affable and tolerant sorts of priest who, in that day and age, could do more for religion than any apostolic zealot.

He had enjoyed considerable success in Tours for, like many middle-class provincial towns, Tours liked peace and quiet. The women were generally pious while most of the men rarely set foot in church. Father Gérard had realized that his most important task was to cause no disruption of family life and had shown unerring skill in achieving that goal. He was made welcome wherever he went; he heard the wives' confessions and played a hand of piquet with their husbands.

"Now, Father, what's your opinion of this chicken?" enquired Madame Robinot.

"Quite delicious . . . I'll take a little salad."

After dessert, coffee and liqueurs were served. Madame Robinot and her daughter withdrew. Father Gérard cheerfully downed a small glass of Chartreuse and, as he was alone with Monsieur Robinot, they both started chatting about an event that was the talk of the town: the elopement of a Tours lady with a young man from Paris.

"A very pretty young woman," said the priest. "Tall, good figure, lovely teeth."

"You were her confessor, I believe?" asked Monsieur Robinot.

But Father Gérard did not seem to have heard the question. His voice took on a fatherly tone: at the family's request, he'd no doubt have to make up his mind to go to Paris to call on the lost sheep and bring her back into the fold. With a sly grin on his face, Monsieur Robinot was trying to embarrass the priest, who finally exclaimed jovially, "Now! Now! You're just a heathen. There's nothing would give you greater pleasure than to make me say something foolish . . . Let's drop the subject."

In fact Monsieur Robinot tried to tease Father Gérard at every opportunity. He enjoyed bringing the conversation round to scabrous subjects and was always looking for new ways to pull his leg in an attempt to make him lose his temper. But the priest always remained imperturbable, exchanged quip for quip and was prepared to discuss any topic, women or anything else, like a man quite untroubled by fleshly desires. In these skirmishes, it was usually Monsieur Robinot who came off second best.

Madame Robinot and Clémentine were waiting in the drawing-room. As soon as the priest came in he went over and sat down between them, while Monsieur Robinot walked outside on to the terrace to smoke his cigar. The priest's manner became quite different and more unctuous as he talked with the ladies about a big procession which was due to take place the following Sunday. He was the confessor of both the mother and the daughter. Lolling back in his comfortable armchair, he toyed with his gold snuff-box as he explained that it would be a most moving ceremony.

Then Madame Robinot turned towards her daughter. Clémentine went to fetch a chasuble that she was embroidering for Father Gérard: it showed mystical green and red flowers on a gold background; the workmanship was superb and the priest exclaimed in admiration as he complimented the girl, who was overcome with delight and confusion. Both women were huddling round him, hanging on his slightest word. When Monsieur Robinot came back, having finished his cigar, he exclaimed, "And there's Father Gérard leading our ladies astray again!"

But the priest intended to have the last word.

"We were talking about you, Monsieur Robinot," he said with his sly smile. "We were saying that you'd be joining in our Sunday procession."

"Me? Good Lord no!"

Without saying anything more, the priest wagged an admonishing finger at him. A few friends now arrived and the drawing-room filled up; as in all provincial drawing-rooms, the ladies had not changed out of their everyday clothes. There was a registrar of mortgages, who was an elderly eccentric and a rabid anti-Jesuit; a rich wheat-merchant who prided himself on his liberalism; and a principal secretary in the Prefecture, a pretty young man who took very seriously his role of skeptical young Parisian male. However, they all shook hands with the priest in a very friendly manner. As for the ladies, they clustered rapturously around him to enquire after his health and to express the hope that his gout was not proving too troublesome. He was able to reassure them and then agreed to have a game of piquet with the registrar of mortgages.

The conversation became general, with Father Gérard interjecting the odd remark between two hands of piquet and carefully avoiding any mention of religion. When one of the men was tactless enough to refer to his cassock, he smiled without saying a word and refused to be drawn. The whole town was still talking about an incident that had just occurred in someone's house when a priest had lost his temper with the registrar of mortgages who was accusing the Jesuits of fostering the use of tobacco in order to stupefy the masses. Father Gérard would certainly have never allowed himself to be provoked into departing from his exquisite manners by anything like that; on the contrary; he would have been greatly amused, for these little fantasies of the registrar of mortgages had the knack of arousing his mirth.

However, the pries could not always avoid being drawn into discussion. When his game of piquet was over, Monsieur Robinot and the rich grain-merchant managed to corner him in a window and brought the conversation round to the part played by religion in a modern society.

"Seriously, Father," Monsieur Robinot exclaimed. "I'm not so fanatically anti-religious as you may think but I am an unbeliever and so I prefer not to go to church. I'd rather be a heathen than a hypocrite . . . Aren't I right?"

The priest bowed but said nothing.

"However," Monsieur Robinot went on, "I do fully recognize that religion is an excellent guardian of morality and as such an indispensable form of discipline for our wives and daughters . . . For example, I prefer my wife to have God on her mind rather than some young cavalry officer."

The principal secretary in the Prefecture, who had joined the group, thought this remark delightful and exploded in a loud guffaw.

"And you do teach them many valuable things—their marital obligations, obedience and so on, and you threaten them with fire and brimstone if they misbehave . . . that sort of thing is very helpful to husbands . . . "

"In a word, we're a police force ensuring that your honor doesn't come to any harm," Father Gérard interrupted.

Once again the principal secretary in the Prefecture went into ecstasies.

"Oh, that's delightful," he murmured.

"Well, as far as I'm concerned," the wheat-merchant exclaimed, "that's the ort of police force I could well do without . . . You must excuse me,

Father, I've no desire to offend you, but if my wife spent less time on her knees in church, she'd spend more time at home with me. And it's not really so very admirable, from the moral point of view, to do your duty merely because you're afraid of hell-fire."

"Now you're going too far," said Monsieur Robinot. "As long as everything is running smoothly at home, you don't need to worry about anything else."

"No need to worry about anything else? Do you think it's a good thing for your wife to spend every day and all day on her knees? It quite upsets my wife and when she comes back from church, all she can think about is the next world."

"But the important thing is that when she comes back from church she's not coming back from anywhere else."

The priest had prudently withdrawn, leaving the wheat-merchant and Monsieur Robinot to fight it out alone; they became quite abusive. Then, when they had calmed down, the priest came back and said in his usual bland voice, "I don't suppose you know about it but you really ought to take part in the procession next Sunday. Just to set a good example, of course, in support of those guardians of morality Monsieur Robinot was talking about a few moments ago."

These two pillars of bourgeois society laughed and declined: it would really be too funny for words to see them carrying candles through the streets of Tours when everyone knew their liberal views . . .

"I won't insist on any candles," the priest retorted in the same joking tone. "Just think of yourselves as taking a stroll behind the canopy and I can assure you that you'll be in very good company for all the local authorities will be there as well as representatives of the town's most distinguished families."

The two men continued to treat the matter as a joke: it was very kind of Father Gérard to invite them but religious processions were really against their principles and they couldn't accept . Courteous as ever, the priest did not insist and as it was striking ten, he took his leave. All the ladies went with him to the door, whispering amongst themselves and following him fondly with their eyes.

"Goodnight, Father, sleep well."

And then Madame Robinot seemed to have remembered something and ran downstairs after him. They could be heard talking together very quietly for some ten minutes.

On the following Sunday, Monsieur Robinot and the corn-merchant were in the front rank of the procession behind the canopy. Father Gérard must have given Madame Robinot the task of persuading her husband, who had, however, agreed only out of sheet middle-class snobbery: he felt very proud at being a member of one of the most distinguished families of the town. But he still intended to maintain his independence and vote against the bishop's candidate at the next municipal elections.

Father Gérard noticed him and gave him a smile, with a glint of triumph in his tiny eyes. For a moment he could imagine himself as the real master of Tours. Not only did he reign over that flock of wives walking along in the procession with downcast eyes and clasped hands; his power even extended to the husbands of Voltairean persuasion who in the privacy of their homes continually made fun of religion. No doubt the reverend father was sufficient satisfaction for him to see them paying lip-service to Catholicism. When churches are growing emptier every day, you need to bring every possible means into play to fill them.

IV

In the Rue de Charonne, in the heart of the Faubourg Saint-Antoine,* a common-law couple was living on the sixth floor of a large and dilapidated old tenement building, housing exclusively manual workers. Every evening the man, a bricklayer called Lambert, came home the worse for drink. The woman, Lisa by name and a stitcher by trade, was so lazy that one by one all the workshops had refused to employ her. They had been living—and fighting—together for the last three years. But their fighting did not prevent them from being fond of each other, in their own way. If they kept continually knocking each other about, this was merely because it was a good way of keeping warm in winter and passing the long summer evenings. The neighbors had ceased to be concerned about them.

However, last winter had been a difficult one. After a more than usually vigorous battering by Lambert, Lisa had been forced to spend six weeks in bed. There had been unemployment and Lambert had not had any work for the last two months. They were without food or heating. One evening in January, Lambert, certainly not a sensitive person, had been reduced to sitting on the floor with his face in his hands, weeping like a little girl.

Without saying anything, Lisa, who was only just recovering, dressed and went downstairs. She was going to beg in the streets to see if she could collect enough money to buy a loaf of bread. So, keeping a sharp lookout for the police, she sidled along in the shadow of the houses, stopping any passers-by who seemed to have kind faces. It was bitterly cold night and the passers-by were reluctant to take their hands out of their pockets; they quickened their pace and made no response. Crying with cold and shame, Lisa was on the point of giving up when she saw a young priest walking quickly along, wearing such a threadbare cassock that his face and hands were purple with cold. Well, she felt pretty certain that he wouldn't give her anything but, having no great liking for priests, she held out her hand purely to see what sort of face he would pull. He stopped, fumbled in his pocket, blushed and said in a hurried voice, "Take me back to your place, but you must be quick, I'm in a hurry."

When Lambert saw her come into the room with this "black beetle", he shot angrily to his feet; he too was not fond of priests. But although he immediately recognized Lambert's indignant reaction, the priest did not seem to be put out by it. He cast a rapid glance round the garret: there was no doubt of their abject poverty. He put his hand into his fob-pocket and pulled out an old silver watch attached to a silk ribbon and handed it to Lisa, saying in the same hurried voice, "Here you are, take this to the pawn shop straightaway. Please be quick. I'll wait here till you come back."

Although bewildered by this strange turn of events, Lisa ran quickly down the six flights of stairs. All the time she was gone, the priest remained standing, pale and deep in thought, in the middle of the room, while Lambert went back to squat in his corner, supporting his head in his hands and glaring at him with burning eyes.

A quarter of an hour later Lisa returned with ten francs. The priest took only the pawn ticket.

"Keep the money," he said. "If you need me, come and ask for Father de Villeneuve at St. Margaret's."

Thereupon he left and went shivering back to his own home to eat his usual evening meal of two slices of bread and butter. Then he settled down to work in his unheated room, wrapping his legs in a blanket.

Father de Villeneuve was tall and thin and his long pale face already bore two deep creases, although he had been born only twenty-eight years ago, in the south of France, into a family of small country gentry, completely ruined. Left an orphan at the age of ten, he had become deeply religious and had entered the seminary with such burning enthusiasm that his teachers had felt compelled to restrain his potentially dangerous fervor; they saw in him one of those excitable spirits who would be incapable of sensible compromise. Later on, he had passed through a period of appalling spiritual struggle: outstandingly intelligent, he had become obsessed with a desire for knowledge and been assailed by doubts. He argued with his teachers and wrestled with his grave misgivings concerning his faith. In an attempt to overcome these doubts, he had imposed on himself the most rigorous acts of penance. But he had remained inwardly torn and unhappy, still harrowed by the violence of his feelings under the mask of serenity which he had forced himself to present to the world. In the diocese, he had been marked out as a young priest on whom a watchful eye would have to be kept and who must be disciplined should the need arise to avoid scandal.

This was why such a highly intelligent man had remained a humble parish priest attached to the church of St. Margaret in a poor inner Paris suburb. He himself had accepted this kind of exile with complete equanimity, his consuming desire being merely to reconcile the modern world and Catholicism. He was anxious to reject neither science nor the new society, while continuing to hold to catholic dogma. He was, indeed, glad to be living in this essentially working-class district, for he felt convinced that the main task of religion should be to win back the hearts and minds of the urban population. He would mingle constantly with the crowds of workers, studying their needs, seeking to convert them with an apostolic fervor and offering them aid and comfort. He had met with deep hostility and, till now, nothing but resentment. He described this situation as a monstrous misunderstanding; but it pierced him to the quick.

He had been deeply moved as well as shocked by the sight of Lisa begging in the streets for a crust of bread and by her look of hatred, starving though she was. A week later, he went back to the Rue de Charonne and found Lisa alone, just about to put a saucepan of potatoes on the stove. She offered him a lukewarm sort of welcome but he sat down and chatted to her. Lisa made no bones about telling him the truth of her situation: she was not married to Lambert; they had come together one evening and it'd last until it came to an end.

"But that's all wrong!" the priest exclaimed. "You must get married."

Lisa laughed and shrugged her shoulders.

"We're better off as we are," she said. "At least, if things don't work out one day, we can leave each other without any fuss . . . Would we have any more money in our pockets if we were married? The answer to that is no, isn't it? So there you are and it's not a matter of being decent or indecent at all."

When he still kept telling her she ought to think it over and talked about morality and the bad example they were setting, Lisa shook her head.

"Look, sir, there's a married couple on our landing. Well, they knock each other about more than we do and they've got a daughter of fifteen who they're already trying to turn into a bad lot . . . Marriage doesn't really make people more respectable, that's for sure."

And when, as he was going out, the priest tried to leave a five franc piece on the table, Lisa asked him not to. Lambert had found work, and charity was for when you were starving and didn't know which way to turn. She pointed down the corridor, where a poor old sick woman lived who hadn't got the money to buy the medicines she needed. He could give his five franc piece to her, it'd be very welcome.

After this, the priest often came for a chat with Lisa. He had sensed that this fallen woman was good at heart and he desperately wanted to persuade Lambert to agree to get married. He felt that he would be conducting a sort of propaganda on behalf of religion and for the revival of religious beliefs in the hearts of the populace. But reality had always led to rude awakenings.

He soon became known in the tenement block in the Rue de Charonne, an enormous stuccoed building in which more than a hundred families were crammed, in cramped little lodgings. Each time he walked through the courtyard and went up the six flights of stairs, eyes would follow him with a malicious gleam. Of the two or three hundred tenants, not one ever went to mass. So, as he went through, the priest ran the gauntlet of a beguiling commentary. Women would say: "What on earth does he think he's doing here?" Or: "Ah well, today's not my lucky day. I've just seen something that'll do me no good." Or: "Well, well, a priest. I suppose he might be going to pay a visit to that curly haired blonde on the first floor. He might at least have had the decency to change out of his cassock . . . " As for the men, they were even more outspoken. They would enquire if it wasn't a real pity to see such a well set-up young fellow, a strapping young man like that, spend his life just gourmandizing and doing damn all.

Nor did their comments stop there: they started accusing the priest of calling on Lisa for very non-canonical reasons: she still had very nice teeth and hair. And it was not only the bad workmen, the drunkards and loafers who placed this interpretation on his visits. Even the good tenants, the respectable workmen, decent fellows, made jokes about him as loudly as all the rest. The more broadminded amongst them said that priests were no different from anyone else, there were good ones and bad ones, but they ought to be made to marry to prevent them from disrupting other people's families.

In the end, after a brawl in the courtyard, a locksmith who had just received a black eye from Lambert shouted to him, "Go and pick up your handout from the priest! Your Lisa's robbing the poor-box with what that black beetle of hers keeps giving her!"

The builder stormed upstairs and started knocking Lisa about, swearing that if he ever caught the priest up to his tricks, he'd do for him. And the very next day, the priest arrived just as Lambert was finishing his supper.

"Don't you touch him!" cried Lisa, terrified at the thought of a scandal. "This gentleman doesn't mean any harm, he just wants us to get married, he says it would be more respectable."

Lambert was too infuriated to listen.

"Clear off and don't you ever come here again," he yelled. "What the hell do you man by interfering and trying to stop people from living the way they want!"

The priest waited calmly for a chance to reply and, speaking in a very quiet voice, tried to appeal to the better nature of this half-demented man: what would become of their children if they ever had any?

"Please listen to me, think of the future and get married."

Lambert cut him short."Why not start by getting married yourself? Get yourself a woman, but not mine, do you understand? And now clear off and sharp's the word!"

Father de Villeneuve hung his head and left. As he went down-stairs, he could hear laughter all around: the neighbors had been listening to the row and were amused to see him beating such an ignominious retreat.

And as he went on his way, the priest imagined all the passersby looking at him and laughing, as if they knew of his discomfiture. Yes, the whole district disliked him and he could feel how completely all these city dwellers lay outside the influence of the church. His dream of reviving the faith of ordinary people and building the new society on it lay shattered. Dear God, were these the modern times that had already come? Would he have to look elsewhere for truth than in Catholic dogma, where he had always tried to find it hitherto? As his doubts increased, his inner struggle grew fiercer. He felt himself already launched on that slippery slope with other fervid and intelligent priests beset by religious scruples and unable to become Christian soldiers supporting the onward march of progress. And so, bruised and bleeding from their struggle, they eat out their hearts in pain and sorrow.

V

Monsignor was sitting in his study hidden away in the remote depths of the Episcopal palace. He had announced that he would not be in for anyone, ad he had a great deal of work that day. His secretary Father Raymond, a young priest of twenty-six, was alone with him, sitting at one end of the big rosewood desk on which the bishop was writing in his large sprawling handwriting.

"Raymond," he said, without looking up, "take that batch of proofs and correct them. It's an article for La Religion that must be sent off to Paris at once. It's due to appear tomorrow."

And he went back to his work. He was writing a pamphlet attacking the materialistic theories of a philosopher with whom he had been waging almost constant war for nearly a decade. He had a vigorous, biblical style; but he made a rather excessive use of anathema.

"Raymond," he said again, after a long pause, "will you find me the word

'neurosis' in the medical dictionary . . . Yes, pass it to me."

He dropped his pen and buried himself in the weighty tome. He read the article on neurosis which covered several pages. A whole section of his pamphlet revolved round the authenticity of certain miracles. Then, having acquired sufficient knowledge of the technical terms, he once again put pen to paper and scratched vigorously on. This scratching pen was the only sound to be heard; the town was plunged in wholesome provincial slumber.

Monsignor was a tall, athletic-looking old man of sixty, as thin as a rake, with a ravaged face to which his narrow nose added a note of implacable determination. He had shapely hands, with long tapering fingers suggesting his aristocratic origins: on his mother's side, he was descended from and old Auvergne family; but his father, a man of peasant stock who had risen in the world through his success in industry, had bequeathed him a far from aristocratic name which he was moreover quite happy to bear, taking pride in having raised it to its present eminence. His determined hands were being elegantly employed in the service of a superior class.

Monsignor had taken orders relatively late in life; he had originally been a colonel in the dragoons. It was not until the age of thirty-six that he had lost his taste for the military life, which had doubtless failed to provide him with the satisfaction he had expected. In the space of a few years he had joined the ranks of the most distinguished doctors of divinity and ever since he had been conducting his fierce and unrelenting struggle against the spirit of his age. He had been immediately acknowledged as an outstandingly vigorous polemicist and had swiftly risen to the upper hierarchy of the Church. If truth be told, he was now feverishly waiting to receive his red cardinal's hat, an ambition which he had fondly nursed ever since he had been ordained.

Monsignor had not disappointed the expectations of his superiors. This ex-colonel of dragoons seemed to think that he was still on the field of battle, smiting his enemy's hip and thigh with his crozier. He fought in the newspapers, he fought with broadsheets, he used every weapon, including the most worldly ones. Above all, he should have been seen in his diocese, where he filled everyone with fear and trepidation. He had vanquished the whole department. He waged pitched battles against the civil authorities and would conduct a three months' campaign in order to obtain the dismissal of a gamekeeper to whom he had taken a dislike. For him, God was a policeman and nothing else; and he would threaten to call Him in at the slightest sign of insubordination amongst the rank and file.

Monsignor had in his study a large ivory figure of Christ on a cross of ebony, somewhat in the same way as you keep a bust of the reigning monarch in a town hall, purely as a symbol of authority. Monsignor rarely went down on his knees before his Christ; he preferred merely to make a rapid sign of the cross. But if there was any sign of revolt amongst the troops, the bishop would hold up his hand to the Christ on the cross as though appealing for help from the armed forces.

Meanwhile, Father Raymond had finished correcting the proofs of the article intended for the newspaper La Religion. Monsignor cast a quick eye over the article, put it in and envelope, rang his bell and had it sent straight off to the post.

"Tell me, Raymond," he said after a moment's thought, "which of these two titles do you prefer: Judas discomfited or The Stupidity of Science?"

But he did not give Father Raymond time to reply before making up his own mind, as he wrote Judas discomfited in large capitals at the top of his manuscript. Then he rang again and gave instructions for it to be sent off to the printers, "and without delay", he added loudly to his usher.

"Excuse me, Monsignor," the later said, "there are a number of people waiting who are very anxious to speak to you."

"They can wait. If I'm free, I'll see them before lunch . . . Oh, and if the Marquis de Courneuve calls, show him in straightaway."

Monsignor stood up and took a few paces round his study. Then he sat down briskly and said, "Pass me my correspondence, Raymond. I'd like you to help me. Wit it."

His secretary placed and enormous bundle of letters on the table and picking them up one by one he opened them with a paper-knife and handed them to Monsignor, who ran his eye rapidly through them; he always insisted on seeing everything for himself. He sorted the letters as he read them, screwing up and throwing on the floor those which he considered unimportant and placing the others in piles.

This voluminous correspondence contained a little of everything: requests for aid, letters relating to diocesan affairs, letters from every corner of France as well as overseas, concerning the propagation of the faith. Occasionally Monsignor would become absorbed in a letter and his sallow face would reflect the complicated calculations of a statesman hatching vast schemes of conquest. The threads of every possible clerical intrigue would end up in this study and decisions affecting the most substantial issues would be reached, questions of war or peace between nations or matters of internal policy in which the material and spiritual welfare of France was constantly at stake.

But on this particular morning, the principal business was happily not a European upheaval but merely the question as to who should have the upper hand on an educational issue, the prefect or Monsignor. The prefect who, although not a republican, prided himself on his liberalism, had set up a lay school in the little town of Verneuil; and Monsignor had sworn to replace it by a Catholic denominational school. The battle had been raging for six months now and both the prefect and Monsignor were digging in their heels. There were already a good score of letters on the subject in the file.

"The Marquis de Courneuve," the usher announced.

Monsignor hurried over to greet the newcomer.

"Well?" he enquired anxiously.

"I'm just back from Paris," replied the marquis. "I saw the Minister but I didn't want to broach the matter openly. If we succeed, the prefect is talking of tendering his resignation and that makes it rather a sensitive issue."

"Anyway, what's the situation?"

"I wasn't able to have a categorical answer but I've asked my mother-in-law to see what she can do and she has promised to let you know as soon as a decision is reached."

Monsignor could not refrain from making a gesture of impatience: he should have gone to Paris himself, for abominable things were taking place in that school.

"Just look at these letters," he said to the marquis. "They've given children books to read in which religion is attacked . . . I'm told that the schoolmaster has a sister who lived in sin with a man for ten years before marrying him . . . I'm assured that at the last municipal elections, that same schoolmaster was a member of a committee of troublemakers . . . Isn't all that enough?"

He went on to attack the prefect. This question of a lay school was an excellent opportunity of getting rid of an official completely lacking in any sort of religious feeling. It so happened that he had just received letters from a number of the town notables, all deeply religious people, who were acting in concert with him against the prefect. He showed the marquis their letters.

Madame de Saint-Luce, whose brother was a member of the Chambre des Députés, had written to say that her brother had been sending her excellent news. Monsieur Baudoin, a local lawyer with a great deal of influence in the town, had assured Monsignor that "anyone who was anybody" was solidly on her side. Monsieur de Mortal quoted the following statements by the prefect: Clericalism is a cancerous growth in the department—dangerous and incautious words that could well be of use if conveyed to the proper government quarters . . . In fact, the prefect seemed all set to take a fall. It would be the third in two years whom Monsignor had succeeded in unseating.

At the moment, the usher came in to inform the bishop that the parish priest of Villeneuve, and old man, had come sixteen miles on foot to present a petition to him.

"Tell him I can't see him now, he'll have to wait!" the prelate cried.

But the door had been left open and the priest himself came in. He was a poor old country priest in a threadbare cassock and wearing heavy dust-covered shoes. He came forward and said in a humble, quavering voice, "Monsignor, you must please forgive me, I shouldn't have come to trouble you on my own behalf, but it's a matter that concerns our dear Lord, Monsignor. Our church at Villeneuve is so old that the recent storms have damaged the roof, the windows are all broken and the doors won't close, so that now the rain comes in on the chancel. The other day we had to put up an umbrella over the altar while I was saying Mass, so that the host shouldn't get wet . . . It's a dreadful state of affairs, Monsignor."

"Well, what do you expect me to do about it? Retorted the bishop, visibly bored by the priest's longwinded explanation.

"You need only to say the word, Monsignor, and they'll repair our church. You have the authority."

"That's where you're wrong, there are endless formalities involved . . . Draw up a proper report and we'll send someone to look at the damage and the matter will be dealt with through the appropriate channels."

He rose to his feet to indicate that the interview was over but the old priest stood his ground, with tears in his eyes.

"Monsignor, I beseech you to help, it's not for my sake, it's for the sake of our dear Lord."

The bishop lost his patience.

"I'm telling you I can't do a thing. Now, stop troubling me, you can see that I'm very busy."

And in the unmistakable voice of a former colonel of dragoons, he snapped:

"Our dear Lord won't melt in the rain, for heaven's sake!"

Completely disconcerted and dismayed by Monsignor's wrath, the old priest backed out of the room, apologizing as he went with his head trembling like a man in his dotage. He would have to walk the sixteen miles all the way back to Villeneuve, haunted by the thought that the rain would be pouring into his leaking church all that winter.

Meanwhile the usher had brought in a letter.

"It's my mother-in-law's handwriting!" exclaimed the Marquis de Courneuve glancing at the envelope.

Victory was theirs! In great excitement, standing by the window, Monsignor reread the letter in which the countess announced that she had seen the Minister and the lay school would be closed. She also informed him that the prefect had sent in his resignation.

"I shall be lunching with the Marquis de Courneuve, Raymond" said the bishop. "Tell the printers that I want the proofs of my pamphlet by tomorrow morning at the latest. We'll read the proofs together."

And as he was making his way towards the door, his eyes happened to fall on his large ivory figure of Christ. He had almost forgotten to associate Him with his victory. So, as he bowed, he spoke these simple words to Monsieur de Courneuve, in the joyful tones of a soldier who has faith in the flag beneath which he serves:

"Marquis, by this sign we shall always defeat our foes!"

MADAME NEIGEON

Eight days have gone by since my father, M. de Vaugelade, allowed me to leave Le Boquet, the mournful old chateau where I was born, in Lower Normandy. My father has strange ideas about the present times; he is a good half-century behindhand. However, I am at last living in Paris, which I scarcely knew at all, having simply passed through it on two previous occasions. Fortunately, I am not over awkward in my ways. Felix Budin, my old schoolfellow at the College of Caen, pretended, on seeing me here, that I was superb, and that the Parisiennes would surely dote on me. This made me laugh. But when Felix had left, I caught myself standing before a looking-glass, contemplating my five feet six inches, and smiling at my white teeth and black eyes. Then, however, I shrugged my shoulders, for I'm not conceited.

Yesterday for the first time in my life I spent an evening in a Parisian drawing-room. Countess de P, who is in some degree my aunt, had asked me to dinner. It was her last Saturday. She wanted to introduce me to Monsieur Neigeon, a deputy for our constituency of Gommerville, who had just been appointed Undersecretary of State, and is on the high road, so people say, to become a Minister. My aunt, who is far more tolerant than my father, plainly declared to me that a young man of my age most not sulk with his country, even if its government were republican. She wishes to get me an official appointment.

'I will undertake to talk to that obstinate old Vaugelade,' she said; 'leave everything to me, my dear George.'

Precisely at seven o'clock I reached the Countess's house. But it seems that people dine very late in Paris. The guests arrived one by one, and some had not yet put in an appearance when half-past seven struck. The Countess informed me with an expression of distress that she had been unable to secure Monsieur Neigeon's company; he was retained at Versailles by some parliamentary imbroglio. Nevertheless, she still hoped that he might look in for a moment during the evening. As a stop-gap she had invited another deputy of our department, 'fat Gaucheraud,' as we call him down there. I knew him already, as we had once gone shooting together.

This Gaucheraud is a short jovial fellow, who has lately let his whiskers grow in the hope of thereby giving himself a serious appearance. He was born in Paris, where his father was a petty solicitor of small means; but, down our way, he has a rich and very influential uncle, whom he somehow prevailed upon to run him as a candidate. I was not aware that he was married; but at table my aunt placed me beside a young fair-haired lady, who looked very pretty and shy, and whom fat Gaucheraud called 'Berthe' at the top of his voice.

The story dates from the time, subsequent to the Franco German War, when the French Legislature met at Versailles.

We were all assembled at last. It was still daylight the drawing-room, which looks towards the west, when all at once we entered the dining-room, which had its curtains drawn and was lit up by a chandelier and several lamps. The change seemed very singular, and as we took our seats some remarks were made about the way in which the last dinners of the winter season are saddened by the lingering twilight. My aunt detested it. And the conversation on the subject was kept up: how mournful, said somebody, did Paris look when you drove across it in the waning light on your way to an invitation. I said nothing myself, but I had not experienced any such impression in my cab, though it had jolted roughly over the paving stones for a full half-hour. As a matter of fact, Paris, seen amidst the first gleams of the gaslight, had filled me with a passionate desire to partake of all the enjoyment with which it would presently blaze.

By the time the entries were served, people raised their voices and politics were discussed. I was surprised to hear my aunt expressing political opinions. However, the other ladies were all conversant with State affairs, called prominent men by their names without any such prefix as monsieur and debated and passed judgment on everything and everybody. In front of me Gaucheraud was taking up an enormous amount of room and talking at the top of his voice while steadily eating and drinking. But all those political matters did not interest me; I did not even understand the true sense of many remarks, and so I ended by devoting all my attention to Madame Gaucheraud, Berthe, as I already called her in my own mind for brevity's sake. She was really very pretty. As she sat beside me her ear struck me as being particularly charming: a pretty little rounded ear it was, with light yellowish hair curling around it. She had one of those fair necks, covered behind with little wavy locks which quite upset one. Every now and then, when her shoulders moved, her dress-body, which was cut very low, gaped a little, and I noticed a supple, feline curve to her back. I did not admire her profile so much, as it was rather sharp. She talked politics with even greater eagerness than any of the others.

'Madame, may I pour you out some wine? Shall I pass you the salt, madame?' I asked, striving to be as polite as possible, forestalling her slightest desires and interpreting her every glance and gesture. She had given me a long look as we sat down to table, as if to judge me once and for all.

'Politics bore you, do they not?' she said to me at last. 'They plague me to death. But then one has to talk about something, and nowadays in society politics are the only thing that people care for.'

Then she darted off to another subject. 'Is Gommerville a pretty place?' she asked. 'Last summer my husband wanted to take me to see his uncle there, but I felt frightened and pretended that I was ill.'

'The country is very fertile,' I replied; 'there are some beautiful plains.'

'Ah! Good. Now I know the truth,' she resumed with a laugh. 'It is a frightful spot, eh? A perfectly flat country with fields following fields, and ever the same fringes of poplar trees rising up at intervals.'

I wanted to protest, but she had started off again, discussing some proposed law on secondary education with the guest seated on her right hand, a solemn-looking man with a white beard. At last, however, the conversation turned to theatricals. Whenever she leant forward to answer a question asked from the other end of the table, the feline undulations of her neck filled me with emotion. At Le Boquet, amidst the covert impatience of solitude, I had dreamt of a fair-haired beauty, but she was slow of gesture and had a noble face; and Berthe's mouse-like mien and little curly hair quite revolutionized my dream. Nevertheless, while the vegetables were being served, I glided into some wild fancies. We were alone, she and I, and I kissed her on the neck and she turned round and smiled at me; whereupon we started together for some very distant land. But the dessert was served, and at that moment she said to me in a whisper, 'Pass me that dish of sweetmeats there, in front of you.'

It seemed to me that there was a caressing softness in her eyes, and the light pressure of her arm on the sleeve of my dress coat gave me a delightful thrill.

'I'm awfully fond of sweetmeats; aren't you?' she resumed, as she nibbled at some candied fruit.

Those simple words stirred me to such a degree that I fancied myself in love with her. As I raised my eyes I noticed Gaucheraud, who had been looking at me while I whispered with his wife. He wore his usual gay expression and smiled in an encouraging manner. The idea of the husband smiling calmed me.

But the dinner was drawing to an end. It did not seem to me that a Paris dinner party sparkled with more wit than one at Caen. Berthe alone surprised me. My aunt having complained of the warmth, the company reverted to their first subject of conversation, discussing the spring receptions, and finally opining that it was only at winter-time that one really dined well. Then we went off to the little drawing-room to take coffee there.

By degrees a great many people arrived. The three drawing-rooms and the dining-room likewise became crowded. I had sought refuge in a corner, and as my aunt passed near me she said to me hurriedly: 'don't go away yet, George. His wife has arrived. He has promised to fetch her, and I will introduce you.'

She was still talking of Monsieur Neigeon, but I scarcely listened. I had heard two young men near me exchanging hasty remarks which filled me with emotion.

They were standing on tip-toes at a door of the big drawing room, and at the moment when Felix Budin, my old schoolfellow at Caen, came in and bowed to Madame Gaucheraud, the shorter of the two asked the other: 'Are they still on the same terms?'

'Yes,' the taller one answered,' more so than ever. It will last till the winter now. I have never known her keep an admirer so long.'

This did not cause me any particular pang, but I felt hurt in my self-esteem. Why had she told me in so soft a voice that she was fond of sweetmeats? I certainly had no intention of contending against Felix, yet I ended by persuading myself that those young men had slandered Madame Gaucheraud. I knew my aunt; she was a person of very rigid principles, and would not suffer women of doubtful repute in her house. Gaucheraud, as it happened, had just sprung forward to greet Felix, whom he tapped in a friendly way on the shoulder while eyeing him affectionately.

'Ah! Here you are,' said Felix as soon as he discovered me. 'I came on your account. Well, will you let me pilot you?'

We remained together in a recess formed by a doorway. I should greatly have liked to question him about Madame Gaucheraud, but I did not know how to do so in an offhand, indifferent way. While seeking a transition I questioned him about a number of other people for whom I cared nothing at all. He named them to me, and gave precise particulars about each of them. He was, I should say, a Parisian by birth, and had merely spent a couple of years at the college at Caen at the time when his father was Prefect of the Department of Calvados. I found him very free in his language, and a smile appeared on his lips when I asked him for information about some of the women present.

'Are you looking at Madame Neigeon?' he suddenly asked me.

To tell the truth I was looking at Madame Gaueheraud. And so, somewhat foolishly, I answered, 'Madame Neigeon, ah I where is she?'

'She's that dark woman yonder, near the chimneypiece. She's talking with a fair woman in a low dress.'

Near Madame Gaueheraud, indeed, there stood a lady whom I had not previously noticed, and who was laughing gaily.

'Ah! So that's Madame Neigeon,' I repeated.

Then I examined her. It was a great pity that she was dark, for she struck me as being charming, not quite so tall as Berthe, but with a magnificent crown of black hair. Her eyes were both bright and soft. Her little nose, her finely modeled mouth, and her dimpled cheeks indicated a lively and yet thoughtful disposition. Such at least was my first impression. But my views became confused as I looked at her, for I soon saw her laughing more loudly and freely than even her friend.

'Do you know Neigeon?' Felix asked me.

'I? Not at all. My aunt is to introduce me to him.'

'Oh! He's a nullity, a downright fool,' Felix continued. 'Political mediocrity in all its perfection—one of those stop-gaps that are so useful in parliamentary government. As he does not possess two ideas of his own, and every prime minister can therefore employ him, he figures in the most contradictory ministerial combinations.'

'And his wife?' I asked.

'His wife? Well, you see her. She is charming. If you want to obtain anything from him, pay court to his wife.'

Felix affected some unwillingness to say anything further. But at last he gave me to understand that Madame Neigeon had made her husband's fortune, and continued watching over the home with a view to its prosperity. All Paris attributed lovers to her.

'And the fair lady?' I suddenly inquired.

'The fair lady,' Felix answered without the faintest show of feeling,' is Madame Gaucheraud.'

'She is a respectable woman, isn't she?'

'Oh I no doubt she's respectable.'

Felix assumed a serious demeanor, but was unable to preserve it. His smile appeared once more, and I even fancied that I could detect on his features an expression of conceit which annoyed me. The two women had doubtless noticed that we were occupying ourselves with them, for they forced their laughter. I remained alone, a lady having led Felix away, and I spent the evening in comparing Madame Neigeon with Madame Gaucheraud, feeling at once hurt and attracted, failing to understand things aright, and experiencing the anxiety of a man who fears lest he may be guilty of some act of foolishness in venturing into a sphere of which he has no knowledge.

'Neigeon hasn't come; what a nuisance he is!' exclaimed my aunt when she again found me in the same corner by the door. 'But it's always like that. True, it is barely midnight as yet, and his wife is still waiting for him.'

I went round through the dining-room and took up a position at the other door of the salon. In this wise I found myself behind the two ladies I have mentioned. Just as I reached the spot I heard Berthe calling her friend ' Louise.' That is a pretty name. Louise was not wearing a low dress. Under her heavy coils of hair I could only see a white strip of neck, but that glimpse of whiteness seemed to me for a moment to be far more fascinating than the exhibition which Berthe was making of her back. Then, however, I no longer knew what to think; they both seemed adorable, and in the perturbed state in which I found myself it appeared to me impossible to choose between them.

But my aunt was looking for me everywhere. It was already one o'clock.

'Have you changed doors?' said she. 'Well, he won't come. Every evening that man Neigeon has to save France. At all events, I will introduce you to his wife before she leaves. And mind that you are amiable, for that is important.'

Without awaiting my answer the Countess placed me in front of Madame Neigeon, giving her my name and briefly acquainting her with my position. I felt rather awkward, and could scarcely find a few words. Louise waited with that smile of hers on her face, and then, seeing that I remained embarrassed, she simply bowed. It seemed to me that Madame Gaucheraud was looking at me contemptuously. Both rose, however, and withdrew. In the antechamber, used as a cloak-room, a fit of wild merriment came over them. However, their free and easy, bold, masculine ways astonished nobody but me. As they passed, the other men drew back and bowed to them with a commingling of extreme politeness and social good-fellowship which stupefied me.

Felix offered me a seat in his cab. But I escaped from him, for I wished to be alone; and I did not hail any driver, for it pleased me to go on foot through the silence and solitude of the streets. I felt feverish, just as one feels at the approach of some severe illness. Was a passion springing up within me? Like the travelers who pay tribute to new climes, I was about to be sorely tried by the atmosphere of Paris.

It was only this afternoon that I met those ladies again, this time at the Salon de Peinture, which, it so happened, opened to-day. I confess that I knew I should meet them there, and that it would be very difficult for me to pronounce an opinion on the value of the three or four thousand paintings before which I promenaded for four successive hours. Felix had promised me yesterday that he would call for me about noon: we were to lunch at a restaurant in the Champs-Élysées and then repair to the Salon.

I have reflected a great deal since the Countess's soirée took place, but I must own that reflection has not brought me much enlightenment. How strange a world is Parisian society, at once so polished and so corrupt! I am not a rigid moralist, but none the less I feel embarrassed when I think of the fearful things that I heard men saying to one another in my aunt's drawing-room. If one was to believe their muttered comments, more than half the women present were disreputable. How was one to tell the truth amidst all those assertions? I had at first thought that, in spite of all my father had said on the subject, my aunt really received a very questionable set. But Felix asserted that things were just the same in most Parisian drawing-rooms. Ladies, even the most severely inclined among them, were compelled to show a great deal of tolerance lest they should find their houses forsaken. Then, my first feeling of revolt having calmed down, I simply felt an impulse to snatch at the facile pleasures placed within my reach.

For the last four days I had never awoke in my little flat in the Rue Lafitte without thinking of Louise and Berthe, as I familiarly called them. A singular phenomenon was at work within me: I ended by confounding them together. I was now certain that Felix was Berthe's lover, but this, instead of wounding my feelings, seemed a kind of encouragement, and though my thoughts and plans remained very vague, I was convinced that I had only to choose between Berthe and Louise to become the master of one or the other.

When we entered the first gallery of the Fine Art show I was amazed at the great crowd that was stifling there.

'The Devil,' muttered Felix; 'we are rather late. We shall have to use our elbows.'

It was a very mixed throng of artists, bourgeois and society people. In the midst of overcoats badly brushed, and frockcoats black and gloomy, there were many light gowns; those spring Paris gowns which look so gay with their soft silk and their bright trimmings. And I was particularly delighted by the quiet assurance of the women, who cut through the thickest of the throng without even a thought of their trains, whose waves of lace always ended by effecting a passage. In this wise they went from one picture to another as if they were simply crossing their drawing-rooms. Only Parisiennes can thus retain a goddess-like serenity in a public crush, as if the words they hear, and the contact they have to put up with, could not possibly reach and soil them. For a moment I watched one lady who Felix told me was the Duchesse d'A. She was accompanied by two daughters of from sixteen to eighteen years of age; and the three of them examined a ' Leda' without so much as blinking, while a party of young painters behind them made merry over the picture with the greatest freedom of language.

But Felix turned into the left-hand galleries, a succession of large square rooms where the crowd was less compact. A white light fell from the glazed roof, a crude light softened by linen hangings. The dust raised by the tramping of the people set, as it were, some slight smoke above the sea of heads. The women needed to be very pretty to bear the effect of that light, that uniform tone, with which the paintings on the four surrounding walls contrasted violently. There one perceived an extraordinary medley of colors, reds, yellows and blues all clashing and running riot amidst the bright gold of the picture-frames. It was becoming very warm. Some bald-headed gentlemen with polished glistening craniums puffed as they walked about, hat in hand. Every nose was raised upward. There was quite a crush in front of certain canvases. And one incessantly heard the tramping of feet over the floor boards, accompanied by a vague, endless clamor like the roaring of waves.

'Ah!' Felix suddenly remarked to me,' there's the big affair that folks talk so much about.'

People stood five rows deep, in contemplation before 'the big affair.' There were ladies with glasses, artists talking spitefully, and a tall lean gentleman taking notes. But I scarcely gave a glance in that direction, for in a neighboring room I had caught sight of two ladies leaning against the handrail and inquisitively examining a little picture on the line. At first there was but a flash of thick black tresses and a mass of fair fluffy hair, showing under stylish hats. Then this vision vanished; a wave of the crowd, a sea of heads hid both ladies from my view. But I could have sworn to them. After taking a few steps, I again caught sight now of the fair hair, now of the black tresses between the ever-moving heads in front of me. I said nothing to Felix; I contented myself with leading him into the next room, maneuvering in such wise that it might seem as if he were the first to recognize the ladies. Had he already noticed them, as I had done? I almost believe so, for he gave me a glance full of delicate irony.

'Ah! What a fortunate meeting!' he exclaimed as he bowed.

The ladies turned and smiled. I awaited the effect of this second interview: it was decisive. Madame Neigeon quite upset me with a mere glance of her black eyes, whereas I seemed to be simply meeting a friend again in the person of Madame Gaucheraud. This time, then, it was the lightning flash. She—Madame Neigeon—was wearing a small yellow hat trimmed with a branch of glycine, and her gown was of mauve silk with trimmings of straw-colored satin, the whole forming a very soft yet showy toilette. However, it was only later that I really scrutinized her. At the first moment she appeared to me in a blaze of light, as if she scattered sunbeams around her.

But Felix was talking. 'Nothing remarkable, eh?' said he; 'I have seen nothing yet.'

'It is the same, mon Dieu, as it is every year,' Berthe declared.

Then, turning towards the wall, she added: 'Look at this little painting which Louise discovered. The gown is so beautifully done! Madame de Kochetail wore one exactly like it at the last ball at the Élysées.'

'Yes,' murmured Louise, 'only the ruches fell squarewise over the table.'

They again studied the little picture, which represented a lady standing before a boudoir mantelpiece, reading a letter. The painting seemed to me very commonplace, but somehow I felt full of sympathy for the painter.

'Why, where is he?' suddenly asked Berthe, as she looked around her. 'He loses us at every dozen yards I'

She was speaking of her husband.

'Oh! Gaucheraud is over yonder,' quietly exclaimed Felix, who could see everybody. 'He is looking at that big Christ in sugar-candy, hanging from gingerbread cross.'

In a peaceful, disinterested way the husband with his hands behind him was indeed making the round of the room on his own account. On catching sight of us he came up to shake hands, and said in his jovial fashion: 'There's a Crucifixion yonder which shows remarkable religious sentiment. Have you noticed it?'

The ladies, however, were walking on. We followed them with Gaucheraud. His presence authorized us to accompany them. We spoke of Monsieur Neigeon, who would no doubt look in at the show if he could only escape early enough from a committee meeting, at which he was to give the Government's opinion on a very important question. Gaucheraud meantime took possession of me with many expressions of friendship. This embarrassed me, for it was necessary that I should answer him. Felix smiled, and gently nudged my elbow, but I failed to understand him. For his part, profiting by the fact that I was keeping the fat man occupied, he walked on in front with the ladies. I only caught snatches of their conversation.

'So you are going to the Varieties this evening?'

'Yes, I have taken a corner box; the piece is said to be amusing. . . . I shall take you, Louise—Oh! I insist on it.'

And further on, 'So now the season is over. The opening of the Salon is the final Parisian solemnity.' 'But you forget the races!'

'Ah! Yes, I've an idea of going to the races at Maisons-Lafitte. It's a very pretty place, I'm told.'

Meantime Gaucheraud was talking to me about Le Boquet, a superb estate, said he, the value of which had been more than doubled by my father. I could tell that he was bent on flattery. But I barely listened to him. I was stirred to the depths of my being each time that Louise's long train brushed against me, as she suddenly stopped before some picture. Under her black hair, her white neck looked as delicate as a child's. However, she retained her masculine ways, which somewhat annoyed me. A great many people bowed to her, and she laughed at them and attracted general attention by her outbursts of gaiety and the quick motions of her skirts. On two occasions she turned round and looked at me fixedly. I walked on as in a dream; I could not say bow many hours I followed her in this fashion, dazed by Gaucheraud's chatter and the leagues of paintings which spread out on right and left. I only knew that towards the end we were all chewing dust and that for my own part I felt horribly fatigued, whereas the women bore up and smiled with all bravery.

At six o'clock Felix carried me off to dinner. And at dessert he suddenly exclaimed: 'I've got to thank you.'

'What for?' I asked him in great surprise.

'Why, for the delicacy you have shown in not paying court to Madame Gaucheraud. So you prefer dark women?'

I could not help flushing, but he hastily added, 'Oh! I don't desire your confidence. You must have noticed that I abstained from intervening. In my opinion, a man ought to make his apprenticeship in life alone.'

He was no longer smiling, but wore a serious, friendly air.

'So you think 'I began.

'I think nothing,' he answered. 'Do as you fancy. You will soon see how things turn out.'

I regarded this remark as a piece of encouragement. Felix had reverted to his ironical tone, and lightly, as if jesting, he pretended that Gaucheraud would have liked to see me fall in love with his wife.

'Oh! You don't know the beggar! You didn't understand why he flung himself so eagerly on your neck. The fact is that his uncle's influence is declining in your district, and if he had to face another election he would be heartily glad of your father's support. Well, as you can understand, I felt frightened directly I saw that you might be useful to him; for he has used me up already.'

'But that's abominable!' I exclaimed.

'Why abominable?' Felix resumed in so quiet a fashion that I could not tell whether he was in earnest or not. 'When a woman is bound to have friends, it is just as well that they should prove useful to the home.'

On rising from table Felix talked of going to the Varieties. I had seen the piece there two days previously; but I dissembled, and expressed a keen desire to become acquainted with it. And what a charming evening we spent! The ladies happened to be in a corner box quite close to our stalls. On turning my head I could read on Louise's features the pleasure she took in the actors' jests. A couple of evenings previously I had found those jests idiotic. But they no longer offended me; I enjoyed them, since they seemed to foster a kind of complicity between Louise and myself. It was a very broad piece, and it was at the most questionable passages that she laughed the loudest. Whenever our eyes met amidst the laughter she refrained from lowering them. I could not help thinking that the piece helped on my interests. Truth to tell, the whole house enjoyed itself; many women in the balcony stalls laughed outright, without even indulging in any fan play by way of hiding their blushes.

We went to pay our respects to the ladies during one of the entr'actes. Gaucheraud had just gone out, so we were able to sit down. The box was very gloomy, and I could feel Louise near me. Her skirts were spread out, and at a sudden movement she made they quite covered my knees. It was entrancing to be thus near her. That contact seemed to me like a first, secret avowal, which bound us one to the other.

Ten days have now gone by. Felix has disappeared, and I can devise no pretext that might bring me and Madame Neigeon together again. My only resource is to buy five or six daily papers in which I read her husband's name. He intervened lately in a serious debate in the Chamber, and delivered a speech about which people are still talking. At any other time that speech would have bored me to death, but nowadays it interests me, because it seems as if I could distinguish Louise's white neck and black tresses behind all the verbose phraseology. I have even had a violent discussion about Monsieur Neigeon—whose incapacity I defended—with a gentleman whom I scarcely know. The malicious attacks of the newspapers quite upset me. That man is an imbecile, no doubt, but then this only proves the superior intelligence of his wife, if indeed it be true, as people say, that she has been the good fairy to whom he owes his fortune.

During these ten days of vain impatience and fruitless rambles I have called quite five times on my aunt, ever in the hope of some piece of good luck, some unforeseen meeting. On the occasion of my last call I managed to displease the countess so seriously that it will be a long time before I shall dare to return to her house. She had taken it into her head to procure me an appointment in the diplomatic service by Monsieur Neigeon's influence; and her stupefaction was intense when I refused the offer on account of my political opinions. The worst was that I accepted it originally, that is, before I had fallen in love with Louise, and had come to the conclusion that I could not decently accept any favors from her husband's hands.

My aunt, who had no notion of the motives of delicacy which actuated me, expressed profound astonishment at what she called my childish capriciousness. Did not many Legitimists, who were quite as scrupulous as myself, represent the Republic abroad? She asked. Indeed, diplomacy was the refuge of the Legitimists. They filled the embassies and rendered useful service to the good cause by keeping possession of high positions which the Republicans envied them.

I was, for good reasons, greatly embarrassed as to how I might answer my aunt, and at last I sought a refuge in ridiculous rigidity of principles, whereupon my aunt ended by calling me a fool, for she felt all the more furious since she had already mentioned the affair to Monsieur Neigeon. But no matter! At all events, Louise will never have cause to think that I court her simply in order to secure a berth from the Government.

People would laugh at me if I were to relate through what a strange succession of feelings I have passed during the last ten days. At first I felt convinced that Louise had noticed the emotion with which she inspired me, and that it was not displeasing to her. Thus conquest on my part seemed quite possible. But on reflection I began to doubt all this. Surely I must be a fool to think that a woman would throw herself at my head so openly and quickly. Madame Neigeon could have no thought of me. It was quite possible that she had already had lovers, but assuredly any intrigue in which she had engaged had been a far more intricate affair than this. There must be a great distance between such a woman as I had dreamt of, a creature of mere elementary passions and instincts, and an artful Parisienne, expert in concealment, such as Louise doubtless was.

Thus she seemed to escape me entirely. I no longer saw her, I no longer knew even if it were indeed true that I had spent five minutes with her in a gloomy box in a theatre, feeling her palpitate beside me. And I became very wretched—to such a point, in fact, that for a moment I thought of hurrying back to Le Boquet and shutting myself up there.

But on the day before yesterday there came to me an idea which I was astonished at not having had before. It was to attend a sitting of the Chamber. Perhaps Monsieur Neigeon would speak; perhaps his wife would be there. But it was written that I was not yet to set eyes upon that singular man. Though it had been decided that he should speak, he did not even put in an appearance. It was related that he had been detained by some committee business at the Senate. On the other hand, as I was sitting down in the rear of one of the galleries I experienced keen emotion, for I perceived Madame Gaucheraud in the front row of the gallery facing me. She saw me and looked at me with a smile. Louise, alas! was not with her. My delight fell. On leaving, however, I contrived to meet Madame Gaucheraud in a passage. She displayed a familiar manner. Felix had certainly spoken to her about me.

'Have you been absent from Paris?' she inquired.

I remained speechless, indignant at such a question. Absent! When I had been scouring the city so furiously!

'Well, one meets you nowhere!' she resumed. 'The last reception at the Ministry was superb, and the Horse Show was marvelous.'

Then, noticing my expression of despair, she began to laugh.

'Well, till to-morrow,' she said, as she walked away. 'We shall see you over yonder, shan't we?'

I answered ' Yes' in a stupid fashion; never daring to ask a question for fear that I might again hear her laugh. She had turned round, and looked at me with a malicious expression. 'Come,' she murmured, in the discreet tone of a friend who had some pleasant surprise in store for one.

A wild impulse came upon me to run off after her and question her. But she had already turned into another passage, and I bitterly reproached myself with my foolish pride, which had prevented me from acknowledging my ignorance. I was certainly quite ready to go 'yonder;' but where might 'yonder' be? The vagueness of the appointment tortured me, and at the same time I felt ashamed at not knowing what everybody else seemed to know. In the evening I hastened to Felix's rooms, with the view of skillfully extracting from him the information which I needed. But Felix was not at home. Then, in my grief, I plunged into the perusal of the newspapers, selecting those which gave the most society news, and striving to guess, amongst the announcements for the morrow, what spot le bon ton would select as a meeting place. But my perplexity increased, for all sorts of functions were announced: an exhibition of paintings by some of the old masters, a charity bazaar at a big club, a musical mass at Sainte-Clotilde, a general rehearsal, two concerts, the veil-taking of an aristocratic novice, without mentioning horse races in all sorts of directions. How could a new arrival in Paris, a provincial conscious of his shortcomings, hope to arrive at the truth amidst such confusion! I understood perfectly well that the proper thing was to attend one of those functions, but which one was it, Oh heaven? Finally, at the risk of wandering about all day consumed with vain impatience if I were mistaken, I dared to make a choice. It occurred to me that I had heard the ladies speak of the races at Maisons-Lafitte, and, an inspiration coming to me, I resolved to repair thither. This decision taken, I began to feel calmer.

What a delightful stretch of country is that formed by the environs of Paris! I was not acquainted with Maisons-Lafitte, which charmed me with its houses so gay of aspect, built on a slope which borders the Seine. Now that we have reached the first days of May, the apple-trees, which are all white, look like big bouquets amidst the tender greenery of poplar and elm.

At first, however, I quite lost my bearings between the walls and the quick-set hedges, for I was unwilling to ask anybody the way. On seeing a great many people take the same train I had felt overjoyed, but the ladies were not there, and as I scanned the passers-by in Maisons-Lafitte itself my heart contracted. I was really losing myself alongside the Seine, beyond all the houses, when all at once keen emotion brought me to a standstill, near a big tuft of nettles. A group of people, still some fifty yards away, was slowly coming towards me, and I recognized Louise and Berthe. Gaucheraud and Felix, those inseparables, followed them at a distance of a few paces. So I had guessed rightly! This filled me with pride. But my emotion was so great that I behaved like a nincompoop. I hid myself behind the tall clump of nettles, full of a nameless shame, dreading .lest I should appear ridiculous. When Louise passed, the hem of her skirt brushed against the bushes. However, I at once realized the folly of my first impulse. And so I made all haste to cut across the fields, and as the others reached a bend in the road I came up in the most natural manner possible— like a man, indeed, who thinking himself alone is yielding to the dreamy mood inspired by the open air.

'Oh! Is it you?' cried Gaucheraud.

I bowed, affecting extreme surprise. We all raised exclamations and shook hands. But Felix laughed in his singular fashion, while Berthe positively winked at me, thereby establishing additional complicity between us. As we walked on, I remained for a few seconds with her, behind the others.

'So you have come?' she said to me gaily, in an undertone.

And without giving me time to answer, she began to jest, saying that I was very happy in still being so young. I felt that I had an ally in her; it seemed to me that she would have been well pleased to help me with her friend. Then as Felix turned round to inquire, 'What are you laughing about?' she replied in all tranquility: 'Oh, Monsieur de Vaugelade has been telling me of his journey in the company of a whole family of English tourists.'

Gaucheraud, however, had again taken Felix by the arm, and was leading him off as if to avoid troubling my Ute-d-tite with his wife. I remained between her and Louise, and spent a most entrancing hour on the shady road which followed the banks of the Seine. Louise was wearing a light silk gown, and her sunshade with its pink lining steeped her face in a warm, shadowless glow. Here in the country there was more freedom than ever in her demeanor; she talked in a loud voice, and looked me full in the face while replying to Berthe, who turned the conversation to rather venturesome subjects with a pertinacity which greatly struck me later on.

'Give Madame Neigeon your arm,' she ended by saying to me. 'You are certainly not gallant; you can surely see that she is tired.'

I offered Louise my arm and she leant on it at once. Then, Berthe having joined her husband and Felix, we two remained together more than forty paces behind. The road ascended the slope, and we walked very slowly. Down below flowed the Seine between meadows stretching out like carpets of green velvet. There was a long slender island, too, intersected by two bridges, over which the trains rushed with a noise like distant thunder. Then across the water there was a vast cultivated plain stretching to Mont Valerien, whose grey buildings could be seen amidst a dust of sunshine on the very fringe of the sky. But what affected me almost to tears was an odor of springtide, spreading all around us as it rose from the herbage on either side of the road.

'Shall you soon go back to Le Boquet?' Louise asked me.

I was foolish enough to answer ' No,' for I did not foresee that she would add: 'Ah! That's annoying, for next week we are going to Les Mureaux, my husband's property, which is only some two leagues from your place, and my husband meant to ask you to call and see us there.'

At this I began to stammer that my father might possibly recall me sooner than I had expected. It had seemed to me that I could feel her arm pressing my own. Was she giving me an assignation, then? With the ideas that I had formed of this Parisienne, so free and coquettish in her ways, I at once built up a perfect romance: an intrigue in the country, a whole month of passion under the trees. Yes, it was doubtless thus; she found in me the qualities of a young squire, and would grant me her love amidst suitable surroundings.

'I have to scold you,' she suddenly resumed, assuming an affectionate, almost maternal manner.

'How is that?' I murmured.

'Yes, your aunt has spoken to me about you. It seems that you will not accept anything from us. That is very discourteous. 'Why do you refuse—tell me?'

I blushed again'; I was on the point of making a declaration, of exclaiming, 'I refuse because I love you.' But she made a gesture as if she understood my intention and wished me to remain silent. And then she added with a laugh: 'If you are proud, if you wish to render service for service, we will willingly accept your protection over yonder. You know that a General Councilor has to be elected. My husband is a candidate, but he fears defeat, which in our position would be very unpleasant. Will you help us?'

It was impossible to be more charming. That election story seemed to me to be a mere pretext devised by a clever woman to enable us to meet again in the country.

'But certainly I'll help you,' I answered.

'And if you succeed in getting my husband returned, it is understood that he in his turn will give you a helping hand.'

'It is a bargain.'

'Yes, a bargain.'

She offered me her little hand, and I tapped it, as the custom goes, by way of sealing our agreement. We made merry together. It really seemed to me most delightful. We had passed the last of the trees, the sunlight streamed down on the crest of the hill, and we walked on, silent, amidst the great heat. But of course that imbecile Gaucheraud must come to disturb that quivering silence under the flaming sky. He had heard us mention the

General Council, and he gave me no more peace, but began to tell me all about his uncle, and to maneuver for an introduction to my father. At last we reached the race ground. They found the races superb. For my part, I stood all the time behind Louise, looking at her delicate neck. And how delightful was the return homeward after a sudden shower! Beneath the rain the greenery had become softer still, the leaves and the earth sent forth a delightful smell, the very scent of love. Louise half closed her eyes, as if tired and penetrated by all the voluptuousness of spring-time.

'Remember our bargain,' she said to me at the railway station, as she entered her carriage which was waiting there. 'At Les Mureaux in a fortnight's time, eh?'

I pressed the hand she offered me, and I fear that I must have been a little rough, as for the first time I saw her become grave, with two little creases as of displeasure about her lips. But Berthe still seemed bent on encouraging me to be bold, and Felix retained his enigmatical smile, while Gaucheraud slapped me on the shoulder, exclaiming, 'At Les Mureaux in a fortnight, Monsieur de Vaugelade. We shall all be there.' The devil take him!

IV

I Have just come back from Les Mureaux, and such contradictory ideas and impressions fill my mind that it is needful I should recapitulate the day I have spent with Louise in order to arrive at a clear opinion.

Although the estate of Les Mureaux is only two leagues from Le Boquet, I knew little of that part of our district. Our own shooting is in the direction of Gommerville, and, as a rather long round has to be made to cross the little Blage River, I had not gone there a dozen times in my life. Yet the slope is delightful, with its climbing road edged by big walnut-trees. Then, after reaching the plateau you dip down again, and Les Mureaux lies at the entry of a dale, whose slopes soon contract into a narrow gorge. The house, a square building of the seventeenth century, is of no great importance, but the grounds are magnificent, with their broad lawns and the snatch of forest land at the far end—such a tangle of trees that the very paths are barred by the branches.

When I arrived on horseback two big dogs greeted me with a prolonged barking and jumping. At the end of the avenue I caught sight of a white spot. It was Louise in a light gown and a straw hat. She did not come down to meet me, but remained motionless and smiling on the large flight of steps that leads to the hall. It was nine o'clock at the latest.

'Ah, how nice of you!' she called to me; ' you, at all events, are an early riser. I am the only one up at the chateau, as you see.'

I complimented her, saying that for a Parisienne she was really courageous. But she added with a laugh, 'It is true that I have only been here five days. I would get up with the chickens the first mornings. Only, as soon as the second week arrives, I gradually relapse into my sluggardly ways and end by coming down at ten o'clock, the same as in Paris. This morning, however, I am still a countrywoman.'

I had never seen her looking so charming. In her haste to leave her room she had negligently knotted her hair, and slipped into the first morning wrap she found. And with her eyes still moist with sleep and her cheeks quite fresh she seemed a young girl again. Some little locks of hair were waving over her neck, and whenever her broad sleeves gaped I could see her bare arms as far as the elbows.

'Do you know where I was going?' she resumed. 'Well, I was going to inspect a screen of convolvuli on that arbor yonder. It is marvelous, it seems, when the sun has not yet closed the flowers. The gardener told me of it, and as I missed the sight yesterday, I don't want to do so to-day. You will come with me, won't you?'

I felt a great inclination to offer her my arm, but I understood in time that it would be ridiculous. She ran on like a school-girl enjoying a holiday. On reaching the arbor she gave a cry of admiration. From aloft hung quite a drapery of convolvuli, a shower of little bells, pearly with dew, and of delicate hues ranging from vivid rose color to violet and pale blue. The whole suggested one of those phantasies of exquisite grace and strangeness that one finds in Japanese albums.

'This is one's reward when one gets up early,' said Louise merrily.

Then she sat down under the arbor, and on seeing that she drew back her skirts to make a little room, I ventured to place myself beside her. I was in a state of keen emotion, for the thought had come to me of bringing matters to a crisis by catching her round the waist and kissing her on the neck. I felt well enough that such roughness was better suited to a young lieutenant dealing with a housemaid, but I could think of nothing else. I don't know whether Louise understood what was passing in my mind; but though she did not get up, her face assumed a very grave expression.

'First of all, shall we talk of our business?' said she.

There was a buzzing in my ears, but I tried to listen to her. It was dim and rather cold in the arbor. Sparks of golden sunshine came in here and there between the foliage of the convolvuli, and on Louise's white wrap they looked like golden flies, golden insects, settling there.

'Well, what is the position?' she asked me with the air of an accomplice.

I thereupon told her of the singular change which I had noticed at my father's. He, who for ten years had never ceased railing at the new state of things and had forbidden me to serve the Republic, had now given me to understand, on the very evening of my return, that a young man of my age owed duty to his country. I suspected my aunt of having effected this conversion. Some women must have been set on him. Louise smiled as she listened, and she ended by saying: 'I met Monsieur de Vaugelade three days ago at a neighboring château where I was making a call. We had a little conversation.'

Then she quickly added: 'You know that the election for the General Council will take place next Sunday. You must start on your campaign at once. With your father's help my husband's success will be certain.'

'Is Monsieur Neigeon here?' I inquired after some slight hesitation.

'Yes; he arrived last night. But you won't see him this morning, for he has gone off in the direction of Gommerville to take lunch with a friend, a landowner who has a good deal of influence.'

She rose up, but I remained seated for yet another moment, deeply regretting that I had not kissed her on the neck, for never should I again find such a dim little nook and such an early propitious hour. It was too late now, and I understood so thoroughly that I should simply make her laugh by falling at her feet on the damp ground, that I put off my declaration till a more favorable moment.

Besides, I had just perceived Gaucheraud's bulky silhouette at the end of the path. On seeing Louise and I come out of the arbor he gave a little sneer. Then he expressed astonishment at our courage in rising so early. For his part, he had only just come down.

'And Berthe?' Louise asked him;' did she sleep well?'

'Well, I really don't know,' he answered; 'I haven't seen her yet.

Then, noticing my astonishment, he explained that his wife had a headache for the whole day whenever she was disturbed in the morning. And he added that they had long found it most convenient to have separate rooms, one for him and one for her. I must confess that this gave me food for thought. I recalled all manner of stories that I had heard and read of Parisiennes in country houses, and when I saw Berthe and my friend Felix come together out of the hall, I could not help thinking that my surmises might be true.

I shook hands with Felix; and, I can hardly account for it, but by the smile which Louise and Berthe exchanged while Gaucheraud stood by, quietly whistling, the idea occurred to me that Louise was not ignorant of the matter I have referred to. And more than ever now I regretted not having kissed her while we were in the dim little arbor.

We had lunch at eleven o'clock. After the meal Gaucheraud took himself off for his siesta. He had opened up himself to me, telling me that he feared he might not prove successful at the next elections, and that he proposed remaining three weeks in the district in the hope of gaining support. Thus, after staying with his uncle, he had desired to spend a few days at Les Mureaux in order to show everybody that he was on the best of terms with the Neigeons, for this, in his opinion, might win him a good many votes. I understood that he was also extremely desirous of being invited to my father's. Unfortunately, it seemed that I did not care for fair-haired women.

I spent a very gay afternoon with the ladies and Felix. Chateau life, with Parisian graces frolicking in the open air amidst the sunshine of early summer, is really charming. The drawing-room spreads out over the lawns. It is no longer the winter drawing-room, where you are virtually cooped up, where the women in low dresses ply their fans while the men in black swallow-tails stand up alongside the walls. It is a kind of holiday drawing room, with women in light garb scampering freely hither and thither, while the men in their short jackets show themselves amiable and natural: a setting aside, as it were, of society etiquette, a familiarity which banishes the boredom born of the stereotyped conversation that one hears at the winter gatherings. Nevertheless, I must confess that the behavior of the ladies still surprised me, reared as I was in the provinces among pious folk. When we took coffee on the terrace after lunch, Louise allowed herself a cigarette, and Berthe talked slang in the most natural manner possible. Later on they took themselves off amidst a great rustling of skirts, and one heard them laughing in the distance, and calling one another, full of a flightiness which greatly disturbed me. It is foolish to own it, but these manners, so novel to one like myself, made me hope that Louise would give me an early assignation. As for Felix, he quietly went on smoking cigarettes, but at times I caught him looking at me in his almost sarcastic way.

At half-past four I spoke of leaving. But Louise immediately protested: ' No, no; you can't go yet. I shall keep you to dinner. My husband will certainly come back, and then you will see him. Really, now, I must introduce you to him.'

I explained to her that my father was expecting me. I was compelled to be present at a dinner he was giving at Le Boquet, and with a laugh I continued: 'It is an election dinner; I have got to work for you.'

'Oh I in that case,' said she, ' make haste. And if you succeed, you know, come for your reward.'

It seemed to me that she blushed as she spoke those words. Did she simply refer to the appointment in the diplomatic service which my father is urging me to accept? I thought I might attribute another meaning to her words, and no doubt I assumed a very conceited air, for all at once, for the second time, I saw her become very grave, with those little creases about the lips which gave her such an expression of proud displeasure.

But I had no time to reflect upon that sudden change of expression. As I was starting a little conveyance drew up before the house steps. I already imagined that the husband had returned. But there were only two children, a little girl about five, and a little boy of four, in the vehicle, accompanied by a maid. They stretched out their arms and laughed, and as soon as they could spring to the ground they "threw themselves among Louise's skirts. She kissed them on the hair.

'Whose pretty children are these?' I asked.

'Why, mine,' she replied with an air of surprise.

Hers! I cannot express in words what a blow that simple answer dealt me. It seemed to me as if she were all at once escaping from me, as if those little beings with puny hands were digging an impassable abyss between her and me. What! She was a mother, and I had known nothing of it! I could not restrain the cry: 'So you have children?'

'No doubt,' she quietly responded. 'They went to see their godmother, two leagues from here, this morning. Allow me to introduce them, Monsieur Lucien, Mademoiselle Marguerite.'

The little ones smiled at me. I must have looked very stupid. No, I could not accustom myself to the idea of it. It upset all my notions. I went off with my head in a whirl, and even at this moment I don't know what to think. I see Louise in the arbor draped with convolvuli, and I see her kissing the hair of Lucien and Marguerite. Decidedly, those Parisiennes are far too intricate for provincials like me. I must get to sleep. I will try to understand things to-morrow.

This is the finish of my adventure. Oh, what a lesson! But let me try to relate things calmly.

Last Sunday Monsieur Neigeon was elected as General Councilor. After the counting of the votes it became evident that without our support he would have failed. My father, who, for his part, has seen Monsieur Neigeon, gave me to understand that a man of such utter mediocrity was not to be feared. Besides, it was a question of beating a Radical candidate. However, after dinner in the evening the old Adam reappeared in my father and he contented himself with saying to me:

'All that is not very clean business. But everybody repeated to me that I was working for you. Well, do what you think fit. For me the only course left is to take myself off, for I no longer understand things.'

On the Monday and Tuesday I hesitated about going to Les Mureaux. It seemed to me that it would be bad taste to go in search of thanks so quickly. The thought of the children no longer inconvenienced me. I had persuaded myself that there was very little motherliness about Louise. Besides, did not people say in our part of the country that the Parisiennes never allowed children to interfere with their amusements, but handed them over to the care of servants, so as to enjoy perfect liberty themselves? So yesterday, Wednesday, all my scruples disappeared. I was consumed with impatience, and set off for the battle at eight o'clock in the morning.

My plan was to reach Les Mureaux as on the first occasion, at an early hour, so as to find Louise alone. But when I dismounted from my horse, a servant told me that Madame had not yet left her room, and made no offer to go and warn her of my arrival. So I simply replied that I would wait.

And, indeed, I waited two long hours. I don't know how many times I made the round of the flower-beds. Every now and again I raised my eyes to the first-floor windows, but the shutters remained closed. Tired, enervated by this long promenade, I ended by sitting down in the bower of convolvuli. The sky was overcast that morning, and the sunshine did not glide in golden dust between the foliage. It was almost night, indeed, amidst the verdure. I reflected, resolving that I must risk everything. I was convinced that if I should again hesitate I should lose Louise for ever. As soon as I should be alone with her I would take hold of her hands and affect great emotion so as not to frighten her too much, but afterwards I would kiss her on the neck, as I had thought of doing on the former occasion. I was for the tenth time perfecting my plan when all at once Louise herself appeared before me.

'Where are you hiding?' she gaily called, looking for me in the dark arbor. 'Oh! You are here, are you? I have been hunting for you for the last ten minutes. I must apologize for having kept you waiting.'

Somewhat huskily I answered that there was nothing unpleasant in having to wait when one's thoughts were of her.

'I warned you,' she replied, without paying attention to my silly compliment,' that I'm not a country woman for more than the first week. I've now become a Parisienne again, and can no longer leave my bed.'

She had remained at the entrance of the arbor, as if she did not wish to risk herself amidst the gloom falling from the foliage.

'Well, aren't you coming?' she ended by asking me. 'We have to talk, you know.'

'But one is very comfortable here,' said I, in a quivering voice. 'We can talk on this bench.'

She again hesitated, just for a second, then bravely replied: 'Oh! As you like. It is rather dark here; still we don't need to see our words.'

Thereupon she sat down near me. I felt like fainting. So the fateful hour had come! Yet another minute and I should take hold of her hands. She, however, still perfectly at ease, continued chatting in her clear voice, in which there was not the faintest sign of emotion.

'I won't thank you in ready-made phrases,' said she. 'You have given us good help, without which we should have been beaten.'

I was in no condition to interrupt her. I was trembling, and exhorting myself to be brave.

'Besides, there is no need of words between us,' she resumed. 'We concluded a bargain, you know.'

She laughed as she said this, and her laugh suddenly emboldened me. I caught hold of her hands and she did not withdraw them. I could feel them so little and so warm in my own. She surrendered them to me in a friendly, familiar way, while repeating: 'Yes, that is so, isn't it? And now it is my turn to carry out my part of the agreement.'

Thereupon I suddenly became audacious and rough, drawing her hands towards my lips. The gloom had increased; a cloud must have been passing over us, and the strong scent of all the plant-life around us intoxicated me in that nest of foliage. But before my lips could reach her, she freed herself with a nervous strength which I should never have suspected, and in her turn caught me roughly by the wrists. And she held me like that without any show of anger, her voice remaining calm, though it assumed somewhat of a scolding tone.

'Come, no childishness,' said she. 'This is what I feared. Will you allow me to give you a lesson while I hold you here, in this little corner?'

She showed the smiling severity of a mother reprimanding a boy.

'I understood you from the very first day. You had been told horrors about me, had you not? And so you conceived fancies which I forgive you, for you know nothing of our sphere of society. You landed in Paris with the ideas of this wolfish region, and perhaps you may say that it is in some measure my fault if you made a mistake. I ought to have stopped you, for you would have withdrawn at a word from me. That's true, and I did not speak that word; I let you go on and you must regard me as an abominable coquette. Do you know, however, why I did not speak that word?'

I began to stammer. The strangeness of the scene paralyzed me with astonishment. She held my wrists yet more tightly and shook me, while remaining so close to me that I could feel her breath on my face.

'I did not say it, because I felt interested in you and wished to give you this lesson. Young men fresh to the world form very erroneous and foolish ideas of women. You don't understand, as yet, but you will reflect and guess. We women are very much slandered. Perhaps we do all that is needed to bring that about. Only, you see, there are some who are perfectly virtuous even amongst those who seem to be the wildest and most compromised. All that is a very delicate matter; but, I repeat, you will reflect and end by understanding.'

'Let me go,' I murmured in confusion.

'No, I will not let you go. Beg my pardon, if you wish me to do so.'

In spite of her jesting tone I could feel that she was growing irritated, that tears of anger were rising to her eyes beneath the affront she had received from me. Within me was springing up a feeling of esteem, of genuine respect for that woman who was at once so charming and so capable. Her Amazonian grace in virtuously enduring her husband's imbecility, her blending of coquetry and rigor, her disdain for evil tittle-tattle, and her skill in playing the man's part in the household amidst seeming flightiness of conduct—all made her a very complex creature, and filled me with admiration.

'Pardon!' I humbly said.

She released me. I at once rose to my feet while she remained quietly seated on the bench, fearing nothing more from the dimness or the disturbing odor of the greenery. And it was in her usual gay voice that she said to me: 'Now, let us come back to our bargain. As I am very honest, I pay my debts. Here is your appointment as a junior diplomatic secretary. I received it last night.'

Then, seeing that I hesitated to take the envelope which she held out to me, she exclaimed with just a touch of irony: 'Well, it seems to me that you may well be my husband's obligation now.'

Such was the finish of my first adventure. When we came out of the arbor Felix was on the terrace with Gaucheraud and Berthe. He pursed his lips as he saw me approach carrying my nomination. He was doubtless aware of everything, and thought me a fool. I took him aside and reproached him bitterly for having allowed me to perpetrate such a blunder, but he answered that experience alone can form young men. And when with a gesture I designated Berthe, who was walking in front of us, by way of questioning him also about her, he shrugged his shoulders with a significance which was extremely clear. Matters being like this, I must confess that in spite of everything I do not yet fully understand the strange morality of society in which the most respectable women show such singular complaisance towards others.

But the last blow was to learn from Gaucheraud himself that my father had invited him and his wife to spend three days at Le Boquet. Felix again began to smile as he announced that for his part he was returning to Paris on the morrow.

Thereupon I ran off, pretending that I had positively promised my father that I would be home for dejeuner. I was already at the end of the avenue when I perceived a gentleman in a gig. It must have been Monsieur Neigeon. No matter! I prefer having again missed him. It is on Sunday that Gaucheraud and his wife are to arrive at Le Boquet. What a horrid nuisance!

SHELLFISH FOR MONSIEUR CHABRE

THE one great grief of Monsieur Chabre was that he had no children. He had married a Mademoiselle Catinot, the fair Estelle, a tall and beautiful girl of eighteen years. And for four years, he had been waiting, anxious, dismayed, hurt that his wishes should be unrealized.

M. Chabre was a retired grain merchant, with a big fortune. Although he had led the virtuous life of a bourgeois absorbed in the one idea of becoming a millionaire, he found himself at forty-five years of age with the heavy dragging steps of an old man. His pale face, lined by money cares, was flat and common-place as a pavement. And he despaired, for a man who has made a fortune that yields an annual income of fifty thousand francs certainly has a right to be astonished that it is more difficult to become a father than to become rich.

The beautiful Madame Chabre was then twenty-two years old. She was adorable with her peachy complexion and her golden hair. Her eyes of a greenish blue were like still water, beneath which it was difficult to read. When her husband complained of the sterility of their union, she drew up her supple figure, displaying the fullness of her hips and of her throat; and the smile that puckered the corners of her mouth said clearly, "Is it my fault?"

Among her acquaintances, Madame Chabre was considered a woman of perfect education incapable of giving grounds for scandal, sufficiently devout; in a word, nurtured in the good bourgeois traditions by a strict mother. Only, the delicate nostrils of her little white nose dilated nervously at times, which would have worried any other husband than a retired grain merchant.

Meanwhile, the family physician, Doctor Guiraud, a stout man, shrewd and smiling, had had several important conversations with Monsieur Chabre. He explained how backward science was still. Ah! No,—a child was not planted like an oak. However, not wishing to discourage anyone, ho promised to think over M. Chabre's case. And, one morning in July he called to say to him, "You should go to the seaside, dear sir. Yes, it is excellent. And above all, eat a great quantity of shell-fish. Eat nothing but shell-fish."

M. Chabre, with rising hope, asked quickly "Shellfish, doctor? You think that shellfish.?"

"Exactly. The treatment has been known to succeed. You understand, every day, eat oysters, mussels, shrimps, sea urchins, winkles, and even lobsters."

Then, as he was leaving, he added carelessly, on the threshold, "Don't bury yourself. Madame Chabre is young and needs amusement. Go to Tronville. The air there is very good."

Three days later, the Chabre household took its departure. But the former grain merchant had thought it unnecessary to go to Tronville where they would spend a large sum of money. One can be just as comfortable anywhere else while eating shell-fish; and, in a secluded place, the shell-fish should be more abundant and cheaper. As for amusements, there would always be more than enough of them. Besides, they were not going on a pleasure trip.

A friend had told M. Chabre of the little beach of Pouliguen, near Saint-Nazaire. Madame Chabre, after a journey of twelve hours found the day passed at Saint-Nazaire very wearisome. They went to visit the port, they strolled about the streets where the shops hesitate between the dark little grocery shops of the villages and the large luxurious shops of the cities. At Pouliguen, there was not a single villa vacant. The little houses of boards and plaster, that seem to surround the bay with the brightly painted booths from a fair, were already occupied by English people and rich merchants from Nantes. Besides, Estelle pouted at those architectures, in which bourgeois artists had given reign to their imaginations.

The travelers were advised to go on to Gueraude for the night. It was Sunday. When they arrived, towards noon, M. Chabre experienced a sensation, although he was not of a poetic temperament. The sight of Guerande, this feudal gem so well preserved, with its fortified walls and its deep-set gates astonished him. Estelle gazed upon the silent city, surrounded by 'the great trees of its promenades; and, in the sleeping waters of her eyes, a reverie smiled. But the carriage rolled along, the horse trotted under a gate, and the wheels danced upon the pointed stones of the narrow streets. The Chabres had not exchanged a word.

"A veritable hole!" at last murmured the former grain merchant. "The villages around Paris are better built."

As the couple left the carriage in front of the Hotel du Commerce, situated in the center of the city, the congregation of a near-by church began filing out from mass. While her husband looked after the baggage, Estelle sauntered up very much interested in the procession of the faithful, of whom a large number wore curious costumes. There were men who live on the salt marshes, dressed in white blouses and full breeches. There were farmers, a distinct race, who wore the short cloth vest and a large round hat. But Estelle was delighted, above all, with the rich costume of a young girl. The cap fitted in at the temples and terminated in a point. On her red bodice were embroidered showy flowers, and a belt embroidered in gold and silver clasped at the waist her three skirts of blue cloth, one over the other, pleated in tight pleats; while a long apron of orange silk was not long enough to hide her red woolen stockings and her little yellow slippers.

"Well, I declare!" said M. Chabre who had just come up behind his wife. "You have to be in Brittany to see such a carnival."

Estelle did not answer. A tall young man of twenty years issued from the church, offering his arm to an old lady. He had very white skin, a proud face, and hair of a tawny blond. He was almost a giant, with broad shoulders and members already knotted with muscles. And he was so tender, so delicate withal that he had the pink face of a young girl without a hair on his cheeks. As Estelle looked at him intently, surprised by his great beauty, he turned his head, looked at her for a second, and blushed.

"Well!" murmured M. Chabre, "there at least is one with the face of a human being. He would make a handsome carabineer."

"It is Monsieur Hector," said the servant from the hotel. "He accompanies his mother, Madame de Plougastel. Oh! A child very gentle, very good!"

During the afternoon the Chabres went out upon the Mall, a vast raised promenade, forming a quarter of a circle, from the east gate to the south gate. Estelle remained thoughtful, gazing upon the admirable horizon that extended for miles beyond the roofs of the suburbs.

"Here is the young man of this morning," said M. Chabre suddenly. "Don't you think he resembles the Larivieres' little one? If he had a hump, the resemblance would be perfect."

Estelle had turned slowly. But Hector, on the edge of the Mall, absorbed by the distant view, appeared unconscious of their regard. Then the young woman resumed the walk slowly. She leaned upon the long stick of her sunshade. After a few steps, the bow on the sunshade became detached. And the Chabres heard a voice behind them.

"Madame, Madame. . . ."

It was Hector who had picked up the bow.

"A thousand thanks, sir," said Estelle with her calm smile.

He was very gentle, very good, this boy. He pleased M. Chabre right away. M. Chabre confided to him his perplexity in regard to a choice of a seaside resort. Hector, very timid, stammered,"I do not believe that you will find what you are looking for either at Croisic or at Batz," he said, pointing out the steeples of those little towns on the horizon. "I advise you to go to Piriac."

And he furnished details. Piriac was about nine miles away. He had an uncle in the neighborhood. Finally, upon a question from M. Chabre, he assured him that shell-fish were found there in abundance.

The young woman prodded the short grass with the tip of her sunshade. The young man did not raise his eyes to her, seemingly embarrassed by her presence.

"Guerande is a very pretty town," said Estelle in her flute-like voice.

"Oh! Very pretty," stammered Hector, suddenly devouring her with his eyes.

One morning, three days after the arrival of the couple at Piriac, M. Chabre, standing upon the pier that protects the little port, placidly watched Estelle as she swam and floated. The sun was already warm; and, correctly dressed in frock-coat and felt hat, he shielded himself with a tourist umbrella lined with green.

"Is it good?" he asked, to appear interested in his wife's bathing.

"Very good!" answered Estelle.

M. Chabre never bathed. He was in terror of the water, but he dissimulated this fear by saying that the doctors had strictly forbidden him sea-bathing. When a wave on the sands rolled up to the soles of his shoes, he drew back with a shudder, as if before a vicious beast that bared its teeth. Besides, the water would have disordered his habitual primness. He found it untidy and inconvenient.

"So it is good?" he repeated, dizzy from the heat, taken with an uneasy somnolence on the end of the pier.

Estelle did not answer, striking the water with her arms, swimming dog-fashion, with boyish daring; she bathed for hours, which greatly dismayed her husband who felt that the proprieties obliged him to wait for her on the shore. At Piriac Estelle found the baths she loved. She disdained the sloping beach; she went to the end of the pier, wrapped in her white fleece gown and, letting it slip off her shoulders, she calmly took a dive. Her bathing-suit, made in one piece without a skirt, outlined her tall form; and the wide blue girdle in compressing the waist rounded out the hips that balanced with a rhythmic movement. In the clear water, her hair imprisoned beneath a rubber cap, from which stray locks escaped, she had the suppleness of a blue fish, with a woman's head disquieting and pink.

M. Chabre had been for a quarter of an hour in the hot sun. Three times already, he had consulted his watch. He finally hazarded the timid remark,—

"You are staying in a long time, my dear. You should come out. Such long baths tire you."

"But I have only just gone in!" cried the young woman. "It is like being in milk." Then, turning on her back,"If you are weary, you can go . . . I do not need you."

He shook his head; he declared that accidents happen so suddenly. And Estelle smiled in the thinking of what great help her husband would be if she were seized with a cramp. But, abruptly, she peered at the other side of the jetty, in the bay that curves to the left of the village.

"Hello!" she said. "What is that over there? I am going to see."

And she swam rapidly, with long, regular strokes.

"Estelle! Estelle!" cried M. Chabre. "Will you not go so far out? You know how I hate imprudence!"

But Estelle did not listen to him; he had to resign himself. Standing on tiptoe to follow the white speck that his wife's hat made on the water, he was fain to content himself with passing the umbrella from one hand to the other, while he suffocated more and more in the overheated air.

"What did she see?" he murmured. "Ah! Yes, that thing that is floating over there. Some dirty thing,—a bunch of seaweed, no doubt. Or a barrel. . . . No. it moves!"

And all of a sudden, he recognized the object.

"Why, it is a man swimming!"

Estelle, in the meanwhile, after a few strokes had also seen that it was a man. So she stopped swimming straight for him; but, out of coquetry, pleased to show her daring, she did not return to the pier; she continued to swim for the open sea. She advanced quietly, pretending not to see the other swimmer. The latter, as if a current had borne him along, drew nearer and nearer to her. Then, when she turned to start back, there was a meeting which appeared quite accidental.

"Madame, how-do-you-do?" said the gentleman.

"Well! It is you, sir!" said Estelle gaily. And she added with a light laugh, — "How we meet again after all!" It was the young Hector de Plougastel. He was still very timid, very strong, and very pink in the water. They swam without speaking, with a decent distance between them. They were obliged to raise their voices to be heard. Nevertheless, Estelle considered it her duty to be polite.

"We thank you for having recommended Piriac. My husband is delighted."

"That is your husband,—is it not—all alone on the jetty?" asked Hector.

"Yes, sir," she answered.

And they were again silent. They looked at the husband, large as a black insect, above the water. M. Chabre, very puzzled, stretched upon his toes, asking himself what acquaintance his wife could have picked up on the open sea. It was unquestionable that his wife was talking to the gentleman. He could see them turn their heads towards each other. It must be one of their friends from Paris. But he searched in vain,—he could think of no one who would have dared venture so far out. And he waited, twirling his umbrella like a top.

"Yes," explained Hector to the beautiful Madame Chabre, "I came to spend a few days with my uncle, whose chateau you can see over there. Every day, for my bath, I leave that point opposite the terrace and swim to the pier. Then I return. Altogether, it is about a mile and a quarter. It is splendid exercise. But you, Madame, you are very brave,—I have never seen a lady so brave."

"Oh!" said Estelle, "when I was very small, I splashed about in the water. It is no stranger to me. We are old friends."

Little by little, they drew closer to avoid shouting. The conversation became more intimate. Hector pointed out several spots of interest on the coast.

'How beautiful!" she murmured. "How beautiful!"

She turned upon her back to rest.

"So, you were born at Guerande?" she asked.

In order to talk more comfortably, Hector also turned over on his back.

"Yes, Madame; and I have been but once to Nantes."

He told her in detail of his education. He had been brought up near his mother, who was of a narrow piety, and who cherished intact the traditions of the ancient nobility. His preceptor, a priest, had taught him what is learned at college, adding a great deal of catechism and heraldry. He could ride, fence,—in fact, was trained in bodily exercise. And still, with that, he seemed to have the innocence of a virgin. He went to communion every week, never read novels, and was engaged to marry, when he should come of age, a cousin who was very plain.

"What! You are only twenty years old!" cried Estelle, glancing at this colossal child.

Her manner became maternal. That flower of the strong Breton race interested her. As they floated, gazing into the transparence of the sky, they were wafted towards each other and he struck against her lightly.

"Oh! Pardon!" he said blushing.

He dived, and reappeared some distance away. She began to swim again, laughing heartily.

"Your husband appears to be impatient," he said in an attempt to pick up the conversation.

"Oh! No," she replied calmly. "He is accustomed to waiting for me while I take my bath."

In reality, Monsieur Chabre fidgeted. He took four steps forward, returned, then started again, the while rotating his umbrella swiftly, evidently hoping to give himself more air. The conversation between his wife and the unknown swimmer began to surprise him.

Estelle suddenly surmised that he had not recognized Hector.

"I am going to call out to him that it's you," she said.

And, as soon as she could make herself heard from the pier, she raised her voice.

"You know, my dear, it is the gentleman from Guerande who was so kind."

"Ah! Very good! Very good!" cried Monsieur Chabre. He lifted his hat.

"Is the water good?" he inquired politely.

"Very good, sir," answered Hector.

The bathing continued under the husband's eyes, and he did not dare complain although his feet were blistered by the burning stones. The young man and the young woman swam about. They advanced with short strokes, making the water foam about them. Then, they glided slowly in, making large circles that heaved and vanished. It was like a discreet and sensual intimacy thus to glide through the same wave. As the water closed up behind the fleeing form of Estelle, Hector sought to follow in the furrow, to place himself where her warm limbs had been.

"My dear, you are going to catch cold," murmured M. Chabre who was dripping with perspiration.

"I am coming out," she answered. And she ran up the slope of the pier and was on the platform enveloped in her bathing-gown by the time Hector raised his head at the sound of the water dripping from her suit. He looked so surprised and vexed that she smiled, while she shivered slightly. She shivered because she knew that she was charming thus shaken, as her tall draped silhouette was thrown up against the sky.

The young man was obliged to take him leave.

"We shall look forward to seeing you again," said the husband.

The Chabres had rented at Piriac the first floor of a large house, with the window looking out upon the sea. As the inns were very second-rate, the Chabres had been obliged to take a woman of the country to do the cooking. It was strange cooking, — roasts reduced to charcoal, and sauces of so disturbing a color that Estelle preferred to dine on bread. But, as M. Chabre said, they had not made the trip for the purpose of gormandizing. He rarely tasted either roast or gravy. He filled up on shell-fish, morning and evening, with the conviction of a man who takes medicine. The worst of it was that he detested those creatures of the sea, with their bizarre shapes; for, having been raised on bourgeois cooking, insipid and light, he had a child's taste for sweet things. The shell-fish, salted and peppered, so surprised his mouth with their strong and unexpected savors, that; he could not prevent grimaces on swallowing them. But he would have swallowed the shells, too, if it had been necessary, so determined was he to become a father.

"My dear, you are not eating," he often cried to Estelle.

He insisted that she eat as many as he. It was necessary for the result, he said. Discussions arose. Estelle maintained that Dr. Guiraud had not spoken of her. But he answered that it was only logical for both of them to follow the treatment. Then the young woman puckered her lips, threw a glance at the sallow obesity of her husband, and a slight smile deepened the dimple in her chin. She said nothing more, not liking to wound anyone. Even after discovering a bed of oysters, she ate a dozen at each meal. Not that she, personally, needed them, but she adored oysters.

The life at Piriac was of a somnolent monotony. There were only three families that went into the water, wholesale grocer of Nantes, an old notary of Guerande, who was deaf and unsophisticated, and a couple from Angers who fished all day long with the water to their waists. This little world made no noise. They bowed when they met, and their relations ended there. On the deserted wharf, the greatest event was to see two dogs fighting in the distance.

Estelle, accustomed to the noise of Paris, would have been bored to death if Hector had not come to see them every day. He became the great friend of M. Chabre after a walk they took together along the shore. M. Chabre, in a moment of expansion, confided to the young man the object of their journey, choosing for his narrative the most chaste terms so as not to offend the purity of the big boy. When he had explained scientifically why he ate so many shellfish, Hector, stupefied, forgetting to blush, looked him over from head to foot, without attempting to hide his wonder that a man should be obliged to follow such a diet. Yet, the following day, he presented himself carrying a small basket of prawns, which the retired grain merchant accepted with an air of gratitude. And, from that day, as he was a skilful fisherman and knew every rock in the bay, he never appeared without an offering of shell-fish. M. Chabre, delighted, no longer obliged to spend a cent, overwhelmed him with thanks.

Now, Hector always had an excuse to call. Each time that he arrived with his little basket, on meeting Estelle, he would say the same thing,"I bring some shell-fish for M. Chabres." And the two smiled, their eyes crinkled up and shining. The shell-fish of Mr. Chabre amused them.

From then on, Estelle found Piriac charming. Every day, after the bath, she went for a walk with Hector. Her husband followed at a distance, for his legs were heavy and the young people walked too fast for him.

At high tide, for a diversion, they went to meet the sardine boats. When a sail came in sight, Hector signaled to the couple. But the husband, after the sixth boat, had declared that it was always the same thing. Estelle, on the contrary, appeared never to tire but to find renewed pleasure in running down to the wharf. Yet, little by little, Estelle and her companion neglected the sardines. They still went to see them, but they no longer looked at them. They started on a run and came back slowly as if weary, the while gazing at the sea in silence.

"Is there a good catch of sardines?" M. Chabre asked each time upon their return.

"Yes, fine," they answered.

Sunday evening, there was a ball in the open air at Piriac. The youths and the girls, with joined hands, whirled for hours, repeating the same verse to the same deep tone strongly accented. Those heavy voices, sounding out of the dusk, gradually acquired a barbaric charm. Estelle, seated on the beach, with Hector at her feet, listened, finally losing herself in a reverie. The sea rose with a noise of caresses. One might have imagined a voice of passion, when the waves beat upon the sand; then, the voice softened suddenly, and the cry died away, with the water that receded, into a plaintive murmur of conquered love. The young woman dreamed of being thus loved, by a giant of whom she would have made a little boy.

"You must be weary of Piriac," M. Chabre sometimes suggested to his wife.

And she hastened to reply, "Why, no, my dear; I assure you I am not."

She enjoyed herself, in this secluded hole. The geese, the pigs, the sardines took on an extreme importance. At the end of two weeks, M. Chabre, who was bored to death, wished to return to Paris. The shell-fish must have taken effect by that time, he said. But she cried out, "Oh! My dear, you have not eaten nearly enough. I know you need a lot more."

One evening, Hector said to the husband and wife, "To-morrow, we shall have a high-tide. We can fish for shrimps."

The proposition seemed to enchant Estelle. Yes, yes, they must go and fish for shrimps! M. Chabre raised objections. To begin with, one never caught anything. Secondly, it was much simpler to buy the shrimps from some woman of the place for a franc piece, and avoid wetting one's self to the waist and skinning one's feet. But he had to give in to the enthusiasm of his wife.

There was considerable preparation. Hector volunteered to furnish the nets. M. Chabre, in spite of his fear of cold water, had declared that he would be of the party. And from the moment that he consented to fish, he intended to fish seriously. In the morning, he had a pair of boots greased. Then, he dressed in light linen; but his wife could not prevail upon him to leave off his cravat, which he tied with loose ends as if he were going to a wedding. That knot was the protestation of a gentlemanly man against the rowdyism of the ocean. As for Estelle, she wore a short loose gown over her bathing suit. Hector, also, wore his bathing suit.

They started out at about two o'clock, each carrying a net over the shoulder. They had a mile and a half to walk over the sand and shingle to reach a rock where Hector claimed were veritable banks of shrimps. He led the party, calm, crossing the puddles, going straight ahead without thinking of the dangers of the path. Estelle followed him boldly, pleased with the freshness of the wet earth in which her little feet paddled. M. Chabre, who came last, did not see any necessity of wetting his boots before arriving at the scene of the fishing. He conscientiously went around the pools, jumped the little streams that the ebbing water left in the sand, chose the dry places with the careful manner of a Parisian who would seek the points of the paving-stones in the rue Vivienne on a muddy day. He was panting already, and he asked every few moments. "Is it still far, Monsieur Hector? Look! Why don't we fish here? I see some shrimps, I assure you. Besides, they are everywhere in the sea,—aren't they? I'll wager that it is only necessary to thrust in your net."

"Thrust it in, sir," answered Hector. And M. Chabre, stopping to catch his breath, dipped his net into a pool as large as his hand. He drew out nothing, not even a weed. Then, he continued the tramp with a dignified air, his lips puckered. But losing the way in an endeavor to prove that there were shrimps everywhere, he found himself considerably behind the others.

The sea was ebbing fast, and was more than a mile from shore. The bottom of shingle and rocks was exposed, spread out like a moist desert, rugged, sadly magnificent, as if devastated by a storm. Estelle gazed upon that naked immensity.

"Oh! How vast it is!" she murmured.

Hector pointed out certain rocks, green boulders, forming bars, worn by the tide.

"Those," he explained, "are uncovered only twice a month, then mussels are gathered from them. Do you see that brown speck over there? That is the "Red Cow," the best spot for lobsters. It is seen during only two tides of the year. But let us hurry. We are going to those rocks of which the tops are beginning to appear."

When Estelle entered the water, she lifted her feet high and splashed about, laughing as the foam spurted up. When the water was up to her knees, she had to struggle against the current.

"Don't be afraid," said Hector. "The water will be up to your waist, but the ocean-bed rises immediately. We shall soon be there." Little by little, they toiled upward, and found themselves upon a group of rocks that the receding water uncovered.

Estelle and Hector were ready for the first dip of their nets when a lamentable voice was heard. M. Chabre, planted in the middle of the small arm of the sea, inquired his way.

"Which way do you go? Straight ahead?" he cried. He was in up to his waist; he dared not take a step, terrified by the thought that he might fall into a hole and disappear.

"To the left," cried Hector. He went to the left, but, as he sank deeper, he stopped again. He lamented.

"Come and give me a hand. I assure you there are holes,—I feel them!"

"To the right, sir; to the right!" cried Hector. And the poor man was so ludicrous in the middle of the water, with his net over his shoulder and his beautiful knotted scarf that Estelle and Hector could not suppress a little laugh.

"I can't swim,—I can't!"

What worried him now was the return. When the young man had explained that they must not allow themselves to be overtaken by the tide, he became more worried.

"You will warn me,—won't you?"

"Have no fear; I'll look after you."

So they all began to fish. With their narrow nets, they rummaged in fissures. Estelle put into her quest all the ardor of a woman. It was she who caught the first shrimps, three large red ones that jumped about violently in the bottom of the net.

"It is curious," said M. Chabre, "I can't catch one."

As he didn't dare risk himself in the clefts, very much bothered besides by his heavy boots filled with water, he dragged his net over the sand and caught nothing but crabs, five, eight, ten crabs at a time. He was scared to death of them and fought with them to drive them out of his net. Momentarily, he turned and looked anxiously at the sea.

"Are you sure it is still going out?" he asked Hector.

The young man contented himself with a nod. He was fishing boldly like one who knows the best places, and he was catching handfuls of shrimps. When he raised his net beside Estelle, he put its contents into her little basket. For two hours, they fished.

"I assure you, the tide is coming in!" cried M. Chabre, agonizingly. "Look! A short time ago, that rock was uncovered."

"Without a doubt, it is coming in," said Hector, impatiently. "It is while it is coming in that one finds the most shrimps."

But Mr. Chabre lost his head. In his last fling with the net, he had brought up a strange fish, a devil of the sea, which terrified him. He had had enough.

"Come along. Let us go," he repeated. "It is stupid to be rash."

"When you are told that fishing is better when the tide turns," said Estelle.

"And it is coming in strong," murmured Hector with a mischievous gleam in his eye. Effectually, the waves were coming in long swells, breaking against the rocks with a loud clamor.

"I am going!" cried M. Chabre, with tears in his voice.

He started, despairingly sounding for boles with the handle of his net. When he had gone a few hundred feet, Hector persuaded Estelle to follow him.

"We are going to have the water to our shoulders," he said, smiling. "A real bath for M. Chabre. See how deep in he is already! You will have to get on my back and I will carry you. Otherwise, you would be soaked. Quick! Climb up!"

He held his back to her. She refused, embarrassed, blushing. But he insisted,—he was responsible for her safety. So she got up, placing her hands upon his shoulders. He, solid as a rock, straightened up as if he had no more than a bird upon his back.

"To the right, isn't it?" cried M. Chabre in a lamentable voice, as the waves broke against his back.

"Yes; to the right, always to the right."

Then, as the husband went forward, shivering as he felt the water rising to his armpits, Hector dared to kiss one of the little hands resting on his shoulders. Estelle tried to withdraw them, but he warned her not to move or he would not answer for the consequences. And he forthwith began covering her hands with kisses.

"I beg of you, don't do that," pleaded Estelle, affecting anger. "You take a strange advantage. I shall jump into the water."

He began again, and she did not jump. He clasped her ankles firmly and devoured her hands with kisses, while he kept an eye on what could be seen of M. Chabre's back, a tragic remnant of a back that threatened to disappear at every step.

"Did you say to the right?" implored the husband.

"To the left, if you wish."

M. Chabre took a step to the left and gave a cry. He sank to the neck, submerging his knotted scarf. Hector seized the opportunity to avow himself.

"I love you."

"Be still, sir, I command you!"

"I love you. I adore you. 'Till now, respect has kept me quiet. . . ."

He continued his long strides, with the water risen to his chest. She could not refrain from laughing, the situation appeared so ridiculous.

"Now, be quiet," she said, maternally, giving him a pat on the shoulder. "Be sensible; and above all, don't stumble."

That little pat filled Hector with enchantment; it was a promising sign. And, as the husband stood still in distress, the young man called out gaily,"Turn to the right now."

When they reached the shore, M. Chabre wanted to explain things.

"I came near staying out there," he stammered. "It was my boots . . ."

But Estelle opened her basket and showed it to him filled with shrimps.

"What! You caught all those?" he cried astonished. "Why, you know how to fish!"

"Oh!" she said, smiling and looking at Hector, "Monsieur showed me how."

The Chabres were to leave Piriac in two days. Hector seemed dismayed, furious, and yet humble. As for M. Chabre, he questioned his health every morning and remained perplexed.

"You cannot leave here without having seen the rocks of the Castelle," said Hector. "We must arrange a tramp for to-morrow."

The rocks were barely a mile out. They would follow the shore, with its caves hollowed out by the waves, for about a mile and a half.

"Well, we'll go to-morrow," Estelle said finally. "Is the walking difficult?"

"No; there are two or three places where you will get your feet wet, that is all."

But M. Chabre did not wish to wet his feet. Since his bath during the shrimp-fishing, he bore the ocean ill-will. So he showed himself hostile to this excursion. Hector, to persuade him, had a sudden inspiration.

"Listen," he said. "You will pass the semaphore of the Castelle. The telegraph operators always have a quantity of superb shell-fish that they will sell you for almost nothing."

"Ah! That's a good idea!" said the grain merchant. "I will carry a little basket, and I'll have one more good fill."

The next day, they waited for low tide. The way was rough. They walked along a beach of dry sand into which their feet sank. The retired merchant puffed like a steer.

"Well! I am going to leave you and walk along the bank," he said finally.

"That is better. Follow the path," said Hector.

They watched him climb to the top of the cliff. Once there, he opened his umbrella and waved his basket, crying, "This is much better! Now, don't be rash! Besides, I am watching you."

Hector and Estelle climbed over huge rocks. The young man, in high boots, went before, springing from boulder to boulder with the grace and skill of a mountain hunter. Estelle chose the same rocks, and when he turned to ask, "Shall I give you a hand?" she answered, "Why, no! I am not a grandmother!"

As they issued from a narrow passage, M. Chabre cried out from the cliff,—

"Ah! There you are! I was uneasy . . . Those chasms are terrifying."

He was six feet from the edge, shaded by his umbrella, his basket on his arm. He added, "The tide comes in rapidly. Take care!"

"We have plenty of time. Don't worry," replied Hector.

"Is that the semaphore, the house with the mast?" asked M. Chabre. "I am going after the shell-fish. I will catch up with you."

Estelle ran over the rocks like a child. She leaped the pools; she approached the sea, seized with a caprice to climb to the summit of a mass of boulders which formed an island at high tide. And, after a laborious climb, she hoisted herself upon the top stone and surveyed the tragic devastation of the coast. She lost herself in reverie, as if she had looked into a mysterious country.

When she returned to the base of the cliff, she found Hector with his handkerchief filled with limpets.

"They are for M. Chabre," he said. "I'll take them to him."

At that moment, M. Chabre returned disappointed.

"They have not so much as a mussel at the semaphore. I didn't want to come,I was quite right."

But, when the young man showed him the limpets, he calmed down. And he was astounded at the agility displayed by the young fellow as he climbed up the face of the cliff by a way known only to himself. His descent was even more audacious.

"That's nothing," he said. "It is a veritable stairway,you only need to know where the steps are."

M. Chabre wanted to start back. The sea was growing restless. The young man laughed and declared that they would have to go on to the end. They had not seen the caves. So, M. Chabre had to resume his walk on the crest of the bluff. As the sun sank, he closed his umbrella and used it as a cane. In the other hand, he carried his basket of limpets.

"Are you tired?" Hector asked softly.

"Yes; a little," answered Estelle.She accepted his offered arm. She was not tired, but a delicious abandonment invaded her more and more. They looked at each other, silent and smiling. The sea arose in short choppy waves, but they did not hear it. M. Chabre, above them, called out and they did not hear him, either.

"But this is crazy!" cried the merchant, shaking his umbrella and his basket of limpets. "Estelle! Monsieur Hector! You are going to be caught! You are walking in the water!" They had not felt the freshness of the little waves.

"What is it?" murmured the young woman.

"Ah! It is you, M. Chabre! This is nothing, don't be afraid. We have only Madame's Grotto to see."

M. Chabre gesticulated despairingly, adding "It is madness! You are going to be drowned!"

They no longer listened to him. To escape the incoming tide, they went over the rocks and finally reached "Madame's Grotto." It was an excavation in a block of granite that formed a promontory. The roof rounded into a dome. During tempests, the water had polished the walls till they gleamed like agate. The gravel on the floor, still wet, retained a transparence that made it resemble a bed of precious stones. At the back, there was a bank of sand, soft and dry, of a pale yellow, almost white.

Estelle seated herself upon the sand and examined the cave.

"One could live here," she murmured.

But Hector, who appeared to be watching the sea, said suddenly, "My God! We are caught! The tide has cut us off. We will have to wait here two hours."

He went out and sought M. Chabre. That gentleman was on the cliff just above the grotto. When the young man announced their predicament, he cried triumphantly,

"What did I tell you? But you wouldn't listen to me! Is there any danger?"

"None," answered Hector. "The sea enters the grotto only five or six yards. Only don't worry, we can't get out for two hours."

M. Chabre became angry. Then, they were not to have dinner! He was already hungry. This was a nice excursion, he must say! Then, grumbling, he sat down on the short grass, placing his umbrella to his left and the basket of limpets to his right.

"I'll wait, there's nothing else to do. Go back to my wife. See that she doesn't take cold."

In the grotto, Hector seated himself beside Estelle. After a silence, he took her hand, and she did not withdraw it. She looked into the distance. The dusk fell. Little by little, the water entered the cave, rolling the gravel with a soft caressing sound. It brought with it the voluptuousness of space, a crooning voice, and irritating odor, charged with desire.

"Estelle, I love you," repeated Hector, covering her hands with kisses. She did not answer; she was suffocated, as if lifted by that sea that rose. On the soft sand, half lying, she resembled a daughter of the sea, surprised and defenseless. And, suddenly, the voice of M. Chabre reached them, thin, aerial.

"Aren't you hungry? I am famished! Fortunately I have my knife. I am eating my limpets."

"I love you, Estelle," repeated Hector who held her clasped in his arms.

The night was black; the white sea lighted the sky. At the entrance to the cave, the sea uttered a low complaint, while beneath the roof, a last remnant of light; was extinguished. Then, Estelle let her head droop upon Hector's shoulder. And the evening breeze bore away their sighs.

Above, by the light of the stars, Mr. Chabre ate his shellfish methodically. He gave himself indigestion eating so many without bread.

ANGELINE

I

Nearly two years ago I was spinning on my bicycle over a deserted road towards Orgeval, above Poissy, when the sudden sight of a wayside house caused me such surprise that I sprang from my machine to take a better look at it. It was a brick-built house, with no marked characteristics, and it stood under the grey November sky, amid the cold wind which was sweeping away the dead leaves, in the centre of spacious grounds planted with old trees. That which rendered it remarkable, which lent it an aspect of fierce, wild, savage strangeness of a nature to oppress the heart, was the frightful abandonment into which it had fallen. And as part of the iron gate was torn away, and a huge notice-board, with lettering half-effaced by the rain, announced that the place was for sale, I entered the garden, yielding to curiosity mingled with uneasiness and anguish.

The house must have been unoccupied for thirty or, perhaps, forty years. The bricks of the cornices and facings had been disjointed by past winters, and were overgrown with moss and lichen. Cracks, suggestive of precocious wrinkles, scarred the frontage of the building, which still looked strong, though no care whatever was now taken of it. The steps below, split by frost, and shut off by nettles and brambles, formed, as it were, a threshold of desolation and death. But the frightful mournfulness of the place came more particularly from its bare, curtainless, smudgy windows, whose panes had been broken by stone-throwing urchins, and which, one and all, revealed the desolate emptiness of the rooms, like dim eyes that had remained wide open in some soulless corpse. Then, too, the spacious garden all around was a scene of devastation; the old flower-beds could scarce be discerned beneath the growth of rank weeds; the paths had disappeared, devoured by hungry plants; the shrubberies had grown to virgin forests; there was all the wild vegetation of some abandoned cemetery in the damp gloom beneath the huge and ancient trees, whose last leaves were that day being swept off by the autumn wind, which ever shrieked its doleful plaint.

Long did I linger there amidst that despairing wail of Nature, for though my heart was oppressed by covert fear, by growing anguish, I was detained by a feeling of ardent pity, a longing to know and to sympathize with all the woe and grief that I felt around me. And when at last I had left the spot and perceived across the road, at a point where the latter forked, a kind of tavern, a hovel where drink was sold, I entered it, fully resolved to question the folks of the neighborhood.

But I only found there an old woman who sighed and whimpered as she served me a glass of beer. She complained of living on that out-of-the-way road, along which not even a couple of cyclists passed each day. And she talked on interminably, telling me her story, relating that she was called Mother Toussaint, that she and her man had come from Vernon to take that tavern that things had turned out fairly well at first but that all had been going from bad to worse since she had become a widow. When, after her rush of words, I began to question her respecting the neighboring house, she suddenly became circumspect, and glanced at me suspiciously as if she thought that I wished to tear some dread secret from her.

'Ah, yes,' said she, 'La Sauvagiere, the haunted house, as people say hereabouts. . . . For my part, I know nothing, monsieur; it doesn't date from my time. I shall have only been here thirty years come next Easter, and those things go back to well-nigh forty years now. When we came here the house was already much as you see it. The summers pass, the winters pass, and nothing stirs unless it be the stones that fall.'

'But why,' I asked,' why is the place not sold, since it is for sale?'

'Ah! Why? Why? Can I tell? People say so many things.'

I was doubtless beginning to inspire her with some confidence. Besides, at heart she must have been burning to tell me the many things that people said. She began by relating that not one of the girls of the neighboring village ever dared to enter La Sauvagiere after twilight, for rumor had it that some poor wandering soul returned thither every night. And, as I expressed astonishment that such a story could still find any credit so near to Paris, she shrugged her shoulders, tried to talk like a strong-minded woman, but finally betrayed by her manner he terror she did not confess.

'There are facts that can't be denied, monsieur. You ask why the place is not sold? I've seen many purchasers arrive, and all have gone off quicker than they came; not one of them has ever put in a second appearance. Well, one matter that's certain is that as soon as a visitor dares venture inside the house some extraordinary things happen. The doors swing to and fro and close by themselves with a bang, as if a hurricane were sweeping past. Cries, moans, and sobs ascend from the cellars, and if the visitor obstinately remains, a heartrending voice raises a continuous cry of 'Angeline! Angeline! Angeline!' in such distressful, appealing tones that one's very bones are frozen. I repeat to you that this has been proved, nobody will tell you otherwise.'

I must own that I was now growing impassioned myself, and could feel a little chilly quiver coursing under my skin. 'And this Angeline, who is she?' I asked.

'Ah I monsieur, it would be necessary to tell you all. And, once again, for my part I know nothing.'

Nevertheless, the old woman ended by telling me all. Some forty years previously—in or about 1858—at the time when the triumphant Second Empire was born, Monsieur de G , a Tuilleries functionary, lost his wife, by whom he had a daughter some ten years old— Angeline, a marvel of beauty, the living portrait of her mother. Two years later, Monsieur de G married again, espousing another famous beauty, the widow of a general. And it was asserted, that from the very moment of those second nuptials, atrocious jealousy had sprung up between Angeline and her stepmother: the former stricken in the heart at finding her own mother already forgotten, replaced so soon by a stranger; and the other tortured, maddened, by always having before her that living portrait of a woman whose memory, she feared, she would never be able to efface. La Sauvagiere was the property of the new Madame de G , and there one evening, on seeing the father passionately embrace his daughter, she, in her jealous madness, it was said, had dealt the child so violent a blow, that the poor girl had fallen to the floor dead, her collar-bone broken. Then the rest was frightful: the distracted father consenting to bury his daughter with his own hands in a cellar of the house in order to save the murderess; the remains lying there for years, while the child was said to be living with an aunt; and at last the howls of a dog and its persistent scratching of the ground leading to the discovery of the crime, which was, however, at once hushed up by command of the Tuilleries. And now Monsieur and Madame de G were both dead, while Angeline again returned each night at the call of the heartrending voice that ever cried for her from out of the mysterious spheres beyond the darkness.

'Nobody will contradict me,' concluded Mother Toussaint. 'It is all as true as that two and two make four.'

I had listened to her in bewilderment, resenting certain improbabilities, but won over by the brutal and somber strangeness of the tragedy. I had heard of this Monsieur de G, and it seemed to me that he had indeed married a second time, and that some family grief had overclouded his life. Was the tale true, then? What a tragical and affecting story! Every human passion stirred up, heightened, exasperated to madness; the most terrifying love tale there could be, a little girl as beautiful as daylight, adored, and yet killed by her stepmother, and buried by her father in the corner of a cellar! There was here more matter for horror and emotion than one might dare to hope for. I was again about to question and discuss things. Then I asked myself what would be the use of it? Why not carry that frightful story away with me in its flower—such indeed as it had sprouted from popular imagination?

As I again sprang upon my bicycle I gave La Sauvagiere a last glance. The night was falling and the woeful house gazed at me with its dim and empty windows akin to the eyes of a corpse, while the wail of the autumn wind still swept through the ancient trees.

II

Why did this story so fix itself in my brain as to lead to real obsession, perfect torment? This is one of those intellectual problems that are difficult to solve. In vain I told myself that similar legends overrun the rural districts, and that I had no direct concern in this one. In spite of all, I was haunted by that dead child, that lovely and tragic. Angeline, to whom every night for forty years past a desolate voice had called through the empty rooms of the forsaken house.

Thus, during the first two months of the winter I made researches. It was evident that if anything, however little, had transpired of such a dramatic disappearance, the newspapers of the period must have referred to it. However, I ransacked the collections of the National Library without discovering a line about any such story. Then I questioned contemporaries, men who had formerly had intercourse with Tuilleries society; but none could give me a positive reply, I only obtained contradictory information. So much so that, although still and ever tortured by the mystery, I had abandoned all hope of getting to the truth, when chance one morning set me on a fresh track.

Every two or three weeks I paid a visit of good fellowship, affection, and admiration to the old poet V, who died last April on the threshold of his seventieth year. Paralysis of the legs had, for many years previous, riveted him to an armchair in his study of the Eue d'Assas, whose window overlooked the garden of the Luxembourg. He there peacefully finished a dreamy life, for he had ever lived on imagination, building for himself a palace of ideality, in which he had loved and suffered far away from the real. Who of us does not remember his refined and amiable features, his white hair curly like a child's, his pale blue eyes, which had retained the innocence of youth? One could not say that he invariably told falsehoods. But the truth is that he was prone to invention, in such wise that one never exactly knew at what point reality ceased to exist for him and at what point dreaming began. He was a very charming old man, long since detached from life, one whose words often filled me with emotion as if indeed they were a vague, discreet revelation of the unknown.

One day, then, I was chatting with him near the window of the little room which a blazing fire ever warmed. It was freezing terribly out of doors. The Luxembourg gardens stretched away white with snow, displaying a broad horizon of immaculate purity. And I know not how, but at last I spoke to him of La Sauvagiere, and of the story that still worried me—that father who had remarried, and that stepmother, jealous of the little girl; then the murder perpetrated in a fit of fury, and the burial in a cellar. V listened to me with the quiet smile which he retained even in moments of sadness. Then silence fell, his pale blue eyes wandered away over the white immensity of the Luxembourg, while a shade of dreaminess, emanating from him, seemed to set a faint quiver all around.

'I knew Monsieur de G very well,' he said. 'I knew his first wife, whose beauty was superhuman; I knew the second one, who was no less wondrously beautiful; and I myself passionately loved them both without ever telling it. I also knew Angeline, who was yet more beautiful than they, and whom all men a little later would have worshipped on their knees. But things did not happen quite as you say.'

My emotion was profound. Was the unexpected truth that I despaired of at hand, then? At first I felt no distrust, but said to him, ' Ah! What a service you render me, my friend I shall at last be able to quiet my poor mind. Make haste to tell me all.'

But he was not listening, his glance still wandered far away. And he began to speak in a dreamy voice, as if creating things and beings in his mind as he proceeded with his narrative.

'At twelve years of age Angeline was one in whom all woman's love, with every impulse of joy and grief, had already flowered. She it was who felt desperately jealous of the new wife whom every day she saw in her father's arms. She suffered from it as from some frightful act of betrayal; it was not her mother only who was insulted by that new union, she herself was tortured, her own heart was pierced. Every night, too, she heard her mother calling her from her tomb, and one night, eager to rejoin her, overcome by excess of suffering and excess of love, this child, who was but twelve years old, thrust a knife into her heart.'

A cry burst from me. 'God of heaven! Is it possible?'

'How great was the fright and horror,' he continued, without hearing me, 'when on the morrow Monsieur and Madame de G found Angeline in her little bed with that knife plunged to its very handle in her breast! They were about to start for Italy; of all their servants, too, there only remained in the house an old nurse who had reared the child. In their terror, fearing that they might be accused of a crime, they induced the woman to help them, and they did indeed bury the body, but in a comer of the conservatory behind the house, at the foot of a huge orange-tree. And there it was found on the day when, the parents being dead, the old servant told the story.'

Doubts had come to me while he spoke, and I scrutinized him anxiously, wondering if he had not invented this. 'But,' said I, 'do you also think it possible that Angeline can come back each night in response to the heartrending, mysterious voice that calls her?'

This time he looked at me and smiled indulgently once more.

'Come back, my friend? Why, everyone comes back! Why should not the soul of that dear dead child still dwell in the spot where she loved and suffered? If a voice is heard calling her 'tis because life has not yet begun afresh for her. Yet it will begin afresh, be sure of it; for all begins afresh. Nothing is lost, love no more than beauty. Angeline! Angeline! Angeline! She is called, and will be born anew to the sunlight and the flowers.'

Decidedly, neither belief nor tranquility came to my mind. Indeed, my old friend V, the child-poet, had but increased my torment. He had assuredly been inventing things. And yet, like all visionaries, he could, perhaps, divine the truth.

'Is it all true, what you have been telling me?' I ventured to ask him with a laugh.

He in his turn broke into gentle mirth. 'Why, certainly it is true. Is not the infinite all true?'

That was the last time I saw him, for soon afterwards I had to quit Paris. But I can still picture him, glancing thoughtfully over the white expanse of the Luxembourg, so tranquil in the convictions born of his endless dream, whereas I am consumed by my desire to arrest and for all time determine Truth, which ever and ever flees.

Eighteen months went by. I had been obliged to travel; great trials and great joys had impassioned my life amidst the tempest-gust which carries us all towards the Unknown. But at certain moments still I heard the woeful cry, 'Angeline! Angeline! Angeline!' approach from afar and penetrate me. And then I trembled, full of doubt once more, tortured by my desire to know. I could not forget; for me there is no worse hell than uncertainty.

I cannot say how it was that one splendid June evening I again found myself on my bicycle on the lonely road that passes La Sauvagiere. Had I expressly wished to see the place again, or was it mere instinct that had impelled me to quit the highway and turn in that direction? It was nearly eight o'clock, but, those being the longest days of the year, the sky was still radiant with a triumphal sunset, cloudless, all gold and azure. And how light and delicious was the atmosphere, how pleasant was the scent of foliage and grass, how softly and sweetly joyous was the far-stretching peacefulness of the fields!

As on the first occasion, amazement made me spring from my machine in front of La Sauvagiere. I hesitated for a moment. The place was no longer the same. A fine new iron gate glittered in the sunset, the walls had been repaired, and the house, which I could scarce distinguish among the trees, seemed to have regained the smiling gaiety of youth. Was this, then, the predicted resurrection? Had Angeline returned to life at the call of the distant voice?

I had remained on the road, thunderstruck, still gazing, when a halting footfall made me start. I turned and saw Mother Toussaint bringing her cow back from a neighboring patch of lucerne. 'So those folks were not frightened, eh?' said I, pointing to the house.

She recognized me and stopped her beast. 'Ah, monsieur!' she answered, 'there are people who would tread on God Himself! The place has been sold for more than a year now. But it was a painter who bought it, a painter named B, and those artists, you know, are capable of anything!'

Then she drove on her cow, shaking her head and adding: 'Well, well, we must see how it will all turn out.'

B, the painter, the delicate and skilful artist who had portrayed so many amiable Parisiennes! I knew him a little; we shook hands when we met at theatres and shows, wherever, indeed, people are apt to meet. Thus, all at once, an irresistible longing seized me to go in, make my confession to him, and beg him to tell me what he knew of this Sauvagiere, whose mystery ever haunted me. And without reasoning, without thought even of my dusty cycling suit, which custom, by the way, is now rendering permissible, I opened the gate and rolled my bicycle as far as the mossy trunk of an old tree. At the clear call of the bell affixed to the gate a servant came; I handed him my card and he left me for a moment in the garden.

My surprise increased still more when I glanced around me. The house-front had been repaired, there were no more cracks, no more disjointed bricks; the steps, girt with roses, were once more like a threshold of joyous welcome; and now the living windows smiled and spoke of the happiness behind their snowy curtains. Then, too, there was the garden rid of its nettles and brambles, the flowerbed revived, resembling a huge and fragrant nosegay, and the old trees, standing amid the quietude of centuries, rejuvenated by the golden rain of the summer sun.

When the servant returned he led me to a drawing-room, saying that his master had gone to the neighboring village, but would soon be home. I would have waited for hours. At first I took patience in examining the room, which was elegantly furnished, with heavy carpets, and window and door curtains of cretonne similar to that which upholstered the large settee and the deep arm-chairs. The hangings were, indeed, so full that I felt astonished at the sudden fall of the daylight. Then came darkness almost perfect. I know not how long I stayed there; I had been forgotten, no lamp even was brought me. Seated in the gloom, I once again yielded to my dreams and lived through the whole tragic story. Had Angeline been murdered? Or had she herself thrust a knife into her heart? And I must confess it, in that haunted house, where all had become so black, fear seized upon me—fear which was at the outset but slight uneasiness, a little creeping of the flesh, and which afterwards grew, froze me from head to foot, till I was filled with insane fright.

It seemed to me at first that vague sounds were echoing somewhere. It was doubtless in the depths of the cellars. There were low moans, stifled sobs, footsteps as of some phantom. Then it all ascended and drew nearer, the whole dark house seemed to me full of that frightful anguish. All at once the terrible call arose, 'Angeline I Angeline! Angeline I' with such increasing force that I fancied I could feel a puff of icy breath sweep across my face. A door of the drawing-room was flung open violently; Angeline entered and crossed the room without seeing me. I recognized her in the flash of light which came in with her from the hall, where a lamp was burning. It was really she, the poor dead child, twelve years of age, so marvelously beautiful. Her splendid fair hair fell over her shoulders, and she was clad in white; she had come all white from the grave, whence every night she rose. Mute, scared, she passed before me, and vanished through another door, while again the cry rang out farther away, 'Angeline! Angeline! Angeline!' And I—I remained erect, my brow wet with perspiration, in a state of horror, which made my hair stand on end, beneath the terror-striking blast that had come from the Mysterious.

Almost immediately afterwards, I fancy, at the moment when a servant at last brought a lamp, I became conscious that B, the painter, was beside me, shaking my hand and apologizing for having kept me waiting so long. I showed no false pride, but, still quivering with dread, I at once told him my story. And with what astonishment did he not at first listen to me, and then with what kindly laughter did he not seek to reassure me!

'You were doubtless unaware, my dear fellow, that I am a cousin of the second Madame de G. Poor woman! To accuse her of having murdered that child, she who loved her and wept for her as much as the father himself did! For the only point that is true is that the poor little girl did die here, not, thank Heaven! by her own hand, but from a sudden fever which struck her down like a thunderbolt, in such wise that the parents forsook this house in horror and would never return to it. This explains why it so long remained empty even in their lifetime. After their death came endless lawsuits, which prevented it from being sold. I wished to secure it myself, I watched for it for years, and I assure you that since we have been here we have seen no ghost.'

The little quiver came over me again, and I stammered, 'But Angeline, I have just seen her, here, this moment the terrible voice was calling her, and she passed by, she crossed this room!'

He looked at me in dismay, fancying that my mind was affected. Then, all at once, he again broke into a sonorous, happy laugh.

'It was my daughter whom you saw. It so happens that Monsieur de G was her godfather; and in memory of his own dear daughter he chose for her the name of Angeline. No doubt her mother was calling her just now, and she passed through this room.'

Then he himself opened a door, and once more raised the cry: 'Angeline! Angeline! Angeline!'

The child returned, not dead, but living, sparkling with juvenile gaiety. ''Twas she in her white gown, with her splendid fair hair falling over her shoulders, and so beautiful, so radiant with hope, that she looked like an incarnation of all the springtide of life, bearing in the bud the promise of love and the promise of long years of happiness.

Ah! The dear revenant, the new child that had sprung from the one that was no more! Death was vanquished. My old friend, the poet V, had told no falsehood. Nothing is lost; renascence comes to all, to beauty as well as love. Mothers' voices call them, those lasses of to-day, those sweethearts of to-morrow, and they live afresh beneath the sun, amid the flowers. And 'twas that awakening of youth that now haunted the house—the house which had once more become young and happy, in the joy at last regained that springs from life the eternal.

HOW WE DIE

I

The Count de Verteuil is fifty-five. He belongs to one of the most famous families in France, and has a large fortune. At odds with the government, he has employed his time as best he could; has contributed articles to serious magazines, which have gained him admission to the Academy of moral and political sciences, has thrown himself into business, has been successively enthusiastic over agriculture, stock farming, and the fine arts. At one time he was even deputy, and distinguished himself by the violence of his opposition.

The Countess Mathilde de Verteuil is forty-six. She is still quoted as the most adorable blonde in Paris. Age seems to ripen her skin. She used to be rather thin; now her shoulders, in maturing, have acquired the roundness of a silky fruit. Never was she more beautiful. When she enters a drawing-room, with her golden hair and the satin of her bust, she appears like a rising star; and women of twenty envy her.

The household of the count and countess is one of those that are not talked about. They married as people in their world oftenest do marry. Some persons will even assure you that they lived together very happily for six years. At that time they had a son, Roger, who is a lieutenant, and a daughter, Blanche, whom they married off last year to M. de Bussac. They approach each other through their children. Since they broke with one another years ago, they have remained good friends, with a vast fund of selfishness. They consult together, treat each other with perfect affability in society, but shut themselves up afterwards in their own apartments, where they receive their intimate friends as they please.

But, one night, Mathilde comes home from a ball about two in the morning. Her maid undresses her; then, just as she is about to withdraw, says, "Monsieur le Count has been a little unwell this evening."

The countess, half asleep, lazily turns her head.

"Ah!" she murmurs.

She stretches herself, and adds, "Wake me to-morrow at ten; I expect the dressmaker."

Next day, at breakfast, as the count does not appear, the countess first sends to ask after him; then she makes up her mind to go and see him. She finds him in bed, very pale and very precise in dress and bearing. Three physicians have been there already, have talked together in an undertone, and left prescriptions; they are to return in the evening. The sick man is cared for by two servants, who go about the room, grave and mute, stifling the noise of their heels on the carpet. The large chamber sleeps in cold severity; not a towel is lying about, not a piece of furniture is out of its place. It is proper and dignified sickness, ceremonious sickness that expects calls.

"So you are unwell, my dear?" asks the Countess, as she comes into the room.

The count makes an effort to smile.

"Oh! A little fatigue," answers he. "I only need rest. . . . I thank you for taking the trouble to come."

Two days pass by. The chamber remains dignified; everything is in its place, the medicines disappear without leaving a spot on the furniture. The servants' close-shaven faces do not even permit themselves to express a sense of boredom. Yet the count knows that he is in danger of death; he has exacted the truth from his physicians, and lets them do their will, without a complaint. Most of the time he lies there with closed eyes, or else looks steadily before him, as if thinking of his loneliness.

"Well? Are you better, my dear?"

"Yes, much better, I thank you, my dear Mathilde."

"If you wished, I would stay with you."

"No, there is no need of that. Julien and Francois do very well. . . . What is the use of tiring you?"

They understand each other; they have lived apart, and mean to die apart. The count has that bitter, selfish satisfaction of the egoist, who wishes to depart alone, without having around his bed the comedies of grief. He abridges as far as possible, for himself and the countess, the irksomeness of the last interview. His last will is to vanish with propriety, as a man of the world who means to trouble and excite repugnance in no one.

Yet, one evening, he has no breath left; he knows that he will not live through the night. Then, as the countess comes up to pay her usual visit, he says to her, calling up a last smile, "Do not go. . . . I do not feel well."

He would spare her the world's tittle-tattle. She, on her part, expected this of him; and she takes her place in the room. The physicians do not leave the dying man. The two servants finish their duty with the same silent assiduousness. The children, Roger and Blanche, have been sent for, and are at the bedside next their mother. Other relatives are in a neighboring room. The night passes so, in solemn waiting. In the morning the last sacraments are brought, the count receives communion in the presence of all, to give a last support to religion. The ceremony is over; he can die.

But he is in no haste; he seems to regain his strength, so as to avoid a convulsive and clamorous death. His breathing, in the large, severe room, gives forth only the broken sound of a clock out of order. It is a well-bred man who is passing away; and, when he has kissed his wife and children, he pushes them from him with a movement of his arm; he falls toward the wall, and dies alone.

Then one of the physicians bends over him, closes the dead man's eyes. He says in an undertone, "It is all over."

Sighs and tears rise amid the stillness. The countess, Roger, and Blanche are on their knees. They weep between their clasped hands; you do not see their faces. Then the two children lead away their mother, who, at the door, sways her body in one last sob, to emphasize her despair; and, from this moment, the dead man belongs to the pomp of his obsequies.

The physicians have gone, rounding their shoulders, and assuming an expression of vague disconsolateness. The parish priest is sent for, to wake with the body. The two servants stay with this priest, seated on chairs, stiff and full of dignity; it is the expected end of their service. One of them espies a spoon that has been left on a table; he gets up, and slips it quickly into his pocket, that the fine orderliness of the room may not be disturbed.

In the room below, the great drawing-room, a noise of hammering is heard; the upholsterers are getting it ready for the dead man to lie in state. The whole day is taken up with the embalming; the doors are closed, the embalmer is alone with his assistants. When they bring the count downstairs, next day, and he is exposed, he is in evening dress; he has the freshness of youth.

At nine, on the morning of the funeral, the house begins to fill with the murmur of voices. The son and son-in-law of the deceased receive the crowd in a parlor on the ground floor; they bow, they preserve the mute politeness of people in affliction. All the notabilities are there: the nobility, the army, the magistracy; there are even senators and members of the Institute.

At ten, at last, the procession sets out for the church. The hearse is a first-class vehicle, adorned with plumes, draped in silver-fringed hangings. The pallbearers are a marshal of France, a duke, an old friend of the deceased, an ex-minister, and an academician. Roger de Verteuil and M. de

Bussac lead the mourning. Next comes the procession, a wave of people in black gloves and cravats, all of them personages of importance, puffing through the dust, and walking with the dull tread of a dispersed flock of sheep.

The whole neighborhood is at the windows; people stand in rows on the sidewalk, raise their hats, and watch the triumphal hearse pass by, with a shake of the head. The street is blocked by the endless line of mourning coaches, almost all empty; omnibuses and wagons are piled up in the cross streets; you hear the coachmen's oaths and the crack of whips. And, all this time, the Countess de Verteuil is at home, shut up in her room, having given out that her tears have overcome her. Stretched out on a lounge, playing with the tassel of her girdle, she looks at the ceiling, relieved and pensive.

At the church the ceremony lasts nearly two hours. All the clergy is agog; ever since early morning, you could see nothing but priests running busily about in surplices, giving orders, mopping their foreheads, blowing their noses with resounding snorts. In the middle of the nave, hung with black, a catafalque is on fire. At last, the cortege has been shown to its seats, the women on the left, the men on the right; the organ peals forth its lamentations, the choristers chant in hollow moanings, the choir boys give shrill sobs; while, in the cressets, green flames burn high, adding their funereal pallor to the pomp of the ceremony.

"Isn't Faure to sing?" asks a deputy of his neighbor.

"Yes, I think so," answers the neighbor, a resplendent individual, given to smiling at the ladies across the aisle.

And, as the singer's voice rises in the thrilled nave, "Ah! What a method, what breadth of style!" he goes on in an undertone, nodding his head in ecstasy.

All present are enraptured. The ladies think of their evenings at the Opera. This Faure really has talent! A friend of the deceased goes so far as to say, "He never sang better! . . . It's a pity poor Verteuil can't hear him, he who liked him so much!"

The choristers, in black copes, walk round the catafalque. The priests, twenty in number, complicate the ceremonial, make genuflections, wave their holy-water sprinklers. At last, the mourners themselves file before the casket, the sprinklers are handed round. And they go out, after shaking hands with the family. Outside, the broad daylight blinds the crowd.

It is a fine June day. Filmy threads fly in the hot air. Then before the church, in the little square, there is jostling and pushing. The procession takes long in re-forming. Those who do not care to go farther vanish. Over two hundred yards off, at the end of the street, you already see the plumes of the hearse nodding and losing themselves in the distance, while the square is still all blocked up with carriages. You hear the slamming of the carriage doors and the brisk trot of the horses on the paving. Yet the coachmen fall into line, the procession makes for the cemetery.

The people in the carriages are at their ease; you might imagine them to be going to the Bois, slowly, in the Paris spring weather. As the hearse is no longer in sight, the burial is soon forgotten; and conversations are started, the ladies talk of the summer season, the men chat about their business.

"Tell me, my dear, are you going to Dieppe again, this year?"

"Yes, perhaps. But it will never be until August. . . . We go on Saturday to our place in the Loire."

"Come now, my dear fellow, he did intercept the letter, and the duel came off. Oh! In the prettiest way in the world; a mere scratch. . . . In the evening, I dined with him at the club. He even let me in for twenty five louis."

'I say, isn't the meeting of stockholders for day after to morrow? . . . They want to propose me on the committee. I'm so busy that I don't know that I shall be able. . . . "

A minute ago, the procession turned into an avenue. A cool shade falls from the trees, and the sunshine sings gleefully amid the foliage. All of a sudden, a giddy lady leans out of a carriage window, and exclaims, "Really! It's enchanting out here!"

Just at this point the procession turns into the Montparnasse cemetery. Voices are hushed; nothing is heard save the wheels grinding on the gravel of the avenues. They have to go quite to the end; the Verteuils' lot is there, on the left, —a large tomb of white marble, a sort of chapel, with much ornamental carving. The casket is set down before the door of this chapel, and the speeches begin.

There are four. The ex-minister retraces the political life of the deceased, whom he represents to have been a modest genius, who would have served his country, had he not disdained intriguing. Next, a friend speaks of the private virtues of him whom the whole world bewails. Then an unknown gentleman addresses the assembled crowd as delegate of an industrial society of which the Count de Verteuil was honorary president. At last, a little grizzly man expresses the regrets of the Academy of moral and political sciences.

All the while, those present take an interest in the surrounding tombs, read the inscriptions on the marble slabs. Those who listen hard catch only a word, here and there. An old man with pursed-up lips, after catching these fragments of sentences, " . . . the noble heart, the generosity and benevolence of a great character . . ." mutters, with a jerk of his chin, "Ah, indeed! Yes, I knew him; he was every inch a skinflint!"

The last farewell flies away into the air. When the priests have blest the body, the people withdraw, and no one is left in that sequestered nook but the gravediggers, who are letting down the casket into the grave. The cords run out with a dull, scraping sound, the oak casket creaks. Monsieur le Count de Verteuil is at home.

And the countess, on her lounge, has not stirred. She is still playing with the tassel of her girdle, her eyes on the ceiling, lost in a reverie which, little by little, brings a blush to her cheeks, beautiful blonde that she is.

II

Madame Guerard is a widow. Her husband, whom she lost eight years ago, was a magistrate. She belongs to the upper bourgeoisie, and has a fortune of two millions. She has three children, three sons, who, at their father's death, inherited five hundred thousand francs apiece. But these sons have grown up like weeds in this austere, cold, and prim family, with appetites and crackbrained crotchets that came no one knows whence. They ran through their five hundred thousand francs in a few years. The eldest, Charles, had a passion for mechanics, and squandered insane sums on extraordinary inventions. The second, Georges, let himself be devoured by women. The third, Maurice, was swindled by a friend, with whom he undertook to build a theatre. To-day the three sons are dependent on their mother, who is willing to feed and lodge them, but prudently keeps the cupboard keys on her own person.

All these people live in a large apartment in the rue de Turenne, in the Marais. Madame

Gubard is sixty years old. With age have come fixed ideas. She exacts, in her home, the quiet and cleanliness of a cloister. She is miserly, counts the lumps of sugar, locks up the half-emptied bottles herself, gives out the linen and crockery piecemeal, according to the needs of the household. No doubt, her sons are very fond of her, and she has maintained absolute authority over them, in spite of their thirty years and their follies. But, when she finds herself alone with these three big devils, she has half-conscious anxieties, she is always afraid they will ask her for money, and does not quite see how to refuse them. For this reason, she has taken care to invest her fortune in real estate: she owns three houses in Paris, and some land in the direction of Vincennes. These pieces of property give her the greatest trouble; only, her mind is at rest, she finds excuses for not giving large sums at a time.

Charles, Georges, and Maurice, however, get as much out of the house as they can. They live on there, quarrelling over every morsel, each one throwing the others' ravenous greed in their faces. Their mother's death will make them rich again; they know it, and find it a sufficient pretext for waiting and doing nothing. Although they never speak of it, their constant preoccupation is to find out how the property will be divided; if they cannot come to an agreement, everything will have to be sold, which is always a ruinous operation. And they let their mind dwell on these matters, without any evil longing, solely because it is well to foresee everything. They are cheery, good-natured fellows, of average honesty; like everybody, they hope their mother will live as long as possible. They are waiting, that is all.

One evening, on getting up from table, madame Guerard does not feel well. Her sons make her go to bed, and leave her with the chambermaid, on her assuring them that she is better, that she has only a severe headache. But next day the old lady has grown worse; the family physician, not without anxiety, asks for a consultation. Madame Guerard is in great danger. Then, for a week, a drama is played by the dying woman's bedside.

Her first care, when she saw herself confined to her room by sickness, was to have all the keys given her, and to hide them under her pillow. She still tries to rule from her bed, to protect her cupboards against waste. Struggles go on within her, she is racked with doubts. She makes up her mind only after long hesitations. Her three sons are there, and she studies them with her dim eyes, she waits for a happy inspiration.

One day she has confidence in Georges. She beckons him to her side, and says in an undertone, "Here, here is the key to the sideboard; take the sugar. . . . You will lock it up safe again, and bring me back the key."

Another day she distrusts Georges, she follows him about with her eye as soon as he stirs, as if she were afraid of seeing him slip the knickknacks on the mantelpiece into his pockets. She calls Charles, entrusts him with a key in his turn, muttering,—

"The chambermaid will go with you.

You will see that she takes out some sheets, and will lock up, yourself."

At death's door, this is her torment, no longer to be able to watch over the household expenses. She recalls her children's follies; she knows them to be lazy, large eaters, crackbrained, open-handed. She has long since lost all respect for them, who have realized none of her dreams, who wound her in her austere and thrifty habits. Her affection alone survives and forgives. In the depths of her entreating eyes can be read that she implores them to wait till she is no longer there, before emptying her drawers and dividing her possessions. This division before her very eyes would be a torture to her expiring avarice.

Meanwhile, Charles, Georges, and Maurice are very kind to her. They arrange among themselves to have one of them always with their mother. A sincere affection appears in the slightest things they do for her. But, inevitably, they bring with them the thoughtlessness of out of doors, the smell of the cigar they have just smoked, their preoccupation with the news of the town. The sick woman's egoism suffers at her not being all in all to them in her last hour. Then, when she grows weaker, her distrust casts an ever-greater embarrassment between the young men and herself. If they were not thinking of the fortune they are to inherit, she would put the thought of this money into their heads by the way she guards it up to her last breath. She looks at them with so keen an eye, in such evident fear, that they turn away their heads. Then she thinks they are standing as spies at her deathbed; and, in truth, they do think of it, they are continually brought back to the idea by the mute questioning of her gaze. It is she who awakens cupidity in them. When she catches one of them looking thoughtful, his face pale, she says to him,"Come here to me. . . . What are you thinking of?"

"Nothing, mother."

But he started. She shakes her head slowly and adds, "I give you a great deal of care, my children. Come, don't worry. I shall soon be here no more."

They surround her, they swear they love her and will save her. She answers no, with an obstinate shake of her head; she plunges still deeper into her distrust. It is a frightful death, poisoned by money.

The sickness lasts three weeks. There have already been five consultations; the greatest medical celebrities have been called in. The chambermaid helps madam's sons take care of her; and, in spite of all precautions, a little disorder has crept into the room. All hope is lost; the physician announces that the patient may pass away at any time.

So, one morning that her sons think her asleep, they are standing near a window, talking among themselves about a difficulty that has come up.

It is the 15th of July; she was in the habit of collecting the rent of her houses herself, and they are in a quandary, not knowing how to get hold of this money. The janitors have already asked for orders. In her weak condition, they cannot talk business with her. Yet, if an accident were to occur, they would need the rents to defray certain personal expenses.

"Good heavens!" says Charles in an undertone, "I'll go if you wish, and call upon the tenants. . . . They will understand the situation, and pay up."

But Georges and Maurice do not seem to relish this plan. They, too, have grown suspicious.

"We might go with you," says the former. "All three of us will have to pay out something."

"Well! I will bring you the money . . . You don't suppose I would run away with it, I hope!"

"No; but it would be just as well for us to be together. It will be more regular."

And they look at one another with eyes in which already glisten the anger and ill-will of sharing. The succession is open; each one wants to secure the largest share for himself. Charles suddenly goes on, carrying out aloud the idea that his brothers are revolving silently in their heads, "Listen: we will sell; that will be best. . . . If we quarrel to-day, we shall come to blows to-morrow."

But a rattling in the sick woman's throat makes them turn their heads quickly. Their mother has risen up in bed, white, with haggard eyes, her body shaken with a fit of trembling. She has heard, she stretches out her lean arms, she repeats in a voice of terror, "My children. . . . My children. . . ."

And a spasm throws her back upon her pillow; she dies with the atrocious thought in her mind that her sons are robbing her.

All three have fallen upon their knees in consternation by the bedside. They kiss the dead woman's hands; they close her eyes with sobs. At this moment, their childhood rises once more in their hearts, and they are, now and evermore, nothing but orphans. But this frightful death remains in the depths of their being, as a remorse and as a hate.

The dead woman is washed and robed by the chambermaid. A sister of charity is sent for to wake with the body. Meanwhile, the sons are running on errands; they go and make their declaration of the decease, order the engraved announcements to relatives and friends, arrange for the funeral ceremony. At night they relieve one another, and watch with the sister. In the room, the curtains of which are drawn, the dead woman lies stretched out on the bed, her head rigid, her hands crossed, a silver crucifix on her breast. A sprig of box hangs over the rim of a vase filled with holy-water. By her side burns a wax candle. And the wake ends in the shivering morning. The sister asks for some warm milk, because she does not feel well.

An hour before the funeral, the staircase fills with people. The porte-cochere is hung with black drapery with a silver fringe. There the coffin is exposed, as in the depths of a narrow chapel, surrounded with candles, covered with wreaths and bouquets. Every one who enters takes a sprinkler from the holy water basin at the foot of the bier, and besprinkles the body. At eleven, the funeral procession sets out. The sons of the deceased lead the mourning. Behind them you recognize magistrates, some large manufacturers, a whole solemn and pompous bourgeoisie, keeping step as they walk, casting side glances at the inquisitive crowd drawn up along the sidewalks. The procession closes with twelve mourning coaches. People count them; they are much commented on in the neighborhood.

Meanwhile, those present are filled with pity for Charles, Georges, and Maurice, in evening dress, gloved in black, walking behind the coffin, their heads bowed down, their faces reddened with tears. For the rest, there is but one exclamation, they are burying their mother in very proper fashion. The hearse is of the third class; it is calculated that they will be in for several thousand francs. An old notary says with a shrewd smile, "If madame Guerard had paid for her funeral herself, she would have saved on six carriages."

At the church, the portal is draped, the organ plays, the absolution is given by the parish priest. Then, when the congregation has filed before the body, they find the three sons drawn up in a single line at the entrance of the nave, stationed there to shake hands with those present who are unable to go to the cemetery. For ten minutes they hold out their arms, press hands without even recognizing people, biting their lips, holding back their tears; and it is a great relief to them when the church is empty, and they resume their slow march behind the hearse.

The Guelards' family vault is in the cemetery of Pere-Lachaise. Many go on foot; others get into the mourning coaches. The procession crosses the place de la Bastille, and follows the rue de la Roquette. The passers-by raise their eyes and take off their hats. It is a rich funeral, at which the workmen of that quarter gaze, as it passes, while they eat their sausages stuffed into slits cut in pieces of bread.

Arriving at the cemetery, the procession turns to the left, and at once finds itself in front of the tomb, in the shape of a Gothic chapel, bearing on its pediment these words, cut in black: Famille Gurard. The ornamented cast-iron door, thrown wide open, discloses an altar table, on which candles are burning. Around the monument are rows of other structures, in the same taste, forming actual streets; it looks like a cabinet-maker's shop front, with wardrobes, chests of drawers, secretaries, newly finished and arranged in symmetrical rows in the show window. The people present are wool-gathering, impressed by this architecture, looking around for a little shade under the trees of the neighboring avenue. A lady has stepped aside to admire a superb rose-bush, growing like a bouquet of fragrant blossoms over a gravestone.

Meanwhile, the coffin has been lifted down from the hearse. A priest says the last prayers, while the gravediggers, in blue jackets, are waiting a few steps off. The three sons sob, their eyes fixed on the gaping vault, the slab of which has been removed; there, in this cool shade, they, in their turn, will one day come to sleep. Some friends lead them away, when the gravediggers come up.

And, two days later, in the office of their mother's notary, they are disputing, with set teeth, dry eyes, and the passion of enemies who have made up their minds not to give in on a single centime. It would be for their interest to wait, not to hurry on the sale of the property. But they cast their bald truths in each others' teeth: Charles would run through it all with his inventions; Georges must have some girl to fleece him; Maurice is surely engaged in another wildcat speculation that would swallow up their whole capital. In vain, the notary tries to induce them to come to an amicable understanding. They separate, threatening to send one another stamped paper.

It is the dead woman awaking in them once more, with her avarice and her terror of being robbed. When money poisons death, from death comes nothing but wrath. There is fighting over coffins.

III

M. Rousseau, at twenty, married an orphan, Adele Lemercier, who was eighteen. Together they had seventy francs on the evening of their setting up housekeeping. At first they sold notepaper and sticks of sealing wax under a doorway. Next, they hired a hole, a shop the size of your hand, where they stayed ten years, adding to their business little by little. Now they keep a stationery shop in the rue de Clichy, worth fully fifty thousand francs.

Adele has not a strong constitution. She has always coughed a little. The close air of the shop and the sedentary life behind the counter are not good for her. A physician they consulted recommended rest and walks out of doors in fine weather. But prescriptions of that sort cannot be followed, when you are bent upon piling up a small income quickly, to live on it in peace. Adele said she would rest and take walks later, after they had sold out and retired to the provinces.

As for M. Rousseau, he is anxious, to be sure, on days when he sees her pale, with red spots on her cheeks. Only he has his stationery business to absorb him, he cannot always be at her elbow to prevent imprudences on her part. For weeks together he cannot find a minute to speak to her about her health. Then, if he happens to hear her little dry cough, he scolds her, he makes her put on her shawl and take a turn in the Champs-Élysées. But she comes back more tired, coughing harder; the bustle of business once more takes hold of M. Rousseau; the sickness is again forgotten till another crisis comes. It is the way in business: you die without having time for treatment.

One day, M. Rousseau takes the physician aside, and asks him to tell him frankly if his wife is in danger. The physician begins by saying that one must trust to nature, that he has seen many much sicker people pull through. Then, cornered with questions, he confesses that madame Rousseau has tuberculosis in a pretty advanced stage. The husband turns white at this avowal. He loves Adele for their long struggle together before they had white bread to eat every day. He has in her not only a wife, but a partner, whose energy he knows. If he loses her, he will be stricken at once in his affection and in his business. Yet he must take heart, he cannot shut up his shop, to weep at leisure. So he shows nothing, he tries not to frighten Adele by letting her see him with red eyes. He resumes his jog-trot life. By the end of a month, whenever he thinks of these sad things, he manages to persuade himself that doctors are often mistaken. His wife does not seem any worse. And so it comes about that he sees her die by inches, without suffering too much himself, his mind taken up with his avocations, expecting a catastrophe, but mentally postponing it to an unlimited future.

Sometimes Adele repeats, "Ah! When we get into the country, you will see how well I shall be. . . . Good Lord! We have only eight years to wait now. The time will go quickly."

And M. Rousseau does not remember that they might retire at once, on smaller savings. To begin with, Adele would not agree to it. When you have made up your mind to a figure, you must reach it.

Nevertheless, madame Rousseau has had to take to her bed twice already. She has got up from it again, and come down to the counter. The neighbors say, "There is a little woman who won't go far"; and they are not wrong. Just at the time for taking account of stock, she is put to bed for the third time. The physician comes in the morning, talks with her, signs a prescription absent-mindedly. M. Rousseau is warned, and knows that the fatal catastrophe is drawing near. But taking account of stock keeps him downstairs in the shop, and it is all he can do to escape for five minutes, from time to time. He goes up, when the physician is there; then he leaves the room with him, and reappears for a moment before breakfast; he goes to bed at eleven in a little room, almost a closet, into which he has put a cot bed. Francoise, the maid, tends the sick woman. A terrible girl, this Francoise, from Auvergne, with great bullying hands, and of dubious civility and cleanliness! She is rough with the dying woman, brings her her medicine scowling, makes an intolerable noise sweeping the room, which she leaves in great disorder; phials, all sticky on the outside, lie about on the chest of drawers, the washbasins are never washed, dishcloths hang over the backs of chairs; you don't know where to set your foot, so littered up is the floor. Yet madame Rousseau does not complain, and is content to rap on the wall with her fist, to call the maid, when the latter does not answer. Françoise has other fish to fry besides taking care of her; she has to keep the shop clean, do the cooking for master and clerks, not to mention errands in the neighborhood and other odd jobs. So that madame cannot require her to be always by her side. She is cared for when there is time.

Besides, even in bed, Adele thinks of business. She follows the sales; asks every evening how things are getting on. The account of stock makes her anxious. When her husband can come up to her room for a few minutes, she never speaks to him about her health; she asks him solely about the probable net profit. She is much chagrined at learning that the year is only middling, fourteen hundred francs behind last year. While burning with fever on her pillow, she still remembers the last week's orders; she sets the accounts straight; she manages the house. And it is she who sends her husband away, if he forgets himself in her room. His being there will not cure her, and it is bad for the business. She is sure the clerks are staring at the passers-by, and she keeps repeating, —

"Go down, dear; I want nothing, I assure you. And don't forget to lay in a stock of copybooks; because the schools open soon, and we must not be short of them."

For a long while she tries to ignore her real condition. She always hopes to get up next day, and take her place at the counter once more. She even makes plans: if she can leave the house soon, they will go and spend a Sunday at Saint-Cloud. Never has she had such a longing to see the trees. Then, of a sudden, one morning, she grows serious. In the night, all alone, open-eyed, she has realized that she is going to die. She says nothing till evening, lying there thinking, her eyes on the ceiling; and in the evening, she detains her husband, she talks quietly, as if she were submitting a bill to him.

"Listen," she says, "you will go tomorrow and get a notary. There is one near here, in the rue Saint-Lazare."

"Why a notary?" cries M. Rousseau; "we surely haven't come to that!"

But she goes on in her calm, rational way, "May be! Only it will make me feel easier to know that our affairs are in order. . . . We married when neither of us had anything, on the plan of holding all our property in common. Now that we have made a little money, I don't want my family to be able to come down on you and plunder you. . . . My sister Agathe isn't so nice to us that I need leave her anything. I would sooner take all with me."

And she sticks to it obstinately; her husband must go to-morrow and get the notary. She questions the latter at length, bent upon having all due precautions taken that the will shall not be contested. When the will is drawn up and signed, she stretches herself out, murmuring, "Now I shall die content. . . . I had well earned a trip into the country; I can't say I am not sorry to give up going to the country. But you'll go. . . . Promise me, when you retire, to go to the place we picked out; you know, the village where your mother was born, near Melun. . . . It will give me pleasure."

M. Rousseau weeps bitterly. She tries to comfort him; she gives him good advice. If he finds life hard, all by himself, it will be proper for him to marry again; only he must choose a woman of a certain age, because young girls, who marry widowers, marry their money. And she points out a lady of their acquaintance, with whom she would be happy to know that he had made a match.

Then, that very night, she has a frightful death-struggle. She is stifling, asks for air. M. Rousseau, standing at the head of her bed, can only take the dying woman's hand and press it, to tell her he is there, that he will not leave her. In the morning, she falls into a profound calm; she is very white, with her eyes shut, breathing slowly. Her husband thinks he can go down with Francoise to open the shop. When he comes up again, he finds his wife still very white, stiffened in the same posture; only her eyes have opened. She is dead.

M. Rousseau has been too long expecting to lose her. He does not weep, he is simply fagged out. He goes down again, sees Francoise put up the shop shutters; and, with his own hand, writes on a sheet of paper, "Closed on account of decease"; then he sticks this sheet on to the middle shutter with four wafers. Up-stairs, the whole morning is taken up with cleaning and putting the room to rights. Francoise passes a cloth over the floor, takes away the phials, puts a lighted taper and a cup of holy-water near the dead woman; for Adele's sister is expected, that terrible Agathe who has the 'tongue of a serpent, and the maid does not want anybody to be able to find fault with her housekeeping. M. Rousseau has sent a clerk to go through with the necessary formalities. He himself goes to the church and discusses at length the funeral tariff. His being in affliction is no reason why he should be cheated. He loved his wife well, and, if she can see him now, he is sure she is pleased at his bargaining with the priest and undertaker's men. Still, for the sake of the neighborhood, he wishes to have a proper burial. At last, he strikes a bargain: he will give a hundred and sixty francs to the church and three hundred francs to the undertaker. He calculates that, with the minor expenses, he will not get through under five hundred francs.

When M. Rousseau comes home, he sees Agathe, his sister-in-law, installed by the dead woman's side. Agathe is a tall, lean woman, with red eyes and thin, bluish lips. The couple quarreled with her three years ago, and has seen nothing of her since. She rises ceremoniously, and then kisses her brother-in-law. In the presence of death, all quarrels are made up. Then M. Rousseau, who could not cry this morning, sobs, finding his poor wife white and stiff, her nose still more pinched, her face so shrunken that he hardly recognizes her. Agathe's eyes are dry. She has taken the best armchair; she casts her eyes slowly over the room, as if making a detailed inventory of the furniture. As yet, she has not brought up the question of her interests; but it is plain that she is very anxious, and is wondering whether there is a will.

On the morning of the funeral, at the moment when the body is to be placed upon the bier, it appears that the undertaker has made a mistake, and sent too short a coffin. His men have to go for another. Meanwhile, the hearse is waiting at the door, the neighborhood is all agog. This is a fresh torment to M. Rousseau. If it could bring his wife back to life again, to keep her so long, it might be! At last, poor madame Rousseau is brought down, and the coffin exposed only ten minutes below, in the doorway hung with black. A hundred people, or so, are waiting in the street, tradespeople of the neighborhood, tenants in the house, friends of the household, a few workmen in overcoats. The procession starts; M. Rousseau leads the mourning.

And, as the funeral passes, the neighbors cross themselves rapidly, speaking under their breath. It's the stationer's wife, isn't it? That little yellow woman who was nothing but skin and bones. Ah! Well! She will be better off underground! But that is the way with us! Business people, very well-to-do, working to enjoy themselves in their old age! She's going to enjoy herself now, the stationer's wife is! And the neighbors' wives are of the opinion that M. Rousseau is doing things in very proper fashion, because he walks behind the hearse, bareheaded, all alone, pale, and his scant hair flying in the wind.

At the church, the priests knock off the ceremony in forty minutes. Agathe, who has taken a seat in the front row, seems to be counting the lighted candles. No doubt, she is thinking that her brother-in-law might have done things with-less ostentation; for, after all, if there is no will, and she inherits half the property, she will have to pay her share toward the funeral. The priests say a last orison, the holy-water sprinkler passes from hand to hand, and the people go. Almost every one goes. The three mourning coaches drive up, and the ladies get into them. Behind the hearse, only M. Rousseau is left, still bareheaded, and thirty others, or so, friends who do not dare to slink away. The hearse is hung simply with black drapery fringed with white. The passers-by raise their hats, and pass on quickly.

As M. Rousseau has no family tomb, he has merely got a five years' grant at the Montmartre cemetery, promising himself to buy a perpetual grant later, when he will exhume his wife, to settle her in her home forever.

The hearse stops at the end of the avenue, and the coffin is carried in men's arms among the low tombstones, up to a grave dug in the soft earth. Those present walk round in silence. Then the priest withdraws, after mumbling twenty words between his teeth. On every hand lie little gardens, closed by ironwork gates, graves decked with carnations, and green trees; the white slabs, in the midst of this verdure, look quite new and gay. M. Rousseau is much struck with one monument, a slender column surmounted by the symbolic urn. That morning a stonecutter had come to bother him with plans; and he thinks of how, when he buys his perpetual grant, he will have just such a column, with that pretty vase, put over his wife's tombstone.

But Agathe leads him away, and, when they have got back to the shop, decides at last to speak about her interests. When she learns that there is a will, she stands up straight and goes, slamming the door. Never will she set foot again in that shanty. M. Rousseau has still, at moments, a great sorrow that chokes him; but what, above all else, stupefies him, makes his head feel empty and his limbs restless, is that the shop is shut on a week-day.

IV

January has been hard. No work, no bread, and no fire in the house. The

Morisseaus have been like to die of want. The wife is a washerwoman; the husband, a mason. They live at the Batignolles, in the rue Cardinet, in a dark house that spreads pestilence through the neighborhood. Their room, on the fifth floor, is so dilapidated that the rain comes in through the cracks in the ceiling; but still they would not complain, if their little Charlot, a boy of ten, did not need good food to make a man of him.

The child is puny; a nothing-at-all throws him on beam ends. When he went to school, if he worked hard, trying to learn everything off-hand, he would come home sick. Very intelligent withal, and such a nice little toad, talking beyond his years. On days when they have no bread to give him, his parents cry like fools. The more so that children are dying off like flies, from the top to the bottom of the house, so unwholesome is it.

There is ice to be broken in the streets. Indeed the father has succeeded in getting a job; he clears the gutters with a pickaxe, and in the evening brings home forty sous. While waiting for his house-building work to begin again, it is always something not to starve on.

But, one day, the man comes home to find Charlot in bed. His mother doesn't know what the matter with him is. She had sent him to Courcelles, to his aunt's, who deals in second-hand clothes, to see if he could not get a jacket that would be warmer than his cotton blouse, in which he goes shivering. His aunt had only two old men's overcoats, both of them too big, and the little fellow had come home all of a tremble, with a tipsy look on him, as if he had been drinking. Now he is very red on his pillow, he talks nonsense, he thinks he is playing marbles, and is singing songs.

His mother has hung a tattered piece of a shawl in front of the window, to stop up a broken pane; at the top, there are only two panes left free, which let in the livid gray of the sky. Want has emptied the chest of drawers, all the linen is at the pawnbroker's. One evening they sold a table and two chairs. Charlot used to sleep on the floor; but, since he fell sick, they have given him the bed, and even there he is very badly off, for the wool in the mattress has been taken, handful by handful, half a pound at a time, to a second-hand dealer, for four or five sous. Now the father and mother sleep in a corner, on a straw mattress that a dog would turn up his nose at.

Meanwhile, both look at Charlot jumping about in bed. What on earth ails the kid, to make him so queer in the head? Like enough, some beast has bitten him, or else he has been given something bad to drink. A neighbor, madame Bonnet, comes in; and, after looking at the boy, says it is chills and fever. She knows all about it, she lost her husband by just such a sickness.

The mother weeps, pressing Charlot in her arms. The father goes out like a madman, and runs for a doctor. He brings one back, very tall and prim looking; he listens at the child's back, he taps him on the chest, without saying a word. Then madame Bonnet must go to her room for pencil and paper, so that he can write his prescription. When he goes, still mute, the mother asks him in a choking voice," What is it, sir?"

"Pleurisy," he answers curtly, without further explanation.

Then he asks, in his turn, "Is your name down at the bureau of charities?"

"No, sir. . . . We were well off last summer. It's the winter that has killed us."

"So much the worse! So much the worse!"

And he promises to return. Madame Bonnet lends twenty sous, to go to the apothecary's. With Morisseau's forty sous they have bought two pounds of beef, some soft coal, and candles. This first night passes off well. They keep up the fire. The sick boy, as if put to sleep by the warmth, has stopped talking; his little hands are burning. Seeing him weighed down by the fever, his parents feel easier; and they are stupefied, next day, in fresh terror, when the physician shakes his head by the bedside, with the wry face of a man who has given up all hope.

For five days there is no change. Charlot sleeps, as if knocked down upon his pillow. In the room the breath of poverty grows stronger, seems to come in with the wind, through the holes in the roofing and window. The second evening, they sold the mother's last chemise; the third, they had to pull out some more handfuls of wool from under the sick boy, to pay the apothecary. Then everything failed them, there was nothing left.

Morisseau is still breaking ice; only his forty sous don't go round as they used to. As this severe cold may kill Charlot, he longs for a thaw, even though he dreads it. When he goes off to work, he is glad to see the streets white; then he thinks of the little boy dying up there, and fervently prays for a ray of sunshine, a bit of spring warmth, to sweep away the snow. If they only had put their name down at the bureau of charities, they would have the doctor and medicines for nothing. The mother has been to the pharmacy; they answered her that there were too many applications, she must wait. Still, she got some bread tickets; a benevolent lady gave her five francs. Then destitution began once more.

The fifth day, Morisseau brings home his last forty sous. The thaw has come; he has been discharged. Then all is over: the stove stays cold, there is no bread, no more prescriptions are taken to the apothecary's. In the room, trickling with dampness, the father and mother shiver opposite the little boy, who is near his last. Madame Bonnet does not come to see them any more, because she has a tender heart, and it makes her feel too low in her mind. The people of the house hurry quickly past their door. At times, the mother, in a fit of tears, throws herself upon the bed, kisses the child, as if to relieve his suffering and cure him. The father, stupefied, stays at the window for hours, raising the old shawl, looking at the thaw running in the gutters, the water dripping in big drops from the roofs, and blackening the street. Perhaps it may do Chariot good.

One morning, the doctor announces that he shall not return. The child is given up.

"This damp weather has finished him," he says.

Morisseau shakes his fist at the sky. So all weathers are death to poor people! It froze, and that did no good; it thaws, and that is worse still. If his wife would agree, they would light a bushel of charcoal, and all three go off together. It would be sooner over.

Yet the mother has gone back to the pharmacy; the people there have promised to send them aid, and they are waiting. What a frightful day! A black chill falls from the ceiling; one corner is dripping with rain; they have to put a pail there to catch the drops. They have eaten nothing since the day before; the child has only drunk a cup of herb tea that the janitor's wife brought up. The father sits at the table, his head in his hands, in a sort of stupor, with a buzzing in his ears. At every sound of steps, the mother runs to the door, thinks it is, at last, the promised aid. Six o'clock strikes; nothing has come. The twilight is muddy, slow and ghastly as a death-agony.

Suddenly, in the deepening darkness, Charlot stammers out some confused words, "Mamma . . . Mamma . . . "

His mother comes to him, feels a strong breath upon her face. She hears nothing more; she vaguely makes out the child, his head thrown back, his neck stiffened. She shrieks, half crazed, imploring, "Light! Quick, some light! . . . My Charlot, speak to me!"

There are no more candles. In her hurry she scratches some matches, breaks them between her fingers. Then, with trembling hands, she feels of the child's face.

"Oh ! My God! He is dead! . . . Say, Morisseau, he is dead!"

The father raises his head, blinded by the darkness.

"Well, then! What would you have? He's dead. . . . It's better so."

At the mother's sobbing, madame Bonnet has made up her mind to come with her lamp. Then, as the two women are making Charlot tidy, a knock is heard: it is the aid, come at last; ten francs, some bread tickets, and a bit of meat. Morisseau gives an imbecile laugh, saying that they always miss the train at the bureau of charities.

And what a poor child's corpse, thin, light as a feather! You might have laid a sparrow upon the mattress, killed by the snow and picked up in the street, and it would not have made a smaller heap!

Meanwhile, madame Bonnet, who has grown very obliging again, explains that it will not bring Charlot back to life, to fast by his side. She offers to go after some bread and meat, adding that she will also fetch some candles. They let her go. When she comes back, she sets the table with sausages, hot and hot; and the Morisseaus, famished as they are, eat greedily beside the dead boy, whose little white face is just visible in the dim light. The stove roars, they are very comfortable. At moments, the mother's eyes grow wet. Great tears drop down upon her bread. How warm Charlot would be! And how he would have liked to eat some sausage!

Madame Bonnet insists upon waking with them. About one, when Morisseau has at last fallen asleep, his head resting on the foot of the bed, the two women make some coffee. Another neighbor, a seamstress of eighteen, is asked in; and she brings the bottoms of a bottle of brandy, so as to stand treat to something. Then the three women sip their coffee, talking in an undertone, telling stories of extraordinary deaths; little by little, their voices are raised, their tittle-tattle takes in a larger field, they chat about the house, about the neighborhood, about a crime committed in the rue Nollet. And, now and then, the mother gets up, goes to take a look at Charlot, as if to make sure that he has not moved.

The declaration not having been made that evening, they have to keep the little body all the next day. They have only one room; they live with Charlot, eat and sleep with him. At moments they forget him; then, when they find him there, it is like losing him over again.

At last, on the next day but one, the coffin is brought, no bigger than a toy box, four boards roughly planed, furnished by the administration, after verifying their certificate of indigence. And all aboard! They set out for the church on the run. Behind Charlot comes the father, with two comrades he has picked up on the way; then the mother, madame Bonnet, and the other neighbor, the seamstress. These people flounder through the mud up to mid-leg. It does not rain, but the fog is so thick that it drenches their clothes. At the church, the ceremony is hurried through; and they start off again over the muddy pavement.

The cemetery is at the devil, outside the fortifications. They pass down the avenue de Saint-Ouen, through the barrier, and get there at last. It is a vast enclosure, a plot of waste land, shut in by white walls. Weeds grow there ; the ground, often dug up, is all in humps; while, at the farther end, grow a row of meager trees, soiling the sky with their black branches.

The funeral moves slowly forward over the soft ground. Now it rains, and they have to wait in the shower for an old priest, who at last makes up his mind to venture forth from a little chapel. Charlot is to sleep at the bottom of the common trench. The field is strewed with crosses overturned by the wind, with wreaths rotted by the rain; a field of wretchedness and mourning, devastated, trampled down, sweating with its overmeasure of dead bodies, heaped up by the hunger and cold of the suburbs.

It is over. The earth is tossed back, Charlot is at the bottom of the hole; and his parents go, without having been able to kneel down in the liquid mud into which their feet sink. Outside, as it is still raining, Morisseau, who has three francs left, of the ten francs from the bureau of charities, invites his comrades and the women to take something at a wine shop. They sit down to table, they drink two liters, they eat a piece of Brie cheese. Then the comrades, in their turn, stand two more liters. When the company gets back to Paris, they are very gay.

V

Jean-Louis Lacour is seventy. He was born at la Courteille, a hamlet of a hundred and fifty souls, an out-of-the-way spot in the wildest sort of country. He has been once in his life to Angers, which is forty-one miles distant; but he was so young that he does not remember it. He has three children, — two sons, Antoine and Joseph, and a daughter, Catherine. The last was married; then her husband died, and she returned to her father's with a little boy of twelve, Jacquinet. The family lives on from seven to nine acres; just enough to give them bread, and let them not go quite naked. When they drink wine, they have sweated for it.

La Courteille is at the end of a valley, with woods on every side that shut it in and hide it from view. There is no church, the village is too poor. The cure of les Cormiers comes over to say mass; and, as the road is five good miles, he comes only once a fortnight. The houses, about twenty ramshackle hovels, are strung along the highway. Hens scratch on the dunghills before the doors. When a stranger goes by, the women stretch their necks, while the children, rolling on the ground in the sun, scamper off in the midst of frightened flocks of geese.

Never has Jean-Louis been sick. He is tall and knotty as an oak. The sun has dried him up, has baked and cracked his skin; he has turned to the color, the roughness and tranquility of a tree. In growing old, he has lost his tongue. He has done with speaking, finding it useless. He walks with long, obstinate strides, with the peaceful strength of an ox.

Last year, he still was stronger than his sons; he would keep the hardest jobs for himself, silent in the fields, which seemed to know him and tremble. But one day, two months ago, his limbs gave way all of a sudden, and he lay for two hours across a furrow, like a felled trunk. Next day, he tried to go to work again, but his arms had gone off, the soil would no longer obey him. His sons shake their heads. His daughter tries to keep him at home. He sticks it out stubbornly, and they have Jacquinet go with him, so that the child can cry out, if his grandfather falls down.

"What are you doing there, lazybones?" asks Jean-Louis of the youngster. "At your age, I was earning my bread."

"I'm tending you, grandfather," answers the child.

This gives the old man a shock. He says no more. In the evening, he goes to bed, and does not get up again. When his sons and daughter go to the fields, next day, they step in to take a look at their father, as they do not hear him moving. They find him stretched out on his bed, with open eyes, as if in thought. His skin is so hard and tanned that you can't even tell the color of his complaint.

"Well, father, out of sorts?"

He gives a grunt, he says no with his head.

"Then you're not coming; we'll go without you?"

Yes, he motions them to go without him. The harvest has begun, every arm is needed. Like enough, if they were to lose a morning, a sudden storm might carry away the sheaves. Even Jacquinet follows his mother and uncles. Old Lacour is left alone. In the evening, when his children come home, he is in the same place, still on his back, with his eyes open and that look of his, as if in thought.

"So, father, you're no better?"

No, no better. He grunts, he shakes his head. What under the sun can they do to him? Catherine suggests putting some wine to boil, with herbs in it; but it is too strong, it all but kills him. Joseph says they will see to-morrow, and they all go to bed.

The next day, before going to harvest, the sons and daughters stop a minute, standing by his bedside. Decidedly the old man is sick. Never before has he stayed on his back like that. Perhaps they really ought to call in a doctor. The trouble is that they will have to go to Rougemont; a good sixteen miles there, and sixteen miles back, that makes thirty-two. They would lose a whole day. The old man, who is listening to his children, fidgets and seems to be getting angry. He doesn't need any doctor; it does no good, and it costs money.

"You don't want one?" asks Antoine.

"Then we'll go to work?"

Of course they must go to work. They wouldn't make him any better by staying there, would they? The soil needs looking after more than he. And three days pass by; the children go to the fields every morning. Jean-Louis does not move, all alone, drinking out of a jug when he is thirsty. He is like one of those old horses that fall down in a corner from weariness, and are left to die. He has worked for sixty years; he may as well go, seeing that he is no longer good for anything, except to take up room and bother people.

His children themselves feel no great sorrow. Tilling the soil has made them resigned to these things; they are too near to it to owe it a grudge for taking the old man. A look at him in the morning, a look in the evening; they can do no more. If their father should pick up again, after all, it would prove that he was fairly stoutly put together. If he dies, it will show that he had death in his body; and everybody knows that, when you have death in your body, nothing will drive it out; not signs of the cross any more than medicines. A cow, now, you can do something for.

In the evening, Jean-Louis gives his children an inquisitive glance about the harvest. When he hears them count up the sheaves and congratulate themselves on the fine weather, his eyes sparkle. Once more, they talk of going for the doctor; but the old man loses his temper, and they are afraid of killing him all the sooner if they thwart him. He only asks to see the district constable, an old comrade. Old Nicolas is his senior, for he was seventy-five last Candlemas. He is straight as a poplar. He conies and gravely sits down beside Jean-Louis. Jean-Louis, who has lost his tongue, looks at him with his little washed-out eyes. Old Nicolas looks at him, too, having nothing to say. And the two old men sit there, face to face, for an hour, without uttering a word, no doubt remembering things far away, in their bygone days. That evening, when his children come home from harvest, they find Jean-Louis dead, stretched out on his back, stiff, and his eyes in the air.

Yes, the old man has died without moving a limb. He has breathed his last straight before him, one breath more in the wide country. Like the beasts that hide themselves and submit, he did not even trouble a neighbor; he did his little business all alone.

"Father is dead," says Joseph, calling the others.

And they all, Antoine, Catherine, Jacquinet, repeat, "Father is dead."

They are not surprised. Jacquinet stretches out his neck in curiosity; the woman pulls out her handkerchief, the two young men walk about, saying nothing, their grave faces turning paler under their tan. He had lasted pretty well; he was rugged, their old father was! And this thought comforts his children; they are proud of the family ruggedness.

They watch with their father up to eleven, then they all give way to sleep; and Jean Louis sleeps alone, with his close-shut face, which seems still to be thinking.

At daybreak, Joseph sets out for les Cormiers, to notify the priest. Meanwhile, as there are still some sheaves to be brought in, Antoine and Catherine go to the fields just the same, leaving the body in Jacquinet's care. The little boy finds the time pass heavily in the old man's company, seeing that he does not even stir; and he goes out, now and then, into the street, throws stones at some sparrows, looks on at a peddler spreading out some silk neckerchiefs before two neighbors' wives; then, when he remembers his grandfather, he runs in again, makes sure that he has not moved, and cuts away once more, to see two dogs fight.

As the door has been left open, the hens come in, walk round quietly, rummaging on the trodden ground with their bills. A red cock stands erect on his feet, stretches out his neck, rounds his live-coal of an eye, anxious about this body, whose presence there he cannot explain; he is a prudent and sagacious cock, who, no doubt, knows that the old man is not used to lie abed after sunrise; and he ends by crowing his sonorous clarion note, singing the old man's death, while the hens go out again, one by one, clucking and pecking the ground.

The cure from les Cormiers cannot come till five. Ever since morning, you could hear the cartwright sawing deal boards and driving in nails. Those who do not know the news say, "How? Can Jean-Louis be dead!" because the la Courteille folk know those sounds well.

Antoine and Catherine have got back, the harvest is over; they cannot say they are disappointed, for the grain has not been so fine for ten years.

The whole family is waiting for the priest, and turn their hands to something, to keep up their patience. Catherine puts the soup on the fire, Joseph draws some water, they send Jacquinet to see if the hole has been dug in the graveyard. At last, but not before six, the priest arrives. He is in a spring tilt-cart, with a young ragamuffin to act as clerk. He gets out at the Lacours' door, takes his stole and surplice out of a newspaper; then puts them on, saying, "Let us be quick; I must be back by seven."

But nobody is in a hurry. They have to go for two neighbors, who are to carry the deceased on the old black wood stretcher. As they are, at last, on the point of starting, Jacquinet comes running up, and screams out that the hole is not finished yet, but that they can come along, all the same.

Then the priest goes first, reading Latin out of a book. The little clerk who follows him holds an old holy-water vase of embossed copper, into which he has dipped a sprinkler. It is only in the middle of the village that another small boy comes out from the barn where mass is said every fortnight, and puts himself at the head of the procession, holding up a cross stuck on the end of a stick. The family walk behind the body; little by little, all the village folk join them; a tail of little ragamuffins, bareheaded, their shirts all unbuttoned, brings up in the rear.

The graveyard is at the other end of la Courteille. So the neighbors set down the stretcher three times; they stand puffing, while the funeral waits; then they go on again. You hear the clomping of their wooden shoes on the hard ground. When they get there, the hole, as Jacquinet said, is not ready; the gravedigger is still in it, and you see him duck down, then reappear, at regular intervals, with every shovelful of earth.

A simple hedge runs round the graveyard. Brambles grow there, to which the boys come, of September evenings, to eat blackberries. It is a garden in the open fields. At one end are enormous currant bushes; a pear-tree in one corner has grown like an oak; a short avenue of lindens casts a shade in the middle, where the old men smoke their pipes in summer. The silence is all a-tremble with life; the sap of this rich soil runs red with the blood of the poppies.

They have set down the bier beside the hole. The small boy who carried the cross has planted it at the dead man's feet, while the priest, standing at his head, keeps on reading Latin from his book. But those present are engrossed, above all, with watching the gravedigger at his work. They surround the grave, follow his shovel with their eyes; and, when they turn round, the cure is gone with the two boys; only the family are left waiting patiently.

At last, the grave is dug.

"It's deep enough, you bet!" cries one of the peasants who carried the body.

And every one helps let down the coffin. Old Lacour can take his comfort in that hole. He knows the soil, and the soil knows him. They will get on well together. Here it is sixty years since it made this appointment with him, on the day when he first struck his pickaxe into it. Their love was to end so; the earth was to take him and keep him; and how good a rest! He will hear only the light feet of the birds bending the blades of grass. No one will walk over his head; he will stay at home, without any one's disturbing him. It is sunlit death, sleep without end in the peace of the fields.

His children have drawn near. Catherine, Antoine, Joseph, take a handful of earth and throw it upon the old man. Jacquinet, who has picked some poppies, throws his nosegay, too. Then the family go home to their soup, the cattle come in from the meadows, the sun sets. A warm night puts the village to sleep.

JACQUES DAMOUR

Over yonder at Noumea, when Jacques Damour gazed at the blank horizon of the sea, he sometimes fancied he saw passing over it all his past history—the miseries of the German siege, the wrath of the Commune, the disruption which had cast him so far, bruised and stunned. It was not a clear vision of memories over which he lingered tenderly; his was the dull brooding of a darkened intellect returning mechanically to certain facts which alone started out sharp and precise from amidst general ruin.

At twenty-seven years of age Jacques had married Felicie, a tall, handsome girl of eighteen, the niece of a fruiter at La Villette, of whom he had hired a room. Jacques was an engraver on metals, and at times earned as much as twelve francs a day. His wife had tried dressmaking, but a baby having come, it was as much as she could do to nurse her boy and look after her household. Eugene was a strong, healthy little fellow, but nine years later a girl was born, who for a long time remained so puny and sickly that she cost a great deal in doctors and physic. Still they were not unhappy. Damour, it is true, would now and then loaf about on a Monday, but when he had been drinking he had the good sense to go to bed, and on the following morning he would return to his work, blaming himself severely as a ne'er-do-well. When Eugene was twelve years old he had learned enough of his father's calling to earn his living, although he could barely read or write. Felicie kept her rooms scrupulously clean; she became a thrifty and clever housewife, somewhat of a screw, the father would say, giving them more vegetables than meat, so as to put by something for a rainy day. They lived at Menilmontant, in the Rue des Envierges, occupying a set of three rooms, one for the father and mother, one for Eugene, and a sitting-room, where the vice, benches, and tools were kept; they also had a kitchen, and a small closet for Louise. The flat was reached by a yard, and was situated in a rear building, but they had plenty of air, as the windows overlooked an open stretch of waste ground, where from morning till night carts came and emptied bricks, stones, and old boards, the refuse of demolished houses.

When war broke out with Germany the Damours had been living for ten years in the Rue des Envierges. Felicie was now nearly forty, but she was still young-looking and plump; indeed, the roundness of her hips and shoulders made her the handsomest woman in the neighborhood. Jacques, on the contrary, was, as it were, desiccated, and the eight years' difference in age between them made him already look an old man beside his wife. Louise, although no longer in danger, was still thin and delicate, resembling her father, while Eugene, then nineteen years old, had his mother's tall figure and broad back. They lived in perfect union, save for those unfortunate Mondays, when father and son lingered in the wine shops, and Felicie sulked, furious at the misspent money. Two or three times they even came to blows, but it did not amount to much, and on the whole there was not a more respectable or more united family in the house. They were quoted as a bright example. When the Germans marched upon Paris, and the terrible stoppage of work began, they had over a thousand francs in the savings bank. This was a large sum for a working couple who had reared two children.

Thus the first months of the siege were not very hard to bear. In the parlor, where the tools lay idle, bread and meat still appeared upon the table. Touched also by the penury of a neighbor, a stalwart house-painter called Berru, who was starving, Damour asked him to share their dinner several times, and soon, indeed, the neighbor dropped in regularly at all the meals. He was a larky fellow, full of chaff and fun, and contrived to get round Felicie, who at first had looked angrily and distrustfully at his big hungry mouth, in which the largest and best morsels vanished. At night they played cards and abused the Prussians. Berru, who was a patriot, talked of digging tunnels, subterranean passages through the country abutting under the enemy's batteries at Citillon and Montretout, and then blowing them all up. He denounced the Government as a pack of cowards, who would throw open the gates of Paris to Bismarck in view of placing Henri V.—the Count de Chambord—on the throne. The Republic as managed by those traitors made him shrug his shoulders. Ah, the Republic! Then, with both elbows on the table and his short pipe in his mouth, he explained to Damour his own ideas of what a Government ought to be—all brothers—all free—all rich—justice and equality reigning everywhere amid high and low.

'Like '98!' he added squarely, not knowing, however, what he meant.

Damour remained grave. He, too, was a Republican, for from his cradle he had heard it asserted that the Republic would one day bring about the triumph of the working classes and universal bliss; however, he had no real notion of the manner in which it was all to happen. He listened attentively to Berru, finding his reasoning exceedingly good, and admitting that such a Republic as he expected would no doubt come some day. He became interested, and even excited in the controversy, firmly believing that if all the Parisians, men, women, and children, had marched to Versailles singing the Marseillaise, the Prussians would have been routed. Yes, the Parisians would have shaken hands with the provinces, and the Government of the people, which was bound to give every citizen an income, would have been established.

'Beware!' said Felicie, with secret misgivings; 'your Berru will lead you into mischief. Feed him, if you want to do so, but let him go and get his skull cracked without your help.'

She, too, wanted the Republic. In '48 her father had been killed on a barricade, but the memory of that death, instead of maddening her, made her reasonable. If she had been the mob, she knew how she would have compelled the Government to be just—she would have behaved irreproachably. Berru's speeches caused her as much indignation as alarm; she found them deficient in honesty. She also noticed uneasily that Damour was changed; that he assumed a manner and used words she did not like; and she became still more anxious when she remarked the somber ardent looks with which her son Eugene listened to Berru. At night time, when Louise had fallen asleep with her head on the table, the young man, after slowly sipping a little glass of brandy, would fold his arms and mutely fix his eyes on the painter, who daily returned from his rambles through Paris with some extraordinary tale of treachery—Bonapartists had signaled to the Germans from Montmartre, or sacks of flour and barrels of powder had been cast into the Seine, so that the city might be forced to surrender.

'What nonsense!' said Felicie to her son as soon as Berru had made up his mind to leave them; 'don't put such stuff into your head, my boy; you know he lies.'

'I know what I know,' answered Eugene, with a furious gesture.

Towards the middle of December the Damours had got to the end of their savings, but as it was hourly pro- t claimed that the Germans had been defeated in the provinces, or that a victorious sortie had at last liberated Paris, the little household was at first not much alarmed, being upheld by the daily hope that work would soon begin again. Felicie accomplished miracles of thrift, and they lived as best they could on the black Biege bread, which little Louise alone could not digest. It was about this time that Damour and Eugene became distracted, or, as the mother said, completely lost their heads. Having nothing to do from morning till night, with all their habits altered, they spent their days in a wearied, troubled idleness, haunted by dreams full of grotesque and sanguinary visions. They had both enlisted in a marching battalion, which, like many others, never left the fortifications, remaining quartered at a spot, where the men spent their time playing cards. It was there that Damour, suffering from hunger, his heart rent by the thought of his family's misery, listened to the reports bandied about on all sides, and acquired the conviction that the Government was determined to exterminate the people and do away with the Republic. Berru was right; everyone knew that Henri V. was at St. Germain, in a house over which the white flag was flying. But all this could not last much longer. Some fine morning they would go and shoot the vermin that starved the working classes and allowed them to be bombarded just to make room for priests and nobles. When Damour and Eugene came home, fevered by the insane delirium of the streets, they talked of nothing but wholesale butchery; while Felicie, pale and dumb, tended little Louise, who had fallen ill again, affected by the bad diet.

At last the siege ended, the armistice was signed, and one day the Germans trooped along the Champs-Élysées. In the Rue des Envierges they again ate white bread which Felicie had gone to buy at St. Denis; still, the dinner proved dreary. Eugene, who had been to look at the Germans, was giving some particulars, when Damour, waving his fork, shouted out furiously that all the generals ought to be guillotined. Felicie thereupon got angry and took his fork away. The following days, as the workshops did not open, Damour decided to begin work on his own account; he had a few articles on hand, among others, a pair of candlesticks, which he meant to finish carefully and try to sell. At the end of an hour, however, Eugene, who felt unable to remain quiet, threw down his tools. As for Berru, he had disappeared since the armistice, having no doubt found more liberal board elsewhere. One morning, however, he returned in a state of great excitement, and related the story of the cannon of Montmartre. Barricades were being erected on all sides, said he, the triumph of the people was at hand, and he had come to fetch Damour, as all good citizens were wanted. Damour at once rose from his bench, utterly disregarding the anxious, troubled looks of Felicie.

The days of March, April, and May followed. When Damour was worn out with fatigue, and his wife implored him to stop at home, he answered: 'And my thirty sous, who would give us bread?'

Felicie silently bowed her head. The thirty sous of the father and the thirty sous of the son, occasionally supplemented by distributions of bread and salted meat, were all they had to live upon. Damour was convinced of the righteousness of his cause, and he fired on the Versailles troops as he would have fired on the Prussians, persuaded that he was saving the Republic and assuring the welfare of the people. After the misery and the fatigues of the German siege, the commotion of civil war gave him a sensation of nightmare amid which he struggled, like an obscure hero who was resolved to die for the defense of Liberty. He did not enter into any of the complex theories about the Commune; in his eyes the Commune was simply the prophesied golden era, the dawn of universal felicity; and he believed with even greater obstinacy that somewhere, at St. Germain or Versailles, there was a king ready to revive the Inquisition and feudal privileges, provided he were permitted to enter Paris. He, who would not willingly have crushed an insect at home, picked off the gendarmes at the outposts without the slightest hesitation. When he returned to Menilmontant exhausted, grimy with sweat and powder, he sat for hours by the side of little Louise's cot, listening to her labored breathing. Felicia no longer attempted to oppose him, but waited for the end of the cataclysm with the calm shrewdness of her practical mind.

One day, however, she ventured to remark that that big, hulking Berru who bragged so loudly had not been such a simpleton as to put himself within gun-shot. He had been shrewd enough to get a post in the commissariat, which did not prevent him, whenever he came in his well-adorned uniform, from exciting Damour with fanatical speeches, talking freely of shooting the Ministers, the members of the Legislature, in fact, all the Reactionaries, as soon as they should be captured at Versailles.

'Why doesn't he go himself, instead of sending others?' argued Felicie, after some such speech.

'Hold your tongue,' answered Damour. 'I am doing my duty; so much the worse for those who don't do theirs.'

One morning, towards the close of April, Eugene was brought back to the Rue des Envierges on a stretcher. A bullet had struck him in the chest, and he expired as they were carrying him up the stairs. When Damour came home at night he found Felicie standing in silence by the corpse of their son. It was a terrible blow for him; he sank to the floor, and remained there sobbing, huddled against the wall. His wife did not attempt to comfort him, she never spoke, for she had nothing to say; still, if she had opened her lips involuntarily, she would have cried, ' It is your doing!' She had closed the door of Louise's closet, so that the noise should not frighten the child. Even now she went to see if the father's sobs had not wakened Louise. When Damour rose up he walked to the mantel-piece, and gazed at a photograph of Eugene, representing the young man in his uniform of the National Guard. Then he took a pen and wrote at the back of the portrait, ' I will avenge you!' adding the date and his signature. After that he felt relieved. The next day a hearse draped with large red flags conveyed the body to the Pere Lachaise Cemetery, followed by an enormous crowd. The father walked bare-headed behind the coffin, and the sight of the flags, of their bloody purple adorning the black bier, swelled his heart with wild, sinister thoughts. Felicie had remained at home with Louise. That same evening Damour returned to the outposts to pick off some more gendarmes.

At last the days of May began. The army of Versailles entered Paris. Damour did not come home for two days, but fell back with his battalion, defending the barricades amid the conflagration. He knew nothing of what went on, but fired through the smoke because it was his duty to do so. On the morning of the third day he reappeared in the Hue des Envierges; his clothes were in rags, and he staggered and seemed stupefied like a drunken man. Felicie was helping him to undress, and washing his hands with a wet towel, when a neighbor rushed in saying that the Communists still held Pere Lachaise Cemetery, and that the Versailles were unable to dislodge them.

'I'll go there, then,' said Damour simply.

He again dressed and caught up his gun. But the last defenders of the Commune were not on the plateau, near the spot where Eugene slept. Damour had vaguely hoped to get killed on his son's grave, but he did not get so far. Bombs were falling, splintering the big tombs. Between the beeches, hidden by the marble whitening in the sun, a few National Guardsmen were still firing in a desultory fashion on the soldiers, whose red trousers were seen advancing. Damour joined his confederates just in time to be captured. Thirty-seven of his companions were shot at once; he himself escaping this summary justice almost by a miracle. As his wife had washed his hands and his gun was not loaded, his life was spared; but in the stupor of his exhaustion and horror he never quite remembered the events that followed, they hovered about in his memory like the perplexing dreams of delirium: long hours passed in dark cells, dreary marches under the sun, yells, blows, staring crowds opening to see him pass. When he at last shook off his crazy imbecility he was a prisoner at Versailles.

Felicie, always pale and calm, came to see him; but when she had told him that Louise was better, they remained speechless, having nothing more to say. As she was going away she informed him, by way of encouragement, that his case was being investigated, and that he would surely come out safe.

'And Berru?' he asked.

'Oh! Berru is all right,' she answered. 'He got away on the day before the troops entered Paris; they won't even trouble him.'

A month later Damour started for New Caledonia; he had been condemned to transportation. As he held no rank, the court-martial before which he appeared would probably have acquitted him, had he not quietly admitted that he had fought and fired from the beginning of the insurrection. During their last interview he said to Felicie, 'I shall come back. Wait for me with the little one.'

And these were the words that Damour heard most clearly amid the confusion of his memory, as he sat with drooping head, before the blank horizon of the sea. At times night fell and found him still in the same spot. Afar a brighter line lingered like the furrow of a ship cutting athwart the increasing darkness, and it seemed to him as if he must rise and walk on that white road, since he had promised to return.

At Noumea Damour behaved fairly well. He found work, and was told that he might expect a pardon. He was gentle and fond of playing with children; he no longer meddled with politics; he kept aloof from his companions, living quite alone. His only failing was that he drank occasionally; still, even in his cups he remained quiet and good-natured, shedding copious tears and retiring to bed of his own accord. His pardon appeared certain, when suddenly he disappeared. The surprise was great when it was found that he had run away with four of his comrades. During his two years of exile he had received several letters from Felicie, regularly at first, but less frequently later on. He himself wrote often. At last, three months having elapsed without bringing him any news, he grew desperate at the thought of waiting for a pardon that might be delayed for two years longer, and in one of those moments of frenzy which are so bitterly rued afterwards he risked everything. A week later, some leagues off, a shattered boat was found on the shore, and near it were the bodies of three of the fugitives—quite naked and in an advanced state of decomposition. Some witnesses declared that one of the corpses was Damour's; it was of the same stature, and the beard looked like his. After a hasty inquiry the necessary formalities were carried out: a certificate of death was drawn up, and at the request of the widow who had been duly informed by the authorities, a duplicate was sent to her. The whole press teemed with this adventure, and a dramatic account of the escape and its tragic ending circulated through the newspapers of the whole world.

Nevertheless Damour was alive. One of his fellow prisoners had been mistaken for him—a circumstance which was all the more singular as the two men were not in the least like one another; only each wore a long beard. Damour and the fourth man, who also had miraculously survived, parted company as soon as they reached Australia. They never met again, and probably the other poor devil died of yellow fever, which very nearly carried off Damour himself. His first intention had been to inform Felicie of his whereabouts by letter, but, having come across a newspaper narrating his escape and death, he thought to himself that it would be imprudent to write; a letter might be intercepted—read, and then the truth revealed. Would it not be better to remain dead to the world? Nobody would then suspect him, and he might quietly return to France and wait for an amnesty before confessing his identity. It was just then that a severe attack of yellow fever prostrated him for many weeks on a hospital bed.

When Damour became convalescent he experienced unconquerable lassitude; for many months he remained very weak and absolutely purposeless. The fever had seemingly swept all his old desires away; he cared for nothing, he wanted nothing; the images of Felicie and Louise were blurred; he still saw them, but at a great distance, in a fog, as it were, and at times he hardly recognized them. Certainly, as soon as his strength returned he meant to start and seek them, but suddenly, when he found himself once more on his legs, another idea possessed him. Before joining his wife and daughter he would make a fortune. What could he do in Paris? Starve over his engraving work, and he might not even find any to do; besides, he felt dreadfully aged. On the other hand, if he went to America, he might, in a few months, gain a hundred thousand francs; a modest sum with which he would rest content, notwithstanding the prodigious tales of millions which were constantly buzzing in his ears. He had been told of a gold mine where every man, even the humblest laborer, had been able to drive a coach and pair before six months had passed. He arranged his future life: he would go back to France with his little pile, buy a small house near Vincennes, and, forgotten, happy, and well rid of politics, settle down there on an income of four or five thousand francs with Felicie and Louise. Four weeks later Damour was in America.

Then began an up-and-down existence, in which chance whirled him at haphazard into a turmoil of adventures at once vulgar and strange; he knew every kind of misery, touched every kind of fortune; three times he thought he had grasped his hundred thousand francs, three times they melted in his fingers; he was robbed, or he ruined himself in the last supreme effort. He suffered, toiled, and at last remained without a shirt to his back. After wandering to the four corners of the world, fate finally threw him on English soil; thence he drifted to Belgium, to the very frontier of France, but he no longer wished to cross it. From America he had written to Felicie, but, as three letters had elicited no answer, he felt justified in thinking that she was either dead or had left Paris. A year later he had made another fruitless attempt to get some news of her. In order not to betray himself, if his correspondence were opened, he had written under an assumed name about some fictitious business, calculating that Felicie would recognize his handwriting, and understand. Her continued silence paralyzed his memory, as it were; he felt dead, as if he belonged to nobody, as if nothing mattered any more. During the year that he spent in Belgium he worked in a coal mine, underground, without seeing the sun, just sleeping and eating, and wishing for naught else. At last, one evening in a pothouse he heard some one say that an amnesty had just been voted, and that all the exiled Communists were returning home. This roused him; he felt a sudden thrill, a desire to look once more upon the street where he had lived so long.

At first it was merely an instinctive impulse; but while he was in the train carrying him to Paris his brain worked, and he realized that he might once again resume his place in the broad daylight, if he could only succeed in finding Felicie and Louise. New hopes dawned in his heart; he was free, he could boldly search for them, and he began to think that he would find them seated quietly in the parlor in the Rue des Envierges, with the cloth laid and waiting for him. Their silence would be easily explained by some simple mishap. Then he would report himself at the municipal offices, and the happy home life would recommence as of yore.

When he alighted at the Northern Terminus in Paris the station was filled with a boisterous crowd. As soon as the travelers appeared, loud acclamations arose, wild enthusiasm prevailed, hats were waved, and names shouted. Damour felt frightened; he could not understand—he fancied that all these people had assembled to hoot him. But presently he caught the name so noisily cheered; it belonged to a member of the Commune who had been with him in the train; an illustrious exile, who was greeted by the crowd with riotous ovations. Damour saw him pass, looking very much stouter, with moist eyes, smiling, and feeling flattered by his reception. When the hero had got into a cab there was a rush to take out the horses; then the mob swayed, and finally the human billows dashed into the Rue Lafayette, the cab slowly rolling along like a triumphal car above a sea of heads. Damour, hurried, hustled, and crushed, experienced great difficulty in reaching the outer boulevards. Nobody noticed him. All his sufferings,

Versailles, the voyage, Noumea, rose up in his throat with a bitter nauseous taste.

When he found himself on the outer boulevards he was strangely affected. He forgot his trials, for it seemed to him that he had just taken back some finished work and was quietly returning to his home in the Rue des Envierges. Ten years of his life, so full of trouble and perplexity, were now closing behind him. And yet he felt a certain wondering strangeness in thus reverting to former habits. Surely the boulevards were wider; and he stopped to read some new inscriptions, surprised at finding them there. Truth to tell, he did not experience any frank delight in setting foot again on that much-regretted ground; the sensation that came to him was half of tenderness musical with old refrains and half of covert apprehension: the uneasiness that one feels in presence of the unknown, and this although the scene before him was a familiar one. His disquietude increased as he neared the Rue des Envierges; his courage wavered, and he felt half-inclined to go no farther, as if indeed he dreaded some impending catastrophe. Why had he returned? What was he to do?

When he at last found himself in the Rue des Envierges, he halted before the house three times without entering it. The pork-butcher's shop, formerly just opposite, had disappeared, being replaced by a greengrocer's; the woman standing at the door seemed so buxom, and so thoroughly at home, that he did not venture to address her as had been his first intention. He preferred to get it all over, and walk boldly to the house-porter's den. How often he had turned to the left at the end of the passage and knocked at the little window-pane.

'Madame Damour, if you please,' he stammered.

'Don't know her. There's no one of that name in the house.'

He stood transfixed. Instead of the door-keeper of his time, who had been extremely stout, he had before him a cross, dried-up little woman who surveyed him distrustfully.

'Madame Damour,' he resumed; 'lived at the back— ten years ago.'

'Ten years! screamed the woman. 'Well, plenty of water has passed under the bridges since then. We only came here last January.'

'Maybe Madame Damour has left her address?'

'No; don't know her.' And then, as he insisted, she got angry and threatened to call her husband. 'Haven't you soon done prying and spying?' she said. 'There are lots of people who sneak in here, anyhow'

Damour colored and went away stammering apologies. He was ashamed of his frayed trousers and his soiled old blouse. He went off along the foot pavement with hanging head, but he soon retraced his steps as if he could not make up his mind to depart; it was like taking an eternal farewell that tore his heart. He lifted his eyes, looked at the windows and examined the shops, trying to reconnoiter the surroundings. In those houses, divided into petty lodgings amongst which evictions rain like hail, ten years had sufficed to change nearly all the tenants; and besides, from a vague sense of prudence not unmixed with shame and terror, he did not wish to be recognized. As he went down the street again, he at last came across some people he had known: the tobacconist, a grocer, a laundress, the baker's wife, with whom he had once dealt. For another fifteen minutes he wavered, passing before the shops, uncertain which to enter, while perspiration came to his forehead from the pain of his inward struggles. With failing heart he finally decided in favor of the baker's wife, a sleepy kind of woman, who looked as white as if she slept in her own flour-bags. She gazed at him without leaving her counter, and she evidently did not know him, with his tanned skin, his bald head scorched by the burning suns, and his long rough beard covering half his face. Emboldened by her manner, he asked for a halfpenny roll, paid for it, and then ventured to ask:

'Haven't you among your customers, madame, a woman and a little girl, Madame Damour?'

The baker's wife pondered a while, and then in her slumberous way answered,' Well, yes; once upon a time, possibly. But that's very long ago. I don't remember; so many people come and go.'

He had to rest satisfied with that answer and go off. During the following days he came to the neighborhood again and questioned other trades people with less timidity; but he always found the same careless indifference, the same oblivion, together with contradictory statements that confused him. All things considered, it seemed positive that Felicie had left the neighborhood some two years after his own departure for Noumea, and just about the time of his escape. Nobody knew her address; some asserted that she had gone to the Gros Caillou, others that she was at Bercy, while, as for little Louise, she was not even remembered. It was a hopeless case. Damour sat down one evening on a bench on the outer boulevard, and wept as he decided to give up his search. What was he to do? Paris seemed empty now, and the little money that he had brought with him was nearly all spent. Once he thought of returning to Belgium and the coal mine, where it was so dark, and where, remembering nothing, he had lived the vacuous happy life of a dumb brute amidst the slumbering earth. However, he stayed on, miserable and starving, unable to procure work, for he was repulsed everywhere, being judged too old. He was only fifty-five, but the decrepitude brought about by ten long years of suffering made him look five-and-seventy. He prowled about like a wolf, roaming over the building-yards of the monuments fired by the Commune, and now in course of re-erection, begging for such jobs as are usually given to children and cripples. A stone-mason employed at the Hotel de Ville works at last promised to procure him the keeping of the tools there, but the promise was slow of fulfillment, and Damour was hungry.

One day he stood on the bridge of Notre Dame looking at the water with the dizziness of those unfortunates who are fascinated by the idea of suicide. But by a mechanical instinct of self-preservation he suddenly loosened his hold of the railings, and threw himself back so violently that he nearly knocked down a passer-by, a tall man in a white blouse, who began to abuse him. 'You brute!'

But Damour had paused aghast, his eyes riveted on the tall fellow.

'Berru!' he stammered at last.

It was indeed Berru—Berru, altered no doubt but to his advantage, for he had a blooming face and looked younger than ever. Damour had frequently thought of him since his return, but then where was he to find the old comrade who had been wont to flit every fortnight? The painter opened his eyes wide, and even remained incredulous, when Damour in faltering accents revealed his name.

'Impossible. What a cracker!'

However, he recognized him at last, and his noisy ejaculations began to attract a crowd around them.

'But you were dead! The deuce, if I expected this!' said he. 'It ain't fair to play such tricks. Come, come, is it quite true that you are alive?'

Thereupon Damour, lowering his own voice, begged Berru to be silent. The painter, who thought the whole thing a capital joke, took his arm and led him off to a wine shop in the Rue St. Martin, plying him with questions and wishing to know all the particulars.

'Presently,' said Damour, as soon as they were seated at a small table in a private room. 'But, first of all, where is my wife?'

Berru looked at him in amazement.

'What do you mean—your wife?'

'Yes. Where is she? Do you know her address?'

The painter's stupefaction increased, and he answered slowly, 'Certainly—I know her address. But you— don't you know the story?' 'No—what story?'

'Ah, there's a go!' burst out Berru. 'A rum go it is, sure enough! So you know nothing, eh? Why, your wife is married again, old man.'

Damour, who had just lifted his glass to drink, replaced it on the table; he trembled so violently that the wine trickled between his fingers, which he wiped upon his blouse while he repeated in a dull, toneless voice, 'what do you say?, married again? Married? Are you sure?'

'Positive. You were dead, and she married again; there's nothing strange in that! Only it's deucedly queer, now that you have come to life again!'

Then while the poor fellow sat there, pale and with tremulous lips, the painter spared him no details. Felicie was perfectly happy. She had married a butcher in the Rue des Moines at Batignolles, a widower whose business she managed with a high hand and level head. Sagnard— the husband's name was Sagnard—was a stout, florid man of sixty, extremely well preserved for his age. The shop—a corner one at the angle of the Rue Nollet—was one of the best patronized in the district; it had tall iron railings painted red, and on either side of the signboard there were two large gilded ox-heads.

'And now what do you intend doing?' asked Berru after each explanation.

The poor wretch, dazzled by the description of the fine shop, answered by vaguely wagging his head—he could not tell.

'And Louise?' he asked abruptly.

'The little one? Ah! I don't know! They have probably sent her somewhere to get rid of her, for I have never seen her with them. That's it. Well, they might anyhow return you the child, as they don't want her. Only, what will you do with a big girl of twenty—for you don't look as if you were in clover, eh? No offence, old man, but anyone passing you in the street would chuck you a copper.'

Damour's head drooped, his throat tightened, and he felt unable to speak a word. Berru ordered a second bottle of wine and began to comfort him.

"The deuce!' he cried. 'As you are alive let's be jolly. It ain't a desperate case—things will mend. What do you propose doing?'

Then the two men plunged into an interminable discussion, in which the same arguments were incessantly repeated. The painter had omitted to mention that immediately after the convict's departure he had attempted to make love to Felicie, and that he harbored a secret grudge against the butcher Sagnard, whom she had preferred to himself, probably because he was well off. After Berru had ordered a third bottle he became excited.

'If I were you,' he said aggressively, 'I'd look them up: square myself in the place and keep Sagnard out if he annoyed me. You are the master; after all the law's on your side.'

By degrees Damour, flushed with wine, felt a glow rise to his white cheeks; he loudly declared that he certainly would do something. Berru kept on urging him to action, slapping his shoulders, and asking him if he were a man! Of course he was a man!—and he had loved that woman so fondly! He loved her still, enough to set Paris on fire in order to get her back. Well, then, in that case, why delay? As she was his, he had only to step out and take her. The two men were nearly drunk by this time, and shouted incoherently in each other's face.

'I'm off,' suddenly said Damour, rising with difficulty to his feet.

'Well done!' cried Berru. 'Don't be a coward I I'll go with you!'

And thereupon they started for Batignolles.

The shop at the corner of the Rue des Moines and the Rue Nollet had a very prosperous appearance, with its red railings and gilded ox-heads. Quartered animals hung there against white sheets, while legs of mutton, partly wrapped in lace-edged paper like nosegays, formed circular garlands round about. Piles of ruddy flesh, joints already cut and trimmed, roseate veal, purple mutton, and scarlet beef streaked with fat covered the marble slabs. The brass pans, the large scales, the steel hooks, shone brightly. The plentifulness of everything, the healthy atmosphere of the premises, paved with white marble and open to the light, the invigorating smell of the fresh meat—all seemed to send a warmer blood to the cheeks of those employed in the shop.

In the centre, and in full view of the street, Felicie sat enthroned behind a tall counter, partitioned off so as to shield her from the draughts. Behind the glass panes and amid the cheerful reflections of all the pink coloring she herself looked young and fresh, with the full mature freshness of a woman who is past forty. And apart from her clear complexion, her smooth skin, her dark hair, and her white neck, she displayed the amiable busy gravity of a clever business woman, who, with a pen in one hand while with the other she fingers the money in the till, represents a shop's integrity and prosperity. Under her eyes the men cut and weighed the meat, and called out the amounts; then the customers passed before the counter; she received payment, and in a deferential voice talked over the news of the neighborhood. A short, sickly-looking woman was at that moment paying for two cutlets, at which she gazed languidly.

'Fifteen sous, isn't it?' said Felicie. 'So you are not any better, Madame Vernier?'

'No, not any better. It is always my digestion—my food never agrees with me. The doctor has at last ordered me to eat meat, but it is dreadfully expensive. Ah! You know that the coal dealer is dead?'

'You don't say so!'

'It wasn't the stomach with him—it was some internal disease, I hear. Two cutlets, fifteen sous! Why, poultry is cheaper!'

'Well, it is not our fault, Madame Vernier. We hardly know ourselves how to make both ends meet. What is the matter, Charles?' she added, turning to one of the men.

While Felicie had been chatting and giving change she had not relaxed in her watchfulness, and had just noticed one of the men talking with two fellows on the foot pavement. As he did not seem to have heard her, she raised her voice to call' Charles, what is wanted?'

But she did not wait for an answer, for as the two men entered she recognized the one who walked ahead.

'Ah! So it's you, Monsieur Berru?'

She did not seem at all pleased, for her lips met with a slightly contemptuous expression. The two men, on their way from the Rue St. Martin to Batignolles, had halted at various wine-shops, for the distance was considerable, and having talked loudly, earnestly, and incessantly, they had frequently felt parched. It was easy to see that the wine had affected them. Moreover, Damour had received a sudden shock when, from across the street, Berru had suddenly stretched out his hand and pointed to Felicie, looking so comely and even young as she sat there at her little counter. 'There she is!' said the painter.

It could not be. That must be Louise, who had always resembled her mother. Felicie was much older. And the sight of the nourishing shop, of the ruddy carcasses, of the dazzling brasses, of that well-dressed woman with her air of middle-class prosperity whose hand was rattling piles of money, robbed Damour of both his anger and his courage, and indeed inspired him with terror. That lady would never consent to take him back; he looked too wretched and abject, with his unkempt beard and filthy blouse. He had already turned on his heels, and was going off in the direction of the Rue des Moines so as to escape notice, when Berru forcibly detained him.

'Thunder!' he cried, ' haven't you any blood in your veins? If I was in your skin I'd make that fine madame wince. I wouldn't go away unless I had share and share alike—yes, half of the joints, and half of everything else. Go ahead, I say, don't be so timid!'

He then compelled Damour to cross the street; and asked one of the men if Monsieur Sagnard was in. And having ascertained that the master had gone to the slaughterhouses, he entered the shop, determined to have it over. Damour followed, feeling dazed.

'What is it you want, Monsieur Berru?' asked Felicie, coldly and unpleasantly.

'I don't want anything,' answered the painter,' but my mate does. He has got some news for you.'

Then Berru stepped aside, and Damour faced Felicie, who looked at him. Suffering tortures, cruelly embarrassed, he lowered his eyes. At first she viewed him with disgust, her calm, happy face expressed strong repugnance for that old drunkard who looked like a pauper; but as she continued gazing at him without a word being spoken on either side, she suddenly turned quite white, stifled a scream, and dropped the money she had been handling, which fell with a silvery ring into the drawer of the till.

'What is the matter? Are you ill?' asked Madame Vernier, who had purposely lingered out of curiosity.

Felicie motioned her away with her hand; she could not speak. With a painful effort she rose up, and walked slowly into the parlor at the back of the shop. Without being told to follow, the two men disappeared behind her, Berru chuckling, and Damour with his eyes still fixed on the sawdust strewing the floor, as if he were afraid of stumbling.

'Well, it's mighty queer,' said Madame Vernier, half aloud when she found herself alone with the assistants.

They had stopped carving and weighing, and looked at each other in astonishment. However, not caring to compromise themselves, they soon resumed their occupations, carelessly indifferent as to the hint of the customer, who went off with her two cutlets in her hand, examining them crossly.

Felicie did not seem to think herself sufficiently alone in the parlor, for she opened a second door and ushered the two men into her bedroom. It was a comfortable, warm, silent apartment, with white curtains to the window and bed; there was a gilt clock, and on the mahogany furniture, shining with polish, not a speck of dust was to be seen. Felicie dropped into a blue rep armchair, repeat ing mechanically: 'You—it is you!'

Damour found nothing to say. He glanced round the room, not daring to sit down, because the chairs looked too fine. Once more Berru took the lead.

'Yes,' he said, airily. 'He has been hunting after you for a fortnight past. He met me by chance, and I brought him here.'

And as if he instinctively felt the necessity of apologizing to her, he added: 'You must see that I couldn't help myself. He's an old chum, and it made my heart jump to see him with one foot in the gutter.'

Felicie was slowly recovering herself. She was stronger-minded and more practical than Damour. When the choking sensation in her throat relaxed, she nerved herself for an explanation which might put an end to this intolerable situation.

'Come, Jacques,' she asked firmly but not unkindly. 'What do you want with me?'

He did not answer.

'It is true,' she continued, 'I married again, but it was no fault of mine, and you know it. I thought you were dead—you did nothing to undeceive me.'

At last Damour spoke.

'I did—I wrote to you.'

'I swear that I did not receive your letter. You know me—you know that I never lie, and I have the certificate of your death—here—in a drawer.'

She went to a desk, opened it feverishly, and pulled out a paper which she handed to Damour, who began to read it with dazed eyes. It was the proof of his death.

Then Felicie resumed: 'I found myself quite alone. I yielded to the solicitations of a man who offered to raise me out of my misery and loneliness. That is my only crime—I allowed myself to be tempted by the prospect of happiness. It was not a sin, was it?'

He listened with bowed head, more humble and more ill at ease than she was. At length, however, he lifted his eyes.

'And my daughter?' he asked.

Felicie started and trembled.

'Your daughter?' she stammered. 'I don't know—I haven't got her.'

'What?'

'I sent her to my aunt, but she ran away, and—and— went to the bad!'

For an instant Damour remained mute; he looked very calm, as if he had not understood. Then suddenly losing his embarrassment, he let his closed fist fall on the chest of drawers with such force that a shell box clattered on the marble top. But before he had time to speak, two children, a boy of six and a girl of four, flung the door open and rushed into Felicie's arms with shouts of delight.

'Good evening, little mother; we have been in the gardens, over there, at the end of the street. Francoise said it was time to come home. Oh, if you only knew— there is some sand there—and ducks on the water!'

'Hush I hush! Run away now,' said the mother sharply; and calling the servant she added: 'Take them out again, Francoise—it is stupid of you to come in so early.'

The children turned away regretfully, and the girl, displeased by her mistress's manner, pushed them angrily before her. Felicie had been seized with the insane fear that Jacques might kidnap the little ones, fling them across his back and hurry away. Berru, who had not been asked to take a seat, but who had unceremoniously stretched himself in the second arm-chair, now whispered to his friend, 'The little Sagnards. Nothing grows so fast as children, eh?'

When the door had closed again behind the little ones, Damour once more struck the marble with his fist and shouted: 'It's neither here nor there—I want my daughter, and I have come to fetch you.'

Felicie shivered from head to foot.

'Sit down,' she said faintly, ' and let us talk. It won't help you to make a fuss. So you have come for me?'

'Yes—you must come with me, and at once. I am your husband, the only real one. Oh! I know my rights. I say, Berru, is it not my right? Come, put on your bonnet, and don't kick up a row if you don't want everybody to know what's up.'

She looked at him, and unconsciously her anguish stricken face plainly expressed that she loved him no longer, that he frightened and horrified her with his hideous, loathsome, old age. Was it possible that she, so fair and clean, accustomed to the comforts of middle-class prosperity, would have to return to the rough, miserable existence of the past with that man who had appeared before her like a ghost?

'You refuse,' said Damour, who read her thoughts in her face. 'Oh! I understand; you have got used to playing the lady behind your counter, and I haven't a fine shop and a drawer full of money to finger and rattle at will. Besides, there are the children that were here just now; they seem better looked after than Louise was. When a woman has lost her daughter, she scorns her husband. But I don't care. I want you to come, and you shall come; or else I'll go to the police and have you brought away between two gendarmes. It is my right, Berru, is it not?'

The painter nodded approvingly. He enjoyed the scene exceedingly. However, when he saw Damour beside himself, intoxicated with excitement, and Felicie exhausted, half fainting and sobbing, he thought it advisable to assume a conciliatory attitude.

'Yes, yes,' he said, in a sententious tone, ' it is your right, but you must pause awhile and consider. I have always conducted myself with propriety, and I say that before coming to a decision it would only be proper to consult Monsieur Sagnard. As he is not here'

He stopped, and resumed in a different voice, tremulous with affected emotion: 'Of course it is hard on my mate to have to wait. Naturally he's in a hurry. Ah, madame! If you knew what he has gone through! And now he hasn't a farthing—not a crust—he's starving—repulsed on all sides. When I met him just now he had not eaten since yesterday.'

Felicie, passing from terror to sudden pity, could not keep back her blinding tears; she was overcome by intense grief, the regret and weariness of life. Involuntarily she exclaimed: 'Forgive me, Jacques!'

Then, when she could command her voice, she continued: 'What is done is done, but I cannot bear to see you so poor. Let me help you.'

Damour made a frantic gesture of refusal.

'Of course,' quickly interposed Berru, 'this house is so plentifully stocked that your wife need not dismiss you with an empty stomach. Admitting that you refuse cash, you can at least accept a present. Supposing you only gave him a bit of gravy beef, eh, Madame Sagnard?'

'Anything he fancies, Monsieur Berru.'

But Damour, still furiously striking the chest of drawers, shouted out: 'Thanks—that's not the sort of grub I live on.'

And walking up close to his wife, he fixed his eyes on hers, saying: 'It is you alone that I want—and I will have you. Keep your meat.'

Felicie had recoiled with renewed fear and loathing. Damour, losing all restraint, became terrible, threatening to smash the whole concern, and vociferating shameful accusations. He would get at his daughter's address, he said; and he shook his wife in her chair, yelling out that she had sold Louise. Felicie, in the awed stupor caused by this outburst, did not attempt to exonerate herself; merely repeating in a broken voice that she did not know the address, but that no doubt it might be discovered. Damour at last took a seat, swearing that the devil himself should not make him leave it; but suddenly he rose, and after a last and still more violent blow on the drawers, he said, hoarsely, 'Well, thunder and hell! I am going. Yes—I go because I choose to go. But you'll lose nothing for waiting. I shall come back when your butcher is at home and I will square you all—he, you, the brats, and the shanty. Just wait, and you'll see.'

He went out, still threatening her with his clenched fist, but in his heart he was relieved to end the scene thus.

Berru, who was delighted at being mixed up in this family affair, lingered behind, to say soothingly, 'Don't alarm yourself; I sha'n't leave him. I'll see that he does no mischief.'

He even ventured to kiss Felicie's hand, but she did not seem to notice it. She was so dazed and exhausted that if at that moment Damour had taken her by the arm she would have followed him unresistingly. She listened to the footsteps of the two men crossing the shop; and heard one of her apprentices sharply chopping a joint of mutton while he hurriedly shouted out some amount. Her business instincts brought her back to her counter, and she sat down, very pale but very calm, as though nothing strange had occurred.

'How much is there to take?' she asked.

'Seven francs and a half, madame.'

Then she gave the change.

The next day Damour had a stroke of luck. His acquaintance the stonemason got him the place of custodian of the building-yard of the Hotel de Ville, and he was set to watch over the edifice which he had helped to burn down ten years previously. His task was easy, his occupation stupid, benumbing, and yet soothing. At night-time he wandered about at the foot of the scaffoldings, listening for stray noises and sometimes falling asleep on the bags of plaster. He never spoke of returning to Batignolles till one day when Berru took him off to lunch, and then he declared after the third bottle that the great flare-up should take place on the morrow. However, when the morrow came he never stirred from the yard. And henceforth it was a regular thing: whenever he was in his cups he got excited and asserted his rights, when he was sober he remained thoughtful and half-ashamed. The painter often chaffed him, and sneeringly declared that he wasn't a man; but he remained gravely indifferent, merely muttering between his teeth: 'That means that I ought to kill them. Well, I'll wait till the fancy takes me.'

One evening he went as far as the Place Moncey, then after spending an hour seated on a bench there he quietly returned to his yard; that afternoon he had thought he had seen his daughter drive past the Hotel de Ville, reclining on the cushions of an elegant landau. Berru had offered to make inquiries, declaring that he could procure Louise's address in twenty-four hours, but Damour had refused the proposal. Why should he know? And yet the supposition that the handsome woman he had seen, beautifully dressed and carried along by two big grey horses, might be his daughter, affected him strangely. His sadness increased, and at last he bought a knife and showed it to Berru, saying that he meant to bleed the butcher with it. This sentence pleased him; he repeated it frequently, adding with a grim enjoyment of his own facetiousness: 'I'll bleed the butcher. His turn next, eh?'

Berru, feeling somewhat alarmed, kept him for some hours in a wine-shop of the Rue du Temple trying to convince him that it was needless to bleed anybody. It would, in fact, be idiotic to do so, for at that game a fellow might run his neck into a noose. Then he wrung his friend's hands, trying to obtain a solemn promise that he would not get himself into trouble; but Damour repeated with a dogged chuckle: 'No, no; his turn next. I'll bleed the butcher!'

The days passed and the bleeding did not take place. But an incident occurred which seemed likely to hasten the end. Damour was dismissed from the yard for inefficiency; for one night during a thunder-storm he had fallen asleep and a shovel had been stolen. He now once more dragged himself about the streets, half-starved but still too proud to beg, though he looked with hungry eyes into the windows of the eating-houses. His poverty, instead of exciting him, made him apathetic with respect to his wife; his shoulders drooped, he walked along meditating. It seemed as if he dared not return to Batignolles now that he no longer had a clean blouse to wear.

At Batignolles Felicie was living in continual terror. She had not dared to mention Damour's visit to Sagnard when the latter came home; and on the next day, frightened by her previous silence, she had felt remorseful, but still had lacked the courage to speak. She every moment expected to see her first husband walk into the shop, and in her distress she conjured up appalling scenes. She fancied, too, that the suspicions of the establishment were aroused, for the men grinned together at times, and Madame Vernier, when she called for her two cutlets, assumed a most unpleasant look while waiting for her change.

At last, one evening Felicie flung her arms round Sagnard's neck, and sobbingly confessed everything. She repeated what she had already said to Damour: it was not her fault, for when people are dead they ought not to come to life again. Sagnard, who was an honest man, hale and hearty, in spite of his sixty years, comforted her. Gracious goodness! It was certainly no joke, but it would all come right. Most things came right in time. Being securely settled in life with plenty of money for his needs, his feelings were principally those of curiosity. He would interview the ghost, and reason with him. The affair interested him; so much so, that a week later, as

Damour did not put in an appearance, the butcher said to his wife: 'Well, what's up? Does he mean to cut us? If I knew where he lived I'd go and look him up myself.'

Then, as she implored him to remain quiet, he added: 'But, my dear, it's only to ensure your peace and happiness. You are fretting and worrying. Let's have it over.'

Felicie was indeed becoming thin, such disquietude did she feel at the thought of the impending tragedy, the postponement of which only made her the more anxious. However, one day, just as the butcher was blowing up one of his men, who had neglected to change the water of a calf's head, she came up to him, deadly pale, and stammered out: 'There he is!'

'All right,' answered Sagnard, suddenly calming down; 'take him into the parlor.'

And then, without hurrying himself, he quietly added, turning to his man: 'Wash it thoroughly, mind—in plenty of water, too; it stinks.'

He then went into the parlor, where he found Damour and Berru. They had met by chance in the Rue de Clichy. Berru had seen less of his old chum lately, having felt bored by his increasing wretchedness. When he discovered that Damour was actually on his way to the Rue des Moines, he became very abusive, declaring that this business was his also. He argued with him, swearing that he would stop his going over yonder to make a fool of himself, and he even stepped in front of him to compel him to give up his knife. However, Damour shrugged his shoulders, obstinately refusing to disclose his intentions, and merely answering again and again,' Come with me if you like, but don't bother.'

Sagnard did not ask the two men to be seated. As for Felicie, she had fled to her room with her children, and double-locked the door; then she crouched against it, frightened, dazed, and clasping the little ones to her bosom as if to guard and defend them. She listened intently, but could hear nothing as yet. In the parlor the two husbands were looking at each other in awkward silence.

'So it is you?' began Sagnard at last, just to say something.

'Yes, it is,' answered Damour.

He was thinking how good-looking the butcher was, and he felt very small before him. Sagnard did not appear to be more than fifty; he was handsome and fresh-complexioned; he wore his hair short, his cheeks and chin were clean shaven. Standing there in his shirt-sleeves with a large apron of snowy whiteness tied round him, he had a joyous air of prosperity.

'However,' said Damour, hesitatingly, 'it is not with you that I want to talk; it is with Felicie.'

At these words Sagnard recovered his composure.

'Come, my friend,' he said quietly, ' let us understand each other. Dash it all, we have nothing to reproach ourselves with—you or I. Why should we quarrel when no one is in fault?'

Damour, with his head bent, fixed his eyes doggedly on the legs of the table. At last he muttered drearily: 'I am not angry with you. Leave me alone; go away. I want to see Felicie.'

'No, you shall not see her,' calmly answered the butcher. 'I don't choose to have her made ill again, as you made her last time. We can settle this without her. Besides, if you are sensible, everything will be all right. You say you love her still; well, consider her position—think it over, and act for her happiness.'

'Hold your tongue,' interrupted Damour, with a sudden burst of rage. 'Don't interfere, or there will be mischief done.'

Berru, feeling convinced that his friend was about to draw his knife, threw himself in front of him with a great show of zeal. However, Damour pushed him aside.

'Hold your tongue, I say! What are you afraid of, you fool?'

'Be calm,' repeated Sagnard. 'When a man is angry he doesn't know what he's about. Listen to me. If I call in Felicie, will you promise to keep quiet? She is very sensitive; you know that as well as I do. We don't want to kill her between us, do we—neither you nor I? Will you promise to behave decently?'

'Eh! If I had come to misbehave myself, I should have strangled you ere this, and stopped all your fine talk.'

He spoke these words in so deep and pained a tone, that the butcher felt sincerely touched.

'Well, then,' he said, 'I'll call Felicie. By nature I'm very impartial, and I quite understand that you wish to discuss the matter with her. It is your right.'

He then stepped up to the bedroom door and knocked.

'Felicie, Felicie!' he called.

Nothing stirred. Felicie, chilled and affrighted by the prospect of the coming interview, was silently pressing her children still closer to her breast. The butcher, however, repeated impatiently: 'Felicie, do come! You are very silly. He has promised to behave sensibly.'

At last the key turned in the lock, and she appeared, carefully closing the door behind her to ensure the safety of her children. Fresh silence and another awkward pause followed. It was the beginning of the end, as Berru styled it.

Damour began to speak in slow entangled sentences, while Sagnard, who had walked to the window and lifted one of the short blinds, pretended to be looking out, as if to show that he was both discreet and magnanimous in this affair.

'Listen, Felicie,' Damour was saying. 'You know that I have never been a bad man; you must own that. Well, I don't mean to begin to-day. True, at first I wanted to smash and murder you all. Then I asked myself how that would better me. I would rather leave you free to choose. We'll do just what you say. Yes, as the tribunals can't help us with their justice, you shall decide what you like best. Answer, Felicie; with whom will you go—him or me?'

But she could not answer; she was speechless with emotion.

'Just so,' resumed Damour in the same husky, desolate voice. 'I understand—you'll remain with him. When I came here I knew how it would be. Oh, I'm not angry with you—you are right after all. I am done for—I have nothing left, and you love me no longer; whereas he makes you happy; and besides there are the two little ones.'

Felicie was weeping uncontrollably.

'Don't cry,' he continued. 'I am not reproaching you. It has happened so—well, that is all; and I had a sort of wish to see you once more, just to tell you that you might sleep in peace. Now that you have chosen, I won't torment you again. It's all over: you'll never hear of me any more.'

He turned to the door, but Sagnard, who felt deeply moved, stopped him, exclaiming: 'Dash it; you are a brick, and no mistake! It is out of the question that we should part like this. Stay and dine with us.'

Berru, amazed at this unlooked-for conclusion, which he considered very droll, looked quite shocked when his friend refused the invitation.

'At least let us drink a glass together,' insisted the butcher. 'The deuce, you can't refuse a glass of wine under our roof!'

Damour did not accept at once. His eyes wandered round the parlor, a clear and cheerful room with its light oak furniture; and when at last they rested on Felicie's tear-stained face, and her imploring earnest glance, he said simply: 'Well, I don't mind if I do.'

Sagnard was delighted.

'Glasses, Felicie,' he shouted. 'We can do without the servant. Bring out four glasses, for you must drink with us. Ah! Mate, you are a good fellow to have accepted. You don't know what pleasure it gives me I love a true heart; and yours is a true heart. I'll take my oath on it.'

Felicie was taking the glasses and a bottle of wine out of the sideboard with trembling hands. Her head was swimming; she could do nothing, and Sagnard had to go to her assistance. When the wine was poured out, and they were all seated round the table, they touched glasses.

'Your health.'

Damour, who sat opposite Felicie, had to stretch out his arm to clink glasses with her. They both looked at each other mutely; all their past was in their eyes. She shook so nervously that, as the crystal rang, one could hear the chattering of her teeth as though she were in a high fever. They were now dead to each other, living only in their memories.

'Your health.'

Then, as they drank, the voices of the children in the next room broke upon the silence. The little ones were playing, chasing each other about with shouts and laughter. Suddenly, too, they knocked at the door, calling: 'Mamma! Mamma!'

'Enough,' said Damour, setting his glass on the table. 'Good-bye, all of you.'

He went away. Felicie, erect and pale, watched him leave the room, while Sagnard politely escorted both gentlemen through the shop to the street.

As soon as Damour got into the street he began to walk so fast that Berru found it difficult to keep up with him. The painter was indignant. On the Boulevard des Batignolles, when his friend finally sank upon a bench, and remained there, with pallid cheeks, dilated eyes, and weary limbs, the painter at last exploded and relieved his feelings. Good heavens! For his part he would at least have boxed the butcher's ears and the woman's too. It was revolting to see a man give up his wife to another fellow without any conditions. It was the act of an idiot, a simpleton, not to use any other word. He quoted various examples in support of his opinion. It was a case for an agreement; none in their senses would allow themselves to be duped and swindled in that manner.

'You can't understand,' answered Damour drearily. 'Go away; go, since you are no friend of mine.'

'What! Not your friend, after all I have done for you? Look at it squarely—what is to become of you? You haven't a soul to look after you; you are like a lost dog in the streets, and you'll starve if I don't come to the rescue. Not your friend? But if I were to forsake you now, all you could do would be to poke your head under your foot, like a fowl weary of living.'

Damour made a gesture of despair. It was true; he had no alternative but to throw himself into the Seine or give himself up to the police as a destitute vagabond.

'Well,' continued the painter, 'I am so much your friend that I'm going to take you somewhere where you'll get a bed and a bite.'

He rose as if impelled by a sudden resolve, and forced his companion to follow him. Damour, half-persuaded, repeated in a dazed way: 'Where? Where do you mean?'

'You'll see. As you refuse to dine with your wife, you shall dine elsewhere. Depend upon it, I won't allow you to play the fool twice in one day.'

He walked rapidly down the Rue d'Amsterdam, and when he reached the Rue de Berlin he stopped before a small house, rang the bell, and asked the footman who came to the door if Madame de Sauvigny were at home. On seeing the servant hesitate, he added:

'Go and tell her that Berru is here.'

Damour followed the painter mechanically. This unexpected visit to this sumptuous residence increased his confusion and perplexity. At last he ascended a flight of stairs and abruptly found himself in the arms of a very pretty, fair, diminutive, young woman, clad in a lace gown.

'Papa! It is papa!' she exclaimed joyfully. 'Ah, how kind of you, Berru, to have persuaded him to come at last t'

She seemed an unsophisticated creature, and did not attach any importance to the old man's grimy blouse; indeed, she was delighted, and clapped her hands in a sudden fit of filial love. Her father, who was greatly startled, had not even recognized her.

'Yes, yes, it's Louise!' said Berru.

Then Damour stammered vaguely, 'Ah yes! You are too kind!'

He did not attempt to be familiar. Louise, however, made him sit down on a sofa, and rang the bell to give orders that she was at home to nobody. Then Damour glanced about the room, which was hung with Indian fabrics, and felt strangely moved. Berru, meanwhile, triumphantly slapped him on the shoulder, saying, 'Will you dare to say again that I'm not your friend? I knew that you'd want your daughter some time or other; so I got hold of her address, and came to tell her all about you. She at once exclaimed, "Bring him to me!"'

'Why, certainly I did, poor dear father!' added Louise. 'Oh, you know, I abhor your Republic! The Communists are a dirty lot, who would ruin us all if they had the chance. But you are my papa. I remember how good you were to me when I was quite little, and so ill. You'll see how comfortably we'll get on together, provided we never talk politics. To begin with, we'll all three of us dine together. Won't it be jolly?'

Her clear eyes were full of laughter, and her pale hair flew round her ears. Damour remained nerveless; he wanted to refuse because he did not think it quite right to accept a meal there; but he had already lost the energy which had hurried him away from the butcher's without once turning his head. His daughter was too soft and gentle, and her little white hands placed on his own held him so fast.

'Now, do say yes,' she pleaded.

'Yes,' he said at last, while two big tears coursed down the furrows with which misery had marked his cheeks.

Berru thought this decision very practical. As the three of them were passing into the dining-room, a footman came to tell his mistress that' Monsieur' was there.

'I can't see him,' she said quietly: 'tell him that I am with my father.'

The dinner was delightful. Berru enlivened it by relating all sorts of stories, and Louise laughed till the tears ran down her cheeks. She fancied herself back in the Rue des Envierges, and enjoyed herself exceedingly. Damour ate heartily and grew heavy with fatigue and food; but each time his eyes met his daughter's his smile became very soft. At dessert they drank some sweet foaming wine like champagne, which affected them all. As soon as the servants had retired they rested their elbows on the table and began to speak of the past with half-maudlin melancholy. Berru had rolled a cigarette for Louise, who smoked it slowly with partly closed eyes and humid lashes while judging her mother's conduct with great severity.

'You understand,' she said to her father,' I do not see her any more—her conduct has been too outrageous. Still, if you like I will go and tell her what I think of the dirty trick she played upon you'

However, Damour gravely declared that Felicie no longer existed for him.

Then Louise rose, exclaiming,' Wait a bit; I must show you something that will give you pleasure!'

She left the room, but presently returned with her cigarette still between her teeth, and handed her father an old yellow photograph broken at the edges. The workman started violently, and, fixing his dim eyes upon the portrait, stammered, ' Eugene, my poor Eugene!'

He passed the photograph to Berru, who looked at it with emotion and murmured feelingly:'It is very like him.'

Then it was Louise's turn. She kept the portrait for a moment in her hand, and then returned it to her father, saying in a tearful voice: 'Oh, I remember him well—he was so kind!'

Overcome by their feelings, they all three began to cry. Twice the photograph went round the table, eliciting pathetic comments. It had become very pale from exposure; poor Eugene in his uniform of the National Guard looked like a phantom rebel. At last, having turned the card round, the father suddenly read what he had written long ago upon the back, 'I will avenge you!' and thereupon, brandishing a dessert-knife over his head, he repeated his oath: 'Yes—yes! I will avenge you!'

Then Damour propped the portrait against his glass, and again gazed at it. By degrees, however, they all became quieter and more practical. Louise, who was easygoing and open-handed, wanted to help her father, and at last she had an inspiration; she asked him if he would consent to look after a small estate which had been bought for her near Mantes in Normandy. There was a small house on the property where he could live very comfortably on two hundred francs a month.

'Come" now, that will be a perfect paradise!' shouted Berru, who accepted for his friend. 'And if he feels dull there, I'll go and cheer him up.'

The following week Damour was settled at Bel Air, his daughter's property; and it is there that he now lives in blissful repose, such as Providence owed him after all his vicissitudes. He is growing stout and florid; he dresses like a well-to-do citizen, and has the honest good-natured face of an old soldier. The peasants salute him respectfully. He shoots and angles; he is often seen sunning himself in the lanes, or watching the growth of the corn with the tranquil conscience of a man who has cheated nobody, but lives on an income laboriously earned. Whenever his daughter visits Bel Air with her friends, he maintains a dignified reserve; his happiest moments are when she runs down alone to see him and they lunch together in the little house. Then he talks to her with the fond foolish prattle of a doting nurse, he looks at her pretty dresses with admiration, and prepares with his own hands various wonderful and delicate dishes, while Louise brings sweets and cakes for dessert in her pockets.

Damour has never tried to see his wife again. His daughter is everything to him; she took pity on him, and she is his only joy. He has obstinately refused to attempt to recover his civil rights. What good would it do to confuse the Government registers? His peace and security are all the more assured since he is unknown. He lives in his nook, lost and forgotten. Being nobody, he accepts the bounty on which he lives without a blush; whereas if he were to resuscitate legally, ill-natured and envious people might comment unfavorably on his position, and he would possibly wince under their blame.

There are times, however, when the little house becomes boisterous. This is when Berru spends four or five days in the country with his old pal. He has, at last, found under Damour's roof a pleasant corner where he can eat his fill and enjoy himself. He shoots and fishes, or else during whole afternoons he lies on his back near the river. At night the two friends talk politics. Berru brings Anarchist papers from Paris, and after reading them they both agree upon the radical measures which are imperatively required, such as shooting the Government, burning Paris again, and rebuilding another city, the real metropolis of the people. They invariably select general extermination as the basis of universal happiness. Finally, when it is time to go to bed, Damour, who has had Eugene's photograph framed, walks up to it, gazes on the faded likeness, and, brandishing his pipe, exclaims: 'Yes —yes, I will avenge you.'

And the next morning, with bent shoulders and placid face, he returns to his fishing; while Berru, stretched out at full length, sleeps buried in the grass.

THE ATTACK ON THE MILL

I

It was High Holiday at Father Merlier's mill on that pleasant summer afternoon. Three tables had been brought out into the garden and placed end to end in the shadow of the great elm, and now they were awaiting the arrival of the guests. It was known throughout the length and breadth of the land that that day was to witness the betrothal of old Merlier's daughter, Francoise, to Dominique, a young man who was said to be not overfond of work, but whom never a woman for three leagues of the country around could look at without sparkling eyes, such a well-favored young fellow was he. That mill of Father Merlier's was truly a very pleasant spot. It was situated right in the heart of Rocreuse, at the place where the main road makes a sharp bend. The village has but a single street, bordered on either side by a row of low, whitened cottages, but just there, where the road curves, there are broad stretches of meadow-land, and huge trees, which follow the course of the Morelle, cover the low grounds of the valley with a most delicious shade. All Lorraine has no more charming bit of nature to show. To right and left dense forests, great monarchs of the wood, centuries old, rise from the gentle slopes and fill the horizon with a sea of verdure, while away toward the south extends the plain, of wondrous fertility and checkered almost to infinity with its small enclosures, divided off from one another by their live hedges. But what makes the crowning glory of Rocreuse is the coolness of this verdurous nook, even in the hottest days of July and August. The Morelle comes down from the woods of Gagny, and it would seem as if it gathered to itself on

The way all the delicious freshness of the foliage beneath which it glides for many a league; it brings down with it the murmuring sounds, the glacial, solemn shadows of the forest. And that is not the only source of coolness; there are running waters of all kinds singing among the copses; one cannot take a step without coming on a gushing spring, and as he makes his way along the narrow paths he seems to be treading above subterranean lakes that seek the air and sunshine through the moss above and profit by every smallest crevice, at the roots of trees or among the chinks and crannies of the rocks, to burst forth in fountains of crystalline clearness. So numerous and so loud are the whispering voices of these streams that they silence the song of the bullfinches. It is as if one were in an enchanted park, with cascades falling on every side.

The meadows below are never athirst. The shadows beneath the gigantic chestnut trees are of inky blackness, and along the edges of the fields long rows of poplars stand like walls of rustling foliage. There is a double avenue of huge plane trees ascending across the fields toward the ancient castle of Gagny, now gone to rack and ruin. In this region, where drought is never known, vegetation of all kinds is wonderfully rank; it is like a flower garden down there in the low ground between those two wooded hills, a natural garden, where the lawns are broad meadows and the giant trees represent colossal beds. When the noonday sun pours down his scorching rays the shadows lie blue upon the ground, the glowing vegetation slumbers in the heat, while every now and then a breath of icy coldness passes under the foliage.

Such was the spot where Father Merlier's mill enlivened with its cheerful clack nature run riot. The building itself, constructed of wood and plaster, looked as if it might be coeval with our planet. Its foundations were in part washed by the Morelle, which here expands into a clear pool. A dam, a few feet in height, afforded sufficient head of water to drive the old wheel, which creaked and groaned as it revolved, with the asthmatic wheezing of a faithful servant who has grown old in her place. Whenever Father Merlier was advised to change it, he would shake his head and say that like as not a young wheel would be lazier and not so well acquainted with its duties, and then he would set to work and patch up the old one with anything that came to hand, old hogshead-staves, bits of rusty iron, zinc, or lead. The old wheel only seemed the gayer for it, with its odd profile, all plumed and feathered with tufts of moss and grass, and when the water poured over it in a silvery tide its gaunt black skeleton was decked out with a gorgeous display of pearls and diamonds.

That portion of the mill which was bathed by the Morelle had something of the look of a barbaric arch that had been dropped down there by chance. A good half of the structure was built on piles; the water came in under the floor, and there were deep holes, famous throughout the whole country for the eels and the huge crawfish that were to be caught there. Below the fall the pool was as clear as a mirror, and when it was not clouded by foam from the wheel one could see troops of great fish swimming about in it with the slow, majestic movements of a squadron. There was a broken stairway leading down to the stream, near a stake to which a boat was fastened, and over the wheel was a gallery of wood. Such windows as there were were arranged without any attempt at order. The whole was a quaint conglomeration of nooks and corners, bits of wall, additions made here and there as afterthoughts, beams and roofs, that gave the mill the aspect of an old dismantled citadel, but ivy and all sorts of creeping plants had grown luxuriantly and kindly covered up such crevices as were too unsightly, casting a mantle of green over the old dwelling. Young ladies who passed that way used to stop and sketch Father Merlier's mill in their albums. The side of the house that faced the road was less irregular. A gateway in stone afforded access to the principal courtyard, on the right and left hand of which were sheds and stables. Beside a well stood an immense elm that threw its shade over half the court. At the further end, opposite the gate, stood the house, surmounted by a dovecote, the four windows of its first floor in a symmetrical line. The only vanity that Father Merlier ever allowed himself was to paint this façade every ten years. It had just been freshly whitened at the time of our story, and dazzled the eyes of the entire village when the sun lighted it up in the middle of the day.

For twenty years had Father Merlier been mayor of Rocreuse. He was held in great consideration on account of his fortune; he was supposed to be worth something like eighty thousand francs, the result of patient saving. When he married Madeleine Guillard, who brought him the mill as her dowry, his entire capital lay in his two strong arms, but Madeleine had never repented of her choice, so manfully had he conducted their joint affairs. Now his wife was dead, and he was left a widower with his daughter Françoise. Doubtless he might have sat himself down to take his rest and suffered the old mill-wheel to sleep among its moss, but he would have found idleness too irksome and the house would have seemed dead to him. He kept on working still, for the pleasure of it. In those days Father Merlier was a tall old man, with a long, silent face, on which a laugh was never seen, but beneath which there lay, none the less, a large fund of good-humor. He had been elected mayor on account of his money, and also for the impressive air that he knew how to assume when it devolved on him to marry a couple.

Francoise Merlier had just completed her eighteenth year. She was small, and for that reason was not accounted one of the beauties of the country. Until she reached the age of fifteen she had been even homely; the good folks of Rocreuse could not see how it was that the daughter of Father and Mother Merlier, such a hale, vigorous couple, had such a hard time of it in getting her growth. When she was fifteen, however, though still remaining delicate, a change came over her and she took on the prettiest little face imaginable. She had black hair, black eyes, and was red as a rose withal; her mouth was always smiling, there were delicious dimples in her cheeks, and a crown of sunshine seemed to be ever resting on her fair, candid forehead. Although small as girls went in that region, she was far from being thin; she might not have been able to raise a sack of wheat to her shoulder, but she became quite plump as she grew older, and gave promise of becoming eventually as well-rounded and appetizing as a partridge. Her father's habits of taciturnity had made her reflective while yet a young girl; if she always had a smile on her lips it was in order to give pleasure to others. Her natural disposition was serious. As was no more than to be expected, she had every young man in the countryside at her heels as a suitor, more even for her money than for her attractiveness, and she had made a choice at last, a choice that had been the talk and scandal of the entire neighborhood. On the other side of the Morelle lived a strapping young fellow who went by the name of Dominique Penquer. He was not to the manor born; ten years previously he had come to Rocreuse from Belgium to receive the inheritance of an uncle who had owned a small property on the very borders of the forest of Gagny, just facing the mill and distant from it only a few musket-shots. His object in coming was to sell the property, so he said, and return to his own home again; but he must have found the land to his liking, for he made no move to go away. He was seen cultivating his bit of a field and gathering the few vegetables that afforded him an existence. He fished, he hunted; more than once he was near coming in contact with the law through the intervention of the keepers. This independent way of living, of which the peasants could not very clearly see the resources, had in the end given him a bad name. He was vaguely looked on as nothing better than a poacher. At all events he was lazy, for he was frequently found sleeping in the grass at hours when he should have been at work. Then, too, the hut in which he lived, in the shade of the last trees of the forest, did not seem like the abode of an honest young man; the old women would not have been surprised at any time to hear that he was on friendly terms with the wolves in the ruins of Gagny. Still, the young girls would now and then venture to stand up for him, for he was altogether a splendid specimen of manhood, was this individual of doubtful antecedents, tall and straight as a young poplar, with a milk-white skin and ruddy hair and beard that seemed to be of gold when the sun shone on them. Now one fine morning it came to pass that Franchise told Father Merlier that she loved Dominique, and that never, never would she consent to marry any other young man.

It may be imagined what a knockdown blow it was that Father Merlier received that day! As was hi 5 wont, he said never a word; his countenance wore its usual reflective look, only the fun that used to bubble up from within no longer shone in his eyes. Franchise, too, was very serious, and for a week father and daughter scarcely spoke to each other. What troubled Father Merlier was to know how that rascal of a poacher had succeeded in bewitching his daughter. Dominique had never shown himself at the mill. The miller played the spy a little, and was rewarded by catching sight of the gallant, on the other side of the Morelle, lying among the grass and pretending to be asleep. Francoise could see him from her chamber window. The thing was clear enough; they had been making sheep's eyes at each other over the old millwheel, and so had fallen in love.

A week slipped by; Francoise became more and more serious. Father Merlier still continued to say nothing. Then, one evening, of his own accord, he brought Dominique to the house, without a word. Françoise was just setting the table. She made no demonstration of surprise; all she did was to add another plate, but her laugh had come back to her, and the little dimples appeared again upon her cheeks. Father Merlier had gone that morning to look for Dominique at his hut on the edge of the forest, and there the two men had had a conference, with closed doors and windows that lasted three hours. No one ever knew what they said to each other; the only thing certain is that when Father Merlier left the hut he already treated Dominique as a son. Doubtless the old man had discovered that he whom he had gone to visit was a worthy young fellow, even though he did lie in the grass to gain the love of young girls.

All Rocreuse was up in arms. The women gathered at their doors, and could not find words strong enough to characterize Father Merlier's folly in thus receiving a ne'er-do-well into his family. He let them talk. Perhaps he thought of his own marriage. Neither had he possessed a penny to his name at the time he married Madeleine and her mill, and yet that had not prevented him from being a good husband to her. Moreover, Dominique put an end to their tittle-tattle by setting to work in such strenuous fashion that all the countryside was amazed. It so happened just then that the boy of the mill drew an unlucky number and had to go for a soldier, and Dominique would not hear of their engaging another. He lifted sacks, drove the cart, wrestled with the old wheel when it took an obstinate fit and refused to turn, and all so pluckily and cheerfully that people came from far and near merely for the pleasure of seeing him. Father Merlier laughed his silent laugh. He was highly elated that he had read the youngster aright. There is nothing like love to hearten up young men.

In the midst of all that laborious toil Francoise and Dominique fairly worshipped each other. They had not much to say, but their tender smiles conveyed a world of meaning. Father Merlier had not said a word thus far on the subject of their marriage, and they had both respected his silence, waiting until the old man should see fit to give expression to his will. At last, one day along toward the middle of July, he had had three tables laid in the courtyard, in the shade of the big elm, and had invited his friends of Rocreuse to come that afternoon and drink a glass of wine with him. When the courtyard was filled with people and every one there had a full glass in his hand, Father Merlier raised his own high above his head, and said,"I have the pleasure of announcing to you that Francoise and this lad will be married in a month from now, on Saint Louis' fete day."

Then there was a universal touching of glasses, attended by a tremendous uproar; every one was laughing. But Father Merlier, raising his voice above the din, again spoke:

"Dominique, kiss your wife that is to be. It is no more than customary."

And they kissed, very red in the face, both of them, while the company laughed louder still. It was a regular fete; they emptied a small cask. Then, when only the intimate friends of the house remained, conversation went on in a calmer strain. Night had fallen, a starlit night, and very clear. Dominique and Francoise sat on a bench, side by side, and said nothing. An old peasant spoke of the war that the Emperor had declared against Prussia. All the lads of the village were already gone off to the army. Troops had passed through the place only the night before. There were going to be hard knocks.

"Bah!" said Father Merlier, with the selfishness of a man who is quite happy, "Dominique is a foreigner; he won't have to go—and if the Prussians come this way, he will be here to defend his wife."

The idea of the Prussians coming there seemed to the company an exceedingly good joke. The army would give them one good conscientious thrashing, and the affair would be quickly ended.

"I have seen them before, I have seen them before," the old peasant repeated, in a low voice.

There was silence for a little, then they all touched glasses once again. Françoise and Dominique had heard nothing; they had managed to clasp hands behind the bench in such a way as not to be seen by the others, and this condition of affairs seemed so beatific to them that they sat there, mute, their gaze lost in the darkness of the night.

What a magnificent, balmy night! The village lay slumbering on either side of the white road as peacefully as a little child. The deep silence was undisturbed save by the occasional crow of a cock in some distant barnyard acting on a mistaken impression that dawn was at hand. Perfumed breaths of air, like long-drawn sighs, came down from the great woods that lay around and above, sweeping softly over the roofs, as if caressing them. The meadows, with their black intensity of shadow, took on a dim, mysterious majesty of their own, while all the springs, all the brooks and watercourses that gurgled in the darkness, might have been taken for the cool and rhythmical breathing of the sleeping country. Every now and then the old dozing mill-wheel seemed to be dreaming like a watchdog that barks uneasily in his slumber; it creaked, it talked to itself, rocked by the fall of the Morelle, whose current gave forth the deep, sustained music of an organ-pipe. Never was there a more charming or happier nook, never did a deeper peace came down to cover it.

II

One month later to a day, on the eve of the fete of Saint Louis, Rocreuse was in a state of alarm and dismay. The Prussians had beaten the Emperor, and were advancing on the village by forced marches. For a week past people passing along the road had brought tidings of the enemy: "They are at Lormieres, they are at Nouvelles ;" and by dint of hearing so many stories of the rapidity of their advance, Rocreuse woke up every morning in the full expectation of seeing them swarming down out of Gagny wood. They did not come, however, and that only served to make the affright the greater. They would certainly fall upon the village in the night-time, and put every soul to the sword.

There had been an alarm the night before, a little before daybreak. The inhabitants had been aroused by a great noise of men tramping upon the road. The women were already throwing themselves upon their knees and making the sign of the cross, when some one, to whom it happily occurred to peep through a half-opened window, caught sight of red trousers. It was a French detachment. The captain had forthwith asked for the mayor, and, after a long conversation with Father Merlier, had remained at the mill.

The sun shone bright and clear that morning, giving promise of a warm day. There was a golden light floating over the woodland, while in the low grounds white mists were rising from the meadows. The pretty village, so neat and trim, awoke in the cool dawning, and the country, with its streams and its fountains, was as gracious as a freshly plucked bouquet. But the beauty of the day brought gladness to the face of no one; the villagers had watched the captain, and seen him circle round and round the old mill, examine the adjacent houses, then pass to the other bank of the Morelle, and from thence scan the country with a field-glass; Father Merlier, who accompanied him, appeared to be giving explanations. . After that the captain had posted some of his men behind walls, behind trees, or in hollows. The main body of the detachment had encamped in the courtyard of the mill. So there was going to be a fight, then? And when Father Merlier returned, they questioned him. He spoke no word, but slowly and sorrowfully nodded his head. Yes, there was going to be a fight.

Franchise and Dominique were there in the courtyard, watching him. He finally took his pipe from his lips and gave utterance to these few words:

"Ah! My poor children, I shall not be able to marry you to-day!"

Dominique, with lips tight set and an angry frown upon his forehead, raised himself on tiptoe from time to time and stood with eyes bent on Gagny wood, as if he would have been glad to see the Prussians appear and end the suspense they were in. Francoise, whose face was grave and very pale, was constantly passing back and forth, supplying the needs of the soldiers. They were preparing their soup in a corner of the courtyard, joking and chaffing one another while awaiting their meal.

The captain appeared to be highly pleased. He had visited the chambers and the great hall of the mill that looked out on the stream. Now, seated beside the well, he was conversing with Father Merlier.

"You have a regular fortress here," he was saying. "We shall have no trouble in holding it until evening. The bandits are late; they ought to be here by this time."

The miller looked very grave. He saw his beloved mill going up in flame and smoke, but uttered no word of remonstrance or complaint, considering that it would be useless. He only opened his mouth to say:

"You ought to take steps to hide the boat; there is a hole behind the wheel fitted to hold it. Perhaps you may find it of use to you."

The captain gave an order to one of his men. This captain was a tall, fine-looking man of about forty, with an agreeable expression of countenance. The sight of Dominique and Francoise seemed to afford him much pleasure; he watched them as if he had forgotten all about the approaching conflict. He followed Francoise with his eyes as she moved about the courtyard, and his manner showed clearly enough that he thought her charming. Then, turning to Dominique, "You are not with the army, I see, my boy?" he abruptly asked.

"I am a foreigner," the young man replied.

The captain did not seem particularly pleased with the answer; he winked his eyes and smiled. Françoise was doubtless a more agreeable companion than a musket would have been. Dominique, noticing his smile, made haste to add, "I am a foreigner, but I can lodge a rifle bullet in an apple at five hundred yards. See, there's my rifle, behind you."

"You may find use for it," the captain dryly answered.

Francoise had drawn near ; she was trembling a little, and Dominique, regardless of the bystanders, took and held firmly clasped in his own the two hands that she held forth to him, as if committing herself to his protection. The captain smiled again, but said nothing more. He remained seated, his sword between his legs, his eyes fixed on space, apparently lost in dreamy reverie.

It was ten o'clock. The heat was already oppressive. A deep silence prevailed. The soldiers had sat down in the shade of the sheds in the courtyard and begun to eat their soup. Not a sound came from the village, where the inhabitants had all barricaded their houses, doors and windows. A dog, abandoned by his master, howled mournfully upon the road. From the woods and the near-by meadows, that lay fainting in the heat, came a long-drawn, whispering, soughing sound, produced by the union of what wandering breaths of air there were. A cuckoo called. Then the silence became deeper still.

And all at once, upon that lazy, sleepy air, a shot rang out. The captain rose quickly to his feet, the soldiers left their half-emptied plates. In a few seconds all were at their posts; the mill was occupied from top to bottom. And yet the captain, who had gone out through the gate, saw nothing; to right and left the road stretched away, desolate and blindingly white in the fierce sunshine. A second report was heard, and still nothing to be seen, not even so much as a shadow; but just as he was turning to re-enter he chanced to look over toward Gagny and there beheld a little puff of smoke floating away on the tranquil air, like thistle-down. The deep peace of the forest was apparently unbroken.

"The rascals have occupied the wood," the officer murmured. "They know we are here."

Then the firing went on, and became more and more continuous, between the French soldiers posted about the mill and the Prussians concealed among the trees. The bullets whistled over the Morelle without doing any mischief on either side. The firing was irregular; every bush seemed to have its marksman, and nothing was to be seen save those bluish smoke wreaths that hung for a moment on the wind before they vanished. It lasted thus for nearly two hours. The officer hummed a tune with a careless air. Francoise and Dominique, who had remained in the courtyard, raised themselves to look out over a low wall. They were more particularly interested in a little soldier who had his post on the bank of the Morelle, behind the hull of an old boat; he would lie face downward on the ground, watch his chance, deliver his fire, then slip back into a ditch a few steps in his rear to reload, and his movements were so comical, he displayed such cunning and activity, that it was difficult for any one watching him to refrain from smiling. He must have caught sight of a Prussian, for he rose quickly and brought his piece to the shoulder, but before he could discharge it he uttered a loud cry, whirled completely around in his tracks and fell backward into the ditch, where for an instant his legs moved convulsively, just as the claws of a fowl do when it is beheaded. The little soldier had received a bullet directly through his heart. It was the first casualty of the day. Francoise instinctively seized Dominique's hand and held it tight in a convulsive grasp.

"Come away from there," said the captain. "The bullets reach us here."

As if to confirm his words a slight, sharp sound was heard up in the old elm, and the end of a branch came to the ground, turning over and over as it fell, but the two young people never stirred, riveted to the spot as they were by the interest of the spectacle. On the edge of the wood a Prussian had suddenly emerged from behind a tree, as an actor comes upon the stage from the wings, beating the air with his arms and falling over upon its back. And beyond that there was no movement; the two dead men appeared to be sleeping in the bright sunshine; there was not a soul to be seen in the fields on which the heat lay heavy. Even the sharp rattle of the musketry had ceased. Only the Morelle kept on whispering to itself with its low, musical murmur.

Father Merlier looked at the captain with an astonished air, as if to inquire whether that were the end of it.

"Here comes their attack," the officer murmured. "Look out for yourself! Don't stand there!"

The words were scarcely out of his mouth when a terrible discharge of musketry ensued. The great elm was riddled; its leaves came eddying down as thick as snowflakes. Fortunately the Prussians had aimed too high. Dominique dragged, almost carried Francoise from the spot, while Father Merlier followed them, shouting, "Get into the small cellar, the walls are thicker there."

But they paid no attention to him; they made their way to the main hall, where ten or a dozen soldiers were silently waiting, watching events outside through the chinks of the closed shutters. The captain was left alone in the courtyard, where he sheltered himself behind the low wall, while the furious fire was maintained uninterruptedly. The soldiers whom he had posted outside only yielded their ground inch by inch; they came crawling in, however, one after another, as the enemy dislodged them from their positions. Their instructions were to gain all the time they could, taking care not to show themselves, in order that the Prussians might remain in ignorance of the force they had opposed to them. Another hour passed, and as a sergeant came in, reporting that there were now only two or three men left outside, the officer took his watch from his pocket, murmuring, "Half-past two. Come, we must hold out for four hours yet."

He caused the great gate of the courtyard to be tightly secured, and everything was made ready for an energetic defense. The Prussians were on the other side of the Morelle, consequently there was no reason to fear an assault at the moment. There was a bridge, indeed, a mile and a quarter away, but they were probably unaware of its existence, and it was hardly to be supposed that they would attempt to cross the stream by fording. The officer, therefore, simply caused the road to be watched; the attack, when it came, was to be looked for from the direction of the fields.

The firing had ceased again. The mill appeared to lie there in the sunlight, void of all life. Not a shutter was open, not a sound came from within. Gradually, however, the Prussians began to show themselves at the edge of Gagny wood. Heads were protruded here and there; they seemed to be mustering up their courage. Several of the soldiers within the mill brought up their pieces to an aim, but the captain shouted:

"No, no; not yet; wait. Let them come nearer."

They displayed a great deal of prudence in their advance, looking at the mill with a distrustful air; they seemed hardly to know what to make of the old structure, so lifeless and gloomy, with its curtain of ivy. Still they kept on advancing. When there were fifty of them or so in the open, directly opposite, the officer uttered one word, "Now!"

A crashing, tearing discharge burst from the position, succeeded by an irregular, dropping fire. Francoise, trembling violently, involuntarily raised her hands to her ears. Dominique, from his position behind the soldiers, peered out upon the field, and when the smoke drifted away a little, counted three Prussians extended on their backs in the middle of the meadow. The others had sought shelter among the willows and the poplars. And then commenced the siege.

For more than an hour the mill was riddled with bullets; they beat and rattled on its old walls like hail. The noise they made was plainly audible as they struck the stonework, were flattened, and fell back into the water; they buried themselves in the woodwork with a dull thud. Occasionally a creaking sound would announce that the wheel had been hit. Within the building the soldiers husbanded their ammunition, firing only when they could see something to aim at. The captain kept consulting his watch every few minutes, and as a ball split one of the shutters in halves and then lodged in the ceiling, "Four o'clock," he murmured. "We shall never be able to hold the position."

The old mill, in truth, was gradually going to pieces beneath that terrific fire. A shutter that had been perforated again and again, until it looked like a piece of lace, fell off its hinges into the water, and had to be replaced by a mattress. Every moment, almost, Father Merlier exposed himself to the fire in order to take account of the damage sustained by his poor wheel, every wound of which was like a bullet in his own heart. Its period of usefulness was ended this time for certain; he would never be able to patch it up again. Dominique had besought Françoise to retire to a place of safety, but she was determined to remain with him; she had taken a seat behind a great oaken clothes-press, which afforded her protection. A ball struck the press, however, the sides of which gave out a dull, hollow sound, whereupon Dominique stationed himself in front of Francoise. He had as yet taken no part in the firing, although he had his rifle in his hand; the soldiers occupied the whole breadth of the windows, so that he could not get near them. At every discharge the floor trembled.

"Look out! Look out!" the captain suddenly shouted.

He had just descried a dark mass emerging from the wood. As soon as they gained the open they set up a telling platoon fire. It struck the mill like a tornado. Another shutter parted company, and the bullets came whistling in through the yawning aperture. Two soldiers rolled upon the floor; one lay where he fell and never moved a limb; his comrades pushed him up against the wall because lie was in their way. The other writhed and twisted, beseeching some one to end his agony, but no one had ears for the poor wretch ; the bullets were still pouring in, and every one was looking out for himself and searching for a loophole whence he might answer the enemy's fire. A third soldier was wounded; that one said not a word, but with staring, haggard eyes sank down beneath a table. Francoise, horror-stricken by the dreadful spectacle of the dead and dying men, mechanically pushed away her chair and seated herself on the floor, against the wall; it seemed to her that she would be smaller there and less exposed. In the meantime men had gone and secured all the mattresses in the house; the opening of the window was partially closed again. The hall was filled with debris of every description, broken weapons, dislocated furniture.

"Five o'clock," said the captain. "Stand fast, boys. They are going to make an attempt to pass the stream."

Just then Francoise gave a shriek. A bullet had struck the floor, and, rebounding, grazed her forehead on the ricochet. A few drops of blood appeared. Dominique looked at her, then went to the window and fired his first shot, and from that time kept on firing uninterruptedly. He kept on loading and discharging his piece mechanically, paying no attention to what was passing at his side, only pausing from time to time to cast a look at Francoise. He did not fire hurriedly or at random, moreover, but took deliberate aim. As the captain had predicted, the Prussians were skirting the belt of poplars and attempting the passage of the Morelle, but each time that one of them showed himself he fell with one of Dominique's bullets in his brain. The captain, who was watching the performance, was amazed; he complimented the young man, telling him that he would like to have many more marksmen of his skill. Dominique did not hear a word he said. A ball struck him in the shoulder; another raised a contusion on his arm. And still he kept on firing.

There were two more deaths. The mattresses were torn to shreds and no longer availed to stop the windows. The last volley that was poured in seemed as if it would carry away the mill bodily, so fierce it was. The position was no longer tenable. Still, the officer kept repeating, "Stand fast. Another half-hour yet."

He was counting the minutes, one by one, now. He had promised his commanders that he would hold the enemy there until nightfall, and he would not budge a hair's-breadth before the moment that he had fixed on for his withdrawal. He maintained his pleasant air of good-humor, smiling at Franchise by way of reassuring her. He had picked up the musket of one of the dead soldiers and was firing away with the rest.

There were but four soldiers left in the room. The Prussians were showing themselves en masse on the other bank of the Morelle, and it was evident that they might now pass the Stream at any moment. A few moments more elapsed; the captain was as determined as ever, and would not give the order to retreat, when a sergeant came running into the room, saying, "They are on the road; they are going to take us in rear."

The Prussians must have discovered the bridge. The captain drew out his watch again.

"Five minutes more," he said. "They won't be here within five minutes."

Then exactly at six o'clock he at last withdrew his men through a little postern that opened on a narrow lane, whence they threw themselves into the ditch, and in that way reached the forest of Sauval. The captain took leave of Father Merlier with much politeness, apologizing profusely for the trouble he had caused. He even added:

"Try to keep them occupied for a while. We shall return."

While this was occurring Dominique had remained alone in the hall. He was still firing away, hearing nothing, conscious of nothing; his sole thought was to defend Francoise. The soldiers were all gone, and he had not the remotest idea of the fact; he aimed and brought down his man at every shot. All at once there was a great tumult. The Prussians had entered the courtyard from the rear. He fired his last shot, and they fell upon him with his weapon still smoking in his hand.

It required four men to hold him; the rest of them swarmed about him, vociferating like madmen in their horrible dialect. Françoise rushed forward to intercede with her prayers. They were on the point of killing him on the spot, but an officer came in and made them turn the prisoner over to him. After exchanging a few words in German with his men he turned to Dominique and said to him roughly, in very good French:

"You will be shot in two hours from now."

III

It was the standing regulation, laid down by the German staff, that every Frenchman, not belonging to the regular army, taken with arms in his hands, should be shot. Even the company's ranches were not recognized as belligerents. It was the intention of the Germans, in making such terrible examples of the peasants who attempted to defend their firesides, to prevent a rising en masse, which they greatly dreaded.

The officer, a tall, spare man about fifty years old, subjected Dominique to a brief examination. Although he spoke French fluently, he was unmistakably Prussian in the stiffness of his manner.

"You are a native of this country?" "No, I am a Belgian."

"Why did you take up arms? These are matters with which you have no concern."

Dominique made no reply. At this moment the officer caught sight of

Francoise where she stood listening, very pale; her slight wound had marked her white forehead with a streak of red. He looked from one to the other of the young people and appeared to understand the situation; he merely added,"You do not deny having fired on my men?"

"I fired as long as I was able to do so," Dominique quietly replied.

The admission was scarcely necessary, for he was black with powder, wet with sweat, and the blood from the wound in his shoulder had trickled down and stained his clothing.

"Very well," the officer repeated. "You will be shot two hours hence."

Francoise uttered no cry. She clasped her hands and raised them above her head in a gesture of mute despair. Her action was not lost upon the officer. Two soldiers had led Dominique away to an adjacent room, where their orders were to guard him and not lose sight of him. The girl had sunk upon a chair; her strength had failed her, her legs refused to support her; she was denied the relief of tears, it seemed as if her emotion was strangling her. The officer continued to examine her attentively, and finally addressed her, "Is that young man your brother?" he inquired.

She shook her head in negation. He was as rigid and unbending as ever, without the suspicion of a smile on his face. Then, after an interval of silence, he spoke again, "Has he been living in the neighborhood long?" She answered yes, by another motion of the head.

"Then he must be well acquainted with the woods about here?"

This time she made a verbal answer. "Yes, sir," she said, looking at him with some astonishment.

He said nothing more, but turned on his heel, requesting that the mayor of the village should be brought before him. But Francoise had risen from her chair, a faint tinge of color on her cheeks, believing that she had caught the significance of his questions, and with renewed hope she ran off to look for her father.

As soon as the firing had ceased Father Merlier had hurriedly descended by the wooden gallery to have a look at his wheel. He adored his daughter and had a strong feeling of affection for Dominique, his son-in-law who was to be; but his wheel also occupied a large space in his heart. Now that the two little ones, as he called them, had come safe and sound out of the fray, he thought of his other love, which must have suffered sorely, poor thing, and bending over the great wooden skeleton he was scrutinizing its wounds with a heart-broken air. Five of the buckets were reduced to splinters, the central framework was honeycombed. He was thrusting his fingers into the cavities that the bullets had made to see how deep they were, and reflecting how he was ever to repair all that damage. When Franchise found him he was already plugging up the crevices with moss and such debris as he could lay hands on.

"They are asking for you, father," said she.

And at last she wept as she told him what she had just heard. Father Merlier shook his head. It was not customary to shoot people like that. He would have to look into the matter. And he re-entered the mill with his usual placid, silent air. When the officer made his demand for supplies for his men, he answered that the people of Rocreuse were not accustomed to be ridden roughshod, and that nothing would be obtained from them through violence; he was willing to assume all the responsibility, but only on condition that he was allowed to act independently. The officer at first appeared to take umbrage at this easy way of viewing matters, but finally gave way before the old man's brief and distinct representations. As the latter was leaving the room the other recalled him to ask:

"Those woods there, opposite, what do you call them?"

"The woods of Sauval."

"And how far do they extend?"

The miller looked him straight in the face. "I do not know," he replied.

And he withdrew. An hour later the subvention in money and provisions that the officer had demanded was in the courtyard of the mill. Night was closing in; Françoise followed every movement of the soldiers with an anxious eye. She never once left the vicinity of the room in which Dominique was imprisoned. About seven o'clock she had a harrowing emotion; she saw the officer enter the prisoner's apartment, and for a quarter of an hour heard their voices raised in violent discussion. The officer came to the door for a moment and gave an order in German which she did not understand, but when twelve men came and formed in the courtyard with shouldered muskets, she was seized with a fit of trembling and felt as if she should die. It was all over, then; the execution was about to take place. The twelve men remained there ten minutes; Dominique's voice kept rising higher and higher in a tone of vehement denial. Finally the officer came out, closing the door behind him with a vicious bang and saying, "Very well; think it over. I give you until to-morrow morning."

And he ordered the twelve men to break ranks by a motion of his hand. Françoise was stupefied. Father Merlier, who had continued to puff away at his pipe while watching the platoon with a simple, curious air, came and took her by the arm with fatherly gentleness. He led her to her chamber.

"Don't fret," he said to her; "try to get some sleep. To-morrow it will be light and we shall see more clearly."

He locked the door behind him as he left the room. It was a fixed principle with him that women are good for nothing, and that they spoil everything whenever they meddle in important matters. Francoise did not lie down, however; she remained a long time seated on her bed, listening to the various noises in the house. The German soldiers quartered in the courtyard were singing and laughing; they must have kept up their eating and drinking until eleven o'clock, for the riot never ceased for an instant. Heavy footsteps resounded from time to time through the mill itself, doubtless the tramp of the guards as they were relieved. What had most interest for her were the sounds that she could catch in the room that lay directly under her own; several times she threw herself prone upon the floor and applied her ear to the boards. That room was the one in which they had locked up Dominique. He must have been pacing the apartment, for she could hear for a long time his regular, cadenced tread passing from the wall to the window and back again; then there was a deep silence; doubtless he had seated himself. The other sounds ceased too; everything was still. When it seemed to her that the house was sunk in slumber she raised her window as noiselessly as possible and leaned out.

Without, the night was serene and balmy. The slender crescent of the moon, which was just setting behind Sauval wood, cast a dim radiance over the landscape. The lengthening shadows of the great trees stretched far athwart the fields in bands of blackness, while in such spots as were unobscured the grass appeared of a tender green, soft as velvet. But Francoise did not stop to consider the mysterious charm of night. She was scrutinizing the country and looking to see where the Germans had posted their sentinels. She could clearly distinguish their dark forms outlined along the course of the Morelle. There was only one stationed opposite the mill, on the far bank of the stream, by a willow whose branches dipped in the water Françoise had an excellent view of him; he was a tall young man, standing quite motionless with face upturned toward the sky, with the meditative air of a shepherd.

When she had completed her careful inspection of localities she returned and took her former seat upon the bed. She remained there an hour, absorbed in deep thought. Then she listened again; there was not a breath to be heard in the house. She went again to the window and took another look outside, but one of the moon's horns was still hanging above the edge of the forest, and this circumstance doubtless appeared to her unpropitious, for she resumed her waiting. At last the moment seemed to have arrived; the night was now quite dark; she could no longer discern the sentinel opposite her, the landscape lay before her black as a sea of ink. She listened intently for a moment, then formed her resolve. Close beside her window was an iron ladder made of bars set in the wall, which ascended from the mill-wheel to the granary at the top of the building, and had formerly served the miller as a means of inspecting certain portions of the gearing, but a change having been made in the machinery the ladder had long since become lost to sight beneath the thick ivy that covered all that side of the mill.

Francoise bravely climbed over the balustrade of the little balcony in front of her window, grasped one of the iron bars and found herself suspended in space. She commenced the descent; her skirts were a great hindrance to her. Suddenly a stone became loosened from the wall, and fell into the Morelle with a loud splash. She stopped, benumbed with fear, but reflection quickly told her that the waterfall, with its continuous roar, was sufficient to deaden any noise that she could make, and then she descended more boldly, putting aside the ivy with her foot, testing each round of her ladder. When she was on a level with the room that had been converted into a prison for her lover she stopped. An unforeseen difficulty came near depriving her of all her courage; the window of the room beneath was not situated directly under the window of her bedroom; there was a wide space between it and the ladder, and when she •extended her hand it only encountered the naked wall.

Would she have to go back the way she came and leave her project unaccomplished? Her arms were growing very tired; the murmuring of the Morelle, far down below, was beginning to make her dizzy. Then she broke off bits of plaster from the wall and threw them against Dominique's window. He did not hear; perhaps he was asleep. Again she crumbled fragments from the wall, until the skin was peeled from her fingers. Her strength was exhausted; she felt that she was about to fall backward into the stream, when at last Dominique softly raised his sash.

"It is I," she murmured. "Take me quick; I am about to fall." Leaning from the window he grasped her and drew her into the room, where she had a paroxysm of weeping, stifling her sobs in order that she might not be heard. Then, by a supreme effort of the will she overcame her emotion.

"Are you guarded?" she asked in a low voice.

Dominique, not yet recovered from his stupefaction at seeing her there, made answer by simply pointing toward his door. There was a sound of snoring audible on the outside; it was evident that the sentinel had been overpowered by sleep and had thrown himself upon the floor close against the door in such a way that it could not be opened without arousing him.

"You must fly," she continued earnestly. "I came here to bid you fly and say farewell."

But he seemed not to hear her. He kept repeating, "What, is it you, is it you? Oh, what a fright you gave me! You might have killed yourself." He took her hands; he kissed them again and again. "How I love you, Francoise! You are as courageous as you are good. The only thing I feared was that I might die without seeing you again; but you are here, and now they may shoot me when they will. Let me but have a quarter of an hour with you and I am ready."

He had gradually drawn her to him; her head was resting on his shoulder. The peril that was so near at hand brought them closer to each other, and they forgot everything in that long embrace.

"Ah, Francoise!" Dominique went on in low, caressing tones, "to-day is the fete of Saint Louis, our wedding-day, that we have been waiting for so long. Nothing has been able to keep us apart, for we are both here, faithful to our appointment, are we not? It is now our wedding morning."

"Yes, yes," she repeated after him, "our wedding morning."

They shuddered as they exchanged a kiss. But suddenly she tore herself from his arms; the terrible reality arose before her eyes.

"You must fly, you must fly," she murmured breathlessly. "There is not a moment to lose." And as he stretched out his arms in the darkness to draw her to him again, she went on in tender, beseeching tones: "Oh! Listen to me, I entreat you. If you die, I shall die. In an hour it will be daylight. Go, go at once; I command you to go."

Then she rapidly explained her plan to him. The iron ladder extended downward to the wheel; once he had got so far he could climb down by means of the buckets and get into the boat, which was hidden in a recess. Then it would be an easy matter for him to reach the other bank of the stream and make his escape.

"But are there no sentinels?" said he.

"Only one, directly opposite here, at the foot of the first willow."

"And if he sees me, if he gives the alarm?"

Franchise shuddered. She placed in his hand a knife that she had brought down with her. They were silent.

"And your father—and you?" Dominique continued. "But no, it is not to be thought of; I must not fly. When I am no longer here those soldiers are capable of murdering you. You do not know them. They offered to spare my life if I would guide them into Sauvel forest. When they discover that I have escaped, their fury will be such that they will be ready for every atrocity."

The girl did not stop to argue the question. To all the considerations that he adduced her one simple answer was: "Fly. For the love of me, fly. If you love me, Dominique, do not linger here a single moment longer."

She promised that she would return to her bedroom; no one should know that she had helped him. She concluded by folding him in her arms and smothering him with kisses, in an extravagant outburst of passion. He was vanquished. He put only one more question to her, "Will you swear to me that your father knows what you are doing, and that he counsels my flight?"

"It was my father who sent me to you," Franchise unhesitatingly replied.

She told a falsehood. At that moment she had but one great, overmastering longing, to know that he was in safety, to escape from the horrible thought that the morning's sun was to be the signal for his death. When he should be far away, then calamity and evil might burst upon her head; whatever fate might be in store for her would seem endurable, so that only his life might be spared. Before and above all other considerations, the selfishness of her love demanded that he should be saved.

"It is well," said Dominique; "I will do as you desire."

No further word was spoken. Dominique went to the window to raise it again. But suddenly there was a noise that chilled them with affright. The door was shaken violently; they thought that some one was about to open it; it was evidently a party going the rounds who had heard their voices. They stood by the window, close locked in each other's arms, awaiting the event with anguish unspeakable. Again there came the rattling at the door, but it did not open. Each of them drew a deep sigh of relief; they saw how it was. The soldier lying across the threshold had turned over in his sleep. Silence was restored indeed, and presently the snoring began again.

Dominique insisted that Françoise should return to her room first of all. He took her in his arms, he bade her a silent farewell, then helped her to grasp the ladder, and himself climbed out on it in turn. He refused to descend a single step, however, until he knew that she was in her chamber. When she was safe in her room she let fall, in a voice scarce louder than a whisper, the words, "Au revoir. I love you!"

She kneeled at the window, resting her elbows on the sill, straining her eyes to follow Dominique. The night was still very dark. She looked for the sentinel, but could see nothing of him; the willow alone was dimly visible, a pale spot upon the surrounding blackness. For a moment she heard the rustling of the ivy as Dominique descended, then the wheel creaked, and there was a faint plash which told that the young man had found the boat. This was confirmed when, a minute later, she descried the shadowy outline of the skiff on the grey bosom of the Morelle. Then a horrible feeling of dread seemed to clutch her by the throat. Every moment she thought she heard the sentry give the alarm; every faintest sound among the dusky shadows seemed to her overwrought imagination to be the hurrying tread of soldiers, the clash of steel, the click of musket-locks. The seconds slipped by, however, the landscape still preserved its solemn peace. Dominique must have landed safely on the other bank. Francoise no longer had eyes for anything. The silence was oppressive. And she heard the sound of trampling feet, a hoarse cry, the dull thud of a heavy body falling. This was followed by another silence, even deeper than that which had gone before. Then, as if conscious that Death had passed that way, she became very cold in presence of the impenetrable night.

IV

At early daybreak the repose of the mill was disturbed by the clamor of angry voices. Father Merlier had gone and unlocked Françoise's door. She descended to the courtyard, pale and very calm, but when there, could not repress a shudder upon being brought face to face with the body of a Prussian soldier that lay on the ground beside the well, stretched out upon a cloak.

Around the corpse soldiers were shouting and gesticulating angrily. Several of them shook their fists threateningly in the direction of the village. The officer had just sent a summons to Father Merlier to appear before him in his capacity as mayor of the commune.

"Here is one of our men," he said, in a voice that was almost unintelligible from anger, "who was found murdered on the bank of the stream. The murderer must be found, so that we may make a salutary example of him, and I shall expect you to co-operate with us in finding him."

"Whatever you desire," the miller replied, with his customary impassiveness. "Only it will be no easy matter."

The officer stooped down and drew aside the skirt of the cloak which concealed the dead man's face, disclosing as he did so a frightful wound. The sentinel had been struck in the throat and the weapon had not been withdrawn from the wound. It was a common kitchen knife, with a black handle.

"Look at that knife," the officer said to Father Merlier. "Perhaps it will assist us in our investigation."

The old man had started violently, but recovered himself at once; not a muscle of his face moved as he replied:

"Every one about here has knives like that. Like enough your man was tired of fighting and did the business himself. Such things have happened before now."

"Be silent!" the officer shouted in a fury. "I don't know what it is that keeps me from setting fire to the four corners of your village."

His anger fortunately kept him from noticing the great change that had come over Franchise's countenance. Her feelings had compelled her to sit down upon the stone bench beside the well. Do what she would she could not remove her eyes from the body that lay stretched upon the ground, almost at her feet. He had been a tall, handsome young man in life, very like Dominique in appearance, with blue eyes and yellow hair. The resemblance went to her heart. She thought that perhaps the dead man had left behind him in his German home some sweetheart who would weep for his loss. And she recognized her knife in the dead man's throat. She had killed him.

The officer, meantime, was talking of visiting Rocreuse with some terrible punishment, when two or three soldiers came running in. The guard had just that moment ascertained the fact of Dominique's escape. The agitation caused by the tidings was extreme. The officer went to inspect the locality, looked out through the still open window, saw at once how the event had happened, and returned in a state of exasperation.

Father Merlier appeared greatly vexed by Dominique's flight. "The idiot!" he murmured; "he has upset everything."

Francoise heard him, and was in an agony of suffering. Her father, moreover, had no suspicion of her complicity. He shook his head, saying to her in an undertone, "We are in a nice box, now!"

"It was that scoundrel! It was that scoundrel!' cried the officer. "He has got away to the woods; but he must be found, or the village shall stand the consequences." And addressing himself to the miller: "Come, you must know where he is hiding?"

Father Merlier laughed in his silent way, and pointed to the wide stretch of wooded hills.

"How can you expect to find a man in that wilderness?" he asked.

"Oh! There are plenty of hiding-places that you are acquainted with. I am going to give you ten men; you shall act as guide to them."

"I am perfectly willing. But it will take a week to beat up all the woods of the neighborhood."

The old man's serenity enraged the officer; he saw, indeed, what a ridiculous proceeding such a hunt would be. It was at that moment that he caught sight of Franchise where she sat, pale and trembling, on her bench. His attention was aroused by the girl's anxious attitude. He was silent for a moment, glancing suspiciously from father to daughter and back again.

"Is not that man," he at last coarsely asked the old man, "your daughter's lover?"

Father Merlier's face became ashy pale, and he appeared for a moment as if about to throw himself on the officer and throttle him. He straightened himself up and made no reply. Franchise had hidden her face in her hands.

"Yes, that is how it is," the Prussian continued; "you or your daughter have helped him to escape. You are his accomplices. For the last time, will you surrender him?"

The miller did not answer. He had turned away and was looking at the distant landscape with an air of indifference, just as if the officer were talking to some other person. That put the finishing touch to the latter's wrath.

"Very well, then!" he declared, "You shall be shot in his stead."

And again he ordered out the firing-party. Father Merlier was as imperturbable as ever. He scarcely did so much as shrug his shoulders; the whole drama appeared to him to be in very doubtful taste. He probably believed that they would not take a man's life in that unceremonious manner. When the platoon was on the ground he gravely said:

"So, then, you are in earnest? Very well, I am willing it should be so. If you feel you must have a victim, it may as well be I as another."

But Francoise arose, greatly troubled, stammering: "Have mercy, sir; do not harm my father. Kill me instead of him. It was I who helped Dominique to escape; I am the only guilty one."

"Hold your tongue, my girl," Father Merlier exclaimed. "Why do you tell such a falsehood? She passed the night locked in her room, sir; I assure you that she does not speak the truth."

"I am speaking the truth," the girl eagerly replied. "I got down by the window; I incited Dominique to fly. It is the truth, the whole truth."

The old man's face was very white. He could read in her eyes that she was not lying, and her story terrified him. Ah, those children! Those children! How they spoiled everything, with their hearts and their feelings! Then he said angrily, "She is crazy; do not listen to her. It is a lot of trash she is telling you. Come; let us get through with this business."

She persisted in her protestations; she kneeled, she raised her clasped hands in supplication. The officer stood tranquilly by and watched the harrowing scene.

"Mon Dieu!" he said at last, "I take your father because the other has escaped me. Bring me back the other man, and your father shall have his liberty."

She looked at him for a moment with eyes dilated by the horror which his proposal inspired in her.

"It is dreadful," she murmured. "Where can I look for Dominique now? He is gone; I know nothing beyond that."

"Well, make your choice between them; him or your father."

"Oh, my God! How can I choose? Even if I knew where to find Dominique I could not choose. You are breaking my heart. I would rather die at once. Yes, it would be more quickly ended thus. Kill me, I beseech you, kill me"

The officer finally became weary of this scene of despair and tears. He cried:

"Enough of this! I wish to treat you kindly; I will give you two hours. If your lover is not here within two hours, your father shall pay the penalty that he has incurred."

And he ordered Father Merlier away to the room that had served as a prison for Dominique. The old man asked for tobacco, and began to smoke. There was no trace of emotion to be descried on his impassive face. Only when he was alone he wept two big tears that coursed slowly down his cheeks. His poor, dear child, what a fearful trial she was enduring!

Franchise remained in the courtyard. Prussian soldiers passed back and forth, laughing. Some of them addressed her with coarse pleasantries which she did not understand. Her gaze was bent upon the door through which her father had disappeared, and with a slow movement she raised her hand to her forehead, as if to keep it from bursting. The officer turned sharply on his heel, and said to her:

"You have two hours. Try to make good use of them."

She had two hours. The words kept buzzing, buzzing in her ears. Then she went forth mechanically from the courtyard; she walked straight ahead with no definite end. Where was she to go? What was she to do? She did not even endeavor to arrive at any decision, for she felt how utterly useless were her efforts. And yet she would have liked to see Dominique; they could have come to some understanding together, perhaps they might have hit on some plan to extricate them from their difficulties. And so, amid the confusion of her whirling thoughts, she took her way downward to the bank of the Morelle, which she crossed below the dam by means of some stepping-stones which were there. Proceeding onward, still involuntarily, she came to the first willow, at the corner of the meadow, and stooping down, beheld a sight that made her grow deathly pale —a pool of blood. It was the spot. And she followed the track that Dominique had left in the tall grass; it was evident that he had run, for the footsteps that crossed the meadow in a diagonal line were separated from one another by wide intervals. Then, beyond that point, she lost the trace, but thought she had discovered it again in an adjoining field. It led her onward to the border of the forest, where the trail came abruptly to an end.

Though conscious of the futility of the proceeding, Francoise penetrated into the wood. It was a comfort to her to be alone. She sat down for a moment, then, reflecting that time was passing, rose again to her feet. How long was it since she left the mill? Five minutes, or a half-hour? She had lost all idea of time. Perhaps Dominique had sought concealment in a clearing that she knew of, where they had gone together one afternoon and eaten hazelnuts. She directed her steps toward the clearing; she searched it thoroughly. A blackbird flew out, whistling his sweet and melancholy note; that was all. Then she thought that he might have taken refuge in a hollow among the rocks where he went sometimes with his gun, but the spot was untenanted. What use was there in looking for him? She would never find him, and little by little the desire to discover his hiding-place became a passionate longing. She proceeded at a more rapid pace. The idea suddenly took possession of her that he had climbed into a tree, and thenceforth she went along with eyes raised aloft and called him by name every fifteen or twenty steps, so that he might know she was near him. The cuckoos answered her; a breath of air that rustled the leaves made her think that he was there and was coming down to her. Once she even imagined that she saw him; she stopped with a sense of suffocation, with a desire to run away. What was she to say to him? Had she come there to take him back with her and have him shot? Oh! No, she would not mention those things; she would tell him that he must fly, that he must not remain in the neighborhood. Then she thought of her father awaiting her return, and the reflection caused her most bitter anguish. She sank upon the turf, weeping hot tears, crying aloud, "My God! My God! Why am I here?"

It was a mad thing for her to have come. And as if seized with sudden panic, she ran hither and thither, she sought to make her way out of the forest. Three times she lost her way, and had begun to think she was never to see the mill again, when she came out into a meadow, directly opposite Rocreuse. As soon as she caught sight of the village she stopped. Was she going to return alone?

She was standing there when she heard a voice calling her by name, softly:

"Francoise! Francoise!"

And she beheld Dominique raising his head above the edge of a ditch. Just God! She had found him.

Could it be, then, that Heaven willed his death? She suppressed a cry that rose to her lips, and slipped into the ditch beside him.

"You were looking for me?" he asked.

"Yes," she replied bewilderedly, scarce knowing what she was saying.

"Ah! What has happened?"

She stammered, with eyes downcast, "Why, nothing; I was anxious, I wanted to see you."

Thereupon, his fears alleviated, he went on to tell her how it was that he had remained in the vicinity. He was alarmed for them. Those rascally Prussians were not above wreaking their vengeance on women and old men. All had ended well, however, and he added, laughing, "The wedding will be put off for a week, that's all."

He became serious, however, upon noticing that her dejection did not pass away.

"But what is the matter? You are concealing something from me."

"No, I give you my word I am not. I am tired; I ran all the way here."

He kissed her, saying it was imprudent for {hem both to talk there any longer, and was about to climb out of the ditch in order to return to the forest. She stopped him; she was trembling violently.

"Listen, Dominique; perhaps it will be as well for you to stay here, after all. There is no one looking for you; you have nothing to fear."

"Francoise, you are concealing something from me," he said again.

Again she protested that she was concealing nothing. She only liked to know that he was near her. And there were other reasons still that she gave in stammering accents. Her manner was so strange that no consideration could now have induced him to go away. He believed, moreover, that the French would return presently. Troops had been seen over toward Sauval.

"Ah! Let them make haste; let them come as quickly as possible," she murmured fervently.

At that moment the clock of the church at Rocreuse struck eleven; the strokes reached them, clear and distinct. She arose in terror; it was two hours since she had left the mill.

"Listen," she said, with feverish rapidity, "should we need you, I will go up to my room and wave my handkerchief from the window."

And she started off homeward on a run, while Dominique, greatly disturbed in mind, stretched himself at length beside the ditch to watch the mill. Just as she was about to enter the village Francoise encountered an old beggar man, Father Bontemps, who knew every one and everything in that part of the country. He saluted her; he had just seen the miller, he said, surrounded by a crowd of Prussians; then, making numerous signs of the Cross and mumbling some inarticulate words, he went his way.

"The two hours are up," the officer said when Franchise made her appearance.

Father Merlier was there, seated on the bench beside the well. He was smoking still. The young girl again proffered her supplication kneeling before the officer and weeping. Her wish was to gain time. The hope that she might yet behold the return of the French had been gaining strength in her bosom, and amid her tears and sobs she thought she could distinguish in the distance the cadenced tramp of an advancing army. Oh! If they would but come and deliver them all from their fearful trouble!

"Hear me, sir: grant us an hour, just one little hour. Surely you will not refuse to grant us an hour!"

But the officer was inflexible. He even ordered two men to lay hold of her and take her away, in order that they might proceed undisturbed with the execution of the old man. Then a dreadful conflict took place in Franchise's heart. She could not allow her father to be murdered in that manner; no, no, she would die in company with Dominique rather; and she was just darting away in the direction of her room in order to signal to her fiancé, when Dominique himself entered the courtyard.

The officer and his soldiers gave a great shout of triumph, but he, as if there had been no soul there but Franchise, walked straight up to her; he was perfectly calm, and his face wore a slight expression of sternness.

"You did wrong," he said. "Why did you not bring me back with you? Had it not been for Father Bontemps I should have known nothing of all this. Well, I am here, at all events."

V

It was three o'clock. The heavens were piled high with great black clouds, the tail-end of a storm that had been raging somewhere in the vicinity. Beneath the coppery sky and ragged scud the valley of Rocreuse, so bright and smiling in the sunlight, became a grim chasm, full of sinister shadows. The Prussian officer had done nothing with Dominique beyond placing him in confinement, giving no indication of his ultimate purpose in regard to him. Francoise, since noon, had been suffering unendurable agony; notwithstanding her father's entreaties, she would not leave the courtyard. She was waiting for the French troops to appear, but the hours slipped by, night was approaching, and she suffered all the more since it appeared as if the time thus gained would have no effect on the final result.

About three o'clock, however, the Prussians began to make their preparations for departure. The officer had gone to Dominique's room and remained closeted with him for some minutes, as he had done the day before. Françoise knew that the young man's life was hanging in the balance; she clasped her hands and put up fervent prayers. Beside her sat Father Merlier, rigid and silent, declining, like the true peasant he was, to attempt any interference with accomplished facts.

"Oh! My God! My God!" Francoise exclaimed, "They are going to kill him!"

The miller drew her to him, and took her on his lap as if she had been a little child. At this juncture the officer came from the room, followed by two men conducting Dominique between them.

"Never, never!" the latter exclaimed. "I am ready to die."

"You had better think the matter over," the officer replied. "I shall have no trouble in finding some one else to render us the service which you refuse. I am generous with you; I offer you your life. It is simply a matter of guiding us across the forest to Montredon; there must be paths."

Dominique made no answer.

"Then you persist in your, obstinacy?"

"Shoot me, and let's have done with it," he replied.

Francoise, in the distance, entreated her lover with clasped hands; she was forgetful of all considerations save one—she would have had him commit treason. But Father Merlier seized her hands, that the Prussians might not see the wild gestures of a woman whose mind was disordered by her distress.

"He is right," he murmured, "it is best for him to die."

The firing-party was in readiness. The officer still had hopes of bringing Dominique over, and was waiting to see him exhibit some signs of weakness. Deep silence prevailed. Heavy peals of thunder were heard in the distance, the fields and woods lay lifeless beneath the sweltering heat. And it was in the midst of this oppressive silence that suddenly the cry arose, "The French! The French!"

It was a fact; they were coming. The line of red trousers could be seen advancing along the Sauval road, at the edge of the forest. In the mill the confusion was extreme; the Prussian soldiers ran to and fro, giving vent to guttural cries. Not a shot had been fired as yet.

"The French! The French!" cried Franchise, clapping her hands for joy. She was like a woman possessed. She had escaped from her father's embrace and was laughing boisterously, her arms raised high in the air. They had come at last, then, and had come in time, since Dominique was still there, alive!

A crash of musketry that rang in her ears like a thunderclap caused her to suddenly turn her head. The officer had muttered, "We will finish this business first," and with his own hands pushing Dominique up against the wall of a shed, had given the command to the squad to fire. When Francoise turned, Dominique was lying on the ground, pierced by a dozen bullets.

She did not shed a tear; she stood there like one suddenly rendered senseless. Her eyes were fixed and staring and she went and seated herself beneath the shed, a few steps from the lifeless body. She looked at it wistfully; now and then she would make a movement with her hand in an aimless, childish way. The Prussians had seized Father Merlier as a hostage.

It was a pretty fight. The officer, perceiving that he could not retreat without being cut to pieces, rapidly made the best disposition possible of his men; it was as well to sell their lives dearly. The Prussians were now the defenders of the mill and the French were the attacking party. The musketry fire began with unparalleled fury; for half an hour there was no lull in the storm. Then a deep report was heard, and a ball carried away a main branch of the old elm. The French had artillery; a battery, in position just beyond the ditch where Dominique had concealed himself, commanded the main street of Rocreuse. The conflict could not last long after that.

Ah! The poor old mill! The cannon-balls raked it from wall to wall. Half the roof was carried away; two of the walls fell in. But it was on the side toward the Morelle that the damage was most lamentable. The ivy, torn from the tottering walls, hung in tatters, debris of every description floated away upon the bosom of the stream, and through a great breach Franchise's chamber was visible, with its little bed, the snow-white curtains of which were carefully drawn. Two balls struck the old wheel in quick succession, and it gave one parting groan; the buckets were carried away down stream, the frame was crushed into a shapeless mass. It was the soul of the stout old mill parting from the body.

Then the French came forward to carry the place by storm. There was a mad hand-to hand conflict with the bayonet. Under the dull sky the pretty valley became a huge slaughter pen; the broad meadows looked on in horror, with their great isolated trees and their rows of poplars, dotting them with shade, while to right and left the forest was like the walls of a tilting-ground enclosing the combatants, and in Nature's universal panic the gentle murmur of the springs and water-courses sounded like sobs and wails.

Franchise had not stirred from the shed where she remained hanging over Dominique's body. Father Merlier had met his death from a stray bullet. Then the French captain, the Prussians being exterminated and the mill on fire, entered the courtyard at the head of his men. It was the first success that he had gained since the breaking out of the war, so, all inflamed with enthusiasm, drawing himself up to the full height of his lofty stature, he laughed pleasantly, as a handsome cavalier like him might laugh. Then, perceiving poor idiotic Françoise where she crouched between the corpses of her father and her intended, among the smoking ruins of the mill, he saluted her gallantly with his sword, and shouted: "Victory! Victory!"

DEATH BY ADVERTISING

I ONCE knew a very nice young man. He died last year. His life had become a sheer martyrdom. Let me tell you the story of a man killed by advertising. Pierre Landry was born in the Rue St. Honoré, near the Central Markets; a paradise for idle loafers. His first reading lessons were given him by his nurse who made him spell out the signs and billposters in the streets. He grew to like those large oblong yellow and blue pieces of paper so conveniently displayed on the walls and later on, as a young lad roaming the streets, he fell in love with some of the posters—the ones printed in enormous characters in queer shapes, on which there is a lot to read. His father, a retired hosier, had completed his son's education by letting him have the advertisement page to read—everyone knows that the large print of the advertisements is easier for children to make out.

At the age of twenty, Pierre Landry was orphaned and found himself quite well-off. He decided to live entirely for his own pleasure and to exploit every aspect of modern progressive civilization for his own personal benefit. His father had been a worker; he was going to relax and enjoy the fantastic luxury of the Golden Age promised him by the advertisements on page four of his paper and on the hoardings. "What a marvelous age we live in!" he mused, "an age of enlightenment and benefits without end. Where can you see anything more moving than those men who devote themselves night and day to the happiness of mankind by producing a constant stream of inventions to provide us with a more peaceful and happy life and who are even so generous as to put all these delightful things within reach of the most modest purse? And to think that these benefactors of mankind even take the trouble to draw our attention to all these wonderful things, great and small, tell us where to find them, and even how much we'll have to pay for them! Some of them we really ought to thank on bended knees for being willing even to lose money on our behalf; and others are quite satisfied merely to cover their expenses. They're working purely in the service of mankind, so that we can live richer, peaceful lives. Well, I've already planned how I want to live. I intend to keep up with progress and enjoy all the advantages of the modern world without any further question. I want a blissfully happy life and for that, all I need is to consult the newspapers and posters, night and morning, and do exactly what they tell me. It's an infallible guide to true wisdom and happiness is guaranteed!"

From then on, Pierre's guideline in life was the advertisements in the papers and on the hoardings. He followed them blindly whenever he had a decision to make and he would never buy or do anything that hadn't been warmly recommended by the publicity men. Every morning he would religiously scan the papers, conscientiously noting down the new discoveries and products. As a result his home became a repository of every crack-brained invention or shoddy article on sale in Paris. Indeed, his basic reasoning was not without logic. By keeping abreast of the times, and choosing the products most enthusiastically praised and recommended in rhapsodic terms by the publicity men, he could claim, with legitimate pride, that he was using the most advanced products of the most highly developed civilization in the world and had thus solved the problem of attaining perfection. However, this was only the theory, and unfortunately the reality became more unpleasant every day. Although everything should have been for the best, in fact it all went from bad to worse and the drama now began which was to make his life a hell on earth.

He had bought a plot of filled-in swampland, into which his house slowly sank. The house itself had been built according to the latest modern principles; when the wind blew, it shook and when rainstorms came, it gently crumbled. The fireplaces, equipped with ingenious smokeless hoods, belched forth asphyxiating fumes; the electric bells remained obstinately silent; the carefully planned modern lavatories turned out to be noisome cesspits; cupboards provided with special mechanical locks would neither open nor shut properly.

In particular, there was a splendid pianola which sounded like a rather inferior hurdy-gurdy, and a burglar-proof and fireproof safe which was quietly removed bodily by burglars one fine winter's night. There was also the country cottage that Pierre had bought at Arcueil, which was quite a different story. Here, he experimented with trees cut out of sheet metal and tried cultivating rare plants which, when they grew, looked like rather poor couch-grass. His architect-designed water tank, widely advertised, collapsed and he was nearly drowned as well as almost crushed to death.

Amid all these trials and tribulations, Pierre continued to smile blandly, his faith quite unshaken. On the contrary, his confidence grew stronger. "Everything isn't yet for the best in the best of all possible worlds," he said to himself, "And the most logical way to avoid all these misfortunes is to follow the march of progress even more closely. The reason my water tank collapsed was that my architect wasn't warmly enough recommended. I must find one recommended more strongly. If I watch the newspapers, I'm bound to achieve perfection and perfect happiness."

Poor Pierre suffered not only in his possessions but in his person. His clothes would split at the seams as he was walking down the street: he had bought them from firms offering vast discounts on stocks being cleared, either because of stock-taking or a takeover. He would seek out such bargains not through meanness but solely in order to enjoy all the benefits of the modern world.

One day when I met him, he'd gone completely bald. In his tireless pursuit of progress, he had hit on the odd idea of changing the color of his hair from blond to dark. He'd applied a liquid which made all his hair fall out, to his great delight, since he could now, he claimed, employ a certain hair lotion guaranteed to give him a head of brown hair twice as thick as his previous one. Incidentally, his cheeks and chin were perpetually covered in gashes from the superior modern razors he used. His hats went out of shape after a week's wear and the clever little springs designed to open his umbrella never worked when it was raining.

I won't mention all his patent medicines. He had always been strong and healthy; he became emaciated and short of breath. And now advertising rally started to destroy him. Thinking he was ill, he began to try out all the wonder-cures advertised in such glowing terms, and to increase their effectiveness, since he was quite at a loss to distinguish between their conflicting claims, all couched in equally high-flown language, he took all the medicines at once. He also consumed enormous quantities of chocolate, unable to resist the blandishments of the various manufacturers. He used toiletries in great abundance and several times went to have teeth pulled out in order to provide work for numerous philanthropic dentists who swore blind that their extraction would be painless, nearly breaking your jaw in the process.

Advertising attacked his mind as well as his body. He had bought an extendable bookcase into which he crammed all the books recommended in newspaper reviews. He invented a very ingenious classification system: he arranged books according to their order of merit, that is to say, according to the degree of enthusiasm displayed by the by the reviewers, all subsidized by the publishers. His shelves groaned under the weight of his collection of rubbish recording all the stupidity and corruption of the age. On the back of each volume, Pierre carefully stuck the blurb which had caused him to buy it, so that each time he opened it he knew in advance how he ought to react: he could laugh or weep according to the instructions.

The outcome of all this was to turn him into a moron, although, having become more selective and difficult to please, in the end he bought only those books described as "outstanding masterpieces," thereby reducing his purchases to some twenty books a week.

We now reach the last act of this harrowing drama. Having heard of a clairvoyant claiming to cure all ills, he rushed round to consult her about his own non-existent diseases. The clairvoyant obligingly offered to restore his youth. All he had to do was to drink a certain liquid and take a bath. Pierre Landry was convinced that such a potion must be the acme of civilization. He swallowed the drug, jumped into his bath and regained his youth to such good effect that two hours later he was discovered there, dead. He had a smile on his lips and the look of ecstasy on his face suggested that he had died worshipping the Great God Advertising. This was no doubt the radical remedy for all ills promised him by the clairvoyant.

Even in death, Pierre Landry remained the humble devotee of advertising. In his will, he had asked to be embalmed in a casket in accordance with a recently patented instant chemical process. At the cemetery, the coffin burst open, tipping his wretched corpse into the mud. He had to be buried higgledy-piggledy with the broken bits of plank. Next winter, the rains rotted the papier-mâché of his imitation marble tombstone, and his grave was left an anonymous heap of moldering refuse.

STORY OF A MADMAN

ISIDORE-JEAN-LOUIS MAURIN was a worthy middle-class citizen, the owner of several blocks of flats in Belleville and residing on the first floor of one of them. He had grown up in the back rooms of this old house, tending his garden and idling away his days like many a Parisian with time on his hands. At the age of forty he was foolish enough to marry the daughter of one of his tenants, an eighteen-year-old blonde whose grey eyes with their occasional sparkle were as shining and gentle as a cat's.

Six months later she had found her way upstairs to the flat of a young doctor who lived on the floor above. This happened as naturally as anything, one evening during a thunderstorm while Maurin had gone out for a stroll along the fortifications of Paris. Their love grew into a devouring passion. They soon found that the few odd minutes they were able to steal together in secret were not enough; they dreamt of living together as man and wife. Their close proximity, the fact that they were separated from each other by nothing more than the thickness of a ceiling, sharpened their desire still more. At night, the lover could hear the husband coughing in bed.

Mind you, Maurin was a decent sort, known in the district as a model husband; he didn't pry and he was as kind and tolerant as anyone could be. But that was exactly what made him such an exasperating obstacle; with his contented nature, he hardly ever left the flat and the very simplicity of his tastes meant that his young wife was a prisoner in the house. After a few weeks, she had run out of excuses for visiting the second floor and so the lovers decided that the old fellow must be got rid of.

They were reluctant to resort to violence or crime. How could your possibly slit the throat of such a tame sheep? Besides, they were afraid of being found out and sent to the guillotine. In any case, the doctor, who was an ingenious young man, hit on a less risky but equally effective method, the bizarre nature of which fired the young woman's romantic imagination.

One night the whole house was aroused by dreadful scrams coming from the owner's flat. They forced open the door and found the young woman in a terrible state, kneeling on the floor, all disheveled and shrieking, her shoulders covered in red welts. Maurin was standing in front of her, trembling and quite bewildered. His speech was slurred like that of a drunken man and when pressed he was quite incapable of replying coherently.

'I can't understand it,' he stammered, 'I didn't go near her, she suddenly started screaming.'

When Henriette had somewhat recovered her composure, she herself stammered something, giving her husband a strange look full of a kind of frightened pity. The neighbors went away greatly intrigued and even rather horrified, muttering to themselves that 'it wasn't at all clear'.

Similar scenes recurred regularly and the whole house was soon living in a state of constant alarm. Every time the scrams were heard and the neighbors forced their way into the flat, they saw the same scene: Henriette was lying on the floor in a state of collapse and trembling like someone who had just been mercilessly beaten, while Maurin was running round the room in a state of bewilderment, unable to offer any explanation.

The poor man became careworn. Every evening he would go to bed trembling with the secret fear that he would be awakened by Henriette's screams. He could not make head or tail of her strange fits: she would suddenly leap out of bed, hit herself violently round the shoulders, tear her hair and roll about on the floor without giving him the slightest idea as to the cause. He concluded that she must be mad and he made a vow to himself not to answer any questions and to keep this private drama to himself. But his easygoing way of life had vanished with his peace of mind; he lost weight and looked pale and ill; his self-satisfied smile had gone for good.

Meanwhile a rumor—the source of which no one quite knew—was spreading in the neighborhood that almost every night the poor man was subject to an attack of fever during which he thrashed the unfortunate Henriette to within an inch of her life. His pale, stricken face and his evasive answers, as well as his sad and embarrassed demeanor, served only to confirm this rumor.

From then onwards Maurin could not do anything that was not interpreted as the action of a madman. As soon as he went out, he became the focus of everyone's eyes, monitoring his every move and leading to strange interpretations of every word he uttered: nobody more resembles a madman than someone who is perfectly sane. If his foot slipped, if he looked up at the sky, if he blew his nose, people would laugh and shrug their shoulders in pity. Street urchins followed him about as though he were some strange animal. At the end of a month, everyone in Belleville knew that

Maurin was mad, stark, staring mad.

People would whisper extraordinary things about him. One woman said she had met him on one of the outer boulevards walking in the rain without a hat. It was quite true: it had just been blown off his head by a gust of wind. Another woman declared that he used to walk round his garden at midnight every night, carrying the sort of candle used in churches and chanting the funeral service. This seemed quite terrifying. The truth was that the woman had seen Maurin on one occasion using a lamp to discover the slugs which were eating his lettuces. Gradually they pieced together a whole indictment of queer actions, an overwhelming dossier of mad behavior. Tongues were busily wagging: 'Such a nice, kind, gentle man! What a shame! But that's how it is! All the same, we'll have to get him put away in the end. He's killing his poor wife, such a wonderful well-bred little woman . . . '

They went to the police and one fine morning, after a dreadful scene, played to perfection by Henriette, Maurin was bundled into a cab on some pretext or other and taken off to Charenton. When he reached there and realized what was happening, in his rage he bit a warder's thumb right off. They put him into a straitjacket and dumped him among the violent madmen.

The young doctor had arranged for the poor man to be kept shut up in a cell as long as possible. He claimed to have been following Maurin's illness and observing such strange symptoms in him that his colleagues thought they had discovered a new form of madness. Moreover, the whole of Belleville was there to provide circumstantial details. Mental specialists conferred and learned articles were written. The lovers slipped away to enjoy their honeymoon in a leafy retreat in Touraine.

It took Henriette eleven months to become tired of her young doctor. Often, in between kisses, her thoughts had turned to her poor wretch of a husband screaming in his cell. She began to feel a growing affection for him now that such a dreadful fate had overtaken him and he was no longer able to go out and look at his lettuces or take his stroll along the fortifications. Women with grey cat's eyes tend to be subject to such whims. She left her lover and went immediately to Charenton determined to make a full confession.

She had often felt surprised that the doctors were taking so long to discover that Maurin was mad. At best, she had relied on enjoying only a few weeks' freedom. When they took her to her husband she saw in a shadowy corner of his cell a pale, thin, filthy, animal-like figure, more ghost than man, who stood up and looked at her with eyes full of mindless, imbecilic horror. The poor man failed to recognize her. And as she stood there in terror, he began to sway to and fro with an idiotic laugh. Suddenly he burst out sobbing and stammered: 'I can't understand it, I can't understand it . . . I didn't go near her!'

Then he hurled himself flat on the floor, exactly as Henriette had done, and kept hitting himself on the shoulders as he screamed and rolled around on the ground.

'He does that trick twenty times a day,' said the warder who had accompanied the young woman.

With her teeth chattering with fear and almost fainting she covered her eyes to avoid looking at the man she had reduced to this brute beast.

Maurin was mad.

A FLASH IN THE PAN

ONCE a month during the fruit season, a swarthy little girl with a mop of black hair would appear in the house of Monsieur Rostand, a solicitor in Aix en Provence, with a basket of apricots or peaches so enormous that she had difficulty in carrying it. As soon as it became known that she was waiting in the large downstairs hall, the whole family would come down to see her.

'Ah, it's you, Naïs,' the solicitor would say. 'You've brought us some fruit. You're a good girl . . . And how's your father?'

'Very well, thank you, monsieur,' the little girl would reply with a flash of white teeth.

Then Madame Rostand would take Naïs Micoulin into the kitchen and question her about the olives, the almonds and the vines. The most important thing was to discover whether there had been any rain on the stretch of coast at L'Estaque, where the Rostands had their property, La Blancarde, which was farmed by their tenant Micoulin. There were only a few dozen almond and olive trees but the question of rain was still the most urgent, for this part of the country was chronically prone to drought.

'There've been a few drops,' Naïs would say. 'The grapes could do with some more.'

Then, having delivered her news, she would be offered a hunk of bread and some leftovers of meat before going back to L'Estaque in the cart of a butcher who came over to Aix once a fortnight. Often she would bring shellfish, a spiny lobster, or a nice fish, for old Micoulin was keener on fishing than on ploughing. Whenever she came during the school holidays, Frédéric, Rostand's son, would run down to the kitchen and tell her when the family would be coming to stay at La Blancarde and remind her to get all the fishing tackle ready. He was on friendly terms with her because he used to play with her when he was quite young; but since the age of twelve, she had started calling him 'Monsieur Frédéric' as a mark of respect. Indeed, every time old Micoulin heard her speak too familiarly to the son of his landlord, he would give her a sound box on the ears. But that did not prevent the children from remaining good friends.

'And you won't forget to mend the nets?' the schoolboy would say.

'Don't worry, Monsieur Frédéric,' Naïs replied, 'We'll have everything ready for you.'

Monsieur Rostand was an extremely wealthy man. He had bought a superb townhouse, the Hôtel de Coiron, in the Rue du Collège, very cheaply. Built in the late seventeenth century, it had no fewer than twelve windows at the front and enough rooms to house a whole community; as the household comprised only five people, including two old servants, it seemed lost in such spacious quarters. The solicitor occupied only the first floor. After advertising the ground floor and second floor for ten years without finding any tenants, he had finally decided to close up those rooms, leaving two-thirds of the house to be taken over by spiders. The gloomy empty house echoed like a cathedral at the slightest sound in the vast entrance hall; it had a monumental staircase and could easily have held a whole modern house. Immediately after buying the house, Monsieur Rostand had erected a partition to divide the Principal drawing-room, some forty feet long and twenty-five feet wide and lit by six large windows; one half of the room he took as his own office while the other half was for his clerks. There were four further rooms on the first floor, the smallest of which measured nearly twenty-three feet by sixteen. Madame Rostand, Frédéric and the two old maidservants had rooms with ceilings as high as most chapels. The solicitor had been forced reluctantly to convert a former boudoir into a kitchen in order to provide a more convenient service, because previously, when the ground floor kitchen had been in use, all the food arrived completely cold after being carried through the damp and icy-cold hall and up the staircase. But the worst feature of these ridiculously large quarters was the totally inadequate furniture. Monsieur Rostand's immense study contained only a sadly inelegant Empire settee and eight matching armchairs in green Utrecht velvet scattered sparsely round the room, while tiny occasional tables of the same period stood in the middle looking like dolls' furniture; on the mantelshelf there was a frightful modern marble clock standing between two vases, while the floor covering consisted of shiny garish red tiles. The bedrooms were even more sparsely furnished. Everywhere you could sense the scornful indifference of the southern Frenchman, however wealthy, for any comfort or luxury, in this sun-blessed country where everybody lives as much as possible out of doors. The Rostands were certainly quite unaware of the desolation and gloom of these vast, deathly cold rooms which had all the sadness of ruins, compounded by the poverty and sparseness of the furniture.

The solicitor was, however, an extremely astute man. He had inherited from his father one of the largest practices in Aix and with an energy rare in a land where people are generally bone-idle; he had succeeded in building it up still further. Small in stature, always on the go, with a ferrety face, he devoted himself wholeheartedly to the advancement of his practice, his pursuit of wealth was, indeed, so single-minded that he did not even take time off to read a newspaper during his rare moments of relaxation at his club. His wife on the other hand had the reputation of being one of the most distinguished and intelligent women of Aix. She had been born a de Villebonne and this had left her with an aura of considerable prestige, despite having married beneath her station. But she was so straitlaced and practiced her religious duties with such stubborn, narrow-minded and methodical routine that she had become, as it were, quite dried up.

So Frédéric was growing up between an inordinately busy father and an excessively puritanical mother. During his school years, he had been a dunce of the first water, going in terror of his mother but with such an unconquerable distaste for work that he would sometimes sit for hours over his books without reading a line, thinking of other things, while his parents, watching him, imagined that he was hard at work. Exasperated by his laziness they finally packed him off to boarding school where, delighted at having escaped his parents' watchful eye, he still managed to work no harder. So, becoming alarmed at the signs of his incipient emancipation, they took him away from the school in order to be able to have him once again under their own observation. In this way he completed his two final years of education, so closely guarded that he was forced to work; his mother would inspect his exercise books and compel him to go over his lessons, standing over him all the time like a policeman. Thanks to the careful supervision, Frédéric failed his school-leaving examination only twice.

The Law Faculty of Aix has an excellent reputation and young Frédéric naturally applied to join it. As the former seat of a High Court, there is no shortage of barristers, solicitors and lawyers of all sorts engaged in the administration of justice; but law is still studied, even by those who have no intention of ever practicing it. Frédéric merely continued to live in the same way as he had at school, giving the impression of working hard while doing as little as possible. Most reluctantly, Madame Rostand had had to allow her son greater freedom. He could now go out whenever he wanted and was expected to be present only at mealtimes; he had to be in by nine o'clock every night except on those days when he was allowed to go to the theatre. He now embarked on the life of the provincial student which is both very monotonous and full of temptations, unless spent wholeheartedly working.

One has to know Aix-en-Provence personally, with its quiet streets, so quiet that grass grows over them, and its general drowsy atmosphere, in order to realize the emptiness of the life of a student there. The ones who work can kill time in studying; but those who are not interested in following their course have only two resources against boredom: going to cafés, where they play cards for money, or going to certain other establishments where they do worse things. As young Rostand turned into an enthusiastic gambler, he spent most of his evenings playing cards, but he ended them elsewhere. With the lustfulness of a schoolboy finally set free, he flung himself into the only sort of debauchery that the town had to offer, since Aix lacked the emancipated girls that you meet everywhere in the Latin Quarter of Paris. When his evenings proved too short, he turned them into nights by stealing a house-key. In such pursuits he passed his years of law school quite agreeably.

Frédéric had also now come to the realization that he must show himself to be an obedient son. Gradually he acquired the imperturbable hypocrisy of all children bullied by their parents. His mother could now proclaim herself fully satisfied: he accompanied her to Mass, behaved impeccably at all times and told her enormous lies without blinking an eyelid and with a note of such sincerity in his voice that she accepted them. So skilful did he become that he was never at a loss, always able to find an excuse and supporting his case by extraordinary stories carefully elaborated in advance. He used to pay his gambling debts by borrowing from his cousins and had a whole complicated system of bookkeeping. Once, after an unexpected win, he even managed to fulfill his dream of spending a week in Paris by arranging an alleged invitation from a friend who owned an estate near Durance.

Moreover Frédéric was a handsome young man, tall, with regular features and a thick black beard. His vices made him attractive, especially to women. Those people who knew of his pranks would give a wry smile but since he had the decency to conceal this shady side of his character, you had to be grateful to him for not advertising his riotous style of living, unlike some less mannerly students who were the talk of the town.

Frédéric was now rising twenty-one and would soon be taking his law finals. His father was still young and unwilling to hand over his practice straightaway, he talked of getting his son into the public prosecutor's office, for he had friends in Paris whom he could persuade to have him made a deputy public prosecutor. The young man did not say no; he never opposed his parents openly; but his lips curled in a slight smile which suggested his firm intention of continuing the life of idleness which was so much to his liking. He knew that his father was rich; he was the only son; why should he give himself the slightest trouble? Meanwhile, he strolled down the Cours Mira beau* smoking cigars, went to gay house-parties in neighboring country-houses and patronized houses of ill fame, daily and in secret. All this did not prevent him from being at his mother's beck and call or showing her every solicitude. When he felt completely fagged out and extremely liverish from some particularly violent excesses, he would come back to his parents' vast, freezing house in the Rue du Collège and enjoy a delicious rest cure. The boredom of the empty and forbidding high-ceilinged rooms was cool and tranquillizing. Here, while pretending to his mother that he was staying home to keep her company, he would recuperate until such time as, having recovered his appetite and his health, he would start plotting some new escapade. In a word, the nicest young man you could ever want to meet, as long as you didn't interfere with his pleasures.

Meanwhile, Naïs used to come to the Rostand house with fruit and vegetables every year and every year she had grown up a little more. She was exactly the same age as Frédéric, perhaps three months older. So each time, Madame Rostand would say to her, 'How grown up you're getting, Naïs!'

Naïs would smile and show her dazzling white teeth. More often than not, Frédéric was not at home. But one day, during his last year at university, just as he was going out, he met Naïs in the hall, holding her basket. He stopped in his tracks in surprise. He could no longer recognize the lanky boyish-looking girl whom he had seen only the summer before at La Blancarde. She was in every way superb: her nut-brown face beneath her thick crop of black hair, the full curves of her figure, her broad shoulders, her magnificent arms, her bare wrists. In the space of a year she had shot up like a young sapling.

'It's you!' he stammered.

'Yes, Monsieur Frédéric,' she said looking him straight in the face with her large, brown, smoldering eyes. 'I've brought you some sea-urchins. When are you coming to La Blancarde? Shall we get the nets ready?'

Still staring at her, he said softly, apparently not having heard what she had said:

'Naïs, you look wonderful! What have you got there?'

The compliment made her laugh. Then, as he playfully took hold of her hands, just as he used to do when they were playmates, her face became serious and, suddenly reverting to the same familiar form of speech of those days, she said in a low, rather hoarse voice' Not now, Frédéric! Your mother's coming.'

A fortnight later, the Rostand family was on their way to La Blancarde. The solicitor had to wait until the courts were in recess and in any case the month of September was the pleasantest to spend by the sea, for the heat was dying down and the nights were becoming deliciously cool.

La Blancarde was not in L'Estaque itself, which is a small town situated close to the outermost suburbs of Marseilles, at the fat end of a bay completely enclosed by rocks. The property stood beyond the town, perched on top of a cliff. Set in a clump of tall pines, the yellow front could be seen from all around the bay. It was one of those heavy, square, old buildings with irregular windows which people call Châteaux in Provence. In front of the house was a broad terrace beyond which the ground fell sheer to a tiny pebbly beach. Behind, there was a large area of poor land where the only plants that could be persuaded to grow were a few vines, olives and almond trees. Also, one of the disadvantages and dangers of La Blancarde was that the sea was constantly battering the foot of the cliff and that underground springs filtered through the mixture of clay and rock, softening it, so that every so often enormous masses of earth would break away and fall with a terrifying noise into the water. The property was slowly being eroded and some of the pines had already been engulfed by the sea.

The Micoulins had farmed the property as tenants for forty years. In accordance with local custom, they did the cultivation and shared the crops with the owner. The crops were poor and they would have starved had they not been able to do a little fishing in the summer; between ploughing and sowing, there was time to set a few nets. The family consisted of old Micoulin himself, a tough and rough old man with a swarthy, deeply-lines face who struck terror in his household; the mother, a tall woman broken down by long hours of working the land in the pitiless sun; a son who was serving on board the Arrogante; and Naïs who had been sent out to work in a tile-factory by her father, despite all the work she had to do in the home. The farmer's house, a tumbledown old cottage clinging to the cliff-face, rarely heard the cheerful sound of a laugh or a song. Micoulin was a taciturn old ogre, endlessly brooding over the vicissitudes of his life. The two women showed him the respect born of fear that wives and daughters owe to the head of the family in southern France. Almost the only sound that ever disturbed the peace and quiet of the house was the furious voice of the mother standing with arms akimbo bawling Naïs's name as soon as she had attempted to make herself scarce. The girl would hear her a good half mile off and have to come back, livid with suppressed anger.

In L'Estaque they called her 'the lovely Naïs'; but she was not a very happy girl. When she was already sixteen, her father, on the slightest pretext, would hit her in the face hard enough to make her nose bleed; and even now that she was turned twenty, she would have bruised shoulders for weeks on end as a result of her father's brutal treatment. He was not an unkind man but merely using his royal prerogative to enforce the strictest obedience, maintaining his legitimate right, inherited from the Roman paterfamilias, of life or death over his family. One day when, during a thrashing, Naïs had dared to lift a hand to defend herself, he had almost killed her. After such punishment Naïs was left inwardly boiling with rage: she would sit on the ground in some dark corner, dry-eyed, brooding over the indignity she had suffered. In her somber fury she would stay like this in silence for hours on end, turning over in her mind plans of vengeance that she would never put into effect. It was her own father's blood in her that was angrily rebelling, in the blind urge always to be on top. She would look scornfully at her cowed old mother trembling with fear as she humiliated herself before her father. She would often say: 'If I had a husband like that, I'd kill him?'

Naïs had even come to prefer being thrashed because at least it gave her a shaking-up; at other times her life was so narrow and restricted that she was consumed with boredom. Her father forbade her to go down to L'Estaque and kept her constantly busy on jobs up at La Blancarde; and even when there was nothing to do, he wanted to keep his eye on her. So she used to look forward impatiently to the month of September, for as soon as the owners moved in, Micoulin was obliged to relax his strict supervision, for Naïs used to run errands for Madame Rostand and was able to make up for the sort of life she led during the rest of the year.

One morning, old Micoulin had realized that this grown-up daughter of his could bring a couple of francs a day into the family. So he released her and packed her off to work in a tile-factory. Although the work was very hard, Naïs was delighted. She would set off in the morning for the other side of L'Estaque and stay there until evening, toiling away in the sun, turning over tiles so that they dried. It was a manual laborer's job and her hands became all rough; but she no longer felt her father on her back all the time; she could enjoy herself in the company of young men without constraint. And in this laborious job, she developed and turned into a beauty. In the hot sun, her face became a deep golden brown and her sturdy neck took on the thick appearance of a rich collar of amber; her jet-black hair grew thick and long, as though to protect her face from the whiplash of her curls; the constant bending and stretching gave her the strong and supple body of a young athlete; and indeed, when she straightened up amidst the red clay tiles spread out on the beaten earth, she looked like some antique Amazon, a terracotta statue suddenly brought into vigorous life by the flaming rays of the sun. When Micoulin saw that his daughter was becoming such a beauty, his beady little eyes started watching her like a hawk. She was too cheerful: he couldn't believe that it was natural for a girl to be so happy. And he promised himself to strangle any sweethearts whom he caught prowling round her skirts. However, although Naïs could have had dozens of sweethearts, she discouraged them and made fun of all the young men she met. Her only good friend was a hunchback who worked in the same tile-factory as herself, a little man who went by the name of Toine. He had been sent as a foundling from Aix and had been adopted by L'Estaque. This little Punch-like figure had a charming laugh and Naïs tolerated him because he was so gentle. She could twist him round her little finger and would often bully him to vent her bad temper after her father had given her a thrashing. In any case, Toine was of no importance; everybody made fun of him. Micoulin once said that he had no objection to his daughter's little hunchback; he knew her too well, she was too proud.

That year when Madame Rostand had moved into La Blancarde, she asked her tenant if he would lend her Naïs as one of her own maids was ill. It so happened that the tile-factory had laid off its workers at the time; moreover Micoulin, however harsh he might be towards his own family, was more forthcoming when it came to his landlord and would have given his consent even had the request for his daughter's services inconvenienced him. Monsieur Rostand had had to go to Paris to deal with some pressing business and Frédéric and his mother were left alone. During the first few days the young man had usually felt the need to take plenty of exercise; the fresh air would tempt him to go fishing with Micoulin, helping him to set or pull up his nets; or else he would go for long walks through the gorges that run down to L'Estaque. Then, after his initial burst of enthusiasm, he would lie day after day drowsing in the shade of the pine trees on the edge of the terrace, watching the monotonous blue sea and eventually growing bored. Generally a fortnight at La Blancarde was all he could stand. After that he would think up some excuse to slip away every morning into Marseilles.

The day after the owners had arrived, Micoulin called up to Frédéric's bedroom as soon as the sun was up. He was on his way to haul up his pots, those long wicker baskets with a narrow aperture used to catch fish that feed on the bottom. But the young man turned a deaf ear to the invitation; he did not seem tempted by the idea of going fishing. When he got up he settled himself under the pine trees, flat on his back, gazing up at the sky. His mother was surprised not to see him go off on one of his long excursions, from which he would return ravenous.

'Aren't you going out?' she asked him.

'No, mother,' he replied. 'As Papa's not here I'll stay and keep you company.'

Micoulin heard this reply and muttered in his dialect, 'Ah well, Monsieur Frédéric will soon be nipping off to Marseilles.'

However, Frédéric did not go into Marseilles. The week went by and still he lay flat on his back changing position only when the sun caught up with him. As a pretext, he took a book with him but he hardly glanced at it; more often than not, it lay unread on the baked earth among the dry pine needles. The young man did not even look at the sea; he kept his eye on the house, seemingly interested in the housework being performed by the maids as they kept coming and going all the time across the terrace; and when it was Naïs who went by, a glint of desire lit up in the young master's eye. Then Naïs would walk more slowly, swaying her hips as she did so without once looking in his direction.

This little game lasted for several days. In his mother's presence, Frédéric would treat Naïs almost rudely if she was serving clumsily; and when he rebuked her, the girl coyly lowered her eyes, almost as if enjoying his irritation.

One day at lunch, Naïs broke a salad bowl. Frédéric flared up, 'What a stupid girl!' he exclaimed. 'What on earth does she think she's up to?'

And he stood up in a rage, saying that his trousers were completely ruined. In fact, a drop of oil had fallen on to his knee; but he made a tremendous fuss, 'What are you staring at?' he shouted. 'Don't just stand there! Bring me a napkin and some water.'

Naïs dipped the corner of a table napkin into a cup of water and knelt down in front of Frédéric to rub out the stain.

'Don't bother,' Madame Rostand was saying. 'There's no need.'

But the girl kept hold of her master's leg and continued to rub it vigorously with her splendid strong arms. He still kept on scolding her.

'I've never seen such carelessness,' he said roughly. 'She couldn't have broken the salad bowl nearer to me if she'd tried . . . Our china wouldn't last long in Aix if she was serving us there!'

His harsh reaction was so disproportionate to the fault that when Naïs had left the room, Madame Rostand felt compelled to expostulate and calm him down:

'What have you got against the poor girl? Anyone would think that you can't stand her. Please try to treat her more politely. Remember that you used to play together as children and she's not like an ordinary servant.'

'Well, she just gets on my nerves, that's all,' replied Frédéric, making sure that he sounded very fierce.

That evening, after dark, Naïs and Frédéric met at the end of the terrace where they could not be seen. They had not yet exchanged a single word alone. Nobody in the house could hear them. In the warm, still air a scent of resin drifted down from the pine trees. In a gentle whisper, falling back into the same familiar way of speaking they had used as children, she asked, 'Why did you lose your temper with me like that, Frédéric? You were horrible.'

His reply was to take hold of her hands, draw her towards him and kiss her full on the lips. She did not protest and then went away, leaving him behind; he sat down on the parapet because he did not want his mother to see him in such a state of excitement. Ten minutes later, Naïs was serving at table with her usual air of rather aloof composure.

Frédéric and Naïs had made no arrangement to see each other again but one night they met at the edge of the terrace under an olive tree, at the top of the cliff; during the meal they had several times looked at each other with burning insistence. It was a warm night and Frédéric had remained standing at his window, smoking cigarettes as he peered into the darkness. At about one o'clock he saw a dim shape slipping along the terrace. He climbed down to a shed roof and then, with the help of some long poles lying in a corner, he clambered down on to the terrace, taking care not to risk waking his mother. Once on the ground he walked over to the old olive tree, certain that Naïs was waiting for him.

'Is that you?' he asked in a low voice.

'Yes.' She replied simply.

He sat down beside her in the short grass and put his arm round her waist. She rested her head on his shoulder. For a moment they did not speak. The old olive tree with its gnarled trunk sheltered them under its leafy roof. In front of them the sea stretched out black and still under the stars. At the end of the bay Marseilles lay hidden in a haze; only the Planier lighthouse on the left kept shining out every minute, its yellow beam piercing the night and then vanishing; and there seemed something gentle and tender in this light that continually disappeared on the horizon only suddenly to return.

'Is your father away, then?' asked Frédéric.

'I climbed out of the window,' she replied in her deep voice.

They did not speak of their love; it had deep roots in their childhood and now they could remember playing together when desire was already stirring in their childish games. Lovingly they began to stroke each other; nothing seemed more natural. They could not put their feelings into words: all they wanted was to make love. He found her lovely and exciting with her country tan and earthy smell; she felt the pride of a girl so often thrashed who was becoming the mistress of her young master. She gave herself to him. When the couple climbed back into their rooms the same way as they had come, day was beginning to break.

It was a wonderful month. There was not a drop of rain and the blue satin of the sky was not speckled by a single cloud. The sun rose pink and glassy and set in a golden haze. Yet it was never too hot, for the sea breeze rose and died away with the sun; then followed the nights, deliciously cool and fragrant with the scent of herbs which, warmed during the day, perfumed the darkness.

The countryside round L'Estaque is superb. Broad promontories of rock project on each side of the bay while the offshore islands seem to block the horizon, turning the sea into a vast lagoon, intensely blue in color when the weather is fine. In the distance, at the foot of the mountains, lies Marseilles with its houses rising in tiers on the foothills; in clear weather you can see from L'Estaque the grey jetty of La Joliette with the delicate mastwork of the ships in the harbor; further back can be seen the house fronts set in clumps of trees, and the dazzling white chapel of Notre Dame de la Garde on a height towering up to the sky. And from Marseilles the whole coast curves round, cut by wide inlets before it reaches L'Estaque and fringed with factories which now and then belch forth long plumes of smoke. When the sun is at its Zenith, the sea, looking almost black, seems to be slumbering between the tow white rocky promontories, set off with warmer tints of brown and yellow. It is like some vast painting, a glimpse of a corner of the Orient rising up in the blinding, shimmering light.

But L'Estaque does not have only this outlook over the sea. The village is backed by mountains and crossed by roads which vanish into the midst of a jumble of fallen rocks. The Marseilles-Lyons railway line runs among the massive rocks, bridging ravines and suddenly penetrating into the rock itself, to emerge nearly three miles further on through the Nerthe tunnel, the longest in France. Nothing can rival these wild and majestic gorges which snake through the hills, the narrow tracks at the foot of precipitous chasms whose arid slopes are planted with pine trees, the walls of rock tinged with shades of rust and blood. Sometimes these gorges open out and you can see a tiny olive grove in the hollow of a valley or an isolated house hiding behind its painted front and closed shutters. Then there are the tracks full of brambles, impenetrable thickets, tumbled boulders, dried up torrents, every imaginable feature to surprise you as you walk through the scrub. And on top, above the black line of pines, the endless silken ribbon of the delicate blue sky.

There is also the narrow strip of coast hemmed in between rock and sea, the red earth where the tile-factories, the main industry of the region, have excavated immense holes to extract clay. The soil is broken up and full of gullies, sparsely planted with a few stunted trees which seem as if their source of life has dried up under a searing gust of passion. Walking along the tracks you could imagine that you are on a layer of plaster in which you sink up to your ankles and the slightest breath of wind sends up clouds of dust which settle on the hedgerows. Little grey lizards lie drowsing at the foot of walls as hot as ovens while flights of chirping grasshoppers, crackling like sparks, flee from the furnace of scorched grass. In the heavy, motionless, slumbering noonday air the only sign of life is the monotonous chant of the cicadas.

For a whole month this countryside of fire and flame was the scene of the young couple's love. It was as if the torrid sky had set fire to their blood. For the first week they were content to meet at night under the same olive tree on the edge of the cliff. Their ecstasy was beyond words; and as the cool night calmed their frenzied lovemaking, they would sometimes lie with their faces and their burning hands turned towards the passing breeze which refreshed them like a mountain stream. Below them at the bottom of the cliff, the sea murmured its delight. The pungent smell of seaweed intoxicated them with desire. Then, as they lay in each other's arms, tired and contented, they would look across the water towards Marseilles glowing in the night and the red lights at the entrance to the harbor reflected blood-red in the sea; the flickering gaslights marking the long sinuous line of the suburbs to right and left; in the middle, over the town, other lights sparkled and glittered while the gardens on Bonaparte Hill showed up as two twinkling lines which sloped up and curved over the skyline. All these lights on the far side of the sleeping bay seemed to be illuminating some dream town that would vanish with the dawn. And the vast bowl of the sky above the dark confused shapes on the horizon cast a spell over them, making them stir uneasily and clasp each other more tightly. The stars overhead flooded them with their radiance; in Provence, on such clear nights as these, the constellations seem like living fire. Trembling at the spectacle of these vast spaces, they would lower their eyes and look only at the single star of the Planier lighthouse, watching its friendly beam affectionately as they once more sought each other's lips.

But one night they found themselves being watched by the round face of the full moon on the horizon. A trail of fire shone over the sea as if the golden scales of a giant fish, some deepwater eel, were gliding in endless rings over the surface and a yellow half-light dimmed the lights of Marseilles as it bathed the hills and inlets of the bay. As the moon rose higher, the light grew brighter and the shadows sharper. This silent witness of their lovemaking embarrassed them. They became afraid that they might be caught if they stayed too close to La Blancarde and next time they met they climbed over a piece of broken-down wall and went in search of all the other hiding-places which the countryside offered. First they took refuge in a disused tile factory: the ruined shed had a cellar underneath in which the mouth of two kilns were still gaping open; but this hole in the ground depressed them, for they preferred to feel the open sky above them. So they explored the red clay quarries and discovered delightful little nooks only a few yards square where the only sound to be heard was the barking of the dogs guarding the homesteads. They went even further afield, straying along the rocky coast going towards Niolon; they also followed the narrow tracks at the bottom of the gorges, looking for caves and remote gullies. For a whole fortnight their nights of love were full of playful adventure. The moon had gone and it was dark once more; but La Blancarde now seemed to have become too small to hold their love, they needed the whole length and breadth of the land to consummate it.

One night as they were walking along a path above L'Estaque, making for the gorge of the Nerthe, they thought they heard a muffled footstep following them behind a small spinney of pine trees beside the path. They stopped and listened uneasily.

'Can you hear that sound?' Frédéric asked.

'Yes, it must be a stray dog,' said Naïs in a low voice.

They went on; but at the next bend in the path, when the spinney came to an end, they plainly saw a black figure slip behind some rocks. It was certainly a human being but of an odd shape, like a hunchback. Naïs gave a slight exclamation.

'Stay here,' she said quickly.

She ran off in search of the shadowy figure. Soon Frédéric heard a rapid whispering. Then she came back, a trifle pale but calm.

'What was it?' he asked.

'Nothing,' she replied.

Then, after a moment's hesitation, she went on:

'If you hear footsteps, don't be scared. It's Toine. You know, the hunchback. He wants to keep guard over us.'

In fact, Frédéric had sometimes felt that they were being followed by a shadowy figure providing a sort of protection around them. Naïs had several times tried to chase Toine away; but the poor creature was asking only to be her watchdog: he wouldn't show himself, he wouldn't make a sound, why not let him do what he wanted? Ever since then, had the lovers listened during their passionate embraces in ruined tile-factories, in the middle of disused quarries or in the depths of remote gorges, they would have detected nearby the sound of stifled sobs. It was their watchdog Toine, crying with his face buried in his hands.

And not only did they want their nights to themselves; they were growing bolder and prepared to take advantage of every opportunity. Often if they met in a corridor or in one of the rooms of La Blancarde, they would exchange a long kiss. Even at meal times when she was serving and he had asked for some bread or a table napkin, he would manage to squeeze her fingers. The straitlaced Madame Rostand noticed nothing and still kept accusing her son of being too strict towards his former playmate. One day she nearly caught them but, hearing the rustle of her dress, the girl quickly knelt down and started dusting off her young master's shoes with her handkerchief.

They enjoyed a thousand and one other little pleasures. After dinner, in the cool of the evening, Madame Rostand often felt like a walk; she would take her son's arm and they would go down to L'Estaque, with Naïs carrying her shawl, just in case. The three of them would walk down to watch the return of the sardine fishermen. Out at sea, lamps were bobbing up and down and soon they could pick out the black shapes of the boats as they slowly rowed in with a muffled creaking of oars. On the days when the catch had been plentiful, there were shouts of joy as the women ran up with their baskets and the three-man crew of each boat began to empty the nets which had been piled up under the thwarts. The nets looked like a sort of broad dark ribbon spangled with silver; the sardines caught in the mesh by the gills were still threshing about, glinting like metal strips before dropping into the baskets like a shower of silver coins in the pale light of the lamps. Madame Rostand would often remain looking at a boat, fascinated by the spectacle; she would let go of her son's arm and stay talking to the fishermen while Frédéric, standing beside Naïs outside the circle of light, would squeeze her wrists with all his might.

Meanwhile, as usual, old Micoulin remained as silent as a dogged, wily animal, whether he was going off to do some fishing or coming to do some digging. But recently, beneath this same sly air, there was an uneasy look in his beady grey eyes. Without saying a word he would keep casting sidelong glances at his daughter. She seemed changed and there was something about her that he could sense but not explain. One day when she dared to stand up to him, he struck her so hard that he split her lip and that evening Frédéric, noticing as he kissed her that her lip was swollen, sharply questioned her.

'Oh, it's nothing, just a slap my father gave me,' she answered.

Her voice was grim; but when Frédéric showed annoyance and said he would do something about it, she replied, 'No, let him be, I can deal with it . . . Don't worry, it won't last for ever!'

She never referred to her father's harsh treatment of her but on the days when he had been hitting her; she clung to her lover more passionately than ever, as though taking revenge on the old man.

For the last three weeks, Naïs had been slipping out almost every night. At first she had been extremely cautious but with increasing confidence she had grown more reckless. When she realized that her father suspected something, she again became cautious and on two successive nights failed to turn up as arranged. Her mother had been telling her that her husband had been unable to sleep at night: instead, he would get up and wander around the house. But on the third day, Frédéric's beseeching look made her throw caution to the winds. She came down to the terrace at about eleven o'clock, promising herself not to stay more than an hour; she was hoping that her father would be so sound asleep in the early part of the night that he would not hear her.

Frédéric was waiting for her under the olive trees. Without mentioning her fears, she refused to go further afield: she felt too tired, she said, which happened to be true since, unlike Frédéric, should could not sleep during the day. They lay down in their usual spot above the sea, facing the lights of Marseilles. The Planier lighthouse was casting its friendly beam and as she lay watching it, Naïs fell asleep on Frédéric's shoulder. He did not move and gradually, overcome by fatigue, his own eyes closed. Clasped in each other's arms, his breath mingled with hers.

Not a sound could be heard but the chirping of the green grasshoppers. The sea was sleeping, like the lovers. Then a dark shape came out of the shadows and approached. It was Micoulin who had been awakened by the creaking of a window and had found Naïs's bedroom empty. He armed himself with a hatchet, just in case, and left the house. When he saw a black patch under the olive tree, he gripped the handle of the hatchet more firmly. But the two young people did not move and he was able to come right up to them, bend down and look at their faces. As he recognized the young master, a stifled cry escaped him. But he could not kill him like that: the blood would spurt out on to the ground and give him away. The price was too high.

He straightened up; two deep creases furrowed the corners of his mouth while his leathery old face was set in grim determination and suppressed fury. But a peasant can't kill his master openly because even when dead and buried, the master is still the stronger. So, shaking his head, old Micoulin crept stealthily away, leaving the two lovers to sleep on.

When Naïs came in shortly before dawn, very anxious at having been out so long, she found the window just as she had left it. At breakfast, as Micoulin looked at her chewing her piece of dry bread, he showed no sign of emotion. She felt reassured; her father did not know anything.

'Aren't you interested in going fishing these days, Monsieur Frédéric?' old Micoulin asked one evening.

Madame Rostand was sitting on the terrace in the shade of the pine trees embroidering a handkerchief while her son was reclining nearby, idly tossing pebbles.

'No, not really,' the young man replied. 'I'm getting lazy.'

'You're missing a lot,' the farmer went on. 'Yesterday our pots were full of fish. You can catch anything you like at the moment . . . It'd give you something to do. Why not come out with me tomorrow morning?'

He seemed so friendly that Frédéric, thinking of Naïs and not wanting to offend him, finally agreed.

'All right, I'll come . . . But I warn you, you'll have to wake me up. At five in the morning I'm still sleeping like a log.'

Madame Rostand had stopped her embroidering and was looking a trifle uneasy. 'And above all, mind you take care,' she said. 'I'm always scared when you're out in a boat.'

Next morning, when old Micoulin called up to Frédéric, his window remained firmly shut, so the farmer said to his daughter, in a voice in which she failed to detect the sarcasm, 'You go up, Naïs . . . Perhaps he'll hear you.'

So it was Naïs who woke Frédéric up. Still half asleep, he tried to pull her into his warm bed but, quickly returning his kiss, she slipped out of his reach. Ten minutes later the young man appeared, dressed in a grey linen suit. Old Micoulin was sitting on the parapet of the terrace, waiting patiently.

'It's quite cool already,' he said. 'You'd better bring a scarf.'

Naïs went upstairs to fetch one. Then the two men went off down the steep steps leading to the sea while Naïs stood looking after them. When they reached the bottom, old Micoulin glanced up at Naïs and again two deep furrows creased the corners of his mouth.

The mistral, that terrible wind from the north-east, had been blowing for the last five days. The previous evening it had died down but at sunrise it had started to blow again, although not very strongly at first. At this early hour, the angry sea, whipped up by the gusty wind, was a deep mottled blue and under the slanting rays of the rising sun, the crest of each wave was tipped with fire. The sky was practically white, like a piece of crystal. In the far distance, Marseilles could be seen so clearly that you might have counted the windows of the houses, while the rocks round the bay were all gleaming in a most delicate shade of pink.

"It's going to be rough coming back,' observed Frédéric.

'Could be,' grunted Micoulin laconically.

He was rowing in silence and did not turn round. The young man looked for a moment at his bent back, his thoughts turning to Naïs; all he could see was the nape of the old man's weather-beaten neck and the two red lobes of his ears, pierced with gold rings. Then he leant sideways and looked with interest down into the sea which was racing past their boat. The water was becoming ruffled and the only things he could see were long wisps of seaweed floating on the surface, barely visible, like some drowned woman's hair. He felt sad and even a trifle frightened.

'I say, Micoulin,' he said after a long pause. 'The wind seems to be getting up. Let's be careful. You know I swim like a lead soldier.'

'All right, I know that,' replied Micoulin in his flat voice.

And he kept on steadily rowing. The boat was beginning to bob up and down and the little fire-tipped tops of the waves had turned into crests of foam blown up into spray by the gusts of wind. Frédéric did not want to show that he was scared; but he did not feel at all easy in his mind and would have given a good deal to be closer to the shore. Becoming impatient he called out, "Where the devil have you put your pots today? Have we got to go to Algiers?'

But old Micoulin replied in the same phlegmatic way, 'We're nearly there, we're nearly there.' He suddenly let go of his oars, stood up and looked towards the shore for his two landmarks; he then had to row on for another five minutes before he reached the centre of the cork buoys marking the position of his pots. Then, before starting to haul them up, he looked back for a few seconds towards La Blancarde; Frédéric followed his gaze and could clearly see a patch of white underneath the pines. It was Naïs' pale dress; she was still leaning over the parapet of the terrace.

"How many pots have you got?' asked Frédéric.

'Thirty-five. We mustn't be too long.'

Micoulin caught hold of the nearest float and heaved up the first basket. The sea was very deep indeed here and there seemed to be no end to the rope. Finally the pot surfaced, together with the large stone which held it on the bottom; and as soon as it was out of the water, three fish started flapping about like birds in a cage. It was like the sound of wings beating. There was nothing in the second pot but in the third there was a spiny lobster violently flipping its tail, a fish not caught very often. Seeing this, Frédéric became quite excited and forgot his fears; he leaned over the side of the boat, his heart beating fast as he waited for the next pot to appear. Each time he heard the sound of wings beating, he experienced the same feeling as a sportsman who has just bagged a bird. Meanwhile all the thirty-five pots were hoisted up one by one, streaming with water, into the boat. There were at least fifteen pounds of fish, a splendid haul for the Bay of Marseilles which for various reasons, chiefly through using nets with too fine a mesh, had been considerably depleted in recent years.

"That's that,' said Micoulin. 'Now let's get back.'

He carefully stowed his pots in the stern. But Frédéric again became rather anxious when he saw that the old man was preparing to hoist the sail and asked whether it wouldn't be wiser to row back, in view of the weather. Micoulin merely shrugged: he knew what he was doing. And before finally hoisting the sail, he cast a glance once more towards La Blancarde. Naïs was still there, in her white dress.

Then, with the suddenness of a clap of thunder, the disaster occurred.

Later on, when trying to explain to himself what had happened, Frédéric remembered that the boat had been caught in a violent squall of wind and immediately capsized. And he could recall nothing else, only a sensation of extreme cold and an overwhelming feeling of terror. He owed his life to a miracle: he had been thrown on to the large sail which held him up. Seeing the accident, some fishermen came to the rescue of him and of old Micoulin, who was already striking out for the shore.

Madame Rostand was still asleep and they did not tell her of her son's narrow escape. Dripping with water, Frédéric and Micoulin were met at the foot of the terrace by Naïs who had witnessed the dramatic incident from afar.

'Just my luck,' the old man was shouting.' We'd picked up our pots and were just starting back . . . You can't win!'

Naïs was as pale as a sheet; she glared at her father.

'Yes, that's right,' she said, in a low voice. 'You can't win . . . but if you yaw with the wind behind you know what happens . . . '

Micoulin flared up.

'Come on, you idle good-for-nothing! What do you think you're doing? Can't you see that Monsieur Frédéric is shivering? Give him a hand quickly!'

A day in bed was all that Frédéric needed to recover. He told his mother that he'd had a sick headache. Next day he found a very grim-faced Naïs. She turned a deaf ear to any suggestion of meeting but when they happened to run across each other in the hall one evening, she spontaneously hugged him and gave him a passionate kiss. She never confided her suspicions in Frédéric but from then on she kept guard over him. Then, after a week, she began to have doubts. Her father was following his normal routine and even seemed gentler than usual, for he struck her less often.

One of the Rostands'outings every year was to go and have a bouillabaisse on the beach in a rocky cove. Afterwards, as there were partridges in the hills, the men of the party would go off on a shoot. This year Madame Rostand decided to take Naïs along to help serve the meal and she refused to listen to the objections of her father whose displeasure was plainly shown in the deep furrows of his brutal-looking face.

They left early. The weather was perfect, neither too hot nor too cold. The deep blue sea stretched out as smooth as a mirror beneath the golden rays of the sun; where there were currents, the blue was ruffled and took on metallic purple tints, while where it was still, the blue was paler, milky and transparent, like a piece of shot-silk stretching far out to the glassy horizon. The boat glided gently through the water, as calm as a mill-pond.

They landed on a narrow beach at the mouth of a gorge and picked a spot on a patch of sunburnt turf to serve as a picnic table.

The preparation of the bouillabaisse was quite a ceremony. First, Micoulin went off by himself to haul up his pots, which he had set the day before. By the time he returned, Naïs had already gathered enough thyme, wild lavender and dry twigs to make a good big fire. Today it was the old man's job to make the bouillabaisse, that traditional fish-soup of Provence the recipe for which was passed from father to son amongst the fishermen along the coast. His was an awesome bouillabaisse, extremely peppery and giving off an overpowering smell of crushed garlic. The Rostands watched its preparation with amused interest.

'Well, Micoulin,' said Madame Rostand, condescending to make a joke for once in honor of the occasion, 'is it going to be up to last year's?'

Micoulin seemed in the best of spirits. First he cleaned the fish in sea-water while Naïs took a big pan our of the boat. The actual cooking took hardly any time at all: the fish was put into the pan and covered in water, with onions, olive oil—half a glassful—garlic, a handful of pepper and a tomato; then the pan was put on the fire, a blazing fire on which you could have roasted a whole sheep. The fishermen say that the secret of making a bouillabaisse lies in the heat; the pan must be completely hidden in the flames. Meanwhile the farmer was solemnly cutting slices of bread into a salad bowl. After half an hour he poured the liquid on to the bread and served the fish separately. The secret of making a bouillabaisse lies in the heat; the pan must be completely hidden in the flames. Meanwhile the farmer was solemnly cutting slices of bread into a salad bowl. After half an hour he poured the liquid on to the bread and served the fish separately.

'Well, that's it,' said Micoulin. 'Remember that it's got to be eaten piping hot.' And the bouillabaisse was eaten to the accompaniment of the customary witticisms.

'I say, Micoulin, how much gunpowder did you put into it?'

'It's first-rate but you need a cast-iron throat.' He sat quietly eating, gulping down a slice of bread in each mouthful. He also showed how flattered he felt at lunching with his landlords by sitting slightly to one side.

After lunch, everyone rested until the sun had lost a little of its heat. Meanwhile the dazzling red-spattered rocks were mottled by the deep shadows of the dark, bushy, evergreen oaks and the pinewoods marched up the slopes of the gorge in regular columns like an army of tiny soldiers. The air was hot and heavy with silence.

Madame Rostand had brought along her everlasting piece of embroidery which never left her hands. Naïs was sitting beside her watching with apparent interest the movement of her needles. But she was keeping a close watch on her father. He was stretched out on the ground a few yards away, having a snooze. Frédéric was asleep; too, a little further away, his face hidden under the turned-down brim of his straw-hat.

At about four o'clock, they woke up. Micoulin swore that he knew of a covey of partridges at the far end of the gorge. He'd seen them again only three days ago. Hearing this, Frédéric allowed himself to be tempted and they both picked up their guns.

'Now please take great care,' called Madame Rostand. 'If your foot slips, you can easily shoot yourself.'

'Yes, it does happen,' said Micoulin placidly.

They went off and disappeared behind some rocks. Naïs suddenly stood up and followed them at a distance, murmuring, 'I'll go and see as well.'

Instead of keeping to the path, when she reached the end of the gorge she took to the bushes and went quickly along to the left, taking care not to set any boulders rolling. At last she caught sight of Frédéric standing at a bend in the track on the other side of the gorge. They had probably already flushed the partridges because he moved on quickly, bending forward with his gun at the ready. Her father was not in sight; but then suddenly she saw him close by, on the same slope as herself; he was crouching down and seemed to be waiting for something. Twice he put his gun to his shoulder. If the partridges were to fly between him and Frédéric, the two might easily hit each other as they fired. Slipping from bush to bush, Naïs finally reached a position directly behind the old man and stood there, anxiously waiting.

Minutes went by. Opposite them, Frédéric had vanished in a dip in the ground. Then he came into sight again and stood for an instant, not moving. Once again, still crouching down, Micoulin took careful aim at the young man. But Naïs leaped forward and kicked up the barrel of the gun which went off with a loud report that reverberated round the gorge.

The old man sprang to his feet and when he saw Naïs, he seized his gun by the barrel as if to brain her with the butt. White as a sheet, the girl stood her ground, her eyes flaming with fury. He did not dare to hit her but merely muttered in dialect:

"Don't worry, I'll get him yet!'

When Micoulin had fired, the partridges had flown off and Frédéric had brought down a brace of them. The Rostands made their way back to

La Blancarde. Their tenant was pulling on the oars, still with the same calm, dogged look on his brutal face.

September had come to an end. After a violent storm, the air had become much cooler, with heavy night dews. The days were drawing in and Naïs was firmly refusing to meet Frédéric at night on the excuse that she was too tired and that they would catch cold lying on the rain-soaked ground. But as she came over to the house at about six o'clock every morning and Madame Rostand rarely stirred until some three hours later, she would go up to the young man's room and stay there for a while, listening all the time for the slightest sound through the door, which she always left open.

This was the period of their love when she showed her greatest tenderness. She would hold Frédéric close, slipping her hand round his neck to bring his face near to hers and look at him passionately with her eyes full of tears. She always had the feeling that she would never see him again. Then she would quickly cover his face with kisses as if promising that she would be able to defend him.

'What's wrong with Naïs?' Madame Rostand kept asking. 'She looks different every day.' And indeed she was losing weight, her cheeks were becoming hollow and her eyes no longer sparkled. There were long periods when she would sit saying nothing and then she would suddenly start up like someone waking from a dream.

'If you're not feeling well, girl,' Madame Rostand kept telling her, 'you must look after yourself.'

'Oh no, ma'am, I'm very well and very happy. I've never been so happy.'

One morning as they were checking the linen, she ventured to ask, 'Will you be staying on late at La Blancarde this year?'

'Until the end of October,' replied Madame Rostand.

And Naïs stood for a moment with a faraway look in her eyes and then, without realizing that she was speaking out loud, she exclaimed 'Still three more weeks!'

A constant struggle was taking place inside her. She longed to keep Frédéric close to her all the time but felt continually tempted to cry out: 'Go away!' She was going to lose him; from their very first meeting she had told herself that their season of love would never return. One evening, when she was feeling particularly depressed, she asked herself whether she should not let Frédéric be killed by her father, so that he would never go with any other woman; but the thought of Frédéric, with his soft white skin and genteel ways, so much more like a little lady than herself, lying dead, was unbearable. No, she would save him without his knowing anything about it; he would quickly forget her but she would be happy in the knowledge that he was alive. In the morning she would often say to him, 'Don't go out; don't go in a boat, the weather's treacherous!' At other times she would advise him to go away from La Blancarde.

'You must be bored; you won't love me any more. Go and spend a few days in town.'

He was bewildered at these changes in her mood, and he was fining his little country girl less lovely now that her face was becoming thin and drawn and he was beginning to be satiated by the violence of their lovemaking. He was hankering after the eau-de-Cologne and face powder of the tarts of Aix and Marseilles.

Her father's words kept ringing in her ears: 'I'll get him yet! I'll get him yet!' She would wake up in the night dreaming that shots were being fired. Her nerves were all on edge and she would cry out if a stone slipped from under her feet. Whenever he was out of her sight, she felt worried about 'Monsieur Frédéric'. And the most terrible thing of all was that from morning till night she could hear Micoulin doggedly muttering to himself: 'I'll get him yet!' He had made no further reference to Frédéric nor said a word nor made the slightest movement. But for Naïs, the old man's eyes, his every gesture, his whole demeanor told her that he would kill his young master at the first opportunity, when there was no risk of being brought to justice. And afterwards it would be Naïs's turn. In the meantime, he kicked her about like some animal that had misbehaved.

'Is your father still as horrible as ever?' Frédéric asked her one day, as he lay smoking a cigarette in bed while she bustled to and fro tidying his room.

'Yes,' she answered. 'He's going out of his mind.'

And she showed him her legs, black and blue with bruises. Then she muttered under her breath the words that she often used, 'It won't go on for ever.'

During the first few days of October, she seemed more depressed than ever. She was absent-minded and her lips kept moving as if she was talking to herself. On several occasions Frédéric saw her standing at the top of the cliff apparently looking at the pine trees around her and trying to measure the depth to the bottom. A few days later he came upon her picking figs with the hunchback Toine in a remote corner of the property. Toine used to come and help Micoulin when there was too much to do on the farm.

He was standing under the fig tree with Naïs perched on a big branch making fun of him by shouting to him to open his mouth and then throwing figs at him which squashed all over his face. The poor creature was opening his mouth and closing his eyes in an ecstasy of delight with an expression of sheer bliss on his big moon-face. Frédéric could hardly feel jealous, of course, but he could not resist the temptation of pulling her leg.

'Toine would give his right arm for us,' she replied sharply. 'You mustn't be unkind to him, we might need him.' The hunchback continued to come every day to La Blancarde. He was working on top of the cliff, digging out a trench to carry water to one end of the property where they were trying to establish a vegetable garden. Sometimes Naïs would go and watch him and there would be a lively conversation between the two. He dawdled so much over his work that in the end Micoulin called him a lazy good-for-nothing and hacked him on the shins, as he did his daughter.

There had been two days of rain. Frédéric was due to return to Aix the following week and had agreed to go out on one last fishing expedition with Micoulin before leaving. Seeing Naïs turn as white as a sheet, he smiled and added that this time he wouldn't choose a day when the mistral was blowing. So, realizing that he was leaving so soon, the girl agreed to have one more meeting with him at night; they met on the terrace at about one o'clock. The rain had washed the soil and a pervasive odor of cool greenery hung in the air. When this dried-up countryside is thoroughly soaked, the colors and scents take on an extraordinary intensity: the red earth bleeds, the pine trees glitter like emeralds and the white rocks gleam like freshly laundered linen. But at night the lovers could smell only the overpowering scent of thyme and lavender.

Force of habit led them towards the olive trees and Frédéric was just about to make for the one under which they had first made love when Naïs, as if suddenly remembering something, dragged him away from the edge saying in a trembling voice, 'No, not there!'

'What's the matter?' he enquired.

At first, she had difficulty in finding words; then she said that after the heavy rains they had had yesterday, the cliff was not safe. She added, 'Last year there was a landslide quite close to here.'

They sat down further away under another olive tree. Naïs seemed uneasy as they lay in each other's arms. All at once she burst into tears but refused to say what had upset her. Then she became silent and cold and when Frédéric teased her about the way she now seemed bored with him, she flung herself wildly into his arms and said in a whisper, 'You mustn't say that sort of thing, I love you too much. But I'm not very well, you know. And then, this is the end for us, you'll be going away . . . Oh God, it's the end!'

He vainly tried to comfort her: he'd be coming back sometimes and they'd have another two months to look forward to next autumn; but she kept shaking her head; she could feel that this was the end. Finally they lapsed into an embarrassed silence and lay looking at the sea with Marseilles twinkling in the distance and the solitary Planier lighthouse now seeming to be shining sadly, all alone; gradually this vast panorama filled them with melancholy. When he left her at about three o'clock, he could feel her shivering, icy-cold, as he again took her into his arms and kissed her on the lips.

That night Frédéric could not sleep. He read until dawn and then, restless from lack of sleep, when day broke he went over to his window. At that very moment old Micoulin was on his way to row out to inspect his lobster pots. As he was passing along the terrace, he looked up, 'Well, Monsieur Frédéric, not coming out with me this morning?' he asked.

'No, not today, Micoulin,' Frédéric called back. 'I've slept too badly. Let's go tomorrow.'

The farmer trudged off; he had to go down and fetch his boat at the foot of the cliff, right under the olive tree where he had caught his daughter and Frédéric together. When he had vanished from sight, Frédéric turned his gaze and was amazed to see Toine already at work: the hunchback was near the olive tree using his mattock to repair the trench that had been damaged by the heavy rains. The air was cool and it was pleasant standing at the window. The young man went back into his room to roll himself a cigarette; but as he was making his way to the window again, he heard a terrible noise, like a clap of thunder. He rushed to the window.

It was a landslide. All he saw was Toine jumping clear in a cloud of red dust, waving his mattock. At the edge of the precipice the olive tree was slipping down out of sight and dramatically plunging into the sea. A column of foam spouted upwards. At the same time a dreadful cry rent the air. And then Frédéric saw Naïs who had dashed to the side and, bracing herself on her arms, was leaning far out over the parapet to discover what had happened down below. She hung there suspended with her wrists as if cemented to the stonework. But she must have sensed that someone was watching her, for she turned her head and, seeing Frédéric, shouted, 'My father! My father!'

An hour later they found the horribly mutilated body of old Micoulin under the pile of boulders. Toine was feverishly explaining how he had nearly been carried away and everybody agreed that a trench should not have been dug there because of the danger of percolating water. Old Madame Micoulin wept bitterly; Naïs followed her father's coffin to the churchyard dry-eyed; her lids were red but she had not been able to shed a single tear.

The day after the disaster Madame Rostand insisted on returning to Aix. Frédéric was very glad to go, too, now that his lovemaking had been disturbed by the tragedy; anyway, country girls were definitely not a patch of local tarts. He began to lead his old life again. Touched by his filial devotion at La Blancarde, his mother now allowed him greater freedom, so he spent a pleasant winter. He arranged for some charming ladies of the town to come and visit him from Marseilles, putting them up in a room that he had rented in the suburbs. He spent nights away from home and did not return to the cold family mansion in the Rue du Collège unless his presence seemed absolutely indispensable; he had hopes that his life would flow on in this delightful manner for ever.

At Easter time, Monsieur Rostand had to go to La Blancarde. Frédéric found an excuse not to go with him. When the solicitor returned, he said at lunch, 'Naïs is getting married.'

'Not really!' Frédéric exclaimed, unable to believe his ears.

'And you'll never guess who to,' Monsieur Rostand continued. 'She gave me all sorts of good reasons for it.'

Naïs was marrying the hunchback Toine. In this way, there would be no change at La Blancarde: Toine would be kept on as the tenant; he had been looking after the property ever since old Micoulin's death.

The young man listened with an embarrassed smile. And then he too agreed that it was an arrangement that suited everyone.

'Naïs has begun to look quite old and ugly,' went on Monsieur Rostand. 'I didn't recognize her. It's extraordinary how quickly they go to see, these girls living by the sea. She used to be very good-looking, young Naïs.'

'I suppose so. Just a flash in the pan,' said Frédéric, and calmly finished off his cutlet.

THE MILLER'S DAUGHTER

CHAPTER I
THE BETROTHAL

Pere Merlier's mill, one beautiful summer evening, was arranged for a grand fete. In the courtyard were three tables, placed end to end, which awaited the guests. Everyone knew that Francoise, Merlier's daughter, was that night to be betrothed to Dominique, a young man who was accused of idleness but whom the fair sex for three leagues around gazed at with sparkling eyes, such a fine appearance had he.

Pere Merlier's mill was pleasing to look upon. It stood exactly in the center of Rocreuse, where the highway made an elbow. The village had but one street, with two rows of huts, a row on each side of the road; but at the elbow meadows spread out, and huge trees which lined the banks of the Morelle covered the extremity of the valley with lordly shade. There was not, in all Lorraine, a corner of nature more adorable. To the right and to the left thick woods, centenarian forests, towered up from gentle slopes, filling the horizon with a sea of verdure, while toward the south the plain stretched away, of marvelous fertility, displaying as far as the eye could reach patches of ground divided by green hedges. But what constituted the special charm of Rocreuse was the coolness of that cut of verdure in the most sultry days of July and August. The Morelle descended from the forests of Gagny and seemed to have gathered the cold from the foliage beneath which it flowed for leagues; it brought with it the murmuring sounds, the icy and concentrated shade of the woods. And it was not the sole source of coolness: all sorts of flowing streams gurgled through the forest; at each step springs bubbled up; one felt, on following the narrow pathways, that there must exist subterranean lakes which pierced through beneath the moss and availed themselves of the smallest crevices at the feet of trees or between the rocks to burst forth in crystalline fountains. The whispering voices of these brooks were so numerous and so loud that they drowned the song of the bullfinches. It was like some enchanted park with cascades falling from every portion.

Below the meadows were damp. Gigantic chestnut trees cast dark shadows. On the borders of the meadows long hedges of poplars exhibited in lines their rustling branches. Two avenues of enormous plane trees stretched across the fields toward the ancient Chateau de Gagny, then a mass of ruins. In this constantly watered district the grass grew to an extraordinary height. It resembled a garden between two wooded hills, a natural garden, of which the meadows were the lawns, the giant trees marking the colossal flower beds. When the sun's rays at noon poured straight downward the shadows assumed a bluish tint; scorched grass slept in the heat, while an icy shiver passed beneath the foliage.

And there it was that Pere Merlier's mill enlivened with its ticktack a corner of wild verdure. The structure, built of plaster and planks, seemed as old as the world. It dipped partially in the Morelle, which rounded at that point into a transparent basin. A sluice had been made, and the water fell from a height of several meters upon the mill wheel, which cracked as it turned, with the asthmatic cough of a faithful servant grown old in the house. When Pere Merlier was advised to change it he shook his head, saying that a new wheel would be lazier and would not so well understand the work, and he mended the old one with whatever he could put his hands on: cask staves, rusty iron, zinc and lead. The wheel appeared gayer than ever for it, with its profile grown odd, all plumed with grass and moss. When the water beat upon it with its silvery flood it was covered with pearls; its strange carcass wore a sparkling attire of necklaces of mother-of-pearl.

The part of the mill which dipped in the Morelle had the air of a barbaric arch stranded there. A full half of the structure was built on piles. The water flowed beneath the floor, and deep places were there, renowned throughout the district for the enormous eels and crayfish caught in them. Below the fall the basin was as clear as a mirror, and when the wheel did not cover it with foam schools of huge fish could be seen swimming with the slowness of a squadron. Broken steps led down to the river near a stake to which a boat was moored. A wooden gallery passed above the wheel. Windows opened, pierced irregularly. It was a pell-mell of corners, of little walls, of constructions added too late, of beams and of roofs, which gave the mill the aspect of an old, dismantled citadel. But ivy had grown; all sorts of clinging plants stopped the too-wide chinks and threw a green cloak over the ancient building. The young ladies who passed by sketched Pere Merlier's mill in their albums.

On the side facing the highway the structure was more solid. A stone gateway opened upon the wide courtyard, which was bordered to the right and to the left by sheds and stables. Beside a well an immense elm covered half the courtyard with its shadow. In the background the building displayed the four windows of its second story, surmounted by a pigeon house. Pere Merlier's sole vanity was to have this front plastered every ten years. It had just received a new coating and dazzled the village when the sun shone on it at noon.

For twenty years Pere Merlier had been mayor of Rocreuse. He was esteemed for the fortune he had acquired. His wealth was estimated at something like eighty thousand francs, amassed sou by sou. When he married Madeleine Guillard, who brought him the mill as her dowry, he possessed only his two arms. But Madeleine never repented of her choice, so briskly did he manage the business. Now his wife was dead, and he remained a widower with his daughter Francoise. Certainly he might have rested, allowed the mill wheel to slumber in the moss, but that would have been too dull for him, and in his eyes the building would have seemed dead. He toiled on for pleasure.

Pere Merlier was a tall old man with a long, still face, who never laughed but who possessed, notwithstanding, a very gay heart. He had been chosen mayor because of his money and also on account of the imposing air he could assume during a marriage ceremony.

Francoise Merlier was just eighteen. She did not pass for one of the handsome girls of the district, as she was not robust. Up to her fifteenth year she had been even ugly.

The Rocreuse people had not been able to understand why the daughter of Pere and Mere Merlier, both of whom had always enjoyed excellent health, grew ill and with an air of regret. But at fifteen, though yet delicate, her little face became one of the prettiest in the world. She had black hair, black eyes, and was as rosy as a peach; her lips constantly wore a smile; there were dimples in her cheeks, and her fair forehead seemed crowned with sunlight. Although not considered robust in the district, she was far from thin; the idea was simply that she could not lift a sack of grain, but she would become plump as she grew older—she would eventually be as round and dainty as a quail. Her father's long periods of silence had made her thoughtful very young. If she smiled constantly it was to please others. By nature she was serious.

Of course all the young men of the district paid court to her, more on account of her eyes than her pretty ways. At last she made a choice which scandalized the community.

On the opposite bank of the Morelle lived a tall youth named Dominique Penquer. He did not belong to Rocreuse. Ten years before he had arrived from Belgium as the heir of his uncle, who had left him a small property upon the very border of the forest of Gagny, just opposite the mill, a few gunshots distant. He had come to sell this property, he said, and return home. But the district charmed him; it appeared, for he did not quit it. He was seen cultivating his little field, gathering a few vegetables upon which he subsisted. He fished and hunted; many times the forest guards nearly caught him and were on the point of drawing up legal papers against him. This free existence, the resources of which the peasants could not clearly discover, at length gave him a bad reputation. He was vaguely styled a poacher. At any rate, he was lazy, for he was often found asleep on the grass when he should have been at work. The hut he inhabited beneath the last trees on the edge of the forest did not seem at all like the dwelling of an honest young fellow. If he had had dealings with the wolves of the ruins of Gagny the old women would not have been the least bit surprised. Nevertheless, the young girls sometimes risked defending him, for this doubtful man was superb; supple and tall as a poplar, he had a very white skin, with flaxen hair and beard which gleamed like gold in the sun.

One fine morning Francoise declared to Pere Merlier that she loved Dominique and would never wed any other man.

It may well be imagined what a blow this was to Pere Merlier. He said nothing, according to his custom, but his face grew thoughtful and his internal gaiety no longer sparkled in his eyes. He looked gruff for a week. Francoise also was exceedingly grave. What tormented Pere Merlier was to find out how this rogue of a poacher had managed to fascinate his daughter. Dominique had never visited the mill. The miller watched and saw the gallant on the other side of the Morelle, stretched out upon the grass and feigning to be asleep. Francoise could see him from her chamber window. Everything was plain: they had fallen in love by casting sheep's eyes at each other over the mill wheel.

Another week went by. Francoise became more and more grave. Pere Merlier still said nothing. Then one evening he himself silently brought in Dominique. Francoise at that moment was setting the table. She did not seem astonished; she contented herself with putting on an additional plate, knife and fork, but the little dimples were again seen in her cheeks, and her smile reappeared. That morning Pere Merlier had sought out Dominique in his hut on the border of the wood.

There the two men had talked for three hours with doors and windows closed. What was the purport of their conversation no one ever knew. Certain it was, however, that Pere Merlier, on taking his departure, already called Dominique his son-in-law. Without doubt the old man had found the youth he had gone to seek a worthy youth in the lazy fellow who stretched himself out upon the grass to make the girls fall in love with him.

All Rocreuse clamored. The women at the doors had plenty to say on the subject of the folly of Pere Merlier, who had thus introduced a reprobate into his house. The miller let people talk on. Perhaps he remembered his own marriage. He was without a sou when he wedded Madeleine and her mill; this, however, had not prevented him from making a good husband. Besides, Dominique cut short the gossip by going so vigorously to work that all the district was amazed. The miller's assistant had just been drawn to serve as a soldier, and Dominique would not suffer another to be engaged. He carried the sacks, drove the cart, fought with the old mill wheel when it refused to turn, and all this with such good will that people came to see him out of curiosity. Pere Merlier had his silent laugh. He was excessively proud of having formed a correct estimate of this youth. There is nothing like love to give courage to young folks. Amid all these heavy labors Francoise and Dominique adored each other. They did not indulge in lovers' talks, but there was a smiling gentleness in their glances.

Up to that time Pere Merlier had not spoken a single word on the subject of marriage, and they respected this silence, awaiting the old man's will. Finally one day toward the middle of July he caused three tables to be placed in the courtyard, beneath the great elm, and invited his friends of Rocreuse to come in the evening and drink a glass of wine with him.

When the courtyard was full and all had their glasses in their hands, Pere Merlier raised his very high and said, "I have the pleasure to announce to you that Francoise will wed this young fellow here in a month, on Saint Louis's Day."

Then they drank noisily. Everybody smiled. But Pere Merlier, again lifting his voice, exclaimed, "Dominique, embrace your fiancée. It is your right."

They embraced, blushing to the tips of their ears, while all the guests laughed joyously. It was a genuine fete. They emptied a small cask of wine. Then when all were gone but intimate friends the conversation was carried on without noise. The night had fallen, a starry and cloudless night. Dominique and Francoise, seated side by side on a bench, said nothing.

An old peasant spoke of the war the emperor had declared against Prussia. All the village lads had already departed. On the preceding day troops had again passed through the place. There was going to be hard fighting.

"Bah!" said Pere Merlier with the selfishness of a happy man. "Dominique is a foreigner; he will not go to the war. And if the Prussians come here he will be on hand to defend his wife!"

The idea that the Prussians might come there seemed a good joke. They were going to receive a sound whipping, and the affair would soon be over.

"I have already seen them; I have already seen them," repeated the old peasant in a hollow voice.

There was silence. Then they drank again. Francoise and Dominique had heard nothing; they had gently taken each other by the hand behind the bench, so that nobody could see them, and it seemed so delightful that they remained where they were, their eyes plunged into the depths of the shadows.

What a warm and superb night it was! The village slumbered on both edges of the white highway in infantile quietude. From time to time was heard the crowing of some chanticleer aroused too soon. From the huge wood near by came long breaths, which passed over the roofs like caresses. The meadows, with their dark shadows, assumed a mysterious and dreamy majesty, while all the springs, all the flowing waters which gurgled in the darkness, seemed to be the cool and rhythmical respiration of the sleeping country. Occasionally the ancient mill wheel, lost in a doze, appeared to dream like those old watchdogs that bark while snoring; it cracked; it talked to itself, rocked by the fall of the Morelle, the surface of which gave forth the musical and continuous sound of an organ pipe. Never had more profound peace descended upon a happier corner of nature.

CHAPTER II
THE PRUSSIANS

A month later, on the day preceding that of Saint Louis, Rocreuse was in a state of terror. The Prussians had beaten the emperor and were advancing by forced marches toward the village. For a week past people who hurried along the highway had been announcing them thus: "They are at Lormiere—they are at Novelles!" And on hearing that they were drawing near so rapidly, Rocreuse every morning expected to see them descend from the wood of Gagny. They did not come, however, and that increased the fright. They would surely fall upon the village during the night and slaughter everybody.

That morning, a little before sunrise, there was an alarm. The inhabitants were awakened by the loud tramp of men on the highway. The women were already on their knees, making the sign of the cross, when some of the people, peering cautiously through the partially opened windows, recognized the red pantaloons. It was a French detachment. The captain immediately asked for the mayor of the district and remained at the mill after having talked with Pere Merlier.

The sun rose gaily that morning. It would be hot at noon. Over the wood floated a golden brightness, while in the distance white vapors arose from the meadows. The neat and pretty village awoke amid the fresh air, and the country, with its river and its springs, had the moist sweetness of a bouquet. But that beautiful day caused nobody to smile. The captain was seen to take a turn around the mill, examine the neighboring houses, pass to the other side of the Morelle and from there study the district with a field glass; Pere Merlier, who accompanied him, seemed to be giving him explanations. Then the captain posted soldiers behind the walls, behind the trees and in the ditches. The main body of the detachment encamped in the courtyard of the mill. Was there going to be a battle? When Pere Merlier returned he was questioned. He nodded his head without speaking. Yes, there was going to be a battle!

Francoise and Dominique were in the courtyard; they looked at him. At last he took his pipe from his mouth and said, "Ah, my poor young ones, you cannot get married tomorrow!"

Dominique, his lips pressed together, with an angry frown on his forehead, at times raised himself on tiptoe and fixed his eyes upon the wood of Gagny, as if he wished to see the Prussians arrive. Francoise, very pale and serious, came and went, furnishing the soldiers with what they needed. The troops were making soup in a corner of the courtyard; they joked while waiting for it to get ready.

The captain was delighted. He had visited the chambers and the huge hall of the mill which looked out upon the river. Now, seated beside the well, he was conversing with Pere Merlier.

"Your mill is a real fortress," he said. "We can hold it without difficulty until evening. The bandits are late. They ought to be here."

The miller was grave. He saw his mill burning like a torch, but he uttered no complaint, thinking such a course useless. He merely said:

"You had better hide the boat behind the wheel; there is a place there just fit for that purpose. Perhaps it will be useful to have the boat."

The captain gave the requisite order. This officer was a handsome man of forty; he was tall and had an amiable countenance. The sight of Francoise and Dominique seemed to please him. He contemplated them as if he had forgotten the coming struggle. He followed Francoise with his eyes, and his look told plainly that he thought her charming. Then turning toward Dominique, he asked suddenly:

"Why are you not in the army, my good fellow?"

"I am a foreigner," answered the young man.

The captain evidently did not attach much weight to this reason. He winked his eye and smiled. Francoise was more agreeable company than a cannon. On seeing him smile, Dominique added, "I am a foreigner, but I can put a ball in an apple at five hundred meters. There is my hunting gun behind you."

"You may have use for it," responded the captain dryly.

Francoise had approached, somewhat agitated. Without heeding the strangers present Dominique took and grasped in his the two hands she extended to him, as if to put herself under his protection. The captain smiled again but said not a word. He remained seated, his sword across his knees and his eyes plunged into space, lost in a reverie.

It was already ten o'clock. The heat had become very great. A heavy silence prevailed. In the courtyard, in the shadows of the sheds, the soldiers had begun to eat their soup. Not a sound came from the village; all its inhabitants had barricaded the doors and windows of their houses. A dog, alone upon the highway, howled. From the neighboring forests and meadows, swooning in the heat, came a prolonged and distant voice made up of all the scattered breaths. A cuckoo sang. Then the silence grew more intense.

Suddenly in that slumbering air a shot was heard. The captain leaped briskly to his feet; the soldiers left their plates of soup, yet half full. In a few seconds everybody was at the post of duty; from bottom to top the mill was occupied. Meanwhile the captain, who had gone out upon the road, had discovered nothing; to the right and to the left the highway stretched out, empty and white. A second shot was heard, and still nothing visible, not even a shadow. But as he was returning the captain perceived in the direction of Gagny, between two trees, a light puff of smoke whirling away like thistledown. The wood was calm and peaceful.

"The bandits have thrown themselves into the forest," he muttered. "They know we are here."

Then the firing continued, growing more and more vigorous, between the French soldiers posted around the mill and the Prussians hidden behind the trees. The balls whistled above the Morelle without damaging either side. The fusillade was irregular, the shots coming from every bush, and still only the little puffs of smoke, tossed gently by the breeze, were seen. This lasted nearly two hours. The officer hummed a tune with an air of indifference. Francoise and Dominique, who had remained in the courtyard, raised themselves on tiptoe and looked over a low wall. They were particularly interested in a little soldier posted on the shore of the Morelle, behind the remains of an old bateau; he stretched himself out flat on the ground, watched, fired and then glided into a ditch a trifle farther back to reload his gun; and his movements were so droll, so tricky and so supple, that they smiled as they looked at him. He must have perceived the head of a Prussian, for he arose quickly and brought his weapon to his shoulder, but before he could fire he uttered a cry, fell and rolled into the ditch, where for an instant his legs twitched convulsively like the claws of a chicken just killed. The little soldier had received a ball full in the breast. He was the first man slain. Instinctively Francoise seized Dominique's hand and clasped it with a nervous contraction.

"Move away," said the captain. "You are within range of the balls."

At that moment a sharp little thud was heard in the old elm, and a fragment of a branch came whirling down. But the two young folks did not stir; they were nailed to the spot by anxiety to see what was going on. On the edge of the wood a Prussian had suddenly come out from behind a tree as from a theater stage entrance, beating the air with his hands and falling backward. Nothing further moved; the two corpses seemed asleep in the broad sunlight; not a living soul was seen in the scorching country. Even the crack of the fusillade had ceased. The Morelle alone whispered in its clear tones.

Pere Merlier looked at the captain with an air of surprise, as if to ask him if the struggle was over.

"They are getting ready for something worse," muttered the officer.

"Don't trust appearances. Move away from there."

He had not finished speaking when there was a terrible discharge of musketry. The great elm was riddled, and a host of leaves shot into the air. The Prussians had happily fired too high. Dominique dragged, almost carried, Francoise away, while Pere Merlier followed them, shouting, "Go down into the cellar; the walls are solid!"

But they did not heed him; they entered the huge hall where ten soldiers were waiting in silence, watching through the chinks in the closed window shutters. The captain was alone in the courtyard, crouching behind the little wall, while the furious discharges continued. Without, the soldiers he had posted gave ground only foot by foot. However, they re-entered one by one, crawling, when the enemy had dislodged them from their hiding places. Their orders were to gain time and not show themselves, that the Prussians might remain in ignorance as to what force was before them. Another hour went by. As a sergeant arrived, saying that but two or three more men remained without, the captain glanced at his watch, muttering, "Half-past two o'clock. We must hold the position four hours longer."

He caused the great gate of the courtyard to be closed, and every preparation was made for an energetic resistance. As the Prussians were on the opposite side of the Morelle, an immediate assault was not to be feared. There was a bridge two kilometers away, but they evidently were not aware of its existence, and it was hardly likely that they would attempt to ford the river. The officer, therefore, simply ordered the highway to be watched. Every effort would be made in the direction of the country.

Again the fusillade had ceased. The mill seemed dead beneath the glowing sun. Not a shutter was open; no sound came from the interior. At length, little by little, the Prussians showed themselves at the edge of the forest of Gagny. They stretched their necks and grew bold. In the mill several soldiers had already raised their guns to their shoulders, but the captain cried, "No, no; wait. Let them come nearer."

They were exceedingly prudent, gazing at the mill with a suspicious air. The silent and somber old structure with its curtains of ivy filled them with uneasiness. Nevertheless, they advanced. When fifty of them were in the opposite meadow the officer uttered the single word, "Fire!"

A crash was heard; isolated shots followed. Francoise, all of a tremble, had mechanically put her hands to her ears. Dominique, behind the soldiers, looked on; when the smoke had somewhat lifted he saw three Prussians stretched upon their backs in the center of the meadow. The others had thrown themselves behind the willows and poplars. Then the siege began.

For more than an hour the mill was riddled with balls. They dashed against the old walls like hail. When they struck the stones they were heard to flatten and fall into the water. They buried themselves in the wood with a hollow sound. Occasionally a sharp crack announced that the mill wheel had been hit. The soldiers in the interior were careful of their shots; they fired only when they could take aim. From time to time the captain consulted his watch. As a ball broke a shutter and plowed into the ceiling he said to himself:

"Four o'clock. We shall never be able to hold out!"

Little by little the terrible fusillade weakened the old mill. A shutter fell into the water, pierced like a bit of lace, and it was necessary to replace it with a mattress. Pere Merlier constantly exposed himself to ascertain the extent of the damage done to his poor wheel, the cracking of which made his heart ache. All would be over with it this time; never could he repair it. Dominique had implored Francoise to withdraw, but she refused to leave him; she was seated behind a huge oaken clothespress, which protected her. A ball, however, struck the clothespress, the sides of which gave forth a hollow sound. Then Dominique placed himself in front of Francoise. He had not yet fired a shot; he held his gun in his hand but was unable to approach the windows, which were altogether occupied by the soldiers. At each discharge the floor shook.

"Attention! Attention!" suddenly cried the captain.

He had just seen a great dark mass emerge from the wood. Immediately a formidable platoon fire opened. It was like a waterspout passing over the mill. Another shutter was shattered, and through the gaping opening of the window the balls entered. Two soldiers rolled upon the floor. One of them lay like a stone; they pushed the body against the wall because it was in the way. The other twisted in agony, begging his comrades to finish him, but they paid no attention to him. The balls entered in a constant stream; each man took care of himself and strove to find a loophole through which to return the fire. A third soldier was hit; he uttered not a word; he fell on the edge of a table, with eyes fixed and haggard. Opposite these dead men Francoise, stricken with horror, had mechanically pushed away her chair to sit on the floor against the wall; she thought she would take up less room there and not be in so much danger. Meanwhile the soldiers had collected all the mattresses of the household and partially stopped up the windows with them. The hall was filled with wrecks, with broken weapons and demolished furniture.

"Five o'clock," said the captain. "Keep up your courage! They are about to try to cross the river!"

At that moment Francoise uttered a cry. A ball which had ricocheted had grazed her forehead. Several drops of blood appeared. Dominique stared at her; then, approaching the window, he fired his first shot. Once started, he did not stop. He loaded and fired without heeding what was passing around him, but from time to time he glanced at Francoise. He was very deliberate and aimed with care. The Prussians, keeping beside the poplars, attempted the passage of the Morelle, as the captain had predicted, but as soon as a man strove to cross he fell, shot in the head by Dominique. The captain, who had his eyes on the young man, was amazed. He complimented him, saying that he should be glad to have many such skillful marksmen. Dominique did not hear him. A ball cut his shoulder; another wounded his arm, but he continued to fire.

There were two more dead men. The mangled mattresses no longer stopped the windows. The last discharge seemed as if it would have carried away the mill. The position had ceased to be tenable. Nevertheless, the captain said firmly, "Hold your ground for half an hour more!"

Now he counted the minutes. He had promised his chiefs to hold the enemy in check there until evening, and he would not give an inch before the hour he had fixed on for the retreat. He preserved his amiable air and smiled upon Francoise to reassure her. He had picked up the gun of a dead soldier and himself was firing.

Only four soldiers remained in the hall. The Prussians appeared in a body on the other side of the Morelle, and it was clear that they intended speedily to cross the river. A few minutes more elapsed. The stubborn captain would not order the retreat. Just then a sergeant hastened to him and said, "They are upon the highway; they will take us in the rear!"

The Prussians must have found the bridge. The captain pulled out his watch and looked at it.

"Five minutes longer," he said. "They cannot get here before that time!"

Then at six o'clock exactly he at last consented to lead his men out through a little door which opened into a lane. From there they threw themselves into a ditch; they gained the forest of Sauval. Before taking his departure the captain bowed very politely to Pere Merlier and made his excuses, adding, "Amuse them! We will return!"

Dominique was now alone in the hall. He was still firing, hearing nothing, understanding nothing. He felt only the need of defending Francoise. He had not the least suspicion in the world that the soldiers had retreated. He aimed and killed his man at every shot. Suddenly there was a loud noise. The Prussians had entered the courtyard from behind. Dominique fired a last; shot and they fell upon him while his gun was yet smoking.

Four men held him. Others vociferated around him in a frightful language. They were ready to slaughter him on the spot. Francoise, with a supplicating look, had cast herself before him. But an officer entered and ordered the prisoner to be delivered up to him. After exchanging a few words in German with the soldiers he turned toward Dominique and said to him roughly in very good French:

"You will be shot in two hours!"

CHAPTER III
THE FLIGHT

It was a settled rule of the German staff that every Frenchman, not belonging to the regular army, taken with arms in his hands should be shot. The militia companies themselves were not recognized as belligerents. By thus making terrible examples of the peasants who defended their homes, the Germans hoped to prevent the levy en masse, which they feared.

The officer, a tall, lean man of fifty, briefly questioned Dominique. Although he spoke remarkably pure French he had a stiffness altogether Prussian.

"Do you belong to this district?" he asked.

"No; I am a Belgian," answered the young man.

"Why then did you take up arms? The fighting did not concern you!"

Dominique made no reply. At that moment the officer saw Francoise who was standing by, very pale, listening; upon her white forehead her slight wound had put a red bar. He looked at the young folks, one after the other, seemed to understand matters and contented himself with adding:

"You do not deny having fired, do you?"

"I fired as often as I could!" responded Dominique tranquilly.

This confession was useless, for he was black with powder, covered with sweat and stained with a few drops of blood which had flowed from the scratch on his shoulder.

"Very well," said the officer. "You will be shot in two hours!"

Francoise did not cry out. She clasped her hands and raised them with a gesture of mute despair. The officer noticed this gesture. Two soldiers had taken Dominique to a neighboring apartment, where they were to keep watch over him. The young girl had fallen upon a chair, totally overcome; she could not weep; she was suffocating. The officer had continued to examine her. At last he spoke to her.

"Is that young man your brother?" he demanded.

She shook her head negatively. The German stood stiffly on his feet with out a smile. Then after a short silence he again asked, "Has he lived long in the district?"

She nodded affirmatively.

"In that case, he ought to be thoroughly acquainted with the neighboring forests."

This time she spoke.

"He is thoroughly acquainted with them, monsieur," she said, looking at him with considerable surprise.

He said nothing further to her but turned upon his heel, demanding that the mayor of the village should be brought to him. But Francoise had arisen with a slight blush on her countenance; thinking that she had seized the aim of the officer's questions, she had recovered hope. She herself ran to find her father.

Pere Merlier, as soon as the firing had ceased, had quickly descended to the wooden gallery to examine his wheel. He adored his daughter; he had a solid friendship for Dominique, his future son-in-law, but his wheel also held a large place in his heart. Since the two young ones, as he called them, had come safe and sound out of the fight, he thought of his other tenderness, which had suffered greatly. Bent over the huge wooden carcass, he was studying its wounds with a sad air. Five buckets were shattered to pieces; the central framework was riddled. He thrust his fingers in the bullet holes to measure their depth; he thought how he could repair all these injuries. Francoise found him already stopping up the clefts with rubbish and moss.

"Father," she said, "you are wanted."

And she wept at last as she told him what she had just heard. Pere Merlier tossed his head. People were not shot in such a summary fashion. The matter must be looked after. He re-entered the mill with his silent and tranquil air. When the officer demanded of him provisions for his men he replied that the inhabitants of Rocreuse were not accustomed to be treated roughly and that nothing would be obtained from them if violence were employed. He would see to everything but on condition that he was not interfered with. The officer at first seemed irritated by his calm tone; then he gave way before the old man's short and clear words.

He even called him back and asked him, "What is the name of that wood opposite?"

"The forest of Sauval."

"What is its extent?"

The miller looked at him fixedly. "I do not know," he answered.

And he went away. An hour later the contribution of war in provisions and money, demanded by the officer, was in the courtyard of the mill. Night came on. Francoise watched with anxiety the movements of the soldiers. She hung about the room in which Dominique was imprisoned. Toward seven o'clock she experienced a poignant emotion. She saw the officer enter the prisoner's apartment and for a quarter of an hour heard their voices in loud conversation. For an instant the officer reappeared upon the threshold to give an order in German, which she did not understand, but when twelve men ranged themselves in the courtyard, their guns on their shoulders, she trembled and felt as if about to faint. All then was over: the execution was going to take place. The twelve men stood there ten minutes, Dominique's voice continuing to be raised in a tone of violent refusal. Finally the officer came out, saying, as he roughly shut the door:

"Very well; reflect. I give you until tomorrow morning."

And with a gesture he ordered the twelve men to break ranks. Francoise was stupefied. Pere Merlier, who had been smoking his pipe and looking at the platoon simply with an air of curiosity, took her by the arm with paternal gentleness. He led her to her chamber.

"Be calm," he said, "and try to sleep. Tomorrow, when it is light, we will see what can be done."

As he withdrew he prudently locked her in. It was his opinion that women were good for nothing and that they spoiled everything when they took a hand in a serious affair. But Francoise did not retire. She sat for a long while upon the side of her bed, listening to the noises of the house. The German soldiers encamped in the courtyard sang and laughed; they must have been eating and drinking until eleven o'clock, for the racket did not cease an instant. In the mill itself heavy footsteps resounded from time to time, without doubt those of the sentinels who were being relieved. But she was interested most by the sounds she could distinguish in the apartment beneath her chamber. Many times she stretched herself out at full length and put her ear to the floor. That apartment was the one in which Dominique was confined. He must have been walking back and forth from the window to the wall, for she long heard the regular cadence of his steps. Then deep silence ensued; he had doubtless seated himself. Finally every noise ceased and all was as if asleep. When slumber appeared to her to have settled on the house she opened her window as gently as possible and leaned her elbows on the sill.

Without, the night had a warm serenity. The slender crescent of the moon, which was sinking behind the forest of Sauval, lit up the country with the glimmer of a night lamp. The lengthened shadows of the tall trees barred the meadows with black, while the grass in uncovered spots assumed the softness of greenish velvet. But Francoise did not pause to admire the mysterious charms of the night. She examined the country, searching for the sentinels whom the Germans had posted obliquely. She clearly saw their shadows extending like the rounds of a ladder along the Morelle. Only one was before the mill, on the other shore of the river, beside a willow, the branches of which dipped in the water. Francoise saw him plainly. He was a tall man and was standing motionless, his face turned toward the sky with the dreamy air of a shepherd.

When she had carefully inspected the locality she again seated herself on her bed. She remained there an hour, deeply absorbed. Then she listened once more: there was not a sound in the mill. She returned to the window and glanced out, but doubtless one of the horns of the moon, which was still visible behind the trees, made her uneasy, for she resumed her waiting attitude. At last she thought the proper time had come. The night was as black as jet; she could no longer see the sentinel opposite; the country spread out like a pool of ink. She strained her ear for an instant and made her decision. Passing near the window was an iron ladder, the bars fastened to the wall, which mounted from the wheel to the garret and formerly enabled the millers to reach certain machinery; afterward the mechanism had been altered, and for a long while the ladder had been hidden under the thick ivy which covered that side of the mill.

Francoise bravely climbed out of her window and grasped one of the bars of the ladder. She began to descend. Her skirts embarrassed her greatly. Suddenly a stone was detached from the wall and fell into the Morelle with a loud splash. She stopped with an icy shiver of fear. Then she realized that the waterfall with its continuous roar would drown every noise she might make, and she descended more courageously, feeling the ivy with her foot, assuring herself that the rounds were firm. When she was at the height of the chamber which served as Dominique's prison she paused. An unforeseen difficulty nearly caused her to lose all her courage: the window of the chamber was not directly below that of her apartment. She hung off from the ladder, but when she stretched out her arm her hand encountered only the wall. Must she, then, ascend without pushing her plan to completion? Her arms were fatigued; the murmur of the Morelle beneath her commenced to make her dizzy. Then she tore from the wall little fragments of plaster and threw them against Dominique's window. He did not hear; he was doubtless asleep. She crumbled more plaster from the wall, scraping the skin off her fingers. She was utterly exhausted; she felt herself falling backward, when Dominique at last softly opened the window.

"It is I!" she murmured. "Catch me quickly; I'm falling!"

It was the first time that she had addressed him familiarly. Leaning out, he seized her and drew her into the chamber. There she gave vent to a flood of tears, stifling her sobs that she might not be heard. Then by a supreme effort she calmed herself.

"Are you guarded?" she asked in a low voice.

Dominique, still stupefied at seeing her thus, nodded his head affirmatively, pointing to the door. On the other side they heard someone snoring; the sentinel, yielding to sleep, had thrown himself on the floor against the door, arguing that by disposing himself thus the prisoner could not escape.

"You must fly," resumed Francoise excitedly. "I have come to beg you to do so and to bid you farewell."

But he did not seem to hear her. He repeated:

"What? Is it you; is it you? Oh, what fear you caused me! You might have killed yourself!"

He seized her hands; he kissed them.

"How I love you, Francoise!" he murmured. "You are as courageous as good. I had only one dread: that I should die without seeing you again. But you are here, and now they can shoot me. When I have passed a quarter of an hour with you I shall be ready."

Little by little he had drawn her to him, and she leaned her head upon his shoulder. The danger made them dearer to each other. They forgot everything in that warm clasp.

"Ah, Francoise," resumed Dominique in a caressing voice, "this is Saint Louis's Day, the day, so long awaited, of our marriage. Nothing has been able to separate us, since we are both here alone, faithful to the appointment. Is not this our wedding morning?"

"Yes, yes," she repeated, "it is our wedding morning."

They tremblingly exchanged a kiss. But all at once she disengaged herself from Dominique's arms; she remembered the terrible reality.

"You must fly; you must fly," she whispered. "There is not a minute to be lost!"

And as he stretched out his arms in the darkness to clasp her again, she said tenderly:

"Oh, I implore you to listen to me! If you die I shall die also! In an hour it will be light. I want you to go at once."

Then rapidly she explained her plan. The iron ladder descended to the mill wheel; there he could climb down the buckets and get into the boat which was hidden away in a nook. Afterward it would be easy for him to reach the other bank of the river and escape.

"But what of the sentinels?" he asked.

"There is only one, opposite, at the foot of the first willow."

"What if he should see me and attempt to give an alarm?"

Francoise shivered. She placed in his hand a knife she had brought with her. There was a brief silence.

"What is to become of your father and yourself?" resumed Dominique. "No, I cannot fly! When I am gone those soldiers will, perhaps, massacre you both! You do not know them. They offered me my life if I would consent to guide them through the forest of Sauval. When they discover my escape they will be capable of anything!"

The young girl did not stop to argue. She said simply in reply to all the reasons he advanced, "Out of love for me, fly! If you love me, Dominique, do not remain here another moment!"

Then she promised to climb back to her chamber. No one would know that she had helped him. She finally threw her arms around him to convince him with an embrace, with a burst of extraordinary love. He was vanquished. He asked but one more question:

"Can you swear to me that your father knows what you have done and that he advises me to fly?"

"My father sent me!" answered Francoise boldly.

She told a falsehood. At that moment she had only one immense need: to know that he was safe, to escape from the abominable thought that the sun would be the signal for his death. When he was far away every misfortune might fall upon her; that would seem delightful to her from the moment he was secure. The selfishness of her tenderness desired that he should live before everything.

"Very well," said Dominique; "I will do what you wish."

They said nothing more. Dominique reopened the window. But suddenly a sound froze them. The door was shaken, and they thought that it was about to be opened. Evidently a patrol had heard their voices. Standing locked in each other's arms, they waited in unspeakable anguish. The door was shaken a second time, but it did not open. They uttered low sighs of relief; they comprehended that the soldier who was asleep against the door must have turned over. In fact, silence succeeded; the snoring was resumed.

Dominique exacted that Francoise should ascend to her chamber before he departed. He clasped her in his arms and bade her a mute adieu. Then he aided her to seize the ladder and clung to it in his turn. But he refused to descend a single round until convinced that she was in her apartment. When Francoise had entered her window she let fall in a voice as light as a breath:

"Au revoir, my love!"

She leaned her elbows on the sill and strove to follow Dominique with her eyes. The night was yet very dark. She searched for the sentinel but could not see him; the willow alone made a pale stain in the midst of the gloom. For an instant she heard the sound produced by Dominique's body in passing along the ivy. Then the wheel cracked, and there was a slight agitation in the water which told her that the young man had found the boat. A moment afterward she distinguished the somber silhouette of the bateau on the gray surface of the Morelle. Terrible anguish seized upon her. Each instant she thought she heard the sentinel's cry of alarm; the smallest sounds scattered through the gloom seemed to her the hurried tread of soldiers, the clatter of weapons, the charging of guns. Nevertheless, the seconds elapsed and the country maintained its profound peace. Dominique must have reached the other side of the river. Francoise saw nothing more. The silence was majestic. She heard a shuffling of feet, a hoarse cry and the hollow fall of a body. Afterward the silence grew deeper. Then as if she had felt Death pass by, she stood, chilled through and through, staring into the thick night.

CHAPTER IV
A TERRIBLE EXPERIENCE

At dawn a clamor of voices shook the mill. Pere Merlier opened the door of Francoise's chamber. She went down into the courtyard, pale and very calm. But there she could not repress a shiver as she saw the corpse of a Prussian soldier stretched out on a cloak beside the well.

Around the body troops gesticulated, uttering cries of fury. Many of them shook their fists at the village. Meanwhile the officer had summoned Pere Merlier as the mayor of the commune.

"Look!" he said to him in a voice almost choking with anger. "There lies one of our men who was found assassinated upon the bank of the river. We must make a terrible example, and I count on you to aid us in discovering the murderer."

"As you choose," answered the miller with his usual stoicism, "but you will find it no easy task."

The officer stooped and drew aside a part of the cloak which hid the face of the dead man. Then appeared a horrible wound. The sentinel had been struck in the throat, and the weapon had remained in the cut. It was a kitchen knife with a black handle.

"Examine that knife," said the officer to Pere Merlier; "perhaps it will help us in our search."

The old man gave a start but recovered control of himself immediately.

He replied without moving a muscle of his face, "Everybody in the district has similar knives. Doubtless your man was weary of fighting and put an end to his own life. It looks like it!"

"Mind what you say!" cried the officer furiously. "I do not know what prevents me from setting fire to the four corners of the village!"

Happily in his rage he did not notice the deep trouble pictured on Francoise's countenance. She had been forced to sit down on a stone bench near the well. Despite herself her eyes were fixed upon the corpse stretched our on the ground almost at her feet. It was that of a tall and handsome man who resembled Dominique, with flaxen hair and blue eyes. This resemblance made her heart ache. She thought that perhaps the dead soldier had left behind him in Germany a sweetheart who would weep her eyes out for him. She recognized her knife in the throat of the murdered man. She had killed him.

The officer was talking of striking Rocreuse with terrible measures, when soldiers came running to him. Dominique's escape had just been discovered. It caused an extreme agitation. The officer went to the apartment in which the prisoner had been confined, looked out of the window which had remained open, understood everything and returned, exasperated.

Pere Merlier seemed greatly vexed by Dominique's flight.

"The imbecile!" he muttered. "He has ruined all!"

Francoise heard him and was overcome with anguish. But the miller did not suspect her of complicity in the affair. He tossed his head, saying to her in an undertone:

"We are in a nice scrape!"

"It was that wretch who assassinated the soldier! I am sure of it!" cried the officer. "He has undoubtedly reached the forest. But he must be found for us or the village shall pay for him!"

Turning to the miller, he said, "See here, you ought to know where he is hidden!"

Pere Merlier laughed silently, pointing to the wide stretch of wooden hills.

"Do you expect to find a man in there?" he said.

"Oh, there must be nooks there with which you are acquainted. I will give you ten men. You must guide them."

"As you please. But it will take a week to search all the wood in the vicinity."

The old man's tranquility enraged the officer. In fact, the latter comprehended the absurdity of this search. At that moment he saw Francoise, pale and trembling, on the bench. The anxious attitude of the young girl struck him. He was silent for an instant, during which he in turn examined the miller and his daughter.

At length he demanded roughly of the old man, "Is not that fellow your child's lover?"

Pere Merlier grew livid and seemed about to hurl himself upon the officer to strangle him. He stiffened himself but made no answer. Francoise buried her face in her hands.

"Yes, that's it!" continued the Prussian. "And you or your daughter helped him to escape! One of you is his accomplice! For the last time, will you give him up to us?"

The miller uttered not a word. He turned away and looked into space with an air of indifference, as if the officer had not addressed him. This brought the latter's rage to a head.

"Very well!" he shouted. "You shall be shot in his place!"

And he again ordered out the platoon of execution. Pere Merlier remained as stoical as ever. He hardly even shrugged his shoulders; all this drama appeared to him in bad taste. Without doubt he did not believe that they would shoot a man so lightly. But when the platoon drew up before him he said gravely, "So it is serious, is it? Go on with your bloody work then! If you must have a victim I will do as well as another!"

But Francoise started up, terrified, stammering, "In pity, monsieur, do no harm to my father! Kill me in his stead! I aided Dominique to fly! I alone am guilty!"

"Hush, my child!" cried Pere Merlier. "Why do you tell an untruth? She passed the night locked in her chamber, monsieur. She tells a falsehood, I assure you!"

"No, I do not tell a falsehood!" resumed the young girl ardently. "I climbed out of my window and went down the iron ladder; I urged Dominique to fly. This is the truth, the whole truth!"

The old man became very pale. He saw clearly in her eyes that she did not lie, and her story terrified him. Ah, these children with their hearts, how they spoil everything! Then he grew angry and exclaimed:

"She is mad; do not heed her. She tells you stupid tales. Come, finish your work!"

She still protested. She knelt, clasping her hands. The officer tranquilly watched this dolorous struggle.

"MON DIEU!" he said at last. "I take your father because I have not the other. Find the fugitive and the old man shall be set at liberty!"

She gazed at him with staring eyes, astonished at the atrocity of the proposition.

"How horrible!" she murmured. "Where do you think I can find Dominique at this hour? He has departed; I know no more about him."

"Come, make your choice—him or your father."

"Oh, MON DIEU! How can I choose? If I knew where Dominique was I could not choose! You are cutting my heart. I would rather die at once. Yes, it would be the sooner over. Kill me; I implore you, kill me!"

This scene of despair and tears finally made the officer impatient. He cried out:

"Enough! I will be merciful. I consent to give you two hours. If in that time your lover is not here your father will be shot in his place!"

He caused Pere Merlier to be taken to the chamber which had served as Dominique's prison. The old man demanded tobacco and began to smoke. Upon his impassible face not the slightest emotion was visible. But when alone, as he smoked, he shed two big tears which ran slowly down his cheeks. His poor, dear child, how she was suffering!

Francoise remained in the middle of the courtyard. Prussian soldiers passed, laughing. Some of them spoke to her, uttered jokes she could not understand. She stared at the door through which her father had disappeared. With a slow movement she put her hand to her forehead, as if to prevent it from bursting.

The officer turned upon his heel, saying, "You have two hours. Try to utilize them."

She had two hours. This phrase buzzed in her ears. Then mechanically she quitted the courtyard; she walked straight ahead. Where should she go?—what should she do? She did not even try to make a decision because she well understood the inutility of her efforts. However, she wished to see Dominique. They could have an understanding together; they might, perhaps, find an expedient. And amid the confusion of her thoughts she went down to the shore of the Morelle, which she crossed below the sluice at a spot where there were huge stones. Her feet led her beneath the first willow, in the corner of the meadow. As she stooped she saw a pool of blood which made her turn pale. It was there the murder had been committed. She followed the track of Dominique in the trodden grass; he must have run, for she perceived a line of long footprints stretching across the meadow. Then farther on she lost these traces. But in a neighboring field she thought she found them again. The new trail conducted her to the edge of the forest, where every indication was effaced.

Francoise, nevertheless, plunged beneath the trees. It solaced her to be alone. She sat down for an instant, but at the thought that time was passing she leaped to her feet. How long had it been since she left the mill? Five minutes?—half an hour? She had lost all conception of time. Perhaps Dominique had concealed himself in a copse she knew of, where they had one afternoon eaten filberts together. She hastened to the copse, searched it. Only a blackbird flew away, uttering its soft, sad note. Then she thought he might have taken refuge in a hollow of the rocks, where it had sometimes been his custom to lie in wait for game, but the hollow of the rocks was empty. What good was it to hunt for him? She would never find him, but little by little the desire to discover him took entire possession of her, and she hastened her steps. The idea that he might have climbed a tree suddenly occurred to her. She advanced with uplifted eyes, and that he might be made aware of her presence she called him every fifteen or twenty steps. Cuckoos answered; a breath of wind which passed through the branches made her believe that he was there and was descending. Once she even imagined she saw him; she stopped, almost choked, and wished to fly. What was she to say to him? Had she come to take him back to be shot? Oh no, she would not tell him what had happened. She would cry out to him to escape, not to remain in the neighborhood. Then the thought that her father was waiting for her gave her a sharp pain. She fell upon the turf, weeping, crying aloud, "MON DIEU! MON DIEU! Why am I here?"

She was mad to have come. And as if seized with fear, she ran; she sought to leave the forest. Three times she deceived herself; she thought she never again would find the mill, when she entered a meadow just opposite Rocreuse. As soon as she saw the village she paused. Was she going to return alone? She was still hesitating when a voice softly called, "Francoise! Francoise!"

And she saw Dominique, who had raised his head above the edge of a ditch. Just God! She had found him! Did heaven wish his death? She restrained a cry; she let herself glide into the ditch.

"Are you searching for me?" asked the young man.

"Yes," she answered, her brain in a whirl, not knowing what she said.

"What has happened?"

She lowered her eyes, stammered, "Nothing. I was uneasy; I wanted to see you."

Then, reassured, he explained to her that he had resolved not to go away. He was doubtful about the safety of herself and her father. Those Prussian wretches were fully capable of taking vengeance upon women and old men. But everything was getting on well. He added with a laugh:

"Our wedding will take place in a week—I am sure of it."

Then as she remained overwhelmed, he grew grave again and said, "But what ails you? You are concealing something from me!"

"No; I swear it to you. I am out of breath from running."

He embraced her, saying that it was imprudent for them to be talking, and he wished to climb out of the ditch to return to the forest. She restrained him. She trembled.

"Listen," she said: "it would, perhaps, be wise for you to remain where you are. No one is searching for you; you have nothing to fear."

"Francoise, you are concealing something from me," he repeated.

Again she swore that she was hiding nothing. She had simply wished to know that he was near her. And she stammered forth still further reasons. She seemed so strange to him that he now could not be induced to flee. Besides, he had faith in the return of the French. Troops had been seen in the direction of Sauval.

"Ah, let them hurry; let them get here as soon as possible," she murmured fervently.

At that moment eleven o'clock sounded from the belfry of Rocreuse. The strokes were clear and distinct. She arose with a terrified look; two hours had passed since she quitted the mill.

"Hear me," she said rapidly: "if we have need of you I will wave my handkerchief from my chamber window."

And she departed on a run, while Dominique, very uneasy, stretched himself out upon the edge of the ditch to watch the mill. As she was about to enter Rocreuse, Francoise met an old beggar, Pere Bontemps, who knew everybody in the district. He bowed to her; he had just seen the miller in the midst of the Prussians; then, making the sign of the cross and muttering broken words, he went on his way.

"The two hours have passed," said the officer when Francoise appeared.

Pere Merlier was there, seated upon the bench beside the well. He was smoking. The young girl again begged, wept, sank on her knees. She wished to gain time. The hope of seeing the French return had increased in her, and while lamenting she thought she heard in the distance, the measured tramp of an army. Oh, if they would come, if they would deliver them all?

"Listen, monsieur," she said: "an hour, another hour; you can grant us another hour!"

But the officer remained inflexible. He even ordered two men to seize her and take her away, that they might quietly proceed with the execution of the old man. Then a frightful struggle took place in Francoise's heart. She could not allow her father to be thus assassinated. No, no; she would die rather with Dominique. She was running toward her chamber when Dominique himself entered the courtyard.

The officer and the soldiers uttered a shout of triumph. But the young man, calmly, with a somewhat severe look, went up to Francoise, as if she had been the only person present.

"You did wrong," he said. "Why did you not bring me back? It remained for Pere Bontemps to tell me everything. But I am here!"

CHAPTER V
THE RETURN OF THE FRENCH

It was three o'clock in the afternoon. Great black clouds, the trail of some neighboring storm, had slowly filled the sky. The yellow heavens, the brass covered uniforms, had changed the valley of Rocreuse, so gay in the sunlight, into a den of cutthroats full of sinister gloom. The Prussian officer had contented himself with causing Dominique to be imprisoned without announcing what fate he reserved for him. Since noon Francoise had been torn by terrible anguish. Despite her father's entreaties she would not quit the courtyard. She was awaiting the French. But the hours sped on; night was approaching, and she suffered the more as all the time gained did not seem to be likely to change the frightful denouement.

About three o'clock the Prussians made their preparations for departure. For an instant past the officer had, as on the previous day, shut himself up with Dominique. Francoise realized that the young man's life was in balance. She clasped her hands; she prayed. Pere Merlier, beside her, maintained silence and the rigid attitude of an old peasant who does not struggle against fate.

"Oh, MON DIEU! Oh, MON DIEU!" murmured Francoise. "They are going to kill him!"

The miller drew her to him and took her on his knees as if she had been a child.

At that moment the officer came out, while behind him two men brought Dominique.

"Never! Never!" cried the latter. "I am ready to die!"

"Think well," resumed the officer. "The service you refuse me another will render us. I am generous: I offer you your life. I want you simply to guide us through the forest to Montredon. There must be pathways leading there."

Dominique was silent.

"So you persist in your infatuation, do you?"

"Kill me and end all this!" replied the young man.

Francoise, her hands clasped, supplicated him from afar. She had forgotten everything; she would have advised him to commit an act of cowardice. But Pere Merlier seized her hands that the Prussians might not see her wild gestures.

"He is right," he whispered: "It is better to die!"

The platoon of execution was there. The officer awaited a sign of weakness on Dominique's part. He still expected to conquer him. No one spoke. In the distance violent crashes of thunder were heard. Oppressive heat weighed upon the country. But suddenly, amid the silence, a cry broke forth:

"The French! The French!"

Yes, the French were at hand. Upon the Sauval highway, at the edge of the wood, the line of red pantaloons could be distinguished. In the mill there was an extraordinary agitation. The Prussian soldiers ran hither and thither with guttural exclamations. Not a shot had yet been fired.

"The French! The French!" cried Francoise, clapping her hands.

She was wild with joy. She escaped from her father's grasp; she laughed and tossed her arms in the air. At last they had come and come in time, since Dominique was still alive!

A terrible platoon fire, which burst upon her ears like a clap of thunder, caused her to turn. The officer muttered between his teeth:

"Before everything, let us settle this affair!"

And with his own hand pushing Dominique against the wall of a shed he ordered his men to fire. When Francoise looked Dominique lay upon the ground with blood streaming from his neck and shoulders.

She did not weep; she stood stupefied. Her eyes grew fixed, and she sat down under the shed, a few paces from the body. She stared at it, wringing her hands. The Prussians had seized Pere Merlier as a hostage.

It was a stirring combat. The officer had rapidly posted his men, comprehending that he could not beat a retreat without being cut to pieces. Hence he would fight to the last. Now the Prussians defended the mill, and the French attacked it. The fusillade began with unusual violence. For half an hour it did not cease. Then a hollow sound was heard, and a ball broke a main branch of the old elm. The French had cannon. A battery, stationed just above the ditch in which Dominique had hidden himself, swept the wide street of Rocreuse. The struggle could not last long.

Ah, the poor mill! Balls pierced it in every part. Half of the roof was carried away. Two walls were battered down. But it was on the side of the Morelle that the destruction was most lamentable. The ivy, torn from the tottering edifice, hung like rags; the river was encumbered with wrecks of all kinds, and through a breach was visible Francoise's chamber with its bed, the white curtains of which were carefully closed. Shot followed shot; the old wheel received two balls and gave vent to an agonizing groan; the buckets were borne off by the current; the framework was crushed. The soul of the gay mill had left it!

Then the French began the assault. There was a furious fight with swords and bayonets. Beneath the rust-colored sky the valley was choked with the dead. The broad meadows had a wild look with their tall, isolated trees and their hedges of poplars which stained them with shade. To the right and to the left the forests were like the walls of an ancient ampitheater which enclosed the fighting gladiators, while the springs, the fountains and the flowing brooks seemed to sob amid the panic of the country.

Beneath the shed Francoise still sat near Dominique's body; she had not moved. Pere Merlier had received a slight wound. The Prussians were exterminated, but the ruined mill was on fire in a dozen places. The French rushed into the courtyard, headed by their captain. It was his first success of the war. His face beamed with triumph. He waved his sword, shouting, "Victory! Victory!"

On seeing the wounded miller, who was endeavoring to comfort Francoise, and noticing the body of Dominique, his joyous look changed to one of sadness. Then he knelt beside the young man and, tearing open his blouse, put his hand to his heart.

"Thank God!" he cried. "It is yet beating! Send for the surgeon!"

At the captain's words Francoise leaped to her feet.

"There is hope!" she cried. "Oh, tell me there is hope!"

At that moment the surgeon appeared. He made a hasty examination and said:

"The young man is severely hurt, but life is not extinct; he can be saved!" By the surgeon's orders Dominique was transported to a neighboring cottage, where he was placed in bed. His wounds were dressed; restoratives were administered, and he soon recovered consciousness. When he opened his eyes he saw Francoise sitting beside him and through the open window caught sight of Pere Merlier talking with the French captain. He passed his hand over his forehead with a bewildered air and said:

"They did not kill me after all!"

"No," replied Francoise. "The French came, and their surgeon saved you."

Pere Merlier turned and said through the window, "No talking yet, my young ones!"

In due time Dominique was entirely restored, and when peace again blessed the land he wedded his beloved Francoise.

The mill was rebuilt, and Pere Merlier had a new wheel upon which to bestow whatever tenderness was not engrossed by his daughter and her husband.

FAIR EXCHANGE

Every Saturday, as regular as clockwork, Ferdinand Sourdis would come into old Morand's shop to stock up on paints and brushes. The shop, which was nothing more than a damp and gloomy ground-floor room, overlooked a tiny square in the town of Mercoeur and stood in the shadow of a former convent, now converted into the local school where Ferdinand had been working for the last year as a very junior assistant master. Ferdinand, who was rumored to have come from Lille, was an enthusiastic painter and spent all his spare time shut away in his room pursuing his hobby, although he never revealed the results of his work. He usually found himself dealing with old Morand's daughter Adèle who was herself a painter of delicate watercolors which aroused much comment in Mercoeur. He would place his order: "Three tubes of white, please, one of yellow ochre and two of Veronese green," and Adèle, who knew all about her father's business, would serve him, never failing to enquire, "Do you need anything else?"

After the ritual "That's all for now, thank you," Ferdinand would slip his little package into his pocket and pay her with the sheepish look of a poor man always afraid of being snubbed. He would then leave the shop. This transaction had proceeded uneventfully on these lines for a whole year.

Old Morand's customers could be counted almost on the fingers of both hands. Mercoeur, a town of some eight thousand souls, was noted for its tanneries but the fine arts were not greatly cultivated, although there were four or five youths who daubed away under the pale eye of a lean Pole with a profile resembling that of a sick bird. The Lévèque girls, daughters of the local solicitor, had indeed taken up "oils" but this was considered quite scandalous behavior.

The only customer of note was the well-known painter Rennequin, a native of Mercoeur, who had achieved enormous success in the capital, winning many medals and commissions, and had recently been decorated. When he came to spend a month in Mercoeur in the summer, he caused an upheaval in the tiny shop in the Place du Collège. Morand would take endless trouble, even having paints sent specially from Paris. He would greet Rennequin hat in hand and enquire deferentially about his distinguished client's latest triumphs. The painter, a large, jovial man had ended by accepting invitations to dinner and would cast a friendly eye over Adèle's watercolors which he declared to be trifle pale but as fresh as a daisy.

"You might just as well do that as embroidery," he would say tugging her ear. "And it's not too bad, either, there's a sort of astringency and determination in them that almost adds up to a personal style . . . So keep at it and let yourself go, just paint as you feel.."

Old Morand did not, of course, make his living from his shop. For him it was in inveterate hobby, a secret artistic bent that had never broken through but was now emerging in his daughter. He owned his house and he had benefited from a series of legacies; people reckoned he had an income of six or eight thousand francs a year. Despite this, he still sold artists' materials in his poky little ground-floor drawing-room whose window was the window of his shop; a narrow shop-window full of tubes of paint, sticks of Chinese ink and brushes and where occasionally some of Adèle's watercolors would appear, sandwiched between small sacred pictures painted by the Pole. Days would go by without a sign of a customer. All the same, old Morand's life was a happy one, surrounded by the smell of turpentine and varnish, and whenever Madame Morand, an ailing old woman who spent most of her time in bed, advised him to get rid of the shop, he would take offence, as a man dimly aware of fulfilling a mission in life. Though a middle-class reactionary at heart and strictly pious, his feeling of being a failed artist kept him attached to his paltry little shop. Where else would the townspeople be able to buy their paints? If the truth be known, nobody did buy any; but it was always possible that they might want to do so. He refused to abdicate.

Mademoiselle Adèle had grown up in this environment. She had just celebrated her twenty-second birthday. Short and a trifle plump, she had a pleasant-looking round face with narrow eyes; but she was so pale and sallow that nobody thought of her as pretty. She seemed like a little old woman; her complexion already had the faded look of a schoolmistress aged by the secret stresses of spinsterdom. However, Adèle was not looking to be married. There had been suitors but she had turned them all down. People thought that she was being haughty; no doubt she was waiting for some Prince Charming to come along; and there were unpleasant stories circulating with regard to the liberties which Rennequin, an old reprobate of a bachelor, might be taking with her. Very "withdrawn", in common parlance, but in fact a thoughtful and taciturn girl, Adèle seemed quite unaware of such scandal mongering. Quite unrebellious by nature, she was used to living in the drab, damp atmosphere of the Place du Collège, having become accustomed since childhood to looking out at all hours of the day on to the same moss-covered paving sets and the same gloomy street crossing which nobody ever crossed; twice a day only, the pupils jostled and scurried along outside the school gates. It was her sole entertainment. Yet she was never bored. It seemed as if she was steadfastly pursuing a plan of action for her life drawn up by herself long ago. She was strong-willed, very ambitious and possessed inexhaustible patience, which led people to fail to understand her true nature. Gradually, they began to speak of her as an old maid. She seemed likely to be spending the rest of her days painting watercolors. However, when the famous Rennequin called and talked about Paris, she would listen in silence, pale-faced but with a sparkle in her eyes.

"Why not send some of your watercolors in for the Salon?" the painter asked her one day, in the unceremonious tone* he always used as an old friend of the family. "I'll see to it that they're accepted."

She gave a shrug and said without false modesty, though not without a touch of bitterness.

"Oh, it's woman's painting . . . It's not worth the trouble, you know!"

The coming of Ferdinand Sourdis had been quite an important event for old Morand's business. It meant an extra customer and an extremely valuable one, for no one in Mercoeur ever disposed of so many tubes of paint as he. For the first month, Morand gave the young man a great deal of attention, surprised to see such a passionate interest in art in one of those "ushers" whom, after observing them going past his front door for nearly half a century, he had come to despise for their grubbiness and sloth. But, according to what he heard, this one came from a good family which had come down in the world, so that after his parents' death he had been forced to accept any situation he could find in order to starve. He was continuing to study painting with hopes of becoming independent, going to Paris and perhaps becoming famous. But a year went by and Ferdinand seemed to have become resigned to being stuck in Mercoeur by the need to earn his daily bread. Old Morand had become used to seeing him around and no longer paid him any special attention.

However, one evening his daughter asked him a surprising question. She had been busy drawing under the lamp, trying to reproduce, with mathematical accuracy, a photograph of a Raphael and after a lengthy silence, without looking up, she said:

"Why don't you ask Monsieur Sourdis to let you have one of his pictures, so that we could put it in the shop window?"

"My goodness, that's right!" exclaimed her father. "What a good idea.

I've never thought of asking to see what he does. Has he ever shown you anything?"

Adèle had begun to be obsessed by Ferdinand. She had been greatly taken by his youthful good looks and his superb head of fair hair, which he wore very short, though his beard was long and silky, the color of gold, and you could see his pink skin underneath. He had very gentle blue eyes while his dainty hands and fingers and dreamy, tender expression suggested a soft, sybaritic temperament. He would seem unlikely to be capable of exercising much will-power, except spasmodically. Indeed, on three previous occasions he had failed to come to work for three weeks; he had dropped his painting and rumor had it that the young man was behaving in a most deplorable manner in a certain house that was the shame of Mercoeur. As he did not return home for two nights running and was dead drunk when he did return one evening, there was talk for a while of dismissing him; but he was so charming when he was sober that they kept him on despite these escapades. Old Morand avoided mentioning these things to his daughter; these "ushers" were all birds of a feather, a completely immoral lot; and as such conduct scandalized his middle-class sense of propriety, he had adopted a distant manner towards the young man, while still keeping a soft spot for the artist.

Nevertheless, thanks to the indiscreet gossip of their maid, Adèle knew all about Ferdinand's dissipated habits. However, she, too, said nothing although she thought a good deal about such matters and had felt so angry with the young man that she had made herself scarce as soon as she saw him coming towards the shop, so that she would not have to serve him. It was at this time that Ferdinand had begun to preoccupy her and all sorts of vague ideas had started stirring in her mind. He had become interesting. Each time he went by, she would follow him with her eyes and then, with her head bent over her watercolors, she would remain meditating for the whole day.

"Well, is he going to bring you a picture?" she asked her father one Sunday, having arranged the day before for her father to serve Ferdinand when he had called to make his purchases.

"Yes, he is," replied Morand, "but he took a lot of persuading. I don't know whether it was false modesty or not but he kept making excuses and saying that they weren't worth exhibiting. He's letting us have the picture tomorrow."

Next day when Adèle came back from a visit to the old ruined castle of Mercoeur where she had gone sketching, she stopped in front of an unframed canvas placed on an easel standing in the middle of the shop and examined it closely. It was Ferdinand Sourdis's picture. It showed the bottom of a wind moat whose high green bank formed a horizontal line against the blue sky; in the moat, a group of schoolboys out for a walk were playing together, while the master in charge of them was lying in the grass reading. The painter had obviously drawn the subject from life; but what Adèle found quite disconcerting was a certain vibrancy of color and a boldness of line which she herself would never have dared to attempt. In her own work she had reached such an extraordinary mastery of technique that she could achieve the elaborate effects of Rennequin and of some other painters whose work she admired; but in this unknown painter's temperament there was a new personal touch which took her by surprise.

"Well, what do you think of it?" asked her father who was standing behind her waiting to hear her opinion.

She was still looking. Finally, with some hesitation but finding the work none the less attractive, she murmured, "It's interesting . . . It's very nice . . . "

She went back to look at the picture several times, with a serious expression on her face. Next day, as she was examining it again, Rennequin, who happened to be in Mercoeur, came into the shop and gave a slight exclamation, "Goodness me! What's that?"

He was gazing at it in amazement. Then drawing up a chair, he sat down in front of the painting and examined it in detail, with growing enthusiasm.

"It's very odd . . . There's such delicacy and truth in the tones . . . Just look at the white of those shirts against the green . . . And there's originality, too, a really individual note! Tell me, little girl, it can't have been you who painted that, surely?"

Adèle was listening, red in the face, as if these compliments were being addressed to herself. She replied hurriedly, "Oh no, it's that young man, you know, the schoolteacher next door."

"Really? It's a bit like your work," the painter went on. "Your work, but with more force . . . Oh, so it's that young man. Well, he's got talent, bags of talent. A picture like that would have a lot of success at the Salon."

Rennequin happened to be dining with the Morands that evening, an honor he paid them each time he visited Mercoeur. He talked painting the whole evening, returning several times to the subject of Ferdinand Sourdis, whom he was promising himself to call on and encourage. Without saying a word, Adèle sat listening to him talking about Paris, and his life and triumphs in the capital. A pensive furrow was creasing her pale, girlish forehead, as though an idea was slowly creeping into her mind and refusing to go away.

Ferdinand's picture was framed and put on exhibition in the shop window; the Lévèque girls came to look at it but found it lacking in "finish", while the very anxious Pole spread the rumor through the town that it represented a new school of painting which rejected Raphael. However, the picture was successful: people found it "nice" and families flocked to identify the schoolboys depicted in it. Ferdinand's situation in the school was, however, not thereby improved. Some of the senior masters were scandalized by the stir caused by the "usher" who had unscrupulously used as models the children placed in his care. Nevertheless, the school agreed to keep him on, on condition that he promised to be more careful in future. When Rennequin called on Ferdinand to offer his congratulations, he found the young man very downhearted, almost in tears and talking of giving up painting altogether.

"Cheer up," he said in his blunt, jovial way. "You've got talent enough to snap your fingers at all those idiots. And don't worry your day will come and you'll be able to escape from your present troubles, just as other fellow painters have done. In my time, I've worked as a bricklayer, you know. Meanwhile, the main thing is to keep on working."

A new life now opened up for Ferdinand. He gradually became a friend of the Morands. Adèle had begun to copy his picture The Walk. She was determined to give up watercolors and try her hand at oils. Rennequin's comment had been very discerning: as an artist, she had the graceful qualities of the young painter but she lacked his masculinity; in any case, her style of painting was already similar to Ferdinand's with an even greater skill and flexibility which made light of technical difficulties. Her slow careful copying of his picture brought them closer together. Adèle took Ferdinand's technique to pieces, as it were, and soon mastered his methods so successfully that he was amazed to see this sort of artistic double who interpreted and gave a literal reproduction of his work with a completely feminine discernment. It was like him, full of charm but in a minor key. In Mercoeur, Adèle's copy had much greater success than Ferdinand's original. Meanwhile, all sorts of scandalous gossip were beginning to circulate about the couple.

In fact, Ferdinand gave little thought to such things. Adèle did not tempt him in the slightest; he had his own vicious habits which he was able to satisfy abundantly elsewhere and this left him completely cold towards this conventional middle-class girl whose sallow complexion and poor figure he found most unattractive. He treated her purely as a fellow painter. Their only conversation was about painting. His imagination was becoming fired; his talk was full of dreams of going to Paris and he would refer bitterly to his poverty that kept him stuck in Mercoeur. Ah, if only he had enough to live on, how he'd love to get away from school-mastering! He felt sure he'd be successful. That miserable question of money and the need to earn his living threw him into a fury of anger. She would listen solemnly, seeming to be examining the question and weighing up his chances of success. Then, without going into any explanation, she would tell him not to be downhearted.

Suddenly, one morning, old Morand was found dead in his shop, struck down by apoplexy while unpacking a case of paints and brushes. A fortnight went by. Ferdinand had avoided intruding on the daughter's and her mother's grief. When he next called, nothing seemed changed. Adèle, dressed in black, was painting; Madame Morand was dozing in her bedroom. So they resumed their former habits, their conversations about art and dreams of triumphant success in Paris. However, the two young people now enjoyed a greater measure of intimacy, though a purely intellectual one, for no word of love or tenderness or over-familiarity ever came to disturb their friendship.

One evening, Adèle, more solemn than usual, after looking long and searchingly at Ferdinand, made up her mind to come to the point, doubtless feeling that by now she knew him well enough and that the time of decision had arrived.

"Listen, Ferdinand," she said, "I've been wanting to talk to you for a long time about a plan of mine. I'm alone in the world now, my mother hardly counts. So I hope you'll forgive me if I speak to you directly . . . "

Somewhat surprised, he sat waiting for her to continue. Then quite without embarrassment, she reminded him how he was always complaining about his lack of money, that he could become famous in very few years if only he could find the initial backing which he needed to work independently and make his mark in Paris.

"Well," she said finally, "let me come to your rescue. My father has left me an income of eight thousand francs a year and I can have it straightaway because he also made provision for my mother. She doesn't need me."

Ferdinand started protesting: he couldn't accept such a sacrifice, he couldn't possibly deprive her of her money. She stared at him, realizing that he had failed to understand.

"We would go and live in Paris," she continued slowly. "We could look forward to the future together."

Then, seeing the scared look on his face, she smiled and, stretching out her hands, said to him in a frank, friendly voice, "Ferdinand, will you marry me? You'd be doing me a favor, because you know I'm ambitious, I've always had dreams of becoming famous and I shall be, through you."

He was at a loss for words, unable to recover from the shock of this sudden proposal, while she meanwhile calmly finished explaining the plan that she had been working out for so long. Finally, she adopted a motherly tone: she would require only one thing as part of her bargain: he must swear to behave properly. Genius was useless without orderliness. And she gave him to understand that she knew about his wild habits and though this did not deter her, she intended to reform him. Ferdinand understood the bargain she was offering him perfectly well: she was putting up the money, he would have to provide the fame for both of them. He didn't love her, he even felt at that moment repugnance at the thought of having to sleep with her. However, he went down on his knees to thank her, although he could find only these words to say to her, which sounded insincere to him as soon as they were uttered, "You'll be my good angel . . . "

Then, despite the coldness of her nature, she felt a sudden surge of emotion: she hugged him and kissed him on the face. Her hitherto dormant passions were awakening; she was captivated by his blond good looks and the bargain she was striking was also providing a release for her long pent-up desires. She was in love.

Three weeks later, Ferdinand Sourdis had ceased to be a bachelor. He had capitulated, not as a premeditated scheme but because he had been driven to it by necessity and a set of circumstances from which he was unable to escape. The goodwill of old Morand's shop had been sold to a small local stationers'. Madame Morand was used to being alone and had accepted everything with great placidity. And so the young couple had set off at once for Paris, taking The Walk with them in their baggage and leaving Mercoeur in a state of shock at this sudden dramatic ending to its speculations. The Lévèque girls went about saying Madame Sourdis would arrive in the capital just in time to have her baby.

It was Madame Sourdis who saw to the setting up of their home. It was a flat in the Rue d'Assas with a big bay-windowed studio overlooking the trees of the Luxembourg gardens. As the couple's resources were limited, Adèle performed miracles in producing a comfortable home without excessive expense. She wanted to keep Ferdinand close at hand and provide him with a studio that he would like. And indeed, in the beginning, their life together in the heart of the great capital was delightful.

Winter was drawing to an end. The fine days in early March were most agreeable. As soon as he learnt of the presence of the painter and his young wife, Rennequin hurried round to see him. Their marriage had not surprised him, although he was usually very critical of such matches between artists; according to him, they always turned out badly, for one of the two was bound to gobble up the other. So Ferdinand would gobble up Adèle and that would be that; and good luck to him, since he needed the money. He might as well have a rather unattractive girl in his bed as have to eat bad meals in cheap restaurants.

When Rennequin went in, he saw The Walk, elaborately framed, on an easel standing in the middle of the studio.

"Ha, ha!" he exclaimed jovially, "I see you've brought the masterpiece with you!"

He sat down and once again launched into an admiring commentary on the delicacy of the tones and originality of conception of the picture. Then, suddenly, "I hope you'll put it in for the Salon. It's bound to be a great success . . . You've come just in time."

"That's exactly what I've been advising him to do," said Adèle quietly, 'but he can't make up his mind , he'd like to make his début with something bigger and more complete."

On hearing this, Rennequin became very annoyed. Youthful works were born under an especially lucky star. Ferdinand might perhaps never again find the freshness of impression, the boldness and lack of sophistication of this first work. Only and idiot could fail to realize that. Adèle smiled at the violence of his tone. Her husband was surely destined for great things and she had every hope that he would go on and paint something better; but she was delighted to hear Rennequin taking such a strong stand against Ferdinand's strange last-minute qualms. So it was agreed that The Walk should be submitted the very next day; the final entry date for the Salon was only three days off. There was no doubt that the picture would be accepted, for Rennequin was one of the judges and extremely influential.

The Walk was indeed accepted and had enormous success. For six weeks, the public thronged in front of the painting and, as often happens in Paris, Ferdinand became famous overnight. He even had the luck to arouse controversy, which doubled his success. While there were no outright attacks, some people criticized certain details which others passionately defended. In a word, The Walk was deemed to be a minor masterpiece and the official authorities immediately offered to buy it for six thousand francs. It had the necessary spice of originality to whet the jaded appetite of the majority of the public without any outrageous display of temperament on the part of the painter which might have offended some people: in a word, the exact mixture of novelty and vigor that the public required. It was a magical balance of pleasant qualities and people acclaimed the advent of a new star in the artistic firmament.

While her husband was suddenly enjoying such rapturous praise from the press and the general public alike, Adèle, who had submitted a few of her Mercoeur works, some very delicate watercolors, received no notice whatsoever, either from the visitors to the Salon or in the newspapers. But she was not envious and did not even feel hurt in her artistic pride; her pride was entirely bound up with her handsome Ferdinand. This withdrawn girl who had been moldering away in the damp and gloomy depths of the provinces for twenty-two years, this frigid, sallow-faced, conventional little miss had suddenly turned into an extraordinarily passionate woman, in heart and mind. She worshipped Ferdinand's golden beard, his pink flesh, the grace and charm of his whole person; she was jealous of him and unhappy when he was away for even a short time; she kept constant watch over his movements, for fear that some other woman might steal him from her. When she looked at herself in the mirror, she was acutely conscious of her inferiority, her dumpy figure and her already fading complexion. It was he, not she who provided the beauty in their marriage and she even felt she owed him what she should have claimed herself. Her heart melted at the thought that everything came from him. She would reflect in admiration on his masterly skill as a painter and would be filled with boundless gratitude at the realization that she was an equal partner in his talent, his success, his celebrity and that she would be able to rise to dazzling heights of fame at his side. All her dreams were coming true, not now through herself but through another self whom she loved as a disciple, as a mother and as a wife. And even, in her heart of hearts, her pride would whisper to her that Ferdinand would be her creation and that after all, everything was owed to her.

During these first few months, life in the studio in the Rue d'Assas was sheer magic, day in, day out. Despite her feeling that so much of what she had came from Ferdinand, Adèle did not feel in the least humiliated, for the thought that it was she who had been instrumental in bringing all this to pass was sufficient. With a tender smile on her lips, she watched the blossoming happiness which she had sought and engineered. Without pettiness or meanness of any sort, she could say to herself that it was her money and her money alone which had made this happiness possible. So she kept her place, realizing that she was necessary. Her admiration and worship was a tribute freely given by a person glad to abdicate her personality in support of a work that she looked on as her own and on which she intended to live. In the Luxembourg gardens, the tall trees were putting on green leaves, the twittering of birds floated into the studio on the warm breezes of the lovely spring days and every morning fresh newspapers would arrive, full of praise. Ferdinand was being photographed and his painting was being reproduced by every possible process and in every possible format. And so with childlike joy, the young newly-weds basked in this blaze of publicity, in the knowledge that, as they sat eating together at their little table in their charming quiet retreat in the Rue d'Assas, Paris, that great and glorious capital, was interested in them.

Meanwhile Ferdinand had not yet begun working again. He was living in so great a fever of excitement that he claimed he was incapable of handling a brush as he would have liked. Three months went by and still he kept putting off his studies for a larger picture which he had long had in mind to paint: a painting which he had baptized The Lake. It would depict an avenue in the Boise de Boulogne, seen at the time of day when the longer queue of carriages drives slowly along in the golden light of the setting sun, He had already been to make a few sketches but he no longer seemed to feel the divine spark that had inspired him during his hard times as a poverty-stricken usher. His present well-being seemed to have quenched his ardor; also he was enjoying his sudden fame too much to want to risk forfeiting it in a fresh work. For the moment, he was always out and about, frequently vanishing in the morning and not reappearing until evening. On two or three occasions, he came home very late. He was always finding different pretexts to go out and not come back: he would be visiting a studio or a show by some contemporary artist; he had to collect material for his future work: above all, he was dining out with friends. He had run across a number of his old Lille friends, he was already a member of several artistic groups; all these activities launched him on a continual round of pleasure and he would come home in a state of feverish exhilaration, with shining eyes and talking very loudly.

As yet Adèle had refrained from making any protest. Although extremely unhappy at his growing self-indulgence which was depriving her of her husband and leaving her constantly alone at home, she was trying to stifle her jealousy and fears: Ferdinand had to manage his own affairs; an artist wasn't a grocer who could stay comfortably by his own fireside; he had to go out into society, he owed it to himself to further his reputation. She almost felt remorse at her secret resentment when Ferdinand put on his act of a man worn out by social obligations, swearing that he was 'fed up' and that he would have given his right arm to be able to stay at home with his darling little wife. Once it was even she herself who sent him off when he was pretending to be reluctant to go to an exclusively male luncheon party where he would be introduced to a very wealthy collector. Then, left alone, Adèle would cry. She was trying to be brave and yet she was continually imagining her husband with other women; she felt that he was being unfaithful and this made her so unwell that sometimes she had to take to her bed as soon as he had left the flat.

Rennequin would often call to pick up Ferdinand and she would try to joke about it, "Now, you'll be good little boys, won't you? You know, I'm putting in him in your charge . . . "

"Don't worry," the painter would laugh. "If someone tries to make off with him, I'll be there . . . In any case, I'll bring back his hat and stick, at least."

She trusted Rennequin. Since he, too, was going out with Ferdinand, the outing must be justified. She'd get used to it. But she would sigh when she remembered their first few weeks together in Paris, before all the upset caused by the Salon and they used to spend their days happily together in the studio. Now she was the only one working there, for she had gone back to her watercolor painting with frantic energy, to while away the time. As soon as Ferdinand had disappeared round the corner of the street with a final farewell wave, she would close the window and settle down to her task. He was gallivanting about all over the town, God alone knew where, visiting all sorts of shady haunts and coming home dog-tired, with bloodshot eyes, while she sat patiently at her little table, all day and every day, doggedly painting the studies for pictures that she had brought with her from Mercoeur, sentimental little landscapes that she was painting with and increasingly impressive skill. She described it, with a wry smile, as her embroidery.

One evening she had stayed up late waiting for Ferdinand, absorbed in a pencil drawing of an engraving, when she was startled to hear a dull thud just outside the studio door. She called out and then decided to open the door, where she discovered her husband slowly getting to his feet, with an inane laugh. He was drunk.

As white as a sheet, Adèle helped him to his feet and half dragged, half lifted him into their bedroom. He kept apologizing; his speech was slurred and incoherent. Without a word, she helped him to undress. Then, when he was drunkenly snoring in bed, completely dead to the world, she spent the rest of the night, wide awake in an armchair, her pale forehead furrowed in thought. Next morning, she made no mention of his scandalous behavior of the previous night. He was deeply embarrassed and still bemused, with swollen eyes and a bitter taste in his mouth. His wife's silence increased his embarrassment and for two whole days he stayed at home and shamefacedly set to work on his painting, like a schoolboy eager and anxious to be forgiven for some misdemeanor. He set about laying out the main lines of his picture, consulting Adèle and trying hard to show how much he valued her judgment. At first, she remained coldly silent, as a living reproach, although still making not the slightest reference to what had occurred. Then, seeing how contrite he was, she became her natural, kindly self again; everything was tacitly forgiven and forgotten. But on the third day, Rennequin came to pick up his young friend to take him to dinner at the Café Anglais* to meet a well-known art critic. Adèle had to wait up until four o'clock for her husband and when he did eventually come home, he was bleeding from an open cut over his left eye, caused by a bottle in the course of a brawl in some low haunt. She put him to bed and dressed his wound. Rennequin had left him on the boulevards at eleven o'clock.

From now on, the pattern was set. Ferdinand could never accept an invitation to dinner or a party or stay out in the evening on some pretext or other without coming home in a revolting state. He would be frightfully tipsy, black and blue from bruises, with his clothes in disorder and reeking to high heaven of spirits or the cheap scents favored by street-walkers. He had got into a vicious rut from which his spineless character made it impossible for him to escape. Adèle maintained her stony silence; each time it happened she would tend him with icy indifference, never questioning him, never even slapping his face for his abominable behavior. She would make him tea, hold a bowl for him to be sick into, clean up after him, refusing to wake the maid in order to keep his condition to herself, since it was too disgusting for a decent person to reveal to anyone. Anyway, what would have been the point of questioning him? Each time it took place, she could easily reconstruct the scene: a few drinks with friends to set him going, a wild rampage through the unsavory night haunts of the capital, drunken debauchery, crawling from bar to bar with stray drinking companions, picking up women on the streets, brawling with soldiers for their favors and finally satisfying his squalid lust in some filthy little artic room. Sometimes she would discover strange addresses stuffed into his pockets and unmentionable objects, all sorts of disgusting evidence which she would hastily burn in order not to learn about such things. When one of his women had scratched him with her nails or he had come home filthy and injured, she would merely take a tighter hold on herself and wash him in such scornful silence that he did not dare to utter a word. Then, the day after these spectacular nights of riotous living, he would wake up and find her as tight-lipped as ever; as neither of them mentioned it, it seemed to them that they had both lived through a bad dream. And so life would begin again as before.

Only once, in a fit of uncontrollable tenderness, Ferdinand had suddenly flung both arms round her neck when he woke up. He was sobbing as he gasped brokenly:

"Forgive me, oh please forgive me!"

Obviously disconcerted, she had pretended to be surprised and pushed him away, saying, "What do you mean, forgive you? You haven't done anything to forgive. I'm not grumbling."

And this dogged refusal to acknowledge his shortcomings and her female superiority in self-control and mastery of her emotions had made Ferdinand feel like a naughty little boy.

In fact, Adèle's attitude was concealing agonized disgust and anger. Both her religious upbringing and her sense of decency and human dignity were completely outraged by Ferdinand's behavior. Each time he came home stinking of vice and she had to touch him with her hands and spend the rest of the night smelling his breath, she was filled with nausea and contempt. But beneath the contempt, there lay a dreadful jealousy directed at his friends and at the women who sent him back to her so soiled and degraded. She would have enjoyed seeing those women dying in the gutter; she thought of them as monsters and could not understand why the police didn't shoot them on sight. But her love was undiminished. When, on certain nights, the man himself filled her with disgust, she would console herself by her admiration for the artist; and this admiration became in a way purified, for with her conventional middle-class notion of the typical man of genius fated to live a wild bohemian life, she had ended by accepting Ferdinand's conduct as being the dunghill on which alone great works of art could flourish. Indeed, if, as a woman, she was shocked by his callous disregard for her own affection and delicacy of feeling, she blamed him perhaps even more strongly for his failure to fulfill his obligations as an artist, for breaking the pact they had made whereby she would supply the material means in return for which he would provide the fame. It was a breach of faith which she deeply resented and she began to cast about to find ways and means of rescuing the painter even should the man sink without trace. It was up to her to be strong for it was she who now had to be the master.

In less than a year, Ferdinand felt himself reduced to the level of a little boy; he had fallen completely under Adèle's thumb. In this survival of the fittest, she had proved to be the male. Each time he had fallen by the wayside and, sternly but without uttering a word of blame, she had condescended to care for him, he had hung his head in shame and humiliation, sensing her contempt. There was no room for lies between them: she represented sweet reasonableness, decency and strength while he was the epitome of weakness and degradation. The thing which he found most painful and made him utterly powerless in her presence was the fact that her implacable condemnation was based on full knowledge of his guilt and her cold contempt was capable of forgiving without feeling the need to reprimand him. It was as if any explanation would destroy their dignity as a couple. She was maintaining her silence in order to remain high above him and not abase herself, with the risk of being sullied by his filth. Had she lost her temper, had she flung his despicable one-night amours in his face like any frantic, jealous wife, he would certainly have suffered less. If she had been prepared to come down to his level, she might have raised him up; but how small he felt, how immeasurably inferior, when he woke up, ashamed and fully aware that she knew all but would never lower herself to utter one word of reproof!

Meanwhile, his picture was progressing, for he had realized that his only superiority lay in his painting. When he was working. Adèle would once again become the tender-hearted wife and bring herself down to his level; she would stand respectfully behind him and study his picture and the better his day's work had been, the more deferential she would become. At such times., it was he who was the master; the male was asserting his proper role in the family. But he was now becoming subject to paralyzing fits of laziness. When he came home exhausted, as if drained of energy by the sort of life he was leading, his hands felt weak, he was full of hesitation, he could no longer paint decisively. Some mornings, his whole being seemed gripped by an overwhelming feeling of impotence. At such times, he would fritter away the whole day in front of his easel, picking up his palette only to fling it down again a moment later, fretting and fuming with rage and unable to do anything at all; or else he would lie down and sleep like a log on the settee, not waking up until evening with an appalling migraine. On these days, Adèle would watch him in silence, creeping around on tiptoe in order not to irritate him or scare away the inspiration that would surely come. She believed in inspiration, that invisible flame that would dart in through the window and settle on the chosen artist's brow. And then she, too, would be seized by discouragement and anxiety at the thought, as yet not clearly formulated, that Ferdinand might fail her, like a defaulting business partner.

It was February and the Salon was approaching The Lake was still not nearly completed. The main part had been done, inasmuch as the canvas was entirely covered; but apart from certain sections that were quite well advanced, all the rest was blurred and unfinished. It was barely more than a rough sketch and could certainly never be submitted in that state. It needed to be pulled together, it lacked the highlights and the finish which gives a work its value as a painting. Ferdinand was now making no progress whatsoever, losing himself in finicky details, undoing in the evening what he had painted during the day, spinning helplessly like a frenzied top. One evening as dusk was falling, when Adèle returned from a distant shopping excursion, she heard the sound of sobs coming from the darkened studio and was moved to see her husband sitting slumped on his chair in front of his easel.

"You're crying!" she exclaimed. "What's the matter?"

"No, nothing's the matter," he replied brokenly.

He had sunk into his chair and for the last hour had sat gazing vacantly at his canvas, even when the failing light had made it invisible. Everything was dancing in front of his blurred eyes. His work seemed to him an absurd, pitiful and chaotic mess and he felt paralyzed, as weak as a child, powerless to bring any sort of order into this confused mass of colors. Then, when darkness had gradually hidden the canvas and even the brighter colors had been obliterated, he had been overcome by an immense sadness which seemed to be throttling him. It was then that he had burst into sobs.

"But you are crying, I can fell it," said Adèle, running her hands over his cheeks bathed in warm tears. "Are you in pain?"

He was choked by a renewed burst of sobbing and was unable to reply. Then, forgetting her resentment and giving way to her compassion for this poor, failed creature, she gave him, in the darkness, a motherly kiss. He was bankrupt.

Next day Ferdinand had to go out after lunch and when he came back a couple of hours later, as he was standing as usual absorbed in front of his painting, he suddenly gave a muttered exclamation:

"Well I'm damned! Someone's been touching my picture."

Part of the sky and a small section of foliage on the left had been finished. Adèle was bending over her table busily concentrating on one of her watercolors and at first made no comment.

"Who on earth can have taken such a liberty?" Ferdinand went on, more surprised than annoyed. "Has Rennequin been in?"

"No," said Adèle at last, 'it was me, I did it just for fun. It's not at all important, I only did some of the background."

Ferdinand gave an embarrassed laugh.

"So you want to collaborate with me, do you? Well, I think you've got the general tone very nicely, only there's one highlight there that needs toning down a bit."

"Where's that?" she enquired, getting up from her table. "Oh yes, I see, it's that branch."

She picked up a brush and made the necessary alteration, while he stood watching her. After a pause, he began to make other suggestions, as though speaking to a pupil, while she went on painting the sky. Without anything being said, it became understood that she would undertake to finish off the backgrounds. Time was short and they had to hurry . . . And he pretended that he was not feeling very well, a statement that she accepted without demur.

"As I'm not very fit at the moment," he would say, "your help is going to come in very useful. The backgrounds aren't all that important."

From that moment, he was completely reconciled to the sight of her standing in front of his easel. Now and again he got up from the settee with a yawn and came over to have a look and pass a brief judgment on the work, sometimes making her go over some of it again. As a teacher, he was very strict. Next day, still complaining that he was feeling even more under the weather, he told her that she should first go ahead with the backgrounds before he finished the foregrounds himself; he felt that that would make the work easier, the situation would be clearer and they would progress more rapidly. So he was able to enjoy a week of utter idleness, spending long periods asleep on the settee while his wife stood all day painting in silence. Then he bestirred himself and tackled the foregrounds. However, he did not want her to go far away and whenever he grew impatient, she would calm him down and herself complete the details as he pointed them out to her. She would often send him off into the Luxembourg gardens to take a breath of fresh air: as he wasn't feeling very well, he must take care of himself; it was doing him no good at all to get excited like that. Her concern was very affectionate. Then, once he was out of the way, she set rapidly to work with feminine determination, not hesitating to get on with the foregrounds as quickly as possible. He had reached such a state of enervation that he did not even notice how much she had done while he was away or, at any rate, he made no comment on it; he seemed to think that the painting was going ahead all on its own. Within the fortnight, The Lake was completed. But Adèle herself was not satisfied. She still felt that something was definitely lacking. When a relieved Ferdinand declared that the picture was very good, she shook her head unenthusiastically.

"What on earth do you want, then?" he snapped angrily. "We can't kill ourselves doing it!"

What she wanted was for him to give the picture his own personal touch and, by dint of patience and willpower, she managed to perform the miracle of infusing him with sufficient energy to do it. For one more week, she nagged at him and encouraged him. He never left the flat; she aroused him with her caresses and intoxicated him with her admiration. Then, once she felt that he was sufficiently stimulated, she thrust his brushes into his hand and kept him standing for hours in front of his picture, talking, discussing and generally putting him into such a state of excitement that he was like a giant refreshed. In this way he reworked the whole picture, going back over what Adèle had done and adding the vigorous individual touch which it lacked. It might not have seemed much but in fact it was everything: the entire painting had come to life.

Adèle was overjoyed. Once again, the future looked rosy. Since working long hours tired her husband, she would help him. It would be a more private mission, a secret happiness which filled her with hope. But she jokingly made Ferdinand swear not to reveal her part in the painting: it wasn't worth mentioning, it would embarrass her. He expressed surprise but made his promise. He felt no jealousy towards Adèle as an artist; he always went about saying that she knew the painter's trade better than he, which was true.

When Rennequin came to see The Lake, he stood looking at it for a long time without saying a word. Then he offered his young friend his very sincere congratulations.

"It's certainly more finished than The Walk," he said. "The background's incredibly light and delicate and the foreground's very spirited and vigorous . . . Yes, it's really good, really original."

He was obviously surprised but he did not reveal the reason for his surprise. This young fellow-me-lad had nonplussed him; he would never have thought him capable of such skilful technique; he also found something new in his painting. All the same, although he did not say so, he preferred The Walk, for although certainly more slipshod and less polished, it was more personal. So, despite the surer, broader, treatment of The Lake, he still found it less attractive because he could detect in it a more conventional, deliberate, approach, with a hint of prettiness and over-elaboration. This impression did not prevent him from saying as he left:

"Remarkable, my dear boy . . . You're going to be a tremendous success."

His prophecy came true. The success of The Lake was even greater than that of The Walk. The women particularly raved about it: it was exquisite. The carriages with their flashing wheels gliding along in the sunshine, the tiny fashionably dressed figures, the bright specks of color bringing out the vivid greenery of the Bois, charmed those members of the public who look upon painting as a decorative art similar to that of a goldsmith. But even severe critics, those who expect vigor and logic from a work of art, were attracted by its painterly skills, an excellent understanding of overall effect and its rare level of execution. But the predominant impression, the one which finally won the total approval of the general public, was the graceful, slightly finical, individuality of the style. All the critics agreed that Ferdinand Sourdis was "coming on well". Only one of them, notoriously outspoken and heartily disliked for his imperturbable way of speaking the truth, dared to write that, should the painter continue to elaborate and emasculate his style, he would give him less than five years to ruin his precious gift of originality.

In the Rue d'Assas, there was great satisfaction. This was no longer the unexpected success of a tyro but a definitive recognition that Ferdinand ranked among the best painters of the age. What is more, he was becoming prosperous: commissions were beginning to flow in from every quarter, and buyers were competing, cash in hand, for the little canvases left lying about in his studio. He had to get down to work.

Amidst this new-found prosperity, Adèle kept her head. She was not miserly but she had been brought up in that provincial tradition of economy which, as they say, knows the value of money. As a result, she showed herself a strict manager and saw to it that Ferdinand never failed to honor his commitments. She would make careful note of his commissions, ensure that they were completed on time, and invest the proceeds. Above all, she exercised relentless pressure on her husband and ruled him with a rod of iron.

She had laid down his way of life: so many hours worked before he could relax. However, she never lost her temper, she remained, as always, dignified and sparing of words; but he had behaved so badly in the past and had allowed her to assume such an ascendancy over him that he was now terrified of her. This was certainly the greatest possible service that she could have done him, for without her willpower to sustain him, he would have let things slide and not produced the works which, in fact, he now managed to produce over a number of years. She was his greatest strength, his guide and support. This fear which she inspired in him did not, however, prevent him from sometimes relapsing into his former disorderly ways; as she refused to pander to his vicious habits, he would break out and launch into wild bouts of debauchery, returning home ill and in a state of stupor that would last three or four days. But each time this happened, he was providing her with fresh ammunition to use against himself. She would look at him with eyes full of an even greater and more pitiless contempt which would chain him to his easel for a week. She suffered too much as wife and woman whenever he betrayed her foe her ever to want him to indulge in these escapades from which he returned in such a repentant and obedient state; all the same, whenever she recognized the symptoms, his pale eyes, his restless, urgent gestures, and realized that he was racked by lust, she could hardly wait to see him come reeling back off the streets, a nerveless jelly of a man who would be like wax in her determined, stumpy hands. With her plain face, her dull complexion, her leathery skin and big bones, she knew that she was indeed no beauty and so she took her revenge on this handsome man, who belonged to her, as soon as his fancy women had bled him white. Moreover, Ferdinand was ageing rapidly; he had been afflicted by rheumatism, and by the age of forty his manifold excesses had already turned him into an old man. Age would inexorably clip his wings.

After The Lake there was a tacit agreement between husband and wife that they should collaborate. They still kept it a secret but behind closed doors, they would set to work on the same picture and make it a joint effort. Ferdinand supplied his masculine gift of inspiration and construction; it was he who would choose the subject, divide it into the appropriate parts and establish the general layout. The execution of the project would then be handed over to the feminine talent of Adèle, although Ferdinand would keep certain vigorous passages for himself to paint. Indeed, at the beginning, he did most of the painting himself and made a point of not letting his wife help him except in minor parts of the picture; but as his strength decreased and he gradually lost heart in his work, he gave up the struggle and let Adèle take over. So, in the nature of things, her collaboration inevitably increased with each new work, without any intention on her part to replace his painting by her own. What she primarily wanted was for the name of Sourdis, which was now hers as well, not to disappear ingloriously, for his fame, which had been this plain, deprived girl's constant dream, not to decline; and, furthermore, she wanted not to let their customers down, to deliver the pictures on the promised date, like an honest business woman whose word is her bond. The result was that she inevitably found herself forced to complete the paintings in a hurry, to fill in the gaps left by Ferdinand and finish the work off when she could see him fuming with impotent rage and unable to hold his brushes in his trembling hands. However, she never gloated and always maintained the pretence of being the pupil, of restricting her task to that of a journeyman working under her husband's instructions. She still respected him as an artist and genuinely admired him, with the instinctive intuition that, despite his degradation, he was still the master without whom she would never have been capable of producing such large-scale paintings.

Rennequin was following with growing surprise and incomprehension this slow supplanting of the male by the female temperament in their work, although they kept their secret from him as from all their other fellow painters. Rennequin felt that Ferdinand could hardly be considered to be strictly on the wrong track since he was, after all, continuing to produce and keep his head above water; but his painting was evolving in a direction that seemed out of line with his earlier work. His first picture, The Walk, had revealed a lively, witty individuality; this had vanished from his later work which was now increasingly swamped in a soft, fluid impasto, very easy on the eye but more and more banal. And yet it was the same hand at work; at least, Rennequin would have sworn that it was, so adept had Adèle become at imitating her husband's technique. She had a genius for taking other people's methods to pieces and adapting herself to them. On the other hand, Ferdinand's paintings were now taking on a kind of vaguely puritanical middle-class feeling of propriety which the old painter found offensive. In the beginning he had welcomed the very great freedom of spirit shown by his gifted young friend and he was now irritated to see this new formality, a sort of starchy prudishness, in his later painting. One evening, in a group of fellow artists, he could no longer restrain himself.

"That fellow Sourdis is turning into nothing more than a preacher!" he exclaimed. "Have you seen his latest painting? It's sheer milk and water. All those tarts of his have squeezed him dry. It's the old, old story: you let some stupid female gobble you up . . . Do you know what makes me really mad? The fact that he can still paint quite well. You may laugh, but I mean it! I'd always imagined that if he went off the rails, he'd do it on a grand scale and finish up an utter shambles, like a man sunk without trace. Not a bit of it! He seems to have found a sort of clockwork mechanism which he can wind up every day and it enables him to churn out his boring stuff ad infinitum. It's a disaster! He's finished; he can't even paint badly!

They were used to Rennequin's paradoxical outbursts and merely laughed. But he knew what he meant and, being fond of Ferdinand, he felt sad about it.

Next day he called in at the Rue d'Assas. Seeing the key in the door, he took the liberty of going in without knocking and stopped short in amazement. There was no sign of Ferdinand and Adèle was standing in front of the easel, deftly finishing off a picture which the papers had already started talking about. She was so completely absorbed in her work that she did not hear the door opening and did not realize that when the maid had come in, she had left the key in the door. Rennequin was thus able to stand watching her for a good minute. She was carrying out her task with a sureness of touch indicative of long practice and putting on the paint with the fluency and facile mechanical perfection which he had been berating the day before. All at once, he understood what had happened and the shock was so great that, realizing the full extent of his indiscretion, he was on the point of going out and knocking on the door before coming in again. But at that moment, Adèle looked round.

"Good gracious, it's you!" she exclaimed. "How did you get in?"

And she went very red in the face. Rennequin, equally embarrassed, replied that he had only just arrived; but, realizing that if he made no reference to what he had seen the situation would be even more embarrassing, he added in his most hearty manner:

"Well, well, I can see that we've been running short of time! You've been lending Ferdinand a hand . . . "

Her complexion had returned to its normal waxen pallor. She replied calmly:

"Yes, this picture should have been handed over last Monday and as Ferdinand has been suffering from his pains again . . . Oh, it's just a couple of glazes, nothing of any consequence."

But she was not deceiving herself; she knew that it was impossible to fool someone as expert as Rennequin. Nevertheless, she made no move but merely stood where she was, still holding her palette and brushes in her hands. He felt obliged to say something, "Don't let me disturb you, just keep going."

She gazed at him for a few seconds before making up her mind what to do. What was the point of further pretence, now that he knew everything? And as she had given her word that the picture would be ready that evening, she quickly set to work again, with a completely unfeminine firmness and boldness of touch. Drawing up a chair, Rennequin followed her work. At this moment, Ferdinand came in. At first he seemed shocked to see Rennequin sitting behind Adèle and watching her at work on his picture. But he looked very tired and hardly capable of any strong reaction. He sank on to a chair beside the older painter, with the sigh of a man whose only need is sleep. Silence fell. Ferdinand did not feel that any explanation was required: that was how things were and he didn't mind. However, after a moment, when Adèle was reaching up and slashing bold stokes of vivid color on to her sky, he leaned over towards Rennequin and said in a voice full of pride, "You know, old man, she's better than me! How about that technique, eh? Isn't she stylish!"

Later, when Rennequin left, perplexed and quite upset, once he was alone on the staircase he gave vent to his feelings out loud:

"There's another good man gone west! She may stop him from going under but she'll never let him reach the top! He's buggered!"

Years went by. The Sourdis had bought a little house in Mercoeur, with a garden looking out on to the Esplanade. At first they came to spend a couple of months there every summer to escape from the stifling Paris heat in July and August. It was a sort of permanent retreat. But, gradually, they lived there more and more. As they settled in and made themselves a home, they felt less and less need for Paris. Since the accommodation was rather cramped, they had a very spacious studio built in the garden and soon enlarged it with further additions. Now they found themselves going to the capital during the winter, tow or three months at most; they lived in Mercoeur and kept only a small flat in Paris, some rooms in a small house which belonged to them, situated in the Rue de Clichy.

This withdrawal to the country had thus taken place gradually, with no particular foresight on their part. When people expressed surprise, Adèle would talk about Ferdinand's poor health and give the impression that her hand had been forced by the need to provide her husband with a peaceful open-air environment. But the truth was that she was fulfilling at last a long cherished dream. As a girl she had sat for hours looking at the wet cobblestones of the Place du Collège and she had indeed dreamt of a brilliant future in Paris, amid the plaudits of the crowd, basking in the fame of the name of Sourdis; but now her dream did not extend beyond Mercoeur, in a quiet little corner of the tiny town surrounded by the respectful admiration of its surprised inhabitants. It was here that she had been born and here that she had felt the continual spur of her ambition to succeed, so much so, indeed, that the amazement of the good women of Mercoeur gossiping on their doorsteps, as she walked by arm-in-arm with her husband, meant more to her than all the praise of the sophisticated denizens of Paris drawing-rooms. At heart, she had remained a provincial middle-class woman concerned at how her little town would view each new triumph; every time she went back there, her heart would beat faster and she would purr with inner satisfaction at the thought of the way in which now surrounded her. Her mother had died some ten years ago and she was merely coming back to recover her lost youth which had been dormant and repressed in her earlier years.

By now the name of Sourdis could hardly have been more famous: at fifty, the painter had received every conceivable award and honor, all the obligatory medals and crosses and titles. He was a Commander of the Legion of Honor and had been a member of the Academy for a number of years. The only thing that was still expanding was his wealth; newspapers had long since fun out of superlatives. There were now ready-made formulas of praise which were trotted out at every opportunity: he was the "prolific master"; he had "exquisite charm which won every heart". But such things no longer seemed to interest him; he was becoming indifferent and wore his halo like an old suit which he had ceased to notice. When the inhabitants of Mercoeur saw him go by, with his eyes glazed, already terribly round-shouldered, their respect was strongly tinged with astonishment for they found it difficult to conceive how this weary, withdrawn old man came to be so famous in the capital.

In any case, by now everyone knew that Madame Sourdis used to help her husband in his painting. She had the reputation of being a most capable woman, although she was so tiny and very stout. Indeed, this was another cause for astonishment in Mercoeur, that such a plump lady could stand all day in front of an easel without her legs giving way by the evening. Must be just a question of habit, opined the worthy citizens of Mercoeur.

This collaboration from his wife had had no adverse effect on Ferdinand's reputation, indeed quite the reverse. With her infallible tact, Adèle had realized that she must not openly expose her husband as a man of straw; he still signed the paintings, like a constitutional monarch who reigns but does not rule. Works by Madame Sourdis would have impressed no one, whereas works by Ferdinand Sourdis retained all their old power over critics and public alike. For this reason, she always showed the greatest admiration for her husband and, strangely enough, this admiration was perfectly genuine. Although he had reached the stage where he very rarely picked up a brush, she still looked on him as the real creator of the pictures now painted almost entirely by herself. In this exchange it was her character which had forced its way into their joint work, to the point of dominating it to the exclusion of her husband; but she nevertheless still felt dependent on his initial impulse; she had replaced him by dint of assimilating him, adopting, as it were, his sex. The result was freakish. Whenever she was showing their works to visitors, she would always say: "Ferdinand did this, Ferdinand's going to do that", even when he had not provided nor would be providing a single brushstroke. She would flare up at the slightest criticism and would not allow anyone to question his genius. Her blind faith in her husband was superb. Her anger in his squalid adulteries, her disgust and contempt, had never managed to destroy her high opinion of him as the great artist whom she had loved and gone on loving even when that artist had declined and she had been forced to step into his shoes to avoid failure. It was a charming touch of blind simplicity, based on her mingled pride and affection, which enabled Ferdinand to live with his secret sense of impotence. His moral decay did not cause him to suffer excessively; he, too, would speak of "my picture", "my work", without thinking how little of his work had gone into the pictures he was signing with his name. And all this had come about so naturally between the tow of them and he felt so little jealousy towards this woman, who had even robbed him of his individuality, that he could not talk for more than a few minutes without starting to praise her. He would keep repeating all the time what he had once said to Rennequin one evening.

"I assure you, she's more talented than me . . . I have the devil of a job with my drawing whereas she does it in a jiffy, as easy as falling off a log . . . You just can't imagine how clever she is! It's a gift. You've either got it or you haven't. I haven't and she has."

People would smile discreetly and see it as a compliment from a loving husband; yet should anyone show that they thought highly of Madame

Sourdis as a person but had no great opinion of her as an artist, he would take umbrage and launch into a long theoretical disquisition on the artistic temperament and the mechanics of painting, always finishing up by asserting, "And I'm telling you that she's better than I am! People must be mad not to see it!"

They were a very united couple. Latterly, age and ill-health had greatly subdued Ferdinand. He could no longer drink, for the slightest excess upset his stomach. Only women were still capable of enticing him into his old habits of debauchery, bouts that would last two or three days. But when the couple finally settled in Mercoeur, the lack of opportunity forced him to become almost completely faithful. After this, Adèle's only danger would be if he took a sudden fancy to one of her maids. She had accepted the fact that she must employ only very ugly ones but that still did not prevent Ferdinand from chancing his arm, if he could persuade the maid to cooperate; in certain moods, he had a pathological urge to satisfy his sexual appetites and gratify his perversions, an urge which he was quite incapable of controlling, however unpleasant the consequences. Adèle merely changed her maids each time she thought she detected too intimate a relationship between master and servant. Then Ferdinand would be contrite for a whole week and, even in their old age, this would rekindle their love. Adèle still worshipped her husband with the same savage jealousy which she had always managed to conceal from him; and he, faced by one of her terrifying silences when she had had to dismiss a maid, would try to obtain forgiveness by a display of cringing affection. At such times, she would dominate him like a little boy. His sallow face was by now fearfully ravaged and deeply lined; but he still had his golden beard, paler but with no trace of grey, so that he looked like some venerable god still possessing the golden charm of youth.

Then on day, in their Mercoeur studio, Ferdinand was suddenly overcome by a deep dislike for painting, a sort of physical revulsion. The smell of turpentine, the feel of the oily brush on the canvas, threw him into a state of nervous exasperation; his hands started to tremble and he was attacked by dizziness. No doubt it was a consequence of his own incapacity, the result of an acute crisis in the breakdown in his artistic faculties, which had been bound to end in this sheer physical impotence. Adèle was very sympathetic and comforted him by assuring him that it must be a passing indisposition from which he would soon recover. She insisted that he should rest and as he was now doing absolutely no work at all on his pictures, he became gloomy and anxious. She thought up a compromise: he would produce the sketch plans in pencil and she would square them up on the canvas and paint them, under his instructions. Henceforth, that was the procedure that they followed and in every work he signed, there was now not one single brushstroke of his own. All the actual painting was undertaken by Adèle while he merely provided the inspiration, the ideas and the pencil sketches, which were sometimes incomplete and even wrong, so that she was forced to correct them, without, however, informing him.

Following his great success in France, orders had poured in from abroad, particularly from America and Russia, and as the art collectors from those distant lands were not very demanding, all that was required was to send off crates of pictures and cash the money, with no questions asked. Gradually, the Sourdis had gone over completely to this convenient form of production. Moreover, sales in France had dropped. When, at rare intervals, Ferdinand sent a picture to the salon, it was still given the same enthusiastic reception by the critics, for, being a recognized and established painter of undisputed talent, he had been able without disturbing the habits of either the critics or the public. For the majority of people, the painter was still the same, only, as he grew older, he had given way to younger, more controversial, painters. Buyers were, however, beginning to lose their taste for his paintings and, though he was still considered a contemporary master, his pictures now sold rather poorly. His whole production was going overseas.

However, one year, one of Ferdinand Sourdis's pictures made a great stir at the Salon. It was a kind of counterpart to his first Salon painting. The Walk. In a cold, white-walled room, school-boys were working, exchanging sly grins and watching flies, while the assistant master in charge of them was absorbed in a novel, seemingly oblivious to everything. It was entitled The Preparation Room. Everyone found it charming and there were critics who, comparing the two works painted at an interval of thirty years, spoke of the progress achieved, of the "prentice quality" of The Walk and the mastery of The Preparation Room. Almost all of them contrived to discover extraordinary finesse in the second picture, exquisite artistry and a perfection of technique that would never be surpassed. However, the great majority of artists protested, Rennequin most vigorously of all. Although by now a man of seventy-five, he had remained young and was still passionately interested in painting.

"For God's sake!" he exclaimed. "I'm very fond of Ferdinand but it really is idiotic to prefer his present works to those he painted as a young man. He's got no spunk, no bite, no originality of any sort. Oh, I grant you it's pretty, it's easy on the eye. But you'd have to be a grocer to enjoy that unimaginative technique, tarted up and titivated into a tawdry mish-mash of every possible style and even the perversion of every style . . . It's not the Ferdinand I used to know who's painting that sort of rubbish."

Yet, although he knew their secret, he still held back from telling the truth about the Sourdis's paintings. You could, however, sense in the bitterness of his remarks the hidden resentment he had always felt against women, those "noxious animals" as he sometimes called them. So he contented himself merely with repeating angrily, "No, that's not the old Ferdinand, definitely not!"

He had been following and analyzing with curiosity the way in which Adèle had slowly taken over from Ferdinand. With each new picture, he had noted the slightest changes, recognizing the parts painted by the husband or by the wife and realizing that the former were steadily and increasingly being superseded by the latter. It was such an absorbing phenomenon that he forgot to be angry and merely enjoyed watching the interplay of personalities, as a man fascinated by life's oddities. He had been conscious of every tiny change in the mutation and he now sensed that this psychological and physiological drama had been played out. The ending, represented by The Preparation Room, was there in front of his eyes. Adèle had gobbled up Ferdinand and that was that.

As in July of every year, Rennequin now decided to go down and spend a few days in Mercoeur. Indeed, ever since the Salon, he had been feeling an irresistible desire to meet the couple again. It would give him the opportunity of seeing for himself whether his reasoning was correct.

When he called on the Sourdis, it was a scorching hot afternoon and the garden was drowsing in the shade. The house and even the flowerbeds looked neat and tidy, the hallmark of middle-class orderliness and peace. Not a sound from the little town could penetrate into this remote corner; all that could be heard was the humming of bees in the climbing roses. The maid told him that the mistress was in the studio.

When Rennequin opened the door, he saw Adèle standing in front of the easel in the same attitude as he had once seen her many years before. Today, however, she was making no secret of the fact that she was painting. She gave a quiet exclamation of pleasure and was about to put down her palette when Rennequin protested:

"If I'm disturbing you, I shall go away . . . Hang it all, I'm a friend of the family. Off you go, keep working."

She let herself be persuaded; she was a woman who knew that time is money.

"Very well, then, since you insist! You know, one never has time to turn round . . . "

Despite increasing age and obesity, she was still tackling her work with determination and extraordinary deftness of touch. Rennequin watched her for a minute then asked, "Is Ferdinand out?"

"Of course not, he's over there," replied Adèle, pointing with her brush towards a corner of the studio.

Ferdinand was indeed there, lying stretched out on a divan. He had been dozing and Rennequin's voice had woken him up; but his mind had become so feeble and sluggish that he did not at first recognize him.

"Oh, it's you, what a nice surprise," he said eventually.

He made a great effort to sit up and held out a flabby hand. The day before, his wife had caught him out with the little girl who came in to do the washing-up and he was in a very contrite mood; he looked scared and worried, not knowing what to do to be forgiven. Rennequin found him more drained and subdued than he had expected. He had become a complete wreck and Rennequin felt pity for the poor man. Wishing to see if he could perhaps rekindle some of his former spirit, he mentioned the great stir that had been created by The Preparation Room at the last Salon.

"Well, young fellow, you can still excite the public. Everybody's talking about you in Paris. It's just like the old days."

Ferdinand gazed at him blankly and then, making an effort to find something to say, "Oh yes, I know, Adèle's been reading me the papers. It's a very good picture, isn't it? Oh, I'm working, I'm still doing a lot of work . . . But I'm telling you, she's better than me, she's got a fantastic technique!"

He blinked his eyes and gave a wan smile towards his wife. She had come up to them and she gave a good-humored shrug of her shoulders as she said, "Don't listen to him! You know that crazy idea of his . . . To hear him speak, you'd think it was I who was the great painter . . . All I do is to help him, and not very well at that . . . Well, since it gives him pleasure to say so . . . "

Rennequin watched without a word this game of pretence which they were playing with each other, no doubt in good faith. But what he saw in the studio told him plainly that Ferdinand's talent had sunk without trace. He was not even producing the little pencil sketches; he had reached the stage of not feeling any need to preserve his self-respect by lies; in his mind it was now enough to be merely Adèle's husband and it was she who composed, sketched and painted the pictures, without asking any advice from him. Moreover, she had, as an artist, entered so completely into his skin that she was able to continue his work without leaving the slightest indication to show where the break had occurred. Now, it was all her own work and all that remained of her female personality was the earlier imprint of Ferdinand's male personality.

Ferdinand gave a yawn.

"You'll stay to dinner, won't you?" he said. "I'm fagged out . . . Can you understand that, Rennequin? I've done damn all today and I'm still completely fagged out!"

"He says he hasn't done anything," interrupted Adèle, "but he works from morning to night. He'll never listen to me and take a good long rest."

"That's true enough." Ferdinand said. "If I take a rest, I don't feel well, I have to keep busy."

He had stood up and wandered about the studio for a minute before sitting down again at the small table on which his wife used to paint her watercolors. He was examining a sheet of paper on which someone had started putting the first washes of a watercolor painting. It was a sort of schoolgirlish subject, a stream turning the wheel of a mill, with a screen of poplars and an old willow. Rennequin leaned over his back and started to smile as he saw the childish clumsiness of the drawing and the colors. It was an almost laughable daub.

"How odd," he murmured to himself.

He stopped short when he saw Adèle give him a sharp look. With a vigorous flourish, not bothering to use a maulstick, she had just dashed off a whole figure in her picture, roughing it in with a quite masterly boldness of brushwork.

"Don't you think that's a really pretty mill? Said Ferdinand, still bending over his sheet of paper. He sounded just like a little boy pleased at the progress he was making. "Of course, you know, I'm only a learner, nothing more."

Rennequin stood there in stunned amazement. It was Ferdinand who was now painting watercolors.

A Note on the Text

The task of assembling the short fiction of Émile Zola has been formidable for a number of reasons. It would be facile to say that any work rendering Zola (or any non-English writer) into English is problematic at the very least, impossible at the worst. We are simultaneously blessed and cursed with existing translations. Blessed because they introduced Zola to a much admiring public; cursed because such translations are so of their time. The Vizetelly family which has always been applauded for their efforts in this regard worked under a threat that few people in the western world face; they were not only fearful of being imprisoned, but were in fact put in jail merely for the act of translating Zola into English. As a result their translations suffer on two counts: they are expurgated almost to the point of nonsense and they are Victorian in the extreme, which is to say that they are insufferably stuffy, overblown and laden with a vocabulary that only the most forsaken scholar living in a cave somewhere and avoiding all contact with contemporary culture could understand.

Translators generally build upon each other's work and it is our misfortune that the foundation of Zola translations are the firm of Vizetelly and Co. I know this will stir the ire of mainly the British scholars of Zola because they are covetous of the prestige which surrounds the "bravery" of the Vizetellys in taking on the task in the first place. But being first does not mean doing a great job; a passable job, yes. A better than no job at all, also yes. But I can be quite certain that their translations destroyed any chance Zola had of being widely accepted in the United States and I can assure you that his influence is so potent as for any student to safely be able to assert that without Émile Zola, American literature from 1880 to 1940 would be completely and utterly different. This influence, however, is based on our American authors' ability to read the master in his original French, a talent widely accepted in the years mentioned but woefully absent today where our literati are considered learned if they have mastered MSWord. Fortunately, the same cannot be said of America's great contemporary film directors who religiously observe French films all to the general good of American cinema.

The problems with translations notwithstanding, there are even greater problems assembling Zola's short works because they were often published in newspapers and other periodicals with a heavy editorial hand. A story such as "Nantas" has at least three variations within the French language itself. So it was with some temerity that I chose the version closest in my opinion to what Zola, hopefully, intended. Most, if not all, of his short fiction was written quickly, under deadline, and with considerably less care than his novels. Many are simply sketches reminiscent of an author's working notebooks where ideas for novels are set down looking to the day when they might be fleshed out. If that day never comes, the sketches or notes will suffice to satisfy the hungry reading public whose appetite has been stimulated by the passion that intelligent readers everywhere have for the novels. Interestingly, many of his stories are so short that in their day they would have been considered ridiculous (and were by many critics.) But today, such short fiction has been "invented" in the form of what is colloquially and now in some more refined circles referred to as "flash fiction."

As a scholar of Zola, but more importantly as an adoring fan (a term I have no qualms with), I would never recommend to any reader unfamiliar with the man to start with his short stories. I think many of Thomas Hardy's short stories, most of William Faulkner's and Herman Melville's and all of Guy DuMaupassant's would make an excellent introduction to those great writers. But unequivocally, Zola is a novelist and even his best stories, while excellent by anyone's standards, pale in comparison to his full-length fiction. Nonetheless, his short works often provide an insight into his genius and, I might say, into his thought processes as a craftsman of fiction. His early stories collected in Stories for Ninon are maudlin, immature, hopelessly romantic and often vicariously embarrassing. But this could be said of any writer, great and small, who for the first time takes up his pen and presents his soul to the world. A careful reading of these stories might remind many readers of their first forays into fiction where wearing one's heart on one's sleeve was not the opprobrium it is today.

The other difficulty in a presentation of so much material is the order in which it is presented. Like any very popular author, publishers scrambled to get work of any kind into print no matter how many times it was rejected when the fellow was unknown. Profit is always the motivating force behind the publishing trade and it is little wonder that works by Jane Austen, Charles Dickens and a slew of others are foisted upon the reading public when, in fact, they were not only unedited by their authors, but not even finished! I have had the good fortune to have had access to a lengthy letter from the London firm of Chatto & Windus which had proposed to the Zola estate a publication of his complete short works. For reasons unknown, the project never proceeded. However, a proposed "table of contents" was included with a precise statement that the order was to be precisely that used in the eventual publication. While I am no fan of the

Chatto & Windus English translations, I much admire their dedication to the master's works and, I might add, they even "updated" some of the expurgations and made some of them a little more accurate and a little less befuddling in the early years of the 20th century. There is a reference in said letter that Zola himself had been consulted on the matter and while there is no evidence that he dictated the order of the stories, it is my opinion that it represents a better version than one I could evolve. It would be very simple to have the order dictated by the chronology of their appearance in print. This would be very difficult indeed and would belie the fact that many were written years before they found their way into print and actually precate others which were written later but published earlier. My own opinion is that by 1900, Zola wouldn't have cared. The fact that he consented to the publication of his early novel, The Mysteries of Marseilles, proves to me at least that whatever brought in a royalty check was good enough for him. And why not? He might have seen that novel and his first, Claude's Confession, with the same affection that many writers view their early work: "Well, this isn't bad at all." His reputation was already made and he could have written a poem sang to the tune of "Yankee Doodle Dandy" and his renown would have suffered not a whit.

What little obeisance I have made to the early translations and to some of the later ones is to retain some of their now obsolete punctuation and archaic syntax. The fact remains that Zola was a writer very much of his time and his MSS indicate that, for example, he often used a colon before a piece of dialogue and not a comma as we universally do today. Sometimes he used single quotation marks, sometimes double. And perhaps his most annoying habit, at least to the eye of a 21st century reader is his absurd overuse of the exclamation point. Today, I'm afraid, we are less apt to license our writers to shout their lines at our sophisticated faces. But in Zola's time when the novel was novel, such excesses were not only permitted but encouraged. Black marks on a white page may be many things but the 19th century reader felt privileged to feel the passion the writer felt and no punctuation accomplishes that so well as the exclamation point!

These volumes of his Complete Stories were years in the making and it is my genuine hope that they entertain, amuse and enlighten the American reader to one aspect of Émile Zola they might not otherwise have encountered.

Stephen R. Pastore, 2011.

www.ingramcontent.com/pod-product-compliance
Lightning Source LLC
Chambersburg PA
CBHW031212020726
47499CB00002B/558
* 9 7 8 0 9 8 3 4 7 3 8 0 0 *